GET A FREE BOOK

Check out Powder Burn the next thriller in the series.

Check out Incoming the most recent in the Zeb Carter Series.

Join Ty Patterson's Facebook group of readers.

ALSO BY TY PATTERSON

Most recent first

Cutter Grogan Series (Zeb Carter Universe)

Two books in the series and counting

Zeb Carter Series

Seven books in the series and counting

Zeb Carter Short Stories

One book in the series and counting

Warriors Series (Zeb Carter Universe)

Twelve books in the series

Gemini Series (Zeb Carter Universe)

Four thrillers in the series

Warriors Series Shorts (Zeb Carter Universe)

Six novellas in the series

Cade Stryker Series

Two military sci-fi thrillers

ACKNOWLEDGMENTS

They say it takes a village to produce a book. In my case, many continents have been involved. Sure, an author's job is a solitary one, but writing is just one part of putting out a book.

My beta readers, who are around the world, are my first responders. I owe a debt of gratitude to them for putting into shape all the words I write.

They are:

Manie Kilan, Mike Duncan, Dori Barrett, Maria Stine, Mike Davis, Larry Kahhan, Linda Thomas, Laura Rachwalik, Jobins MJ, Simon Alphonso, Steve Panza, Ann Finn, Don Waterman, Kimber Krahn, Robin Eide Steffenson, Blanca Nichols, Loz Yeung, Charlie Carrick, Martin Pingere, Terrill Carpenter, Kathryn Defranc, Dave Davis, Mike Duncan, Donna Young Hartridge, Shadine Mccallen, Shell Levy, Wanona Koeppler, Marion McNulty Hulse, Gerry Kenny, Rob Fox, Dan Gherasim, Toni Osborne, Theresa Ann Kari, JoAnn Cates Lewis, Cathie M Jones, Debbie McNally, Sylvia Foster, Beth Perry, Mike Davis, Pat Barling, Mary Kauffman, John Spiller, Dave Campbell, Mark Campbell, Cathy Silveira, Franca Parente, Jan Fisher, Nancy

Schmit, Claire Forgacs, Pete Bennett, Eric Blackburn, Margaret Harvey, Jim Lambert, Jimmy Smith, Suzanne Mickelson, Brad Werths, Allan Coulton, Paula Artlip, Pat Ellis, Linda Collins, Tricia Cullerton, Alun Humphreys, Wa Reedy, Tania Reed, Matt Bell, Jeane Jackson, Gary Bristol, Gary Rounds and Jennifer Anderson.

Donna Rich, my proofreader, and Doreen Martens, my editor, have been invaluable in polishing the book.

Lastly, a special thanks to Debbie Gallant, Tom Gallant, Michelle Rose Dunn and Cheri Gerhardt, who have supported me since the beginning.

To my wife and son for their sacrifices in supporting me

If you are free, you need to free somebody else. If you have some power, then your job is to empower somebody else.

— Toni Morrison

I

Everything could be used as a weapon.

The covers and spine of a hardback novel. A rolled-up newspaper. The points of a folded sheet of paper. Any everyday object could be used to either attack or block.

Cutter Grogan's eyes took in the surroundings as he walked down Lafayette Street, noting what could be used for offense or defense. That umbrella someone had discarded in a trashcan. The empty cartons on the sidewalk outside a store. That vandalized phone booth on the corner with Grand Street—it could be used as cover.

It was automatic, a habit so deeply ingrained from years of training and experience in far-off dusty and dangerous lands that he wasn't even conscious of it.

New York in the summer. The insistent and never-fading sounds of traffic and the smell of fumes. He jaywalked the street to get to the sunlit side of Lafayette and closed his eyes momentarily to bask in the warmth.

'It's not a park!' a passerby yelled at him and brushed past in a huff.

He grinned. He had been to the world's top cities. Paris, London, Berlin, Rio, Jakarta, Tokyo—wherever he went, he felt at home. But New York? It was where he began and where he ended. He donned his shades and carried on. Waited at the intersection with Grand for the lights to turn and, when they did, proceeded to his destination, a bodega.

There were many within walking distance, some even closer, but this particular one was his favorite. It was neatly maintained, tidy, and had the light smell of incense in the air. He knew its owners. But the deal-clincher was the dessert counter. Fluffy pastries and cakes, chocolates that melted in one's mouth, all of them freshly baked by the owner's wife. They would set off calorie-counter alarms, if fitness gear had those.

He glanced at his watch and hurried. An oven-fresh batch would be coming, and he wanted to be first in line. Not many knew of the store's delicacies. However, word of mouth was a thing, and the desserts often ran out as soon as they were displayed.

He removed his shades, folded them and placed them in an inner pocket as he squinted at the scaffolding outside the bodega. Construction on the building's upper floors cut visibility.

A bell jangled when he entered.

'Chang,' he greeted the Chinese man behind the counter.

'Cutter,' the owner responded, his face creasing in a smile. He was in his fifties, his hair still thick and black, experience and hardship lining his face with tiny wrinkles. 'Long time. You been going to some other store?'

'Only if Lin Shun has run away with someone else. I come only for her pastries. You know that.'

'I dunno what she sees in him,' said an elderly man from the next aisle, where he was mopping the floor. 'I've proposed to her several times.'

'Have you considered that perhaps you're old?'

'Me? Old?'

Cutter stood silently, enjoying their humor. Moshe, the arrival, was joint-owner with Li Shun and Chang. An unlikely partnership on the face of it. The elderly man outranked the Chinese-American couple by close to three decades, though he was so fit only his wrinkled face and arms gave his age away.

That night brought us together.

Cutter had been on a late run several years ago, the streets deserted, when the sounds of a scuffle had caught his attention. A narrow alley behind the bodega, where buildings stored their trash bins. It opened into Center Street. Several shadows moving in the dark.

At the sound of his arrival, the figures had burst out and fled, but not before he had taken one man down and crippled him with a blow to the temple.

A mugging gone wrong. Chang and Lin Shun's young son left bleeding on the ground. Moshe, then, a passerby who had tried to help, injured as well.

Cutter called 911 and stayed with them until the cops and first-responders arrived. He was with them when the paramedics shook their heads almost imperceptibly. Daniel Shun, the son, had died.

He had waited in the hospital's hallway while Moshe was undergoing surgery that helped him survive the near-fatal knife wound to his kidneys.

Cutter joined the bodega owners in their mourning, and as time healed, got close to them. Moshe became part of them when he stayed in touch and became a business partner as well when he bought in to the store.

Cutter clapped the elder man on his shoulder and looked at him critically. 'He's still got all his teeth,' he told Chang. 'That ought to count for something, shouldn't it?'

'Teeth! That's all he's got.'

Moshe was in incredibly good shape for his age. He ran half-marathons and was an active participant in neighborhood walks. Any other person would be content with being a silent partner in the business. Not the elder man. He helped out wherever he could. Stacking shelves, cleaning up, even behind the checkout counter if needed, though he didn't prefer it.

He feels claustrophobic there. He doesn't like it.

Cutter stepped around the older partner when he resumed wiping the floor. Moshe's sleeves slid up his forearms, and there it was: faded numerals tattooed on the inside of his left arm. Many thought it was old ink, badly done. Cutter knew what it was and the horrors behind it.

Moshe was an Auschwitz survivor.

He had been six when he was deported to the camp along with his parents and elder sister, ten when the camp was liberated. The only member of his family to survive.

Cutter went to the dessert counter and inhaled the aromas. A woman came from inside the store and wiped her hands on her white apron. She hugged him hard and checked him out. He could see his reflection in the glass covering the delicacies.

Six feet one. Styled, dark hair. Green eyes. Clean-shaven. Tee tucked into his jeans. Lightweight sports jacket. Rubber-soled sneakers.

Because of his deep tan, he could easily pass for someone from the Mediterranean region. Or the Middle East, South America, North Africa—a vast range of geographies. Only a handful knew what his genealogy was. Lin Shun, Chang and Moshe were among them.

'Haven't seen you for a while.' Lin Shun went behind the display cabinet and waited expectantly.

'Been away.'

'Vacation?'

'Something like that.' *Rescuing a hostage from a Colombian cartel. That was some holiday!*

Her eyes sharpened at his tone. They lingered on him. 'No injuries?'

'Nothing gets past you, Lin Shun,' he admitted ruefully. 'None, this time.'

She looked at him searchingly and then got down to business.

'Pineapple and banana pastries. New recipe. They have come out well. You should try them out.'

'I'll take two of them, and my usual.'

Coconut-sprinkled fruit cupcakes were his go-to dessert. He licked his lips unconsciously as Lin Shun packed them in a brown paper bag.

He was taking it from her when it happened.

2

'YOU! HANDS IN THE AIR!' a voice yelled.

Lin Shun gasped. Her eyes widened, her hands trembled as she raised them.

Cutter turned slowly, bag in his left hand, as the blinds on the store window came down, darkening the interior.

The dessert display was the short leg of an L-shaped counter that ran down the side of the store and ended where Chang stood behind the register.

One man faced him, a black bandana over his nose and mouth, baseball hat covering his head, shades over his eyes. A gun in his hand, waving in the air.

Just him? Who rolled down the blinds?

As if in reply, another man came into view. Similarly dressed, with a grey scarf around his face, gun on Moshe, who shuffled from behind the central display stand, mop still in hand.

Two.

'HANDS. RAISE THEM!' the first man shouted.

Cutter lifted his slowly. *Three,* he corrected himself, when a balaclava-wearing hood came around the center stand and covered him and Lin Shun with a weapon.

'MONEY!' Bandana screamed. 'EVERYTHING YOU HAVE. QUICK.'

'Who else here?' Balaclava jerked his gun. 'WHO?'

'Just us.' Lin Shun trembled. 'Inside rooms are empty.'

'YOU'LL DIE FIRST IF THERE'S SOMEONE ELSE.'

Three gunmen. One to Cutter's right, six feet away, weapon angled away, in the baker's direction. Two others about twenty feet away, standing close to each other. Bandana facing Chang, Grey Mask watching the entrance, gun on Moshe, who stood calm, silent, his hands high above his head.

'YOU! JACKET MAN,' Balaclava raged. 'YOU THINK THIS IS A JOKE? OUR GUNS ARE EMPTY? LIFT YOUR HANDS. STAND STILL.'

Time slowed. The world blurred and reduced to the counter, the central display, and three gunmen.

'Are you sure you want to do this?' Cutter asked softly. Taking everything in. The mole on Balaclava's wrist. The bead of sweat coming from beneath the mask, going down his neck, over what looked like a tattoo just visible above the edge of his shirt. Moshe, looking at him, still calm, as if it was a routine event. Chang hustling over the counter, sweeping its contents into a plastic bag with shaking fingers. Lin Shun breathing hard.

Fight or stand down? Three against one. What were the odds there?

'WHAT DID YOU SAY? SHUT YOUR MOUTH.' Balaclava lunged forward, his face twisting beneath his mask in anger, the gun rising to barrel-whip Cutter.

Fight it was.

It came over Cutter instantly, a detachment of his mind from his body as it observed dispassionately, got neurons to fire impulses to axons that released chemicals that triggered muscles, all without conscious thought, in nanoseconds.

One long step to his right. Letting go of the brown bag, whose fall caught Balaclava's attention. Right-hand fingers folding to extend knuckles, which throat-punched the attacker as his left hand came down, clamped the gun wrist in a vise-like grip and twisted it away from Lin Shun, and as the gunman fell, choking, gasping, the weapon came free and into Cutter's hand, which extended in a straight line, tilted slightly to give better control, eye to sight, sight to body mass of Grey Mask, who was half-turned, mouth opening in shock, as Moshe dropped to the floor.

The first round sent the gunman staggering back; the second slammed into Bandana's chest. One more, to make sure he stayed down. A brutal kick to Balaclava's head to prevent him from rising, crouch-walking over to the payment counter to check that Bandana wouldn't be a threat. Grey Mask wasn't a problem. Moshe had jammed the handle of his mop against the man's throat and a leg over his chest as the man moaned in agony.

Cutter's worldview widened to take in Chang, who had sagged against the wall, sweat streaming down his face. Time caught up as Lin Shun rushed to her husband and held him tight.

Moshe shook his head reproachfully. 'You should have warned us.'

3

NYPD rolled up with sirens and flashing lights, the full treatment. Paramedic wagons turned up as well and pronounced that Bandana, Grey Mask and Balaclava would live.

The cops questioned Cutter and the bodega owners. Went through CCTV footage. Took his prints, measured distances and bagged the gun and shell casings. Threw several speculative looks at Cutter.

The detectives arrived half an hour later in an unmarked car. They conferred with the first-responders, inspected the interior of the store, watched the camera recordings and made several calls.

Checking if we are in the system, Cutter thought as he stood outside the store with the bodega owners. One of the new arrivals, a Hispanic-looking woman, threw him a sharp glance as she spoke into her phone. Her partner drew close to her and they talked in low tones before heading towards them.

'They've found out about you, Cutter,' Chang murmured. Moshe grunted in agreement.

'Difiore,' the woman introduced herself and gave out her card. 'That's Griffen,' she said, introducing her partner, who seemed to be younger. No first names. The older cop had that look. *Like she's seen it all. Nothing surprises her anymore.* Her companion nodded at them briefly as he chewed gum and rocked on his heels.

'You don't know the perps?' He removed his shades and tucked them into his pocket.

'Nope.' Lin Shun nodded her head at the cops in the background. 'They took our statements.'

'You knew they would be coming?'

'How would I know that?' Cutter growled, knowing the question was directed at him.

'That was good shooting.' Griffen ignored his reply. 'Someone else's weapon. Three shots, all of them on the upper body, none of them fatal. All made under pressure. That's some skill.'

Cutter didn't comment. He had recognized the gun in Balaclava's hand, a Glock 19. The same model he owned, which had been with him on all his military tours. As for the shooting, that had come instinctively.

'You were in the military, Mr. Grogan?' No expression in Difiore's voice.

'Yeah.'

First SFOD-D, Special Forces Operational Detachment–Delta. Known as Delta Force, or just Delta. One of the US military's Tier One Special Mission units.

'You could have gotten yourself killed. Your friends, too.'

No. I knew what I was doing. He didn't say that, however.

'Everyone else would have held their hands up and let themselves be robbed.' Griffen, thumbs hooked in his belt, mouth working as he chewed. 'Safest option. No one plays the hero, everyone stays alive.'

'Is that a question?' Moshe asked softly. 'Do we need our lawyers?'

'What do you do, Mr. Grogan?' Difiore threw her partner a sharp glance.

'I'm sure you know,' Cutter replied, tired of the games. 'You will have checked who we are. You would have seen the NYPD knows me.'

'A fixer.' Griffen, who seemed to have gotten over his partner's nonverbal rebuke. 'That's what you said last time. When you were questioned. That's still what you do?'

'Yeah.'

'You saw these thugs come in and went into fixing mode? Is that how it works?'

'We're done here,' Chang cut in. 'You got any more questions, ask them with our lawyer present.'

'You seem okay. Any civilian who got held up at gunpoint and witnessed a shooting would be shaken. But you, your wife and Mr. Sternberg seem perfectly fine.'

'You want us to feel sorry for the thugs?' Lin Shun retorted scornfully.

'No, ma'am, but,'—Griffen's eyes glinted—'other people would have shivered. They would have gone into shock. You folks ... it's as if you've had a day in the park.'

'You've looked us up,' Chang sneered. 'You know this isn't our first time. We've been held up before. We've also been mugged.'

'Mr. Grogan came to your rescue. Yeah, that's in our files.'

Cutter felt rage wash over him. *That wasn't much of a save. They lost their son.* He was about to speak when Moshe sensed his fury and put a hand on his forearm. He controlled himself and breathed in deeply, once. 'Time was when cops didn't harass the innocents.'

Difiore stiffened at that. Her face flushed. She threw a hard look at her partner. 'We're done here. We'll take statements from the gunmen and might want you to come down if we have any more inquiries.'

'We aren't going anywhere,' Chang replied brusquely, hard eyes on her partner.

Cutter watched them leave, the older cop's back straight and stiff as she spoke softly to her partner, seeming to rebuke him.

Griffen's lips curled when their eyes met, and then he was inside the car. Their tires squealed and they were away.

'Cops!' Moshe shook his head.

'Many of them are good.'

'That one has issues.'

Can't argue with that. 'You all ...' He turned toward his friends. 'You're okay?'

'Of course,' said Lin Shun, who had gone inside the store and returned to answer his question. 'We kicked some ass. And you dropped my pastries. Here.' She handed him another brown bag. 'Don't lose this one.'

'I won't, ma'am.' He mock-saluted her, and that was when the TV crews and reporters arrived.

4

Cutter escaped the journalists' scrum after an hour of being interviewed by local media organizations.

Fixer. The reporters loved that word and questioned him in detail on what he did for a living.

'That will be the headline,' Chang had said, winking at him as he was leaving. 'Fixer saves bodega.'

He didn't mind the brief publicity. Name recognition was good in his business. It was how clients heard of him. They came to him because law enforcement couldn't help them. Or wouldn't.

Someone was kidnapped. Their folks or partners came to Cutter for help. A wife was leaving her husband and needed a bodyguard temporarily to protect her from his threats. Corporate espionage. Security advice. Recovering stolen items. Driving out a neighborhood gang. Cutter took on all those jobs.

He got referrals from the NYPD, FBI and several other authorities, too. Cold cases where they couldn't afford to throw in any more manpower. Political complications where they were ordered to stand down. Cases where the law sided with the criminals and the victims wanted justice. He had good friends in law enforcement who mentioned his name to those who wanted closure.

The military came to him from time to time. Generals in the Pentagon, or his former commanding officers, who knew him well and needed his specialist skills.

None of that was on his mind. He was savoring Lin Shun's pastry, unable to resist the temptation, when he reached his loft office on Lafayette Street.

An opaque glass door. His name etched discreetly on the brass plaque to the side. It opened smoothly to reveal a reception office. Warm lighting. Couch, coffee table, magazines, and behind the desk, Arnedra Jones. Her instant smile dimmed when he entered. Her dark eyes narrowed at the brown bag he was carrying and at the sight of his hand hastily wiping his mouth.

'There had better be some left for me.'

'Saved the best for you.' He handed her the bag.

She scoffed and opened the bag, and when her smile burst, it was as if the sun had risen.

He went past her through another opaque glass door to the inside office. Hardwood floor, high, exposed beams, exposed brick, colored throws and rugs, comfortable seating. He went to his desk, brought the screen to life, grunted on finding there was nothing requiring urgent attention, and leaned back in his swivel chair.

He shook his head when he saw Arnedra's silhouette outlined. She sat out there by choice, despite his insistence that she occupy the larger office, alongside him.

He had come across her as she was being violently robbed in Central Park, late one night. The muggers had been beating her up when he arrived. He had broken the arm of one of them in the brief scuffle that followed, and kicked the groin of the other. They had escaped when he turned his attention to the fallen woman. She was bruised and bleeding from a split lip and gashed eyebrow, but grabbed him when he made to call the cops.

'Don't,' she told him.

When he looked at her in astonishment, she glared fiercely.

'They'll question *me*. What a black woman is doing alone this time of night in Central Park. Some of them will imply I brought the mugging on myself. I don't need the hassle.'

Cutter had tried to protest, but she had remained adamant. He helped her stand and got her painkillers and bandages from the nearest pharmacy and escorted her to the Columbus Circle subway.

They met the next day, over coffee. Arnedra had lost her husband a year earlier to cancer. He had been a licensed private investigator; she had managed the business side of it. She was in the process of winding down the business, which required several visits to the Lafayette office. There had been nothing sinister about her walk through Central Park. She had wanted to clear her mind. Nothing more.

'I've met bad cops,' she grimaced. 'Too many of them, when Curtis was alive. A few used to harass us when his cases conflicted with their investigations.' Those experiences had hardened her.

Cutter got to know her and, after several months, proposed a partnership. He would buy into the business, as an equal partner with her.

'Private investigations?' She had raised her eyebrows. 'We'll restart Curtis's business?'

'No.'

He hadn't wanted to go through his backstory, but Arnedra had a way about her.

'I've been to prison,' he explained, bringing up his past. Everything. No holding back. Only a handful knew of it.

Her eyes were moist when he finished. She held out her hand and, when he shook it, ordered another round of drinks.

'But, what shall we do?' she asked when their coffees arrived.

'I want to help people,' he had said.

. . .

'You're a celebrity,' Arnedra said as she walked over to him. She picked up a remote from his desk and turned on the wall-mounted TV. Tuned to a local news channel, a journalist reporting from outside the bodega, who described Cutter's actions and interviewed Chang, Moshe and Lin Shun, all of whom called him a hero.

'That should get the phones ringing.' She switched off the screen and sat next to him.

'How was Colombia?' She side-eyed him, noting the faint lines around his eyes.

'I'm here. The daughter is safe, back with her family. We got a bonus check.'

'You had to shoot it out?'

'A few cartel thugs. No one I'll lose sleep over.'

She caught his chin, turned him to face her and examined him. Was satisfied when she saw nothing but exhaustion. Nothing that a good sleep couldn't cure.

'You need to find someone,' she said softly.

She followed his eyes when they dropped involuntarily to the drawer. She opened it and took out the photo. A woman laughing into the sun. Black curly hair falling onto her chocolate shoulders. Eyes dancing in mischief. Riley Grogan, Cutter's wife. Arnedra shivered involuntarily when she recalled how she had lost her life. She caressed the photograph, put it back in the drawer and shut it.

She laid her hand on his forearm and sat with him as the sun set in the city and darkness enveloped it.

Cutter had helped her during her darkest days. She would never leave his side.

5

Carmel Ward caught the clip on the news channel when she was having dinner.

Alone in her two-bedroom apartment in Brownsville. All by herself, because Darrell, her fifteen-year-old son, hadn't returned home yet. Ten pm, and he was still out. He had messaged her that he would be with friends, catching up on schoolwork. That she should not wait for him.

She thought of calling him. Nope. That wasn't a good idea. Lately they had been arguing all the time. No conversations. No family time. Just one fight after the other. Nothing else.

She sniffed and wiped the stray tear rolling down her cheek.

Three years ago, he had been different. That was when her no-good husband was still around. Her boy had been a bright student, getting top grades in school, had a good set of friends.

It had fallen apart with her finding out her husband was cheating on her. She had ended their sixteen-year marriage and asked him to leave. Weeks of screaming fights ended in sudden, abrupt silence when he left.

She and Darrell made new arrangements, lifestyle changes to

deal with the aftermath. Carmel had to find a second job to supplement her law clerk income. That meant she came home late from Manhattan, where both jobs were, to Saratoga Avenue, where they lived.

Her son, mature beyond his years, had to manage on his own. Go to school in the morning, which thankfully was a few blocks away, walking distance. Return, make his own dinner, study. If she was lucky, she arrived just before he went to sleep.

Shawna, their next-door neighbor, another single parent, kept an eye on him. Invited him for dinner occasionally while her children, younger than Darrell, kept him company.

It had worked for a while. Then he became argumentative. Questioned everything she did. Sulked and withdrew into himself. His grades started falling, and when she urged him to work harder, he talked back insolently.

It got worse when he graduated to high school. He became moody. Hung out with people she didn't know. Shawna had her own problems and got busy dealing with them.

Their relationship broke down when she discovered the weed in his room. Stuffed beneath his bed, underneath dirty laundry.

She had confronted him. He had turned defensive. Swore he never smoked it. Didn't do drugs. Didn't even drink. He was holding it for his friends.

'YOU'RE HANGING OUT WITH DEALERS?' she yelled, and a shouting match ensued. She begged and pleaded with him to give up the bad company, to get back to the smart student he had been. Got a defiant, 'I'm grown. I'll make my own decisions,' in reply.

They became sullen strangers, mother and son. She was tempted to take a day off, follow him, check out who his friends were and challenge them. She wasn't afraid of street gangs and neighborhood dealers. She held herself back, however. That was the surest way to lose him.

. . .

Carmel pushed the despairing thoughts to the back of her mind. She went to the kitchen sink, rinsed her dishes and placed them in the washer.

A plan formed in her mind.

That reporter lady said that Fixer dude was on Lafayette Street. That was just a block away from her law firm's offices. She could meet him during her lunch break. She didn't know how he could help or whether he would, but at this stage, she would willingly clutch at straws.

She checked her watch. Romaine, her brother, would still be awake. He worked downtown too, in a hotel, as a security guard. She would take him along. He was big and could look mean. It wouldn't hurt to have him for the meeting.

She prepared meals for the next day and packed them in boxes. One for Darrell and one for her.

Showered and hit the bed. Tossed and turned until she heard the front door open and Darrell's stealthy footsteps. Midnight.

What was he up to? Where had he been?

She refused to cry. She had shed enough tears.

She punched her pillow into shape angrily and forced herself to sleep.

6

Cutter was cleaning his Glock the next day when he heard voices in the outer room. He slid his weapon into a drawer when Arnedra knocked on the door and opened it.

'You've got visitors,' she announced and stepped aside to let the arrivals in. 'Carmel Ward, and her brother, Romaine.'

He came around from his desk, shook their hands and escorted them to a couch. 'Coffees?' he asked.

'I'll get them,' Arnedra said and made to move to the kitchen.

He frowned at her. Telegraphed an order with his eyes. *STAY HERE!* She wasn't his EA, his executive assistant. Even if she was, he didn't believe in women having to take on the hospitality duties.

'My turn.' He flashed a smile and hustled faster than her. Inhaled the aroma of Jamaican Blue Mountain. They never ran out of it. Good friends of his, on Columbus Avenue, bought enough of the coffee and regularly sent over sufficient stock so that they never ran out. Those cookies in the glass jar came from that office, too. Homemade, baked with love and care by a grandmother his friends had helped.

He brewed the coffee, poured it into cups, arranged the cookies on a plate and took the serving tray out. He handed over their cups and settled himself next to Arnedra.

'I saw you on TV yesterday,' Carmel Ward said as she played with a loose thread on her cuff. 'You said you're a Fixer. What does that mean?'

'Cutter helps people, Ms. Ward,' Arnedra cut in smoothly. 'In whatever way he can. Companies come to him for security advice. Someone gets kidnapped, the cops aren't able to do much, they come here. Those kinds of problems. Not domestic disputes. No family matters. No spying on husbands, wives, partners. Cheating, affairs, that isn't what he does.'

'Like a private investigator? Is that who you are?' Romaine checked out the office carefully.

'You could say that, but I'm not licensed.' Cutter observed them, automatically taking them in. The brother was in a dark uniform, a hotel's name embroidered on his chest. *That's a couple of blocks away. Neat place.* He could read people quickly. *It's not the brother. That's not why they're here. It's her who's got the problem.*

Strands of silver in her hair. Lines of age and experience around her eyes and mouth. Smartly dressed in a dark suit. Polished suit. Neatly cut nails. She felt his eyes and fidgeted.

'Carmel. Please call me that. I work in a law firm on Grand. Jamieson Partners. I'm a legal clerk there.'

He waited.

'I have a son. Darrell. I think he's hanging out with a street gang. I discovered weed in his room.' The words came out in a rush, as fast as she could speak, as if a dam had broken inside her and they could no longer be contained.

'That's not the kind of work I do,' Cutter said gently when she had finished.

'I told you!' Romaine glared at him and then at his sister. 'Why would he help us?'

'Why don't you go to the cops?'

'Cops!' the brother sneered. 'They would arrest Darrell. What good would that do?'

'They're more likely to question him. Get details of who he hangs out with and let him off with a stern warning. They're taking a softer approach these days.'

'You live in a different world,' Romaine snapped. 'You watch the news, dude? You got any idea how cops treat people like us?'

Cutter made a hand gesture when Arnedra made to speak. He knew what she would say. *She'll defend me.*

He was pushing their visitors' buttons deliberately. To see how they'd react. Some of his clients had ulterior motives in coming to him. *Don't need those kinds.* On top of that, clients sometimes found they had bitten off more than they could chew, after engaging him. An early assessment helped in identifying how far clients were willing to go. It looked like Carmel was a mom in distress. Nothing more.

'You could talk to the school. They have a duty to investigate drug dealing on their premises.'

Romaine shook his head incredulously and got to his feet. 'Come on, sis. We've wasted enough time.'

Carmel Ward didn't move. She looked at Cutter searchingly and then her shoulders slumped. Defeat etched on her face, swiftly replaced by a hard expression. She made to rise too, her mouth set tightly.

'Please sit.' He stopped them. 'I think you should talk to your son—' he raised his hand to stop Romaine's retort. 'However, let me check the school out. See if I can find out who his friends are. We can then decide how to proceed. Going to the school or the cops might be the best move, but we can make that call later.'

He winced inwardly at the look on Carmel Ward's face. *Don't want to give her false hope.*

'Ma'am,' he said, choosing his words carefully, 'I may not be able to help much. I'll have to find out.'

'I have money.' Her lips trembled. 'We can discuss fees—'

'Later. Once I know what we're dealing with.'

'Thank you. You don't know how much this means to me. I haven't been able to sleep—' She stopped herself. Regained control. When she stood up, her voice was businesslike, professional. 'You'll let us know.'

'I will, ma'am.'

ARNEDRA SIDE-EYED CARMEL WARD AS SHE LED THEM OUT. She had no kids, but she could relate to the mother. *She's alone, too. Just like me. I know that feeling of helplessness.*

Romaine stopped in the reception area. Sneered at her. 'Is this like a white knight thing for him?' He jerked his head toward the inside office.

She stared at him.

Cutter's father had been an alcoholic, a bystander who was killed in a gang shootout in Brooklyn. His mother had fallen into depression and had turned to drugs. ACS, Administration for Children's Services, had taken him away when he was four years old. She overdosed and killed herself.

His childhood memories were of being bounced from one foster family to another. Years later, when he was in the military, he traced his roots as far as they would go.

Sierra Leone, Native American, Irish, Italian, French Canadian ... his genes were from all over. 'I represent the United Nations,' he had told Arnedra, chuckling, in one of their early meetings. He had changed his surname to his mother's: Grogan. No one recollected who had given him his first name, but it fit.

'White knight?' Arnedra repeated. She ignored Romaine and turned to Carmel. 'If you believe that, call it off.'

'No.' The mother shook her head decisively. 'We're good. We'll wait for Mr. Grogan's finding.'

'Cutter,' Arnedra corrected her. 'We don't do formality here.'

Perhaps one day they would learn who he was. It wouldn't be from her, however. *It's not my story to tell.*

. . .

'WHAT WAS THAT ABOUT?' CUTTER ASKED WHEN SHE returned.

'Nothing. Small talk. She's distressed.'

'Yeah.'

'We can help her?'

'I don't know,' he shrugged. 'If it's school kids messing around, sure. If it's an organized crime gang ...'

'You've taken those on, too.'

'Let me do a surveillance run.'

'We need to look her up as well.'

Standard practice, checking into who their clients were. Not just to see whether they could pay, but also to make sure there was no shady past.

I have enough of that in my background. He grinned to himself. *Don't need any more.*

He went to his screen and began typing. Stopped. He had access to several databases and had sources within the NYPD. Heck, he knew Bruce Rolando, the Commissioner. They had good history.

But there was an easier way to do a background check.

'I need some information,' he said when his call connected.

'What do you think we are?' Beth Petersen snapped from the Columbus Avenue office. 'Your personal assistants?'

7

Carmel Ward's employer occupied the sixth floor of a red-brick building. Lamar Jamieson, founder, headed the firm and worked with five other partners. Class action, property disputes, complaints against the city, housing. No criminal or divorce cases. The firm usually represented the less privileged, and while it wasn't the biggest in the city, had a good reputation.

'Clean,' Beth had told him.

Cutter grinned as he sipped a drink and checked out the front of the building.

She and her twin, Meghan, worked in the Agency, a covert US intelligence outfit that carried out counter-terrorism operations around the world. Its lead operative, Zeb Carter, was a good friend, as were the rest of the agents.

The sisters were the glue in the firm and provided Arnedra and him with an endless supply of coffee and cookies.

And intel. They had access to databases all over the world, and more connections than he had. The twins griped whenever he called, but he knew it was for show. There was nothing he wouldn't do for them.

Cutter finished his drink and hung around for a few more

hours, but nothing aroused his interest. He checked his watch. Getting to Darrell's high school would take half an hour. *He'll be in classes*. He would time it so that he arrived when the teenager finished for the day.

He got out of his car and fed the meter. Loped down the street to where his favorite food truck was parked. It served Turkish food, and the aroma, as he got closer, made his mouth water.

'Fahid,' he greeted the owner, who nodded and began preparing Cutter's lunch. Lahmacun, a pizza kind of dish, with vegetable toppings instead of the usual meat, with a generous splash of olive oil.

He took the food, went to an upturned barrel and munched slowly as New York passed him by.

He was midway through his food when he grew aware of it: Two women at the next barrel. A burly man and his friend eyeing them. Making audible comments. Not that loud that Fahid or the other customers could make them out.

He studied them. Both had short hair; the large one had a tattoo on his neck—a snake spitting at a pack of cards. Both were in Tees and jeans. Sneakers. No briefcases or bags, just them, making lewd comments.

Cutter glanced at the women, who were Asian-looking. One with glasses, the other with short, black hair. Both stylishly dressed and, judging by the cameras around their necks and the maps on the barrel, tourists. They had their heads down and were eating as fast as possible, clearly uncomfortable.

He waited a beat. Fahid could easily deal with unruly customers. *Don't need to get involved.* Besides, they might not want his intervention.

One of the women raised her head, met his eyes, a look of embarrassment and pleading, before ducking down again.

'Can I join you?' he asked in English and repeated it in Mandarin.

Surprise on their faces. Tentative smiles.

'Yes,' they replied in the same language.

Cutter took his paper plate and went to their barrel. Turned to the men and eyed them.

'If you keep doing that,' he told them coldly, 'I will break your jaws, then your fingers, and dislocate your knees. You won't walk for a month; you won't eat that kind of food for a long time. You'll have to be fed through a tube.'

Everyone around him froze. Shocked glances his way. The men looked startled. Then, a red flush spread over their faces.

'Don't,' he warned them. 'You won't win. You won't even hurt me.'

He knew how he looked. Utterly confident of carrying out his promise, of wreaking intense violence.

'Cutter,' Fahid called from his van, 'are those two a problem?'

'They were. Not anymore. They're leaving.'

The men read the mood. The big one cursed under his breath and slunk away, followed by his companion.

'Thank you,' the one with glasses said, breathing a sigh of relief. 'They were rude.'

'Yeah. I heard them.'

They peppered him with questions as he ate. Asked how he knew Mandarin. "Several business visits," he replied. They were from Shanghai, he learned, ran a boutique clothing outlet and were visiting the US for the first time. He gave them directions to their next site, his number. And when they were out of sight, went to the counter.

'Those men, they're regulars?'

'Nope,' Fahid replied. 'I know what they look like, now.' He nodded at the discreetly mounted cameras under the awning of his truck. 'I won't be serving them.'

It was when Cutter was driving to Brownsville that it came to him. It was the big thug who had jogged his memory. That tattoo on his neck reminded him of another one he had seen.

Balaclava had one. The gunman who had accosted Lin Shun and him at the bodega. It had looked like a lion's head, red, but he couldn't be sure. Only a small part of it had been showing above the man's shirt. Chang's CCTV hadn't shown it. Wrong angle.

He searched his pockets; yeah, the detective's card was there.

He dialed her number one-handed.

'Difiore, NYPD.' Flat tone. No greeting.

'Cutter Grogan.' He gave her a moment to place him.

'Yeah, the Fixer. How can I help you, Grogan?'

'Those men, what happened to them?'

'All three got bailed.'

A car honked angrily from behind when he instinctively jammed on the brakes. It overtook as the driver flipped him the finger.

'Bailed? How the heck is that poss—'

'Their lawyer, yeah, one slick dude representing all of them, made a good argument. That it was a holdup, nothing more, and they didn't start the shooting. Besides, none of them have priors. Judge set it high and let them go. They're tagged. We know where they are at any point.'

'Those men I shot? They were let go, too?'

'All of them. Injuries not serious. You placed well. No vital organs damaged.' Staccato bursts of words. No emotion. Dry recital.

'Any gang affiliations?'

'Nope. All of them unemployed. Families are middle-class. Pillars of the community kind.'

'Their being white had nothing to do with bail, I guess.'

'I'm not the judge.'

'Why did they pick that bodega?'

'Randomly. The idea was a dare among their friends. Came up during a drinking session with friends. We're questioning them. Guns belonged to their fathers.'

'You have their names?

'Sheely Boyce, the one closest to you.'

Balaclava. Cutter nodded unconsciously.

'Travis Pupius, first man you shot.' Grey Mask. 'Chad Tuttle, the second gunman.' Bandana.

'Why are you sharing so much?'

A long silence. Only the sounds of his tires humming and the surrounding traffic.

'Because they're out.'

'You'll let me know how the investigation goes?'

'No.' She hung up.

Cutter took the Manhattan Bridge as he pondered Difiore's revelations. Sighed, finally. *She's not at fault.* The detective had to deal with the system, like anyone else. *They'll go to trial and get convicted for sure.*

It was when he was parked near Darrell's high school that he remembered.

I didn't ask her about the tattoo.

8

Darrell's school was on Pitkin Avenue. A half-hour walk from Carmel's apartment. Cutter parked his car in a vacant space on Saratoga Avenue and strolled the same route that the mother said her son took.

At three pm, he was lounging against a wall of an office building, ball cap jammed low over his head, shades over his eyes, waiting as if he was one of the several parents who had come to pick their kids up.

A tiny camera in the buttonhole of his jacket was feeding images to his cell phone, which relayed the feed to the cloud. All in high definition.

Teenagers surged out of the school. The street was filled with their clamor and the honks of vehicles forced to move slower.

Darrell was one of the last to emerge, with a bunch of similar-age teenagers. Different ethnicities, no girls.

He high-fived many of them, slung his backpack over his shoulder and joined three boys, all taller than him.

They walked down the avenue, laughing, shouting, kicking at an empty soda can. One of them broke out a bag of chips and shared it. No sign of drugs or weapons.

Cutter shadowed them down East New York Avenue, moving

with the flow of other pedestrians, using cover wherever it was available, urban following coming to him as naturally as stealth movement in the jungles of the Congo.

None of the students looked back, however.

At the intersection to Eastern Parkway, Darrell broke away. More high-fives as he left the group and ran across a patch of green. He brought out his phone, appeared to message someone, and went to an apartment building on Park Place.

Cutter sprawled on a bench, found a discarded newspaper and engrossed himself.

Darrell emerged at eight pm. Looked neither left nor right. Headed towards Saratoga Avenue and went inside his building without stopping or making any more calls.

A bedroom window lit. His shadow moved across the curtain. The light turned off, but he didn't emerge.

Cutter bought a hot dog from a street stand and wolfed it down in his car. *Living it up*.

A shadow moved at ten pm. Slow. Head bowed. Weary. Carmel Ward. She entered the building and another street-facing window lit up minutes later.

Cutter gunned his engine and drove back to Manhattan. To his apartment, which was on the same street as his office.

He showered, turned off the lights, sat on the windowsill and watched as the city slept.

9

Carmel invited Arnedra and him for dinner the next day, when he checked in and reported nothing alarming had happened.

'Don't you get back late?'

'I'll come early.'

'Will Darrell be there?'

'I hope.'

Cutter hung up and rocked in his chair. *Might be useful to see the inside of their home. Get a feel for how Darrell lives.*

'We're going for dinner,' he said, going to the outer office.

'Lord!' His partner made a show of fluffing her hair. 'It took you this long to ask me out.'

He rolled his eyes. Beth. Meghan. Arnedra. They loved to yank his strings.

THE HOUSE WAS WARM AND COZY WHEN THEY ARRIVED AT seven pm. Carmel graciously accepted their bottle of wine and ushered them into the living room. Went to the kitchen and returned with a tray of appetisers and glasses of wine.

'Cutter doesn't drink. He'll take whatever juice you might have, though.'

'You quit?'

'No, ma'am. I never started.'

She laughed and returned with a glass of orange juice. He thanked her and checked out the books on a shelf while the women talked. Philosophy, some fiction. Academic texts.

'Darrell used to read. A lot,' Carmel said from behind.

Cutter nodded, noting the past tense. He wandered to the window. Yep, that was the one with the street view. Three stories above ground level.

'You want to look at his room?'

'Won't he mind?'

'It's my house.' Her eyes flashed.

She led him down the hallway, past the kitchen, a bedroom, and opened the door to a second one.

Cutter nodded when she excused herself and went to join Arnedra. First impressions registered. A desk filled with books. Chair skewed at an angle. Posters of rappers on the wall. Laundry on the floor, neatly heaped in one corner. A closet whose doors were ajar. He opened them further with a finger and noted the folded clothing on shelves. The room was surprisingly well kept, despite the pile on the table. Shoes arranged against the wall, bed made up, night lamp turned off.

He dropped to one knee and peered underneath the bed. Nothing but a storage box that seemed to contain childhood toys. He went to the desk and tapped the space bar on the laptop's keyboard. A screensaver sprang to life. A random, system-generated picture.

Cutter rejoined his host and sat at the dining table at her beckoning. She asked about his past. He skirted around it, and then Arnedra launched into stories about her times with Curtis. The conversation flowed easily after that.

. . .

Darrell entered the house when they were on coffees. He greeted them sullenly when his mom introduced them. 'They're helping me with something.'

He nodded, didn't ask what it was about.

'You joining us for dinner?'

'I had something at Shane's,' he replied and disappeared into his bedroom.

Carmel's shoulders slumped briefly. She smiled automatically when she felt Cutter's eyes on her.

'Were you like that, at that age?'

I was trying to survive in foster homes. 'All teenagers go through that,' he lied smoothly. He didn't tell her about his surveillance report.

What's there to tell? Besides, that was just one day.

It was different the next day.

10

Brownsville, part of Brooklyn, wasn't the kind of New York neighborhood featured in travel brochures.

Tourists weren't interested in seeing its public housing. It had one of the highest crime rates in the city. Lack of new development, empty lots and abandoned housing projects contributed to an air of grimness.

Cutter had seen enough desperate localities in his life that the seedy, rundown, trying-to-survive character of the area didn't register.

He was shadowing Darrell the next day. After school. The teenager had hung out with the same bunch of students from the day before, but after a while had set off with a Hispanic-looking one.

The two walked and talked, doubling over occasionally at a joke. Straight down Pitkin, a right on Rockaway Avenue, where they stopped at an abandoned parking lot. A group of young men hanging around. Late teens. Many of them puffing on spliffs. Light catching on their jewelry. One of them greeted Darrell's companion and slapped palms with the student.

Cutter slowed. A long line of cars on the street, many of

them damaged. There wasn't much cover for him. *I can sprawl on the sidewalk. Act like a homeless person.*

He didn't have to, however. A smaller group peeled off from the men and sauntered down the street, Darrell between them.

Down Belmont, other passersby skirting around the group, a few women talking back angrily at their comments. One of the youths shoved Darrell towards a pharmacy. He stumbled. His smile faded and turned sullen when the man gestured. He went to the store and returned with a water bottle.

Cutter didn't spot any money changing hands. The student hurried to catch up, a reluctant grin lighting his face at a joke. *How does he know them?* Through his friend who was at the head of the group, talking softly with a couple of men? Were these boys from school too? He shrugged mentally. It didn't matter.

He kept his distance, occasionally stepping out on the street, walking against oncoming traffic.

They rarely looked back, however, and when they did, it was to gesture or point out women.

The peeling off happened again at Mother Gaston Boulevard. Darrell and his school friend turned left, while everyone else went the other way.

A nail salon. A takeout joint and then a long stretch of open space behind a barbed-wire fence. A developer's lot, according to the signs on it. Awaiting permissions or stuck in some bureaucratic red tape. The sidewalk in front of it seemed to be a no-go zone. Empty bottles, litter and the stench of urine. Broken-down cars on the street. Far ahead was the signage of another takeout.

In the darkening gloom were six men. These were older, not students.

Time to be a drunk.

Cutter made to stumble, fell against the wall of an empty building and slid to the ground slowly. He reached into his pocket and drew out a flask that he carried for just such occasions. His hands shook as he held it to his lips and sipped the tomato juice. He wiped his lips and adjusted his position.

Turning sideways so that he could watch Darrell and his fellow student join the men. A hundred feet away.

Are those dudes white? He wasn't sure. He adjusted his jacket just so for the camera to capture all of them.

Fist bumps of greeting. Faint voices. He caught *bro* mentioned a few times. It looked like the boy knew the group. There was an air of deference about him, as if he looked up to them.

Lights flared red. A car eased into a vacant space in front of them. One of the men straightened, looked up and down the street and went to a rolled-down window. The exchange was so swift that Cutter almost missed it.

That's a drug deal!

Street dealing had become sophisticated. Cars didn't just roll up to a bunch of shady-looking people and inquire. There were social media groups, photo identities of buyers in some cases, secure messaging apps, to coordinate a sale.

Darrell was among the rest of the men, and even through the growing darkness, Cutter could make out the boy's unease.

The car rolled away. The dealer returned to his friends and slipped something to another person. *Roll of cash.* All of it so fast and smooth that only someone watching closely would have made it out for what it was. And even then, it could be mistaken for a bunch of friends in a car making small talk.

No one on the boulevard looked their way. Pedestrians seemed to have given up on that section of the sidewalk. As if there were warning signs that only they could see.

Cutter knew how it was for the residents. *Many of them are in survival mode, living from paycheck to paycheck.* They wouldn't have the energy or the will to get involved. *The cops? They have bigger fish to fry,* he thought cynically.

One of the men cracked open a can, drank from it and threw it on the sidewalk. It rolled lazily. Another man kicked it beneath a parked car.

Another vehicle drove up. An SUV with tinted windows. A

different seller went to its window. The soft conversation turned loud. He straightened and yanked the door open and dragged out a man, who yelled and struggled, and then he and another thug were on him, kicking, punching.

Cutter blinked. He shook his head in bemusement. Nope, he wasn't dreaming. There was a man getting beaten on the street and no one was responding. *That line of parked vehicles is cutting off the view from passing traffic.* The rest of the men had surrounded them, blocking pedestrian traffic on the sidewalk. Darrell was fidgeting, trying to look away, but his school friend had a hand on his shoulder, clamped firm.

Cutter whipped out his cell, the burner that he always carried in addition to his usual phone, and dialed 911 instinctively. 'Man being attacked in Brownsville. I can see guns and knives,' he embellished and gave the location. 'Oh my God! They've cut him!' he cried out in alarm and hung up.

That will bring the cops.

He pulled out a bandana and wrapped it around his face. Was getting ready to rise when the victim was hauled to his feet. He was punched and shoved back to the vehicle. The seller pushed him inside the SUV, reached deep inside and snatched out a backpack. Slammed the door shut and pointed something dark and metallic-looking at the driver, who took off, tires squealing.

One of the hoods, seemingly the oldest of them, took the bag, unzipped it, checked its contents, zipped it up and gave it to Darrell. The student protested. He was pushed. He shook his head. He was slapped so hard his head rocked. He took the backpack reluctantly and slung it over his shoulders and slipped away, in between two cars with his friend.

Cutter sagged back when the boy disappeared from sight. He could hear sirens in the distance. The boy wouldn't be around when the cavalry showed up. That was a small win. He would take that.

Four of the thugs split. They jogged down the boulevard

toward the takeout in the distance and merged with the gloom and the thick of people.

The leader straightened as the sirens grew louder. He conferred with the remaining hood and was readying to leave when Darrell returned. Alone, with the bag in hand, presenting it to the thug.

What the—?

Cutter swore softly. Cops would arrive at any moment. If they found the backpack on the student, and it contained drugs or cash ...

He cursed again, and thought turned to action as he heaved himself up, took several strides, narrowing the distance to the gangbangers.

'Hey!' he called out. 'I saw what happened. You're dealing. I'll report you to—'

'Mind your business, dude,' the leader warned.

Seven steps away. The two hoods fanning out to face him. Darrell's wide eyes looking at him. The flash of red and blue lights down the boulevard, still a couple of blocks away.

'I saw you punch that guy. Sell drugs to that car.'

'Get away, old man,' the second hood snarled. 'Cross the street. Forget what happened.'

'What's in that backpack?' Cutter lunged at Darrell, got his right hand on its strap and jerked it hard.

The student shouted in pain. He stumbled back, freeing the bag.

Just as the hoods attacked.

Cutter was anticipating their moves.

He spun on his heel and swung the backpack in an arc. Connected with the nearest man's nose, which broke. Brought his knee up at the same time into the incoming groin and twisted away to let the man go sprawling.

'YOU—' the leader swore and drew a gun.

Cutter hadn't stopped moving. He dropped the backpack, ducked easily beneath the straightening arm, caught it at the elbow in a double-handed grip and dislocated the joint with a snap. He stepped aside nimbly and used the hood's momentum to send him staggering into the side of the nearest vehicle. Smashed the thug's face on its roof to finish him.

The cruisers were close by then, their sirens loud, their lights painting the street, scattering vehicles out of their way.

'GO!' Cutter yelled at Darrell. One second to yank up the leg of his jeans, withdraw his ankle-strapped Benchmade. A snip of the sharp blade and the backpack's strap, the one that he had been holding, came away.

He grabbed the boy, who was frozen, staring wide-eyed, and dragged him along with him as he burst into a sprint down the boulevard.

He had turned the corner when the first cruiser squealed to a stop at the fallen hoods. Left on Osborn Street, through a maze of housing projects, darting through spaces between shoppers, brushing past office-goers, running across lights and leaving curses and angry honks in their wake, and only when they were several blocks away did he slow down and let go of the boy.

Darrell staggered to the wall of a store and rested against it. He sucked air harshly and wheezed.

'You,' he gasped when he had gathered his breath. 'Are you following me?'

And only then did Cutter realize his bandana had slipped off.

11

Cutter mopped his face with the scrap of cloth and stuffed it into his back pocket.

'Let's go,' he nudged Darrell. 'We've got to keep moving.'

The student glowered at him and didn't move.

'Your choice.' He shrugged. 'The cops will fan out. Question people. They will find out two people bugged out of there.' He sized the teenager up. 'One of them with a backpack. Your choice.' He set off at a brisk pace. Stifled a grin when the boy caught up with them. They cut through lanes, doubling back several times until they reached Saratoga Avenue.

'Why are you following me?' the boy demanded as they approached his house.

'I wasn't. I was in the neighborhood. I was heading to that takeout joint beyond your group when I recognized you.'

'I don't believe you. Did my mom set you up? To watch me?'

'Believe what you want.'

An occasional passing car lit them up. Darrell's features pinched, his lips clamped, as he hurried to keep up with Cutter.

'You're going to tell her, aren't you?'

'I'm considering it.'

'Why don't you start, to warm me up for her,' he said bitterly. 'Warn me about gangs and drugs.'

'Do you need a warning? I'm sure you know how you'll end up.'

'Yeah? Why don't you tell me?'

'Dead or in prison.' He didn't hold back. 'That's where most hoods end up.'

'You don't know that.'

'I do.'

'Who are you to lecture me?' Darrell rounded on him. 'You've no idea what it's like for me. What I have been through.'

'Why don't you tell me?'

'So that you'll rat on me to Mom?'

'I know what it's like for you. You feel lost. Alone. Your mom comes home late. She's always tired. You think she's never there for you. When you and she talk, it's always to fight. It was different when your dad was around. You've lost that feeling of family. That gang—there's a feeling of belonging. You're a part of them. They make you feel valued. You're someone with them. I've seen it. I have lived it myself.'

'I knew you would do that. Make stories up for me.'

'Darrell,' Cutter said, softening his voice. 'You think you're all alone. That it's you against the world. The gang is your escape. It's never like that. Those dudes? They're using you. They wanted you to carry that backpack. What was in it? Baggies? Money? You're a mule for them. You're young. A high school student is not a priority for the cops. You'll get off lightly if you're caught. I bet those men, the ones who attacked me, have priors. They'll be facing hard time, longer sentences if they're arrested. It's business for them. With your mom? She would kill for you.'

'You think I haven't heard this before? I hear enough of it at school. There's nothing else Mom talks about. That and my grades. It's the same at Manuel's home, too.'

Is that his school friend?

'Who is he?'

The student bit his lip. Wiped sweat from his face. He squirmed under Cutter's intense gaze. 'A friend,' he said sullenly.

'Was he the one with you?'

'You *were* following me!'

'I was at the traffic lights at Mother Gaston. At the nail bar. I saw you down the street with your friend. Didn't recognize you initially.'

'You were there all along? We didn't see anyone.'

You wouldn't. Your buddies didn't show any street skills.

'I must have crossed the boulevard. Like I said, I was there on business. Manuel, he must be some friend. He stayed out of it. Why didn't he take that backpack?'

'He was arrested once. He was let off with a warning.'

'And you're clean.'

Darrell flushed. He looked to his right, at his apartment building far down the street.

'I can make my own decisions.'

'I can see that.'

'You don't have the right to—'

'Yeah. And I'm not telling you any more. You'll die or go to prison. Not my business,' he said callously. 'Tell me something. If that gang means that much to you, why did you refuse to take that backpack? They had to force you. And why did you return? You had second thoughts?'

A stubborn look came over the student. He set off down the street.

He doesn't want to admit that. He thinks it will make him look weak. Back off, Cutter told himself. *Yet another lecture isn't what he needs.*

'Why did you cut that?' Darrell nodded at the strap in his hand.

'It's got your prints. Mine, too. And unlike you, I have no interest in jail time.'

Been there. Did that.

That silenced the boy until they reached his building. He reached the door, hesitated and turned back.

'Will you tell my mom?'

Darrell's face shone with perspiration. His shirt was dirty and stuck to his lean body. His trousers and shoes were scuffed and his school bag kept slipping off his shoulder. He jammed his hands in his pockets, but not before Cutter saw them shake.

He's scared.

He read the boy for what he was in that moment. A fifteen-year-old whose world had collapsed when his folks split up. A teenager who had gotten himself in deep and didn't know how to extricate himself.

'It will break her.'

The boy nodded dumbly, a pleading look on his face.

'Call me. Any time.' He handed over his card. 'For anything.'

He walked away in the darkness, wondering what he would tell Carmel Ward.

And how he could get Darrell out of the gang.

12

Cutter was in his apartment an hour later. He washed up, went to the kitchen and rummaged through the refrigerator.

Removed three eggs and made a French omelet. A generous sprinkle of spices, a taste for which he had developed while in Asia. Poured himself a glass of juice and settled down for his dinner.

Home was a three-bedroom apartment on Lafayette, a brisk walk from his office. Funded from the proceeds of fixer missions for millionaire clients.

A long couch in the sitting room. A Persian rug on the floor. Mahogany dining table. Kitchen outfitted with modern fittings. No decorations. Just the one photograph of Riley by his bedside. That was enough. He carried her within himself. What more did he need?

He turned on the TV and followed the news as he ate. Kevin Rubin, presidential candidate, being interviewed on a talk show.

Cutter turned the volume up and listened.

He was running as an independent and, despite his outsider status, had gathered an enormous following all over the country. He got more screen time than the candidates from the mainstream parties. President Morgan, serving out his second term, got far less coverage.

He had a fascinating backstory.

Family who had made it big in oil. Inherited wealth. White supremacist in his early years. Gained notoriety while in college and at the start of his career in hedge funds. He went on radio shows and drew fans. Built on that platform and started his own newspaper. He was a celebrity. Dated Hollywood stars, those who didn't mind associating with him. Lived a flashy life. By the time he was in his thirties, there wasn't anyone in the US who hadn't heard of him.

And then it came crashing down.

He was arrested for white-collar crime. He had defrauded his business partners in an investment firm. He served a year in prison and came out as a reformed person.

He rejected his supremacy beliefs. Told the world that he had been young, naïve and foolish. Became an ethical investor, backed companies that made a positive difference to society. A few of his companies made it big, and that catapulted him to billionaire status.

That was when he discovered his love for politics and threw his hat into the presidential race.

Rubin was charismatic, and his strong oratorical skills spread his message around. Strong government and community focus.

His poll performance had surprised everyone. He was trailing the Veep, Bryan Thyssen, who was the lead contender, but had beaten all other candidates. Many analysts figured that if elections were to be held the next day, he just could end up being the country's second truly independent president, after George Washington.

Experts also believed many senior politicians from one or both the major parties would come out and support him once he increased his lead in the polls.

Cutter listened to him for a while as the candidate

expounded on his beliefs. *Hollywood couldn't have scripted his story better.*

He turned off the TV when he finished his dinner and cleaned up. He extracted his Benchmade and washed it. Wiped it dry and inserted it back in its kydex sheath. He had cut the strap to small pieces, which were now part of the city's sewage.

He turned on his laptop and opened his cloud account. Yeah, his jacket camera had worked. All its videos were in there.

He played the one from Mother Gaston. Good picture quality. Decent audio, too. The surveillance device had captured his fight, too.

His smile faded when the leader's face came up during the attack. He did look Caucasian. No scars, no tattoo—whoa!

Cutter straightened and paused the video. Wound it back and played it again.

His camera had captured Leader's profile when he had sidestepped just before crashing him against the car. There, on the neck.

A lion's head. Well etched.

Similar to the one he had seen at the bodega.

He tore his eyes away from the screen and made a call to a cop who owed him favors.

'Mother Gaston? Yeah, we found a backpack underneath a car. Full of baggies. Some oxy, most of them meth.'

'And the dealers?'

'No one there. Someone reported a knifing but no bodies, no perps, just the drugs.'

Leader and his man got away.

13

'What will you tell her?'

Arnedra, the next day in their office, when he had finished recounting his surveillance.

'Carmel?' Cutter made a face. 'Nothing for now. I think I connected with Darrell at the very end. He just might quit the gang. I'll shadow him some more. See what he gets up to.'

'If he's still hanging out with them?'

'I might confront him.'

'Leaving criminals isn't easy.'

'I know.'

'You'll work something out.'

He shook his head at the utter confidence in her voice.

'It's not as straight up as giving up a club membership.'

'You'll come up with something.'

'DIFIORE,' THE DETECTIVE BARKED WHEN HE CALLED HER.

'No howdy? No, how are you? No, I missed you?'

'I didn't miss you.'

Cops were like that. They loved him but pretended they hated his guts.

'I'm hurt.'

'I meant to ask you the other day,' he continued when she didn't respond. 'Boyce, the man I shot. Did he have a tattoo on his neck?'

'Why?'

'Come on, Gina,' he coaxed. 'Yes or no?'

'Difiore,' she told him bluntly, 'we aren't friends. It won't end there. You'll ask what kind, if I say yes. You'll ask more questions.'

Finding out her first name hadn't been hard, with his contacts.

'So, that's a yes?'

'Why do you want to know?'

Do I tell her about the gang? Can I keep Darrell out of it?

'Off the record?'

'I'm an NYPD detective. Nothing's off the record.'

'You know I have contacts. I can find out easily enough.'

'Ask them.'

She hung up.

Cutter sighed. He had been doing a lot more of it ever since he had come across this detective.

He ran through the list of people he knew. Nope. He couldn't ask Rolando. He was too high up, and besides, he didn't want to compromise his friend.

There was another detective. Someone he had helped.

'Wayne?'

'Cutter! How are you, buddy?'

That was more like it. Gina Difiore had probably skipped NYPD's *Tips on Being Polite* training.

'I'm good. How are the kids?'

'Killing me,' responded Wayne Poser, detective second grade with SID, Special Investigations Division. 'Why did I think I had to shoot for three?'

'How's Milly?'

Milly Poser, the cop's wife. Ran a charity for street kids, one of whom Cutter had helped leave a gang.

'She's spending more time at the shop. You think she's got someone on the side?'

'I'm sure of it.'

Twelve years of marriage hadn't dimmed the couple's romance.

'You made the news. The kids told their friends about you. They're the cool crowd now.'

'I haven't seen them in a while. Hey, you know Difiore?'

'Gina, yeah. She was my mentor a while ago.'

Cutter grimaced. Of all the cops to pick on, he had to call Wayne. *He'll be close to her.*

'A problem?'

'No, nothing to do with her. I'm chasing a lead and it reminded me of the holdup. I called her and, you know—'

'Yeah, she's a badass. She didn't help?'

'Nope.'

'You want to know something?'

'Not if it will put you in a tight spot.'

'Ask me. I'll decide.'

'That holdup. One of the dudes had a lion's tattoo. Or something that looked like it.'

'You want to see what exactly it was?'

'Yeah.'

'I can do that. But you got to turn up for dinner.'

'Deal.'

Keys clicked. Poser hummed beneath his breath. He grunted abruptly. His chair squeaked.

'You'd better talk to Gina.'

'Huh?'

'That's all I can tell you.' And he hung up.

. . .

One Police Plaza, OnePP, downtown Manhattan. HQ to the NYPD, where Major Cases, a SID team was based.

Cutter frowned as he approached the brutal-looking concrete building, which stood out from its surroundings. Major Cases didn't investigate bodega holdups. *Bank robberies, hijackings, kidnappings—that's what they deal with. Why's she looking into this?*

He walked around the building to the Avenue of the Finest, where the exit of the parking lot met Pearl Street. Bought a drink from the coffee joint and leaned against the metal framework of the awning overhead.

He fingered his phone. He could ask Poser, but he doubted the detective would give him any more intel. Not from the way he hung up. He could ask Beth or Meghan, and they could easily check out why Difiore was investigating a small case. They could also look up the tattoo. Nope to that, too. They had their missions.

He sipped his coffee as he considered what he knew of Difiore. Detective First Grade, the senior-most rank. Recipient of several medals and awards. Got covered in national media for her role in taking down a bank robbery gang. Highly reputed cop who was going places.

No one mentioned her attitude, he thought, grinning to himself. *Or maybe that's just for me.*

He straightened at seven pm, when he spotted her car, a silver Chevy, nosing past the concrete barriers.

She's alone. That was good. He stepped out on the exit road, drink in hand. Hoped that she wouldn't shoot him or run him over.

The detective seemed to say something to herself, and then her flasher lit and she rolled to the side.

She rolled down her window. 'Are you stalking me?'

'Nope. I—'

'How did you know I would be here? That this is my car?'

'I have my ways.'

'Like calling your friend, the commish?'

Commish, aka NYPD Police Commissioner.

Cutter squeezed the paper cup involuntarily. *Relax*, he admonished himself. *Anyone would want to know, in her position.*

'He's not the only one I know,' he replied mildly.

She checked him out with hostile eyes and then seemed to make a decision.

'What is it?'

'That tattoo. Boyce had one, didn't he?'

'Yeah.'

He fist-pumped internally. Getting her to acknowledge that was a win, however small.

'What kind?'

'Why do you want to know? Why are you interested?'

'I thought I saw another such tattoo.'

She gave him an incredulous look. 'You realize this city has eight million people. Several million will have tattoos. Chances are, thousands will have a lion's head inked on their necks.' She clamped her lips tight when she realized what she had admitted.

'Did it look like this?'

He showed her the sketch he had made.

She took it warily and inspected it. Her eyes flicked at him in surprise. 'This is very good. You did this?'

'Yeah.' *Not much else to do in a super-max prison.*

'Yes. This is how his tattoo was.'

'No gang connection, you said.'

'Yeah. What do you know that I don't?'

'Nothing.'

She was out of her car in an instant, her face darkening in fury.

'Listen,' she hissed. 'You're holding something back.'

'You have to trust me. Please.'

'Trust you?' she scoffed. 'You're interfering in an active NYPD investigation.'

'Yeah, about that. You're with Major Crimes. Why are you looking into this?'

'Ever heard of Task Force, dude?' she sneered. 'And, don't change the subject. TELL ME!' She slammed her palm on her roof. The cop in the security hut at the concrete barrier came out, nodded once when she waved at him and returned to his position.

'I can't. Not now. I need to run something through.'

'I can bring you in, and all your high-powered contacts won't stop me.'

'Look, Difiore. I can guess what you think of me. That I'm sorta like a vigilante—'

'You are.'

'I'm sure you spoke to various cops who know me. What did they say?'

She refused to answer.

'They said I was *unorthodox*,' he quoted what Rolando had told him once, 'but I didn't break the law and helped the cops whenever I could, didn't they?'

She didn't look at him.

'That tattoo. I saw it on a gang member.' He decided to give a little.

'Where?' She whipped her head around.

'Can't tell you.'

'Grogan,' she grated through clenched teeth, 'if I find out—'

'You'll know what I know. Give me some time.'

'One day.'

'A week.'

'No—'

'I'll need that much. Meanwhile, you can question Boyce and his friends again. Where he got that ink done. Whether he's hiding that he's part of a gang.'

'I can't. They're all dead.'

14

Cutter stared at her dumbly, then went to the coffee window and got two more drinks. Handed one to her wordlessly, took his first swallow and cleared his throat. 'Dead? How? When?'

'The day you called me,' she spit out savagely, 'they went for dinner. The three of them, in Queens. That's where they lived. Friends since high school. They were T-boned by a box truck.'

'That can't be an accident.'

'It was,' she said wearily. 'Driver was drunk. Well over the limit. He gave himself up immediately. He's got a few drunk-driving violations. Nothing else.'

'That gang—'

'Grogan, read my lips. This wasn't a gang killing.'

Cutter drank the rest of his coffee, crushed the cup and dumped it in a bin. He shook his head in disbelief. 'It's too coincidental.'

'That happens.'

Her lips twisted in a sly smile. 'Poser sits behind me. I can hear his calls. I knew he was talking to you. I messaged him. Asked him how he would like to get back to patrol. He hung up on you.'

'He's my friend.'

'And he's my mentee.'

'Used to be, I understand.'

'That relationship never ends.'

He sighed. There would be only one winner in a headbutting contest with her. *It won't be me.*

'That bodega holdup,' he said, changing tack. 'Have you looked up any other attacks?'

'Hundreds of such crimes in the city.'

'I mean, where the owners were targeted.'

'Like how?'

'Racially targeted.'

She straightened. Gave him an impassive look. 'We're done talking. You'll get nothing else from me until you tell me what you know. You've got my number.'

He watched until her car joined the traffic on Pearl Street. *What did she mean by that?* There are more such crimes? Or was Difiore just being herself, stubborn, unreadable?

Cutter gave up. He had two threads to pursue. He decided to follow up on the easiest one.

'WHO IS HE?' PEYTON QUINDICA, FBI SAC, SPECIAL AGENT in Charge, jammed her phone between shoulder and ear as her fingers flew over her keyboard.

'He calls himself a fixer,' Difiore replied over a clank of metal. 'Hostage rescue. Missing persons. That kind of thing.'

'Like a PI?'

'He's not licensed, and he takes on more dangerous work than most investigators. I've sent his file across to you. He must be in your system too. He's well-connected. There are senior people in the NYPD who vouch for him.'

'How senior?'

'All the way to the top.'

Quindica blew hair out of her eyes as she considered the detective's words.

'Cops have referred him to some victims. I think he's gotten a few clients that way from you folks as well.'

'FBI?'

'Yeah.'

'How much does he know about the Task Force?'

'Nothing. But he could find out, with his contacts.'

'He won't,' Quindica assured her. 'Like I said before, we are as covert as we can get. Only a handful of people, at the very top at your end and mine, know of us.'

'Let's hope it stays that way.'

'Yeah. Grogan. You think we should shake him?'

'Nothing would give me more pleasure,' Difiore declared. 'But I gave him my word. Let's wait to hear from him.'

'Keep on top. Let's sweat him if he doesn't turn up with anything.'

'I sure as heck will.'

Quindica grinned at the enthusiasm in the detective's voice and hung up. She stifled a yawn and stretched. Rubbed her eyes and returned to her screen.

SHE HEADED THE MULTI-AGENCY TEAM THAT HAD BEEN formed when her case overlapped with Difiore's.

She had been looking into white supremacists infiltrating law enforcement. The detective had been investigating a string of crimes that seemed to have racial connotations.

Bart Jamison, the FBI Director, had convened a meeting with NYPD's Commissioner, which resulted in creation of the task force.

When they met, the FBI SAC liked what she saw in the detective. She recognized another super-smart, dedicated law enforcement officer. Both of them came from minority backgrounds: Quindica with her Chinese-Polynesian roots, Difiore with her Latin background. They had to overcome systemic and institutional biases, along with certain societal views. They'd had to wear invisible armor as they rose through the ranks to reach their positions.

The detective had further impressed her when she didn't start any turf wars within the task force. Instead, she saw the joint investigation as an opportunity. With the FBI's reach and resources and the NYPD's street savvy, they could get things done.

Quindica's only concern had been Griffen. 'He's a great cop,' Difiore had assured her. 'That act he puts on, getting in people's faces, is just that.' The SAC didn't make a fuss, and as she came to know the NYPD team, she found the detective was right.

Progress had been slow, and there was little to show for their suspicions. *Other than Gina's cases.* She cracked her knuckles and massaged a crick in her neck. They had come across the red lion tattoo on some of those arrested, all of them white perps. *No known link to any gang, however.*

Some of those criminals had gotten away with light sentences, and in at least one case the thug had walked because his crime had been recorded wrongly.

They seemed to have reached a frustrating dead end until Cutter Grogan turned up.

She logged into her email and opened the file Difiore had sent. Sucked in her breath at the redactions in the fixer's military details. Searched for him in the FBI's various databases. No arrests. No criminal records, however his name was tagged by several staff, from field agents to SACs. Her eyebrows shot up at one name. Bob Mulhoney, the Deputy Director, to whom she reported.

She checked her watch and dialed his number.

'Bob, you heard of Cutter Grogan?' she asked when they had finished the small talk. 'In New—'

'Cutter? Yeah. Not many with that name. Why?'

'He's come up in a case we're looking at. Looks like he's withholding some intel. I want to come down hard and heavy on him, but Gina wants to wait.'

'You want to know if we can trust him?'

'Yeah.'

'I know Cutter well. But you should talk to Bart.'

'The Director?'

'Yeah.' Mulhoney chuckled at her astonishment. 'He knows our friend even better.'

'How?'

'Ask him. I'll give him a heads-up to expect your call.'

'I WAS CUTTER'S CO,' THE FBI DIRECTOR TOLD HER. IT WAS nine pm, but he had taken her call promptly. 'Commanding Officer. On a few missions. What do you want to know about him?'

'Can we trust him, sir?'

'Have you seen his file?'

'The one I have is heavily redacted, sir.'

A long silence.

'Get on to ARTEMIS.'

The program was for sharing highly classified files. All parties had to log on to it, verify themselves biometrically, and turn their screen cams on. The sender then delivered the requested documents to the rest and stayed online until it was read. The program registered the movements of the readers' irises and flipped the pages automatically, based on the reading speed. Note-taking and photography weren't allowed.

'Yes, sir.'

Quindica froze when, moments later, a file appeared on her screen.

'Sir, I don't have clearances for this.'

'You do, now.'

She skipped through the sections she already knew. Found

that it was still redacted, but now she could read the commendations from various officers and ... her eyes slowed when she read about the Distinguished Service Cross and the Purple Heart. Both of them awarded in secret for clandestine missions.

'Sir, there are still many blacked-out parts. Like, a lot.'

'Yeah, you don't need to know about any of his operations. Skip to the last.'

'That's his civilian life, sir. Why is it in his file?'

'You'll see.'

Quindica skimmed through it quickly. Cutter getting married to Riley, a paramedic with FDNY, Fire Department of New York. A few photographs of the couple and their friends. A honeymoon in Yanartas, Turkey, a remote part of the country. She felt she was intruding. Uneasy that such personal details were included in the record. Was about to end the program when it came up on screen.

Terrorists bursting into their hotel room. Capturing and taking them to an abandoned village. Tayyib Mansoor, a Daesh terrorist, torturing them. Raising his knife to behead Riley when she lunged forward and impaled herself on it.

The SAC slowed her reading. No, she hadn't made a mistake. The report said Grogan's wife had deliberately thrust herself on the blade.

Mansoor and his men left Grogan's bullet-ridden body in the village, thinking he was dead. A goat herder found him barely conscious and nursed him back to life.

Quindica sat back and rubbed her brows. There wasn't much more in his file. His rehabilitation, return to the US. His new life.

'Sir.' She cleared her throat, aware how hoarse she sounded. 'There are a couple of years missing. After his return to New York.'

Her boss filled her screen when he terminated the program. He was still in his Hoover Building office in DC. In his white shirt, sleeves rolled up to reveal powerful forearms. Looking as if his day was beginning, not ending.

'I shared that file with you so that you get a measure of him,' Jamison said, evading her question. 'Whether you trust him ... that's your call to make.'

'You would?'

'With my life. There's something you should know that's not in the file.'

I bet there's a lot more that's not in there.

'Riley was pregnant when she died.'

The SAC exhaled slowly as if the weight of the world was on her shoulders.

'How does one live through all that without going insane?'

It was a rhetorical question, but her boss answered.

'Cutter's not an ordinary person.' He smiled gently, his eyes distant. 'I tried to recruit him into the FBI. He turned me down flat. Said he was done with working in structured environments. He wanted to be free.'

'Permission to share those details with Difiore, sir?'

'I cleared you for that file.' He drummed his fingers and then nodded. 'Okay. I'll clear her as well. Your task force might lead you to places where you might need such security clearances. However—'

'Yes, sir. If we leak that info, we'll be cleaning toilet bowls in Idaho.'

'Both of you.'

'Understood, sir. Why's that file so detailed?'

'Welcome to the world of covert ops, Quindica.' He smiled thinly but didn't elaborate.

'Does he do any contract work for the CIA, sir?'

'No. That operator life is well behind him, which is why the file ends there.'

'Sir, didn't we capture Mansoor?'

'Yeah. A joint manhunt with the Brits and Germans. We captured him in Lebanon and brought him Stateside for trial.

He's doing life in a supermax.' Something crossed her boss's face. A fleeting expression that disappeared so fast that she wasn't sure if she had seen it or if it was a screen flicker.

'About those missing years?'

'You'll have to ask him yourself. If you do, let him know I let you read his file.'

QUINDICA WAS STILL THINKING ABOUT THE FILE'S CONTENTS when she reached her small apartment in Brooklyn. She freshened and had her dinner, thinking of Riley Grogan and how she had died.

She poured herself a glass of milk and went to her bedroom window. If she stood on her toes, she could see the lights of the bridge above the rooftops.

She was a veteran herself. She had served in the 82nd Airborne and had one tour of Afghanistan under her belt. She had left the army on her return, wanting to try a different life, and applied to join the FBI. She passed the selection test and the rest was history.

She and her girlfriends had vacationed in Yanartas, famous for its natural fires that burned from vents in the rock.

It was splendid isolation. Nothing but the sky and nature. Ideal for bonding with the earth and with friends.

She finished her milk, rubbed the calluses on her fingers absently, and, as the night grew, thought about what made people who they were.

15

Cutter Grogan, unaware of who Peyton Quindica was and her insight into him, was tailing Darrell Ward the next day.

The easier of the two lines of investigation he could pursue.

He had worked it out.

The only way to protect the boy from his involvement was to present that leader to the cops. Which meant he had to find out where the thug hung out. He could ask Darrell, but there was no saying the student would cooperate.

Which was why he was back on the street. A false nose and contacts in his eyes to hide their natural green. A disguise that would fool even keen observers.

Following them in his rental vehicle, watching them in his mirrors as they walked briskly down the sidewalk.

Keeping up with them wasn't a problem. Traffic was slow on account of the school. A car went the other way, a pounding beat pouring from its speakers and open windows, filling the street. The driver reached his hand out and stylishly high-fived his friends as he drove.

That's why gangs thrive. He followed the car in his mirror as it continued down the street, honking as it turned the corner. Gangs offered image, status, and a feeling of belonging to those who were vulnerable.

He put the thought behind him as he located Darrell, who was with Manuel again. The other student was talking earnestly, gesticulating as they walked.

They were going a different route. Down Pitkin, left at the lights at Herzl Street and toward Betsy Head Park. Past it, beneath the overhead subway line on Livonia, and there the two students stopped. Behind a line of cars, leaning against the metal fence, chewing gum.

Tailing them was a practiced art. He overtook them, slid into vacant spaces and waited for them to catch up.

A train passed above, its rattling and clanking drowning every other sound, and in that flood of noise, a dark car rolled to a stop next to the boys.

Leader got out from the passenger side, a bandage on his forehead. The rear door opened and two hoods emerged.

Same dudes from Mother Gaston.

The three men approached the students, stopped a couple of feet away.

Cutter noted the way the thugs formed a protective shield around Leader, hiding his actions from the street as much as possible.

Darrell dropped his eyes when the man confronted him, kept his head down. He flinched when the thug jabbed his shoulder with a finger.

Leader looked around casually. Didn't seem to spot anything threatening. Backhanded the boy, splitting his lip. Raised his hand to strike again when Manuel intervened, talking fast. The other hoods closed in. One of them, the man who had pulled a gun the other night, spoke softly at his boss and nudged him towards the car.

Leader went, but not before gesturing savagely.

Cutter was too far away to lip-read, but it was obvious what the man was saying.

He's angry. Blaming Darrell for the lost drugs. Probably threatening him as well.

He watched as Manuel pulled the boy away from the railing. They jaywalked across Livonia and went down Strauss Street. He watched the teenager's slumped shoulders until the line of cars hid the students. When he looked up, Leader's car was pulling out.

Cutter nosed out and let an SUV go past. The vehicle carried just the driver, and through its rear and front windows he could see inside the dealer's car.

Leader was still raging. He waved his hands angrily as he addressed his men.

His elbow sure healed fast. Or, I didn't dislocate it. He could guess why the man was furious. *He's got to answer to his boss. Make the loss good.*

Was Darrell in danger?

He thought about it as he tailed them to Rockaway, hung a right and maintained a car length's distance.

Nope. They would have acted sooner if he was a threat. They still need him as a mule.

The thugs circled aimlessly in Brownsville for an hour. Hegeman Avenue, East Ninety-Eighth Street, Sutter Avenue and Julius Street. A wide loop they repeated continuously.

They're killing time until their next meeting.

No other explanation. It wasn't a counter-surveillance operation to shake off any tails. There was no attempt to double back, switch lanes or stop abruptly.

Cutter was familiar with Brownsville, but the neighborhood never failed to jolt him when he visited. The resigned look on many people's faces as they went about their lives. Chasing the American dream had fallen by the wayside.

The neighborhood had one of the highest concentrations of public housing in the county. One TV channel had dubbed the stretch of Rockaway leading to the intersection with Livonia as the most dangerous street in the city.

He shook his head unconsciously. He had been fostered by such families. He knew how hard it was to keep hope afloat when the system and circumstances conspired against people.

Taillights flared ahead, rousing him. Leader's car was heading to Livonia. He jammed the gas, cut ahead of a family vehicle, and fell behind them.

Deepening evening. Traffic growing as office-goers returned home. Explosion of red again as the thugs' vehicle singled and turned into at a bar's parking lot.

Cutter checked it out as he drove past. Big parking lot. That was a plus. That would give him cover. He drove on, cursed under his breath when Powell Street came up. One-way street, no right turns on it. He had to go on Junius to turn, circle all the way to get to Livonia.

He drove into the lot, searched swiftly, and located Leader's car in a corner. Cutter parked in the same row, several spaces away, and brought his phone out. Clear line of sight through the windows of the vehicles in between.

Gunman and driver were out, leaning against the vehicle, puffing spliffs. Leader was on his phone as well. Nodding a lot. Deference in his posture.

They made no move to leave.

Cutter waited as well.

Ten pm. The bar was emptying. Cars beeped as their owners keyed their fobs and headlights came on. Two cars still between the hoods and him. Still no move to leave.

Must be a gang-owned or -controlled joint. That's why they aren't worried.

Headlights flashed and painted the lot brightly before they dimmed. A Suburban. Dark as coal, shining under the dim lighting of the lot. He pretended to speak angrily, throwing his hands up in the air when it drove past.

Can't make out who's inside. Tinted windows.

It returned and slowed. Backed into a space next to Leader's vehicle.

Bummer. That blocked his view. He was opening the door when a dome light came on. Leader's. It turned off, and a shadow moved. The thug came around the hood of the Suburban, whose driver window rolled down.

Cutter checked his surroundings swiftly. No one was looking in his direction. He glanced down at himself. Nope, the jacket camera wouldn't work. He was sitting too low for it to capture the meeting. He raised his cell phone slowly and fingered its camera button just as the large vehicle's interior light switched on.

Leader shifted on his feet uneasily, which briefly exposed the interior of the vehicle to Cutter's view. A hatchet-faced man in the driver's seat. A larger man beyond him, his face bathed in shadow. Bald. He leaned forward to speak to the thug, and then the light went off.

Cutter kept taking photographs as something stirred inside him. A distant memory. Did he know the driver? And that bald man ... he hadn't seen his face, but there was something familiar in the shape of his head and the way he had moved. He racked his brains as he captured the meeting, but no names or faces came to mind.

More indistinct movement inside the Suburban. Leader reached out and grabbed a large travel bag. Hefted it in his hand and nodded his head. The Suburban's headlights turned on before he crossed over to his vehicle. Cutter turned away when its windows rolled up and slid down in his seat. He yelled into his phone as he looked blindly out of the window. Hatchet's profile showed up when his car's headlights fell on the passing SUV: sharp features, lean face, hollow cheeks. And then the vehicle disappeared, leaving him with that feeling again. That he had seen the man somewhere.

Cutter risked a quick glance when Leader's car didn't follow. *He's checking the bag. Got to be drugs in it. Making up for the stock they lost when I attacked them.* Distribution lines had to be supplied and end customers had to be kept satisfied. There was no loyalty in the business. A user could find any other gang to buy from.

'I've seen a drug deal go down,' he spoke hurriedly, panic in his voice when he got the operator on the emergency number. 'In the parking lot of a bar. Livonia Avenue.' He gave the address and upped the anxiety. 'Hurry. They're still here. THEY'VE SEEN ME—'

He hung up and drove out. Got lucky when a parking space opened up as a pickup truck left. Slid into it quickly and climbed out. That food truck over there, that would do nicely. It was doing brisk business even at that time of the night. He joined the line, his mouth watering at the smells coming from it. A slight angle of his head and he could side-eye the parking lot's exit. The thugs were still inside.

He was at the counter, placing his order, when the cops arrived. Flashing lights, sirens, several vehicles, the works. Four Police Interceptors and three patrol cars surged into the parking lot, while the others ranged out on Livonia.

'Wow!' Cutter spoke around a mouthful of burger. 'Wonder what went down?'

'Drug bust,' said the apron-clad vendor leaned over his counter to look. 'Or a murder. Not much else happens in Brownsville.'

Cutter joined the crowd of curious spectators, watched and ate. Grunted in satisfaction when he made out Leader and his thugs in the Interceptors when they emerged.

'It won't make any difference,' the vendor said cynically when he returned for paper towels. 'They'll be back on the street. Nothing changes here.' Several bystanders nodded at his words.

Cutter didn't argue with them. *They live here; they know how it is. I'm not from their world.*

He wiped his hands and reached his car. Drove back with the windows down and the night air swirling inside his rental. He hoped the vendor was wrong and that Difiore would find out about the arrest and investigate the lion tattoo.

He thought of the two men in the Suburban as he crossed Brooklyn Bridge, the lights of the city spread out on each side of him.

Do I know them? How?

16

Doug Mease knew something was wrong from the way Jeff 'Gunner' Sheller listened to his incoming call in silence. He drove quietly, carefully, sticking to the speed limit, waiting at the lights.

He usually had a driver, but he missed getting behind the wheel and took every opportunity he could.

'What is it?' he asked when his companion hung up.

'Davis.' He spat out the name like a curse.

'What happened to him?'

'He and his men got arrested. At the bar where we met.'

Mease froze. He scanned Park Avenue rapidly, and when Gunner pointed at a vacant space, drove into it.

'That's not good.' His voice sounded calm, still. That was good. Panic and fear were the enemy of reasoning. He was famous for never losing his cool. He breathed quietly and placed his hands lightly on his thighs. They didn't tremble. 'He's seen me.'

'You are not a public figure. He doesn't know your name.'

'He'll be able to recognize me.'

'I told you to stay in the backseat. Don't drive. You didn't listen—'

'Gunner.' Mease didn't raise his voice, but Sheller stopped talking immediately.

'Davis needs to be taken care of.'

'He's important to us. His gang controls a big part of Brownsville.'

'I'm not asking.'

'It won't be easy.'

'We have our cops in the NYPD.'

'We can't risk them.'

'We can't risk him giving me or you up.'

'He won't do that. He's been in the business for a long time. Neither he nor his people have ever revealed they're part of us.'

'You don't know he'll keep it that way.'

'We have a code.'

'We also have a code for punishing people when they make mistakes.'

'It'll be difficult.'

Mease looked at him impassively. Gunner was smart. People often took in his big size and mean-eyed look and thought he was all brawn. Those folks were wrong.

'We have a few people in the 73rd Precinct. That's where they'll be taken.'

'Do it. You and I, both, have our contacts in the NYPD—high up. Many of them are Lions as well. We can get them to cover this action.'

Gunner made a few calls, seemed to find the right police officer, and issued instructions.

'I spoke to our friend, in OnePP.'

Mease nodded. He knew who the gang leader was referring to. A senior leader in the ranks who had sworn allegiance to the outfit.

That was how they worked.

'He'll find a cop in the precinct who'll do the job.'

'Remind me who this man is, the prisoner.' Mease

commanded when the gang leader had finished. 'All I know is you had to give him some stock.'

'Do you really want to know? You want to keep distance between us and you and our friend.'

'I want to know anything that might affect his chances.'

'This has nothing to do with him.'

'I'll be the judge of that.'

'I told you. Davis is our chapter head in Brownsville. He's good. I was thinking of promoting him to take over all of Brooklyn.'

'He lost a shipment, didn't he?'

'We aren't selling soap or screen wipes. There's some loss in our business.'

Gunner didn't drop his eyes or look away when Mease pinned him with his stare. That was good, too. The man wasn't scared. He was a bull. He ran his nationwide gang with an iron fist. Nothing happened on the streets, his turf, without him knowing it. Every thug of his swore allegiance to the Lions and were aware of the dangers of violating the code.

Mease's eyes lingered on the patch of pale skin, lighter than the surrounding flesh, on the man's neck, which shone in the lights of a passing car.

Where once a lion's tattoo had been inked.

Police Officer Pete Martinelli licked his lips as he went to the holding cells. The instructions he had received were specific. He went closer to the barred door and surveyed Davis. Walked down the hallway and returned, just as he would for any other well-being check on arrested suspects.

He turned his back on the nearest camera and found that this time, his shuffling had woken the prisoner.

'Take my gun.' His lips barely moved. He brought his hand up to scratch his neck and in doing so, pulled down his collar to show the lion's head. 'Hold me hostage.'

Davis didn't move.

The cop went out and returned an hour later. Repeated the same action. Thrust his right hip forward to present his weapon.

The prisoner got up.

He acted on the officer's third pass.

His fingers shot through the bars, caught hold of the gun and whipped it out.

Martinelli didn't react the way he had expected.

'GUN!' the officer yelled and dived to the side. 'HE'S GOT MY GUN.'

Davis looked perplexed. 'What—'

'DROP IT!' an officer roared as cops flooded the hallway and covered the prisoner.

'But—'

'DO IT. NOW!'

Davis moved.

'HE'S GOING TO FIRE!' Martinelli screamed.

His warning was drowned in the crash of shots.

17

Cutter caught the news when he was finishing cleaning up after breakfast the next day.

Prisoner shot in 73rd Precinct, the caption ran. CCTV footage that the channel had somehow obtained.

His plate fell into the sink with a clatter. He wiped his hands on his jeans and lunged toward his phone.

Surely it was a coincidence. *Let it not be Leader*, he prayed as he thumbed numbers and dialed. The prisoner was indistinct in the clip as it played on repeat.

His call connected just as the man's name came on screen. Leon Davis. It meant nothing to him.

'Brian, Cutter, yeah, yeah,' he cut through the greetings. 'Davis, the prisoner who was shot at night. Where was he arrested?'

He swore loudly when his worst fears were confirmed. Apologized to the cop and hung up. Dialed another number.

'Difiore.'

'That's the second prisoner you've lost,' he told her bitterly.

'What? Grogan? That you? What are you talking about?'

'Leon Davis, the prisoner who was killed in the 73rd Precinct.'

'I heard that. What about him? It's not my case.'

'Check his body, Difiore,' he raged. No more first names. He ended the call before she could retort.

He washed his dishes, the mechanical actions calming him. *Fool,* he told himself when he had regained composure. He hadn't lost it when outnumbered and under heavy fire in Syria or Iraq. There was no reason to take out his anger on the detective.

He made to call her but stopped himself.

She'll call me.

DETECTIVE FIRST GRADE GINA DIFIORE WAS SEETHING WHEN Grogan hung up on her. Who did that fixer think he was? She glared at Poser, who was looking at her curiously. Counted to twenty and got her pulse back to normal.

Okay. What was all that about? Why would he care about some prisoner? And why should she check his body?

She read the shooting report. Several precinct officers were on administrative leave pending an investigation. That was standard procedure for an incident of that nature.

She read about Leon Davis. A few priors for possession and dealing. Served time. Was violent and ruthless. He ran his own gang. She tapped her teeth with a pen. That wasn't normal. There were very few independents in the city. Almost every thug belonged to a larger gang. Why would it be different in Davis's case?

No, she decided, the more she thought of it. The previous detectives hadn't recorded gang affiliations, or Davis had been a good liar. Her eyes narrowed at Davis's description. He was white, but that wasn't what held her attention.

Now she knew why Grogan mentioned his body.

Another lion tattoo.

'There has to be some connection,' Quindica surmised when the detective broke it down for her. 'Nothing in our system, though.'

'Grogan knows something.'

'There's something you should know about him.'

'What?'

'Not on the phone.'

THEY MET IN BATTERY PARK, THE FBI SAC AND THE detective, both women radiating such authority that tourists skirted widely around where they were seated.

'What did you find out about him?'

'It's classified. I ran it past my grand boss and he cleared you to receive it.'

'Grand Boss? The Director?'

'Yeah.'

'He can do that?'

'There isn't much Bart Jamison can't do.'

Difiore nodded. The FBI Director was a legend in law enforcement circles. *America's Sheriff* was how Time Magazine had described him once.

'Color me surprised and interested.'

Quindica went through Grogan's file, leaving nothing out, and when she had finished the detective was silent. They watched ferries depart with travelers, some bound for Ellis Island and the Statue, others for a loop of the city, all of them packed with camera-wielding tourists and excited families. Making memories that would linger in their minds. And, if those memories started to fade, there were digital proofs to fall back on.

'That's ...' Difiore trailed off, her face pensive. 'Yeah,' Quindica nodded understandingly. 'I had to read it a few times to take it all in.'

'Why did Jamison share it with you?'

'He wants us to know who Grogan is. What makes him tick.'

'And perhaps he wants us to team up with Grogan?'

'That thought crossed my mind. However, the fixer's an

external party. A civilian. The only part he plays is by telling us what he knows.'

'Good. We're agreed, then.'

'Yeah. We cut him no slack.'

18

Cutter went for a run after his call with the detective.

Early morning in Central Park was his preferred time and route. That was when the city was still slow and the air the freshest. A fast five-mile lap, followed by sets of martial arts moves, wing chun, jiu jitsu, alternating between fast and slow until sweat poured like a river over his body. Over time he had gained a few fans, regulars who stopped to watch him practice, and a few kids tried to ape his moves.

He didn't go to the park. He hit the streets, a backpack over his shoulders, strapped tightly, threading through people, running in automatic mode, letting his mind float free of his body, heading to the East River and then the Hudson, a wide loop that spanned the breadth of the city. He walked the last few blocks, allowing his body to cool.

His footsteps echoed in the basement car park of his building. Lines of vehicles, a few vacant spaces, no other person. He went to his SUV and brought out the empty water bottles for refilling.

'We've been waiting—'

He let go of the bottles, which crashed to the concrete and

rolled away. He dived to the floor, twisting his body as he fell, reaching back with his left hand to yank his backpack to the side, his right hand reaching inside its partly open mouth to come out with his Glock. He landed on his chest, one hand to brace his fall, the other straight and true, training the weapon on the speaker. Muscles and limbs and eyes and brain working together seamlessly in one long, smooth move, executed flawlessly and completed even before the fallen bottles had stopped moving.

He relaxed when he took in the figures his barrel was pointing at.

Two women, both in suits. One of them was Difiore; the other, a stranger.

'Impressive,' the detective's companion said.

'Grogan has many talents.'

'As we are finding out.'

Cutter got to his feet and returned his Glock to his backpack.

'I hope you've got a permit for that.' The cop stopped a rolling bottle and kicked it back toward him. He ignored her comment. Stooped and collected them with one hand.

'You were waiting for me?' He took in the second woman. Silky, dark hair cut straight to her shoulders. Black eyes that studied him expressionlessly. Light complexion. No makeup. Lips thinned in a flat line. The same height as Difiore. The same build, even. Lean, straight posture, the suit's well-cut jacket falling to her waist. A glint of a belt buckle. Leather shoes that gleamed in the garage lights.

'Nah, we were out, taking in the sights,' the detective replied sarcastically.

'How can I help you?'

'You can tell us what you know about this tattoo,' the stranger said.

'You got Davis,' he replied, addressing Difiore. 'You can start from there.'

She's some kind of cop as well. Senior. But heck, he wasn't going to respond to the newcomer. *Not unless she's introduced.* He could play their game.

'He's dead.'

'I can't help you anymore.'

'You wanted a week.'

'And I delivered in two days.'

The detective's brows came together in amazement. Then her face cleared. 'You called it in!'

He didn't answer.

'Grogan,' the other woman said softly, dangerously, 'You had better tell everything you know. NOW!'

A man entered the car park from the elevator entrance. He looked at them, startled. Read their body language and skirted wide of them before heading to his car.

'And you are?' he challenged her.

'FBI. Special Agent in Charge Peyton Quindica.'

Cutter sized her up, and then the detective. 'Task Force.' He recalled what the cop had said when they had met at her parking lot.

'Yeah, Peyton heads it. I report to her.'

'What's this about?'

'Need to know,' the SAC sneered. 'And you don't need to know.'

'It was good meeting you,' he told them and headed to the elevator.

'Grogan,' Difiore sighed. 'We need ...'

'I'm listening.'

'You're obstructing a federal investigation,' Quindica growled.

'Arrest me.'

'Don't think I won't.'

'Grogan, you do us a favor, we might be able to help you sometime,' the cop cut in quickly.

'I won't need your help.'

'We know about Yanartas.'

That detached feeling swept over him instantly as he spun on his heel, his hand instinctively reaching for his backpack to draw his weapon.

STOP!

His hand fell away limply. He breathed. In, out, in, out, until the thundering of his blood faded and the city's sounds returned.

They're doing their job. I would have used that intel if I was in their shoes.

The door behind him opened. Another office-goer, talking loudly on his phone. He barely gave them a glance as he ordered someone to buy all the stock of some company.

'We can go to your apartment. Sixth floor, isn't it?' The detective waited until Stock Buyer drove out. 'This place will get busy.'

'Only my friends come to my apartment,' he told her pointedly.

'We're stuck. Dead end.' Quindica's hands twisted in the smallest gesture of helplessness.

Cutter thought about it for a moment. *What do I have to lose?* He was good as long as he didn't mention Darrell or Carmel. Besides, it didn't hurt to have more cop and FBI contacts.

He nodded and led them to the elevator and up to his apartment. Noticed the way they took it in quickly. Saw the surprise in their eyes, which they hid just as quickly.

They must have thought I live like a slob.

'I need to shower,' he told them. 'Kitchen's over there.' He nodded toward the hallway. 'Help yourself to coffee.'

'This place would go for millions,' Quindica mused. 'How is it that a soldier can afford it?'

'Money laundering. That's my main gig. The fixer business, that's just a cover.'

He couldn't help but chuckle at her look. Pinned Difiore with his eyes. 'Don't steal the silverware.'

'We're the good people,' she told him cuttingly. 'It's the other side that does that.'

'Yeah, and all cops are clean, aren't they?' he tossed back.

He had meant it flippantly, but his smile evaporated at the fast look they exchanged.

Crooked cops? That's what the task force is about?

19

They had made him a cup of coffee as well when he returned to the living room.

He took an appreciative sip. Difiore on the couch idly flipping through a magazine, Quindica at the window, looking out pensively.

'Nope.' The SAC felt his eyes on her. 'We didn't steal anything.'

'There would have to be something to grab in the first place,' the detective said with a smirk. 'Clearly, Grogan is into minimalism.'

He sighed. One snarky detective he could just about deal with. Now there was Quindica, too.

He was halfway to the kitchen before he stopped. Living alone for too long did that. Made him forget his manners.

'Let's talk there,' he jerked his head. 'I'm going to rustle up something. You want to join me?'

'Depends.' The detective patted her belly, which rumbled loudly. 'Are you a good cook?'

'He might poison us,' the SAC said.

He threw his hands up and went to his fridge. Brought out several wraps, bell peppers, onions, baby spinach and a chunk of cheese. Placed them on the island. Grated the cheese efficiently while they pulled up chairs and watched him silently. He sliced and diced the veggies and spread them over each wrap. Added generous dollops of hummus and sprinkled spices. Rolled the wraps tightly and cut each end. Placed them on a tray with bowls of salsa and brought out fresh plates and cutlery.

'Mexican pinwheels,' he presented the preparation to them.

'Talk,' Quindica ordered after her first bite.

'You're in my house, eating my food,' he told her. 'You go first.'

'I can shoot him,' Difiore told her companion. 'We can make it look like he was threatening us.'

The SAC wiped her lips. Exchanged an indecipherable look with the detective and reached for the orange juice Cutter had poured them. She took a swallow and settled back.

'We are investigating white supremacists in various police forces in the country. NYPD is my focus.'

'Not just that,' the cop joined in. 'Racial crimes as well. We have a broad remit.'

Cutter was still when his visitors outlined how the two threads they had been pursuing merged and became the task force.

'We came across that tattoo in some earlier cases. All white men. Holdups, burglaries, assaults, a few killings as well. No links to any gangs, however.'

'Not just that,' the FBI agent said bitterly. 'Many of them walked with very light sentences. Heck, some of them weren't even arraigned.'

'Dirty cops?' He turned cold.

'Dirty judges as well, we suspect, but there's nothing we can prove. It's too circumstantial.'

'Can't you question those perps?'

'We would, if we could find them.'

'Or if they were alive. Yeah,' Difiore read his look. 'Those who walked or served their sentences have dropped off the radar. Those who were in prison, died in fights.'

Cutter took their empty plates and cutlery, rinsed them and placed them in the dishwasher. He wiped the kitchen island and washed his hands. Enough time for him to get his thoughts in order.

There were always dirty cops, bad apples, who were dealt with harshly when they were discovered.

But what they are talking about is much more than a few individual cases.

'Your turn,' Quindica glowered at him. It looked like his lunch hadn't mellowed his guests.

'They're called the Rising Lions,' he briefed them. 'A white supremacy group started in prison. That tattoo was their symbol. Its leader is dead. A ruthless killer. He served twenty-five years, and when he was released, was killed in Florida. Stabbed, decapitated, body burned. The gang died with him. There was no other leader to take over. The few you arrested, if they were all white, must have been part of the gang.'

'Yeah,' Difiore nodded. 'They were all ex-cons. They served time in various prisons across the country.'

'Who was the leader?'

'Jeff Sheller. Gunner, that's what they called him.'

'Killed his stepfather when he was seventeen years old.' Quindica looked up the name on her phone. 'Assaulted a prison guard and got into several fights. Sentence got reduced when he turned snitch. He was released four years ago. His intel led to the arrest of a serial killer, brought down a drug gang and the release of a few wrongfully convicted innocents.'

'Where was he in prison?' the detective asked.

'Colorado. ADX Florence.'

The federal supermax prison was the most secure in the country. Colloquially known as the Alcatraz of the Rockies, it was where the most notorious and dangerous convicts were sent to. The Unabomber, the Boston Marathon Bomber, and El

Chapo were among its inmates. A hundred miles south of Denver. No prisoner had escaped from the facility in its twenty-six-year history.

'How do you know all this?' the FBI agent turned to Cutter.

'I was an inmate there.'

20

Cutter couldn't help grinning at their slack-jawed expressions.

'You were in ADMAX?' Difiore gasped.

United States Penitentiary, Florence Administrative Maximum Facility. The official name for USP Florence ADMAX, shortened to ADX because the formal name was a mouthful.

'Two years.'

'The missing two years,' Quindica breathed.

Cutter cocked his head at them, wondering what she meant, and then nodded when he connected the dots. 'You read my file.'

'Yeah.'

'That's classified. You're not senior enough to have the clearances.'

'The Director shared it with me.'

He eyed her and the detective thoughtfully. It looked like Difiore knew about his past, too, judging by the lack of surprise on her face.

'Bart shared all of it?'

'Your missions were redacted. Your return to civilian life, that's all I could read.'

'ARTEMIS?'

She nodded.

The program had been designed for just that purpose. To allow highly confidential intel to be shared between agencies even if the readers didn't have the requisite clearances.

He felt reassured. His former boss hadn't stepped out of line.

'You know what'll happen if you two spread it?'

'All kinds of hell.'

How much do I tell them?

He weighed the pros and cons. He was fiercely protective of what had happened in the past and only a handful of civilians were aware of his full backstory. He had told the bodega owners because they had become part of his life. Bruce Rolando and Bart Jamison, Zeb and his crew, they knew as well. He didn't regard them as civilians, however.

'We get it.' Difiore read his silence. 'Most people won't understand what you went though. They'll show sympathy. You don't want that.' Her lips curled into a warm smile briefly. 'You won't get it from us. You know something that could help us. If those two years are relevant, we want to know.'

Cutter sized them up. *They have been through a lot too.* He could guess how it was for them. *They've had to work twice as hard. Unwanted attention from men. Lewd humor. They've had to put up with all that.*

'This doesn't go beyond you.'

'We're law enforcement, Grogan,' Quindica replied flatly. 'Not journalists.'

'I was undercover in ADX. To get close to Mansoor and other terrorists there. We suspected there were several sleeper cells in our country, however we had found nothing.'

'That's true,' the SAC told the detective. 'I remember that hunt. We spent hundreds of man hours, kicked down so many doors, but got nothing. Zilch. But all the while, the chatter was strong. That these cells were planning an attack.'

'Why you?' Difiore wondered. 'Mansoor would have recognized you and ... I can't even imagine the state you were in.'

'They'—he didn't clarify who that meant; they weren't read into how the special operations world works and he wasn't going to educate them—'didn't want a trail that would lead back to our military, or any agency. This was after my return to the States and leaving the military. I was a civilian, was highly motivated, and had the experience.' He shrugged.

IT HADN'T BEEN THAT EASY. THERE HAD BEEN HEATED discussions with intelligence officers. *Too personal* had been tossed back at him several times. *It is,* he had shot back, *but do you have anyone better?* His linguistic skills and looks had been the clincher. He spoke not only Arabic but also several other Middle Eastern languages fluently and could easily pass for someone from the region.

An elaborate cover had been prepared for him. He was a Daesh terrorist captured in Syria who had been convicted in a closed-door trial and sent to ADX. The CIA, the Defense Intelligence Agency, and several other clandestine outfits flooded the dark net with mentions of him. Bots spread the message of his heroic attacks against the West. That embellished his legend.

There was no risk of Mansoor seeing him, because the terrorist was in solitary and was never in the presence of other prisoners.

'AS FOR BEING RECOGNIZED,' HE GESTURED AT HIMSELF, 'I didn't go looking like this. I had a burn scar on my face. A beard. No one could link who I was to Cutter Grogan.

'I used to see Sheller in the yard. The workout space.' He didn't use the gangster's more memorable nickname. That would have been normalizing who the criminal was. 'We used to work out there. The only recreation we had. He was like a bull. Large, bald ...' he trailed off, remembering the man in the SUV. The one who handed Davis his stash. *Nope. Can't be him. He's dead.* 'No one messed with him. It was when I was there that he started the Lions. He was recruiting. He wanted it to be a bigger gang than the Aryan Brotherhood. He was charismatic. Great speaker. Several cons joined. He made it like an exclusive club. Not just everyone could join. They had to prove themselves, had to pass hazing rituals.'

His listeners didn't move when he paused for breath. They were listening with rapt attention. 'They tattooed themselves. What he was selling had appeal. Word spread to other prisons, and that's how you saw those lions on those perps. There was a rigid code, however. No one was allowed to speak about the gang to the public. Enforced by death. Which is why there's no coverage.'

'How's that possible? If the gang spread to other prisons, people would have known. There would be talk.'

'There was, and those who were indiscreet were killed. That code—it was a blood oath. Anyone who violated any rule was killed. Viciously. No mercy. Sheller was one of the most dangerous men I came across. As ruthless as any terrorist.'

'Did he approach you?'

'Me? He hated me. I was Daesh. There was no love between us. We had a few words. That escalated over days. He threatened that he would saw my head off. He and his group attacked me and the other terrorists a few times. I saved them, that's how I got close to them. Sheller didn't like that. He ruled ADX, and here I was, challenging his authority. But the other terrorists were behind me, and he couldn't do much, short of attitude, words, and random fights.'

Cutter's visitors hung on to every word, taking everything in. His neighbors' voices filtered from outside, a car honked loudly on the street, his fridge sighed in the kitchen, but they weren't distracted.

'There was another fight. A big one. Sheller and his men were attacking another inmate. Jake Horstman. Ripper, they called him. He had killed his girlfriend and her boyfriend for cheating on him. He had joined the gang initially but then backed out. He had found religion. Sheller didn't like that. It went against his code. No one left his gang, and he decided to make an example of Jake. I intervened.' Cutter rubbed his chest unconsciously, remembering the brutal showdown. 'I saved Horstman and got him sent to solitary, where he would be safe. We became close. The one friend I made there. And Sheller's hatred for me grew.'

He got to his feet and stretched. He brewed more coffee and brought their cups over.

'Is that all?' Difiore asked impatiently.

'That's all you'll get from me.'

'He left you alone after that?'

'He didn't.'

'What happened?'

He shook his head.

He wasn't going to tell them about the long nights when he forced himself to stay awake, listening keenly for the slightest movement. The hurried showers in the bathrooms. The cozying up to the terrorists. No, his time at ADX was a bleak, violent stretch of time. He wasn't going to relive his memories for anyone.

The detective changed tack. 'Why didn't the Lions survive after him?'

'Sheller was everything. He was the leader, the organization ... he ran everything. The smuggling, the cell phones, the paid killings, the recruitment in other prisons, everything went through him. He was the sole decision-maker. Other gangs had a structure, an organization that wasn't dependent just on their founders. The Lions had the same philosophy as other white-supremacist prison gangs, but without Sheller they were nothing.'

'You're sure he's dead?'

'He is.' Quindica held up her phone. 'I checked. Sheller was killed in Miami shortly after his release. A bar fight that escalated in the parking lot. Gruesome murder.'

'The gang could still be around,' Difiore mused.

'They aren't,' Cutter insisted. 'I followed up on Sheller's death. Besides,' he turned to the FBI agent, 'they would have come up on your radar.'

'Not if they were still operating to their code,' the detective objected. 'Don't forget Boyce. He didn't have a criminal record. He must have heard of the Lions somewhere.'

'That's a common tattoo. We don't know if he was in the gang. Davis was a lead, but—'

'Don't go there,' the detective warned.

'The cops who shot him—'

'You heard what I said.'

Cutter looked at her impassive face, flat eyes. *Those officers are on her radar. She'll check if they have lions on their necks. She'll tear their lives apart, see if they're dirty.*

'The NYPD, the Feds, you hadn't heard of the Rising Lions before today. Why?'

Her scowl showed that the thought had struck her.

'Is there anyone who could know about the Lions?' Quindica broke the silence. 'We'll reach out to our informants.' She looked at Difiore, who nodded. 'But chances are they won't know anything.'

There is someone, he thought, but he didn't say anything.

'Grogan,' Difiore warned ominously. 'You're holding out on us again. I can feel it. No,' she said when he made to protest. 'Don't lie.'

'We're on the same side,' the SAC urged.

'We are?' He looked at them in mock surprise. 'News to me.'

He raised his hands in surrender when the detective's face darkened.

'Jake might know.'

'Jake?' Quindica asked, confused.

'That man he saved,' the cop replied absently, 'from Sheller in ADX. Why would he know?'

'He became something like a priest to the inmates. They went to him, unburdened themselves. He gained their trust because he never snitched, and that helped him when I left. He became untouchable. Even from Sheller. Any inmate who raised a finger to him would get it from the other convicts.'

'Let's go ask him.' Difiore slapped her palm on the island and got to her feet. 'Where is he?'

Her face fell at Cutter's reply. 'In ADX. He's serving life.'

Silence. The women looked at each other and then at him.

'He won't talk to us, will he?' Quindica guessed.

'Nope.'

'He'll talk to you, though.'

'He might.'

Difiore sighed. 'Will you go ask him?'

'That's missing the magic word.'

'You were going to, weren't you?' the SAC cut in quickly before the cop exploded.

'Yeah. I'll let you know what I find out.'

He wondered who would ask him the question. Bet with himself that it would be Difiore. Not because Quindica was any less smart, but the cop knew him longer.

'Did you get the intel from the terrorists?' the detective asked.

Yep, her. He congratulated himself for guessing right.

'Yeah. We shut down several cells. No,' he clarified when the SAC's brow wrinkled. 'We made it look like intel from anonymous sources, concerned citizens. That's how we hid the ADX connection from the Feds.'

'What about Mansoor?' Difiore again, persistent. He could see why she was a highly regarded cop.

'I killed him.'

The detective sat down in her chair heavily. 'But ... I don't understand. He's still in ADX.'

'That's what the world thinks.'

'At some point, there will be a small news item that he died of natural causes,' Quindica guessed.

'Something like that.'

'So that he doesn't become a martyr to his people.'

'Was it worth—' Difiore's face flamed in embarrassment, and she waved her hand as if to retract her question.

'Mansoor coming at us in Turkey was no accident. He was hunting me. I had wiped out several of his people. Had destroyed his camps. My name got leaked somehow. Terrorists knew who I was. I was on their kill list.'

'That wasn't in your file,' Quindica frowned.

'Nope. Not everything goes in there. It's not like Hollywood shows it.' He breathed deeply. 'I can only guess that's why Riley ... did what she did. She wanted to take the act away from him.'

'Closure?' he smiled bitterly. 'That's what you were asking, right? That's a selfish thought. It doesn't bring the victims back. Am I glad he's dead? Heck, yeah!

'So, now you know.' He regarded them impassively.

'But not everything. We don't know how your prison record doesn't show up in the system. I'm guessing ADX won't have anything at its end, either. How did you get close to Mansoor? You said he was in solitary ...'

'No. You won't get those details. Not from me. Ever.' *How it went down with the terrorist* ... no civilian would know that.

'We both took an oath,' Quindica nodded at her companion, 'Gina and I. When we joined our organizations. You weren't worried when you told us what you did?'

'No.'

'Because?'

'It isn't the first time you've looked the other way.'

'How do you know that?' Difiore fired at him.

'I can see it in your eyes. Besides,' he grinned, 'you aren't the only ones who have contacts.'

'You met me for the first time today.' Quindica narrowed her eyes.

'You think I was only bathing when I went to take a shower? I know the kind of cops you are.'

'What kind is that?'

'My kind.'

'We aren't friends, Grogan,' Difiore told him decisively. 'We'll never be. I still think you're a vigilante.'

With that, she strode out of his apartment, along with Quindica.

21

Cutter was back at what was turning out to be his usual after Difiore and Quindica left.

Shadowing Darrell.

He was in the same big-nose disguise and in another rental car. The student came out when school finished for the day. He hung about with his friends and, when Manuel turned up, spoke briefly with him. Shook his head several times when the boy spoke and turned his back on him and walked away.

Is he quitting the gang?

His friend watched him uncertainly and then went the other way, toward Mother Gaston, while Darrell headed home.

Cutter followed him until the boy went inside his building. Four-thirty pm. His mother would have a pleasant surprise when she returned.

Unless he goes out again.

Darrell didn't.

He remained inside when it turned dark and was still at home when a dark figure came up the street, climbed the steps to the building tiredly and went inside.

Cutter watched her shadow move in the apartment. Another

silhouette appeared on the curtain. They hugged, and then the room turned dark.

He was driving in Manhattan when his phone rang. He thumbed it and put it on speaker.

'Thank you,' she said softly.

'For what, ma'am?'

'For whatever you did. He was home when I returned.'

'I didn't do anything, ma'am.'

'I knew that's what you would say,' she scoffed. Her voice dropped. 'What was he involved in?'

He stared blindly ahead as a red light approached. Slowed to a stop. She was his client, but he had promised Darrell.

'I'm still working on it, ma'am,' he evaded her question. 'It's going to be a long, hard journey. Today is not indicative.'

'I know,' she sniffed, 'you are not going to tell me, are you?'

'It's complicated.'

'I knew it.' She sighed. 'How bad is it?'

'Ma'am. Your son's at home?'

'Darrell's sleeping.'

'Go look at him and then go to bed yourself. He's with you. That's all you need to know for now.'

'Your fees?'

'Later.'

This isn't over yet.

He rolled down the window when she hung up and let the night air swirl inside.

Darrell must have heard of Davis's death. *Is that why he was ignoring Manuel? He's now finding out gang life isn't glamorous?*

Time would tell.

In the meantime, he had a visit to Florence ADMAX to arrange.

22

Doug Mease sat in his robe the next morning and read the morning newspapers.

Kevin Rubin had held a big rally in upstate New York the previous night. Well-attended. Many cops had cheered when he declared the police forces needed more support. A huge roar from the crowd when he said he would make the country safer.

No policy details. His campaign was based on popularity and rhetoric. Candidates from both major parties opposed him, but that didn't seem to dent his polling. The Veep, whom the president was backing, was still ahead with a double-digit-point lead over him, but commentators said Rubin could narrow the lead soon.

Mease folded the papers carefully and placed them on his breakfast table. Adjusted the edges so that they were parallel to the table's. Perfection mattered.

Went to his bedroom and dressed. Blue shirt, striped tie, dark trousers, dark jacket. A briefcase in his hand. He opened it and checked his files were present. He brought out a burner phone and dialed a number. It bounced through several proxies and rang at an assistant chief's desk. A white nationalist who had sworn allegiance to the Lions once he had known Gunner was alive.

'It's me,' he introduced himself. No names were necessary. The officer hung up wordlessly. Mease knew he would go to a secluded area, their security protocol. He called after ten minutes.

'Tell me about those cops.' He didn't elaborate. He didn't need to. The man would know he was calling about the 73rd Precinct.

'I told all this to ... our mutual friend.'

Gunner.

'I want to know as well.'

'He doesn't update you?'

'Tell me,' he retorted.

'Investigation's still underway. The officers are on administrative leave.'

'Complications?

'Martinelli's likely to face disciplinary action. He was too close to the cage.'

Cage. Old-school cops still used the term for the cells.

'Will he snitch?'

The assistant chief lowered his voice. 'I've personally reminded him of his oath.'

Mease grunted. He didn't say what steps would have to be taken if the cop turned informant. Action would be quick and brutal.

'Keep us in the loop.'

'Will do.'

He pocketed the phone and glanced at his watch. At precisely ten am, he left his apartment in Queens. He had a family, a wife and two kids, but they were back in Texas. Work had brought him to the city, where he lived alone.

He walked two blocks, hailed a cab, and gave the driver an address on Fifth Avenue.

'That's the Frick Collection.'

'Yeah.'

'Should have said the name to start with,' the driver grumbled as he joined the traffic.

Mease put on his shades and looked out of the window as the city slid past. He paid in cash at his destination and entered the art museum. Broke away from the line and pretended to take a call. Left the building and strode briskly towards East 79th. He slowed as he approached a grey stone building three blocks from the Frick.

He went to a side entrance on 74th and pressed the buzzer to a law firm. Went in when the door opened. Nodded politely when he joined a bunch of people in the elevator. Exited his floor. Took the fire stairs, climbed two floors, and pressed the buzzer to the hallway door.

Two hard-faced men faced him when it opened. Both with weapons in their hands. One frisked him while the other watched. He went on into the thickly carpeted corridor, his shoes sinking in the softness.

Chandeliers and walnut paneling. Two elevators, both of them manned by more armed men. A large door with a knocker. He didn't approach it. He went down the hallway, to another entrance meant for the help. He placed his palm against a screen and it unlocked. He entered a reception area manned by another security guard, who checked him out, and went past a door, another hallway, the kitchen where white-aproned staff bustled about, not one of them looking at him. Another carpeted hallway. More rooms on each side that looked like they could have been featured in style magazines. They had.

A suited man standing at a door nodded at him.

Mease knocked on the door and entered.

Kevin Rubin greeted him. 'You saw the polls?'

23

'Yeah. You got a great reception.'

'Scott says I need a big wave to come close to the Veep.'

Scott Farley, Rubin's campaign manager.

'He got any ideas?'

'He's thinking of a few. He's testing them out with the data scientists and the behavioral people.'

'What about Brad?'

Brad Parsons, chief of staff.

'You know what he's like. He's digging, seeing if there's any dirt on the others.'

'You rejected that.'

'I did. But no harm in seeing what comes out.' Rubin went to a side table and poured them coffees. Brought them back on a silver tray and served Mease. The personal touch, because the two men went a long way back.

THEY HAD MET IN OTISVILLE, THE WHITE-COLLAR PRISON eighty miles north of the city.

The federal institution was minimum security, had no

perimeter fence or barbed wire. It had lockers for personal belongings, microwaves, ice machines to keep cool, and was once dubbed one of the cushiest prisons in the country. It was one of many such low-security facilities where Wall Street convicts—lawyers, accountants—served time.

Mease, a partner in an accounting firm, had been convicted of tax fraud and had met Rubin while serving his time.

His first sentence to the other man was: 'I'm a registered member.'

'Of what?'

'Your club.' Mease lowered his voice.

They had bonded over prison life. Had found they had similarities; both strongly believed that they were born to rule and those from other ethnicities were to be ruled. Both were razor-sharp smart and ambitious. They complemented each other. Rubin was a big-picture man, while Mease was into details. The former was an extrovert, while the latter was reserved and hid his ego deep.

It was in the third month that Mease brought up the idea.

'You're wasting your life,' he said over lunch. Roast beef, potatoes, taco salad.

'How so?' Rubin chewed his food.

'What will you do when you get out? Go back to your family? Preach on the radio?'

'Pretty much. I'll get back into investing. Back startups.'

'You're capable of much more.'

The celebrity stopped eating. Gave him all his attention.

'Politics. You're a natural. Look how you've drawn people to you here. We've already got a few converts.'

'You've got to be kidding. Politics? With my background?'

'You've got to distance yourself from it, of course. Reject it outright.'

Rubin stared at him.

'You're serious?'

'No one ever elected a white supremacist,' Mease replied drily.

He didn't push. He let the idea take root. Gave time for Rubin to think about it and broke into a grin when the man approached him a week later.

'What you were saying the other day ...'

So, the disgraced celebrity's transformation began.

The two men made a list of their most trusted confidantes. All of them in high positions in government, law enforcement and business. Used code to communicate. There was cautious support from several quarters.

'Financing, that's where you'll stall,' said one doubter, a mayor in one of the country's largest cities. 'No one will back you.'

'I don't need it,' Rubin scoffed. 'Have you heard of my family? How much I've inherited?'

Everyone they reached out to said they wanted to know more. They wanted details.

That was something Mease excelled at. They got working. Rubin on a five-year, high-level plan, the accountant on the minutiae that would catapult the heir into the most powerful role in the world.

'Worst case,' Rubin flashed his trademark brilliant smile, 'we'll have become national figures.'

'That will give us power to influence,' Mease agreed.

And that was what they were after.

Power.

24

Their plan accelerated once they got out.

Rubin began a carefully orchestrated series of media appearances. He renounced his white supremacy beliefs. Said he had been ignorant and a fool. That prison had opened his eyes. He declared he would be an ethical investor and set up a fund, to which he was a major contributor.

A few TV channels commented that he seemed to back only white male founders. He laughed, shrugged apologetically and said that was how the technology sector was. There was a preponderance of such people in that sector. He didn't decide who founded companies; that wasn't in his control. He promised to back minorities, too, however, and made a big show of women-founded companies. In the hype that followed, the fact the women were white too was barely noticed.

Mease put together the plans. The funding required, the TV ads, the prominent backers they could go to, the PACs, Political Action Committees and Super PACs that their supporters could form. The swing states, the poll leads, this was what he was good at.

Several meetings followed thereafter. With high-net-worth individuals who secretly shared their beliefs. Corporation CEOs, wealthy families, politicians, government and law enforcement officers. All conducted in secret, security organized by Mease, who personally vetted every guard.

And then they met Jeff 'Gunner' Sheller.

They had heard of the Rising Lions and their founder while in prison. There was quite some distance between ADX and Otisville, and the two institutions were radically different. However, inmates had a way of communicating; news and gossip had a way of spreading, like jungle drums. There were a few Lion tattoos even in the white-collar camp.

Sheller shared their philosophy, and while there were many such prison gangs, they felt his outfit was unique.

It was Gunner who made the gang different from other white nationalist ones. From what they had heard, the founder was as smart as they were.

Mease confirmed that for himself when they got out of Otisville. On a whim, he set up a meeting with the Lions' founder in ADX. He posed as a distant cousin and pulled a few strings with high-level contacts, and that gained him face time.

It was a meeting of minds in terms of shared beliefs, and while it was brief, he came away convinced that Gunner was no ordinary thug.

They hadn't thought of integrating the Lions into their plans, however. Not initially. It was just shared beliefs. Mease had quickly dampened Rubin's interest in getting inked.

'Not now, or ever. The world is watching. Your tattoo will ruin everything we're aiming for,' he warned, and that had convinced the wealthy heir.

It was the gang leader who reached out once he left prison.

Seen you a lot on TV. He sent a message through a courier. *I know you haven't changed.*

'You think he's blackmailing us?' Rubin showed the note to Mease.

The strategist, which was what the candidate called the accountant, frowned and inspected it. Written neatly, all in caps. Black ink.

'How did you get it?'

'There was a crush of people at the last rally. Ricky found it in his pocket. Someone must have slipped it to him. He knew it was meant for me when he read it.'

Ricky Schillum was the head of security. Former special operations forces, a trusted man. He had been with Rubin for years. Mease didn't blindly take on that relationship, however. He subjected the man to the same screening everyone in the inner circle underwent.

Background checks, psychological interviews, lie-detector tests, which were repeated every few months. They had to not only believe in white supremacy but also renounce those views publicly.

Mease fingered the note as he paced. What if Sheller exposed them?

'He's got nothing. No proof,' he thought out loud. 'The people we met, they won't snitch. They've got as much as us to lose. Their reputations, lives, families, businesses, jobs—they'll lose everything if they leak. Nope, I don't think he wants to finger us.'

'You met him when he was inside.'

'A brief meeting. It didn't mean anything. Let's hear him out.'

Mease organized it in Florida. A dinner in a restaurant outside Miami. He booked the entire venue and got Schillum to mount security.

The Lions' man arrived with four companions. All of them hard-eyed and ex-cons, judging by their looks and the ink on their bodies. They submitted themselves to the pat down. Their guns and phones were taken away, and they were wanded to check for recording devices. The four men waited outside with Schillum while their leader proceeded inside.

Sheller seemed to fill the dining room with his size. The tattoos on his bare arms—serpents, dragons, crosses—writhed whenever he moved, and his biceps filled out his shirt. The lion on his neck rippled when he drank or swallowed.

Mease was struck again by his presence, by the feeling that he was capable of immense violence. It wasn't the first time that Rubin had met hard-core criminals, but he could sense the candidate was impressed, too.

'Long time, Mease,' the Lions' founder said softly. His smile was a mere twist of his lips. 'Call me Gunner.' He nodded at Rubin.

'That note.' The strategist cut to the chase. His previous meeting with the Lions' founder had been so brief that there was nothing to catch up on. 'What did you mean?'

'What I wrote. I can see through you. Both of you. I know what you're doing.'

'What's that?'

'Power grab. If Rubin wins the elections, and that's a big if, you can change this country.'

'How?'

Gunner looked at the bar, where photographs of the staff were mounted on the wall. Many of them African Americans, a few of Asian and Hispanic origin.

He didn't say a word. His cold smile conveyed what he meant.

'Relax,' he rumbled after a moment. 'I'm not here to out you. And save your protests.' He held up a palm the size of a shovel when Rubin made to protest. 'Finch, in Arizona, he told me about both of you.'

Mease considered his words. The man Gunner had mentioned was a multimillionaire who owned a chain of retail stores. He was one of their secretive backers.

'How do you know him?'

'Let's say my people helped him out with a problem. Something the cops couldn't do.'

The strategist played with his fork absently as his thoughts raced. Rubin was still, silent, at his side, but he knew the candidate was also thinking hard.

If Finch had told Gunner about the meeting it meant he knew the Lions' man well. And trusted him.

'What do you want?'

'I want in. When everything shakes out, I want to be at the dining table with you.'

'What does that mean?'

'I don't know at this stage, and neither do you. The size of the meal'—he grinned mirthlessly—'depends on how the elections turn out. We can work out the details then.'

'I don't think—' Rubin broke his silence.

'You need me.'

Mease looked at the gangbanger as if seeing him for the first time. There was more to the man, much more than his appearance suggested.

'Explain.'

'I can help,' Gunner replied simply. 'I have fifty thousand people in my gang across the country. Some of them in prison, many of them out.'

'Yours is a criminal outfit,' Mease retorted. 'We've distanced ourselves from our past. We can't afford to be linked to gangs.'

'I didn't say we need to parade our alliance. No one needs to know about it.'

'I'm waiting for that explanation. How you can help us.'

'You need the muscle we can provide. You need our activities.'

'How so?'

Gunner wrapped his fingers around his glass and drank his wine. He wiped his lips with a paper towel and threw it on the table.

'You need a platform. We can provide it.'

'Be specific.' Rubin shook his head. 'What do you mean?'

Gunner's smile was feral. 'My people can start a crime wave in the country. Target minorities and their businesses. Take that and run with it. Strong government. Strong cops. That will be your message.'

Mease stared at him. Of course!

25

Mease took the cup from the tray and sipped his coffee.

They had hired Farley and Parsons once the campaign gained momentum. The same vetting procedure, along with a new wrinkle. Everyone in the campaign had to sign a tight confidentiality agreement.

The men were good, experienced campaigners who had worked on several high-profile candidacy runs and delivered.

They brought in the experts, fundraisers, the people profilers, pollsters, videographers, influencers, media managers, bloggers. Key campaign team members traveled with Rubin all over the country and appointed volunteer cells to statewide activity.

TV ads, billboards, newspaper advertising, leaflets—the Rubin campaign had everything that the mainstream parties had.

No one other than a highly vetted inner circle of people on the candidate's team knew of Mease's existence. One of Rubin's companies, a technology firm in Silicon Valley, had erased the Rising Lions' internet history. That had effectively turned Gunner and his people into ghosts. It had removed all traces of Mease as well, after his release from prison. Nothing existed of him on the internet. DMV had no record of him, since he didn't own a vehicle or have a license. Social Security had a name for the address he lived at, but it wasn't Doug Mease.

'I met our friend.'

The candidate's eyes sharpened.

'I think we agreed we wouldn't meet him. Not until this was over.'

'He's in town.'

'I know that.'

'I needed to get out of the apartment. Needed some air. Relax. No one saw us. I followed security procedures.'

'How is he?'

'He's good.'

He didn't tell the candidate about Davis. That was a detail Rubin didn't need to know. Not when he was embarking on a tour of several cities.

'This wave Scott's talking about,' he mused. 'Our friend could help.'

'Like what he proposed when we met him first?'

'Yeah.'

'I like it,' Rubin said after a while. 'Does he have the people?'

'The Lions have grown; you know that. One reason for that is the way Gunner works. He'll bail out anyone who goes to prison. If the judge doesn't grant that, he'll work on his connections and ours and try to lighten the sentence. Worst case, someone goes to prison, he'll make sure their families are taken care of. That's how he gets loyalty. And that oath.'

'He's taken on some disposables as well, hasn't he?'

Disposables. Youngsters of different ethnicities. Labeled that, because that's what they were for the gang. They used them for street-level activity, no great loss if they were arrested or killed. Those recruits never rose higher in the gang.

'Yeah. He needs to, to expand.'

'Do it. Whatever idea Scott comes up with will be on top of Gunner's.'

. . .

MEASE MET THE LIONS' MAN IN MELROSE, IN THE PARKING lot of an abandoned building. Just the two of them, with several Lions guarding the place. It was owned by one of Rubin's companies and was empty that time of night.

The car rocked on its springs whenever the large man shifted.

'A problem?' he asked.

'The polls,' the strategist explained. 'We're behind.'

'Isn't that how it's supposed to be? The lead narrows as the election nears.'

'It'll be difficult to make up if the gap's too big. The Veep hasn't done anything wrong so far.'

'That's because Morgan's campaigning for him,' Gunner scoffed. 'The President's popular. It's natural that some of that will rub off on the vice president.'

'Agreed, but nothing we can do about it.'

'You want us to get active on the street?'

'It will help. You have people you can afford to lose?'

Gunner's nails rasped on his stubble as he scratched his jaw. 'I'll need to send felons,' he figured aloud. 'That will get the maximum impact.'

'Yeah, and they'll have to be white.'

'I can find those. Good people who won't squeal. Jew-owned joints? Black, Indian, Chinese as well?'

'That will help. Not too many, though. We might need more waves later on. I'll work on the cops and judges, the ones who know about us, once there are arrests.'

'Do that.'

'What about Tizzard? You're in touch with him?'

'Eric? We're best buds.'

Eric Tizzard, another felon, a prominent white nationalist in the country.

'Get him to organize a rally. Anywhere.'

'I can make it turn violent.'

'That'll be even better.'

'Heck, I would have gone on the stage myself, but I'm dead!' he snickered.

It had been Mease's idea, once Gunner had joined forces with them. Killing him had been easier to arrange than anticipated. There *had* been a bar fight, which spilled over into the parking lot.

It had been carefully orchestrated. A Cuban gang was cutting into the Lions' business in Miami. Gunner had decided to take him out. He and his lieutenant started the fight with the man, dragged him out and killed him. They slashed his face beyond recognition, cut his head off and burned his body, leaving its charred remains. The lieutenant was the sole witness and testified that the dead man was his former boss, Jeff Sheller. Friendly cops ensured that his witness statement held.

Mease had also convinced the Lions' founder to erase his tattoo. Gunner cottoned on instantly. He got his ink lasered away and ordered his highest ranks to do the same. New, white recruits were explicitly forbidden from tattooing themselves. That was part of the oath, too.

He put a new structure in place. He personally appointed every street-level boss, who could recruit members however they wished, as long as a significant percentage were white. The leaders could call their gangs anything except the Lions. No one bucked his orders. His authority was such that no arrested or convicted gang leader gave up the outfit's real name.

Gunner lived in the shadows, never appearing on law-enforcement radar. He had proven a worthy ally, Mease and Rubin's invisible ace.

'I'll get onto it,' he promised. 'I'll make contact with Eric. The earlier the better, I guess?'

'Yeah. What about Davis?'

'I've sent a replacement. He's taken over that gang. He's smart. Our business won't suffer in Brownsville.'

Mease gripped his shoulder and left the rendezvous. He hit

the street and shivered in the cool air. Drew his jacket tight around him and raised its collar.

There were benefits to being anonymous. No one associated him with Rubin. He could walk the streets alone without being followed by reporters.

He looked up at the night sky and spotted a shooting star. Mease was neither spiritual nor religious, however that sight felt like an omen to him.

Destination White House was coming together.

26

Paperwork.

When Cutter had joined Arnedra and started the fixing business, he hadn't anticipated the filing, the invoices, the ledger maintenance that came along with it. All the small things that made a business tick.

He worked with his partner for several hours in the morning and, when everything was in order and to her satisfaction, sat back and stretched.

'Darrell?' she reminded him.

'He's stayed away from the gang.' He had shadowed the student the previous day. Another early return home for the boy.

'He's done with the gang?'

'Can't say. He's stubborn.' He opened a drawer and took out his Glock and kydex holster. 'I'll be gone a couple of days.'

'ADX?'

'Yeah.' He had told her about Difiore and Quindica's visit. There were no secrets between them.

'Those two sound feisty.'

'They are,' he said with feeling. 'It was bad enough having Difiore on my case. Now there's a Fed too!'

Her peal of laughter accompanied him as he went down to the basement.

Nope, no cops, this time. He checked the line of parked vehicles just in case. These law enforcement officers were wily.

He climbed into his vehicle and set the navigation to Newark Liberty International Airport. Twenty minutes. The satellite didn't give him a quicker route.

He drove through Soho and Hudson Square and out of the city through the Holland Tunnel, lights reflecting off its ceramic tiles, casting a glow on his face.

He tuned his radio when he emerged. Found Arethra Franklin, the Queen.

When the river was deep, I didn't falter.

Powerful lyrics that had comforted him when he was lost after Riley. They carried him to the airport.

He parked his SUV in the long-term lot and went to the terminal building. Of all the airports that served the city, he disliked Newark the most. It was small, in a perennial state of construction, and didn't have the feel of other airports. He got no sense of adventure when he traversed through it.

He cleared security and searched for his gate. Strode to it, a tall figure flowing through human traffic like a stream of water, naturally finding the easiest passage.

He paid for an upgrade: a window seat and more leg room. It didn't make much of a difference, considering the size of the aircraft, but he would take whatever little luxuries he could get.

He looked out as the aircraft took off, defied the laws of gravity, and surged into the sky. The city grew tiny and disappeared from sight, though he could still feel its pull.

A gravitational force that seemed to draw people from all over the world to it.

DENVER, FIRST STOP. TIME FOR COFFEE AND A COMFORT break. He brushed off conversational attempts by another passenger, grabbed his paper cup, took his first swallow, and searched for the gate.

There was just enough time to finish his drink before his boarding call was announced.

The second leg of travel was so short that it felt as though he had barely buckled in before his flight was landing at Colorado Springs Airport.

When he emerged from the aircraft, which had parked close enough to the terminal that passengers could walk in instead of taking a shuttle bus, he breathed in the crisp air. Brilliant blue sky and bright sunlight and a vast expanse of space, the kind of which he never saw in his home city. And there in the distance was Pikes Peak, the highest mountain in the Southern Front Range of the Rockies. A fourteener, the summit was supposedly the second most visited peak in the world.

Cutter had his doubts about that claim, but heck, who was he to argue with the state's tourism board?

He hired a vehicle in the airport. Four pm. Not enough time to get to the prison. He drove to the city and stayed overnight.

He met Horstman the next day.

27

Before flying, Cutter had called a three-star general at the Pentagon, who had pulled strings that resulted in a member of the security personnel looking up from his screen and nodding when Cutter arrived at ADX. His name was on the visitor list.

He folded his shades and was escorted inside by a prison officer, someone new to him, to a small room next to the warden's office, not where the inmates met family and friends.

Two chairs, a metal table separating them, the furniture bolted to the floor. A jug and two glasses of water were the only embellishments.

'You need anything?' the prison officer asked.

Cutter couldn't help smiling. *The general's got juice, that's why he's being polite. Warden must have instructed him.*

'Nope.'

He waited. Watched a spider crawl up the wall. Similar insects had kept him company in his cell.

A clanking of chains and a shuffle of footsteps. Two guards escorting the man he wanted to meet. They pushed him inside the room indifferently and shut the door. *They'll be waiting outside, alert for any noise, ready to break up any fight.*

'Jake.' He greeted his friend and hugged him over his cuffed hands.

'You missing this place?' the inmate responded sardonically.

Cutter studied him. The prisoner was lean, pale from the lack of sunlight, stubble over his cheeks. His eyes were sunken, but bright. Faded tattoos on his arms and above his vest.

Horstman had stopped inking himself once he found his faith. He didn't preach it. Didn't force his beliefs on others. Accepted that his religion wasn't the only one. His calm manner was what drew other inmates, and his explaining his faith, breaking it down in simple, relatable language, was why he had gained respect.

'I missed you.' Cutter reached out and held his friend's hands, which gripped him back. 'How are you holding up?'

'You know me, Cutter. One day after the other. Prisoners come and go. I'll die in here.'

No drama in his voice. He had long accepted what he had done and the consequences. Knew that whatever he did wouldn't bring back the couple. He carried that burden every moment of his life, but at the same time, didn't allow that to drag him down.

'You made a life for yourself?'

'Yes. I take on cases ... where I can help people.' He broke it down for his friend, what he did in New York.

'A fixer, huh?' Horstman smiled. 'I like it.' His face turned serious. He jerked his head in the direction of the cells. 'What you did there ... it brought you peace?'

I told him who I was once Mansoor was dead. He had secured a last meeting with the convict before leaving prison and then had revealed his identity and why he had been in ADX. The inmate hadn't been surprised.

'I knew there was something different about you,' he had replied.

. . .

'You didn't come here all the way from New York just to see me.'

'No. It's Gunner. I need to know everything about him.'

Horstman's face tightened. He glanced involuntarily at the ceiling.

'Recording devices are turned off.'

'You can do that?'

'Yes.'

'Gunner's dead, last I heard.'

'His Lions are still here?'

'Some. They're serving life too. That gang's disbanded, though. They don't even call themselves that anymore. Is that why you're here?'

'A few Lions have surfaced in New York. They targeted Jews, Asians—you know who they go after. Those arrested got light sentences, a few died, and some even got away.'

'They said they were from that gang?'

'No, but their ink gave them away.'

'That's a common enough—'

'Yeah, I know. But their victims. All of them minority communities. Feels like Gunner's outfit is back in play.'

'You think someone's started the gang again?'

'It's possible.'

'I would have heard something.'

A shadow crossed his face.

'What is it?'

Horstman lifted a finger for quiet. He looked away, his eyes deep in thought, and then sighed.

'Bull.' He leaned forward, his lips barely moving. 'One of the prisoners here, on life. He was a Lion.' He snapped his fingers, remembering. 'You know him!'

Cutter searched his memory. Nicknames and faces. 'Slim build? Broken nose? They call him that because he's not built like one?'

'That's him. He comes to me often. We talk. He said something that didn't make sense. Not until you came here.'

'What?'

'We were talking about life after death and I told him there were religions that believed we had several lives. Beliefs, faith, that kind of discussion. He said he knew one person who had come back from the dead on this earth, in this world. No magic about it. I made a joke and he turned serious, insisted that it was true and said I knew that person. He clammed up when I pressed. I let it go. Didn't think much of it. You know how it is in here. It's not hard to lose touch with reality.'

'How close was he to Gunner?'

'Very. He was in the kill group, to get me. You fought them off, remember?'

Cutter nodded. 'Can you find out? Discreetly?'

'I'll try.'

No protests. No pushback that prisoners confided in him and he couldn't misuse their trust. Ripper had his own code. Doing right was part of it.

'Leave a message with the warden. He'll get back to me. Don't be obvious about me.'

'I've been here a long while, Cutter,' Horstman said with a wry smile. 'I know how communication works here.'

CUTTER DIDN'T PAY ATTENTION TO THE SCENERY ON THE drive back to Colorado Springs. The mountain range was in the distance, fleecy clouds around it, postcard-perfect. But none of it registered.

He was thinking about the bar on Livonia, the parking lot and the Suburban. That large silhouette, the bald man.

It was Gunner. He was sure of it.

The man had come back from the dead.

28

'Difiore.'

'We need to meet.'

'You found something?'

'Lunch. There's a bar near Trinity Church.'

'We'll be there. If you're buying.'

'I am sure you and Quindica can claim expenses.'

'We can't feed taxpayers, Grogan. Meaning you.'

Cutter shook his head and hung up. The cop always had to have the last word.

HE HAD RETURNED LATE THE PREVIOUS NIGHT. HAD READ UP on what the media had covered about Gunner's death. It was cut and dried.

Had woken up and perused the same headlines and articles. They hadn't changed overnight.

And yet he's alive.

. . .

DIFIORE AND QUINDICA SHOWED UP AT TWELVE-THIRTY. 'It had better be good.' The detective slid down on the leather seat, the SAC next to her.

'It will be.'

'I mean the food.'

'Don't look at me like that.' Quindica raised her hands. 'She's gotten worse ever since she met you.'

'The steak's good. Fish, too. Almost everything here.'

'How would you know?' the detective challenged him, without looking up from the menu. 'You're a vegetarian.'

How does she know that? He tried to figure it out, gave up and placed his order.

'He's alive. Sheller,' he said bluntly when the server had left.

Difiore blinked. Quindica sipped the drink she had ordered. No theatrics. No surprised exclamations, but he could see the interest flaring in their eyes.

'That's not much to go on,' the SAC said thoughtfully when he had finished briefing them. 'Just the word of a prisoner.'

'Vague at that,' Difiore added.

'I saw him.'

That got their attention.

'When? Where?' the detective demanded.

How much could he share?

'Where Davis was captured.'

'I knew it. You were involved somehow,' she muttered. 'Sheller was there?'

He told them about the SUV, its occupants.

'You didn't see him clearly,' Quindica said. 'It could be any bald man.'

'It's him.'

'Who was the other man?'

'I don't know.'

He hadn't placed the driver, even though that feeling of having seen him before persisted.

'Why were you there?'

'I was driving past,' he lied, 'got a call and drove inside to take it.'

Difiore didn't believe him. Her expression was scornful, but she didn't push him.

'Why would he go through that?' Quindica again, tracing the lines on the table with a finger. 'Stage his death, go to all that trouble. He could have run the Lions just as he was. Many gang leaders do.'

'Good question. There's another you should ask yourselves. Who does he know inside the system? How far does his reach go? That killing, he couldn't have done it himself. The coroner, the cops, Davis's death ...'

He trailed off when Difiore went impassive, the wooden face that he was becoming familiar with fast.

'The thought's crossed our minds,' she ground out.

They picked at their food silently when it arrived. He paid for it, and when they were leaving, Quindica caught his sleeve.

'Thanks,' she said. 'You'll let us know when your friend gets back?'

'Yeah.'

'Grogan,' Difiore warned him, 'stay out of this. You've helped, great, but that's the end of your involvement.'

He nodded.

He wouldn't stay out of it. He had to be sure Darrell left the gang. That there would be no blowback.

Sheller's out there, too. *If he's based here, he must know I'm here, too.*

The man would come for him at some point if he recognized him from their prison days.

If that happened, their enmity would spill over to the street.

29

Cutter swore when he saw Darrell with Manuel that evening. The two boys were loping down Pitkin Avenue and headed towards Mother Gaston.

'Have you lost your senses?' he said savagely in the silence of his car.

He parked it after a light and felt his false nose. Yeah, it was in position, as were the pads on his chest and belly, to give him a heavyset look, and his Glock in his ankle holster.

He put on his shades and got out of his vehicle. Followed them at a distance to the same stretch of sidewalk in front of the developer's lot.

He couldn't risk pretending to be a drunk again. He turned on his jacket cam and proceeded. Looked dubiously at the group of thugs and stepped to the street and went past them with the line of vehicles in between. A wary civilian who wanted no truck with the bunch of hoods on the sidewalk.

Where are the cops? he wondered. Wouldn't they patrol this area after what happened? They would. But the gang was also there, which meant they were fearless or stupid. *Or they have a pass.* Which seemed most likely, given that Sheller was alive.

Cutter went down several car lengths and then patted his

pocket and brought out his cell phone. He leaned against a vehicle and checked the recording. Made a face when he found there were no close-ups of the gang members. He had to know who had come in place of Davis.

Forty yards between him and the Lions. He could make Darrell out, a small figure who kept his distance from the bunch on the sidewalk. He shook his head when Manuel turned to him and beckoned.

Doesn't look like he's committed to them. Cutter faced them to allow his jacket cam to take everything in. Brought his phone to his ear and started speaking with a nonexistent caller.

No thugs looked his way. It didn't look like the new leader, a taller man around whom many men were bunched, had put in place any surveillance.

'You waiting for someone?'

Cutter turned around slowly and found out how wrong he was.

The speaker was short, bearded, in a loose Tee over jeans. One hand hooked loosely in his pocket, something hard and flat outlined at his waist. A gun. Ink all over his arms and up his neck.

He must have been crouching between cars. Watching the street from sidewalk level. Excellent tradecraft.

'Hold up a moment, Pete,' Cutter spoke loudly and held his phone away from his ear. 'Yeah? You said something?' he queried the arrival.

'What are you doing here?'

'Me? Can't you see? What business is it of yours?'

The speaker's face hardened. He took a step closer. 'Move. Take your call somewhere else.'

'Huh? Who are you—'

'What's that on your jacket?'

Cutter looked down. Cursed mentally when he saw the camera had slid out of its buttonhole.

'That's ... you're a ... COP!' the man hollered, his face twisting in anger. He started reaching for his weapon.

'Who? Me? No—'

'COPS!' the man yelled again furiously, his hand emerging from beneath his Tee.

Cutter risked a glance down the sidewalk.

The Lions had heard the call. They split up. Some of them leapt over the barbed wire and fled through the open lot. Darrell was a distant figure. It looked like he had run at the caller's first shout. Some heavies hustled down the sidewalk, determined looks on their faces, looking to support the sentry. The leader ... there he was, along with a few hoods. He had threaded through the parked vehicles. *Can't let him escape through the traffic Need to find out who he is.*

No time to fight.

'GUN!' Cutter roared. 'SHOOTER ON STREET. CHRIST! HE'S FIRING.' He shoved the startled thug against the vehicle as several passersby screamed. He leapt over the vehicle's hood and landed on the street. A car blared angrily. Tires squealed.

'CALL THE COPS,' he shouted and pointed wildly at the thugs on the sidewalk. 'THEY'RE SHOOTING.'

Word spread. Cars honked. People cleared away from the street.

Cutter didn't stay to watch. He ran through the traffic. Prayed that the drivers had more sense than him. They did, but not before several cursed him loudly through rolled-down windows. He didn't pay them any attention. His eyes were on the tall man who was fleeing with three hoods.

Can't let him get away.

He put on a burst of speed. Yells behind him. Spotted the caller and one more thug in a storefront's reflective window. Chasing him.

Cutter put them out of his mind as he sprinted through an opening, landed on the sidewalk and raced to catch up with the leader. Down Mother Gaston, shoving past shoppers, leaping over a baby stroller, the mother's angry shout burning his ears.

Right on Livonia, and then the hoods veered suddenly to the right. Into a housing project, over a metal fence, through a children's play area. Past grim-looking buildings and narrow lanes. The sounds of their footsteps echoing in the small passageways.

No one else present. Just the gang's leader and his men, who had spotted their pursuer, and more hoods behind.

A left and a sudden right, and Cutter slithered to a stop.

A dead end. A storage alley lined with trash bins. Several doors, all of them shut.

Two hoods standing, grinning wickedly, their guns by their sides.

No sign of Leader.

Pounding footsteps behind him.

Caller turned the corner and entered, along with another hood.

One against four mean-looking hitters. All of them armed, flanking him.

Flight wasn't an option.

'I'm a cop.' Cutter raised his hands. 'Backup should be here soon.'

'Nails and Serro?' Caller asked.

'Got away.' One of the two thugs nodded at a door.

The sentry reached for his gun.

Violence it would be.

30

Cutter had no fear of being killed.

He had faced down that enemy a long time ago, after Riley died. If he had to meet his end in the housing project, however, killed by punks, it wouldn't be alone. He would take as many as he could with him.

He ran at Caller with a ferocious yell, drawing his Glock with blinding speed as the emptiness filled him.

The sudden move gave him a fractional advantage. No one charged at a gun-wielding assailant. Caller was startled and was late in raising his gun.

His first shot caught the sentry in the shoulder, and then he was in the air. He landed on the two men, full body contact. Lashed out with his legs and caught the second shooter in the face. Swiped wildly with his Glock and felt it connect with the man's nose.

He landed on his feet. Stumbled, and that saved his life when a round buzzed angrily over his head. Another spat into a concrete wall as the roar of shots filled the narrow passage.

MOVE!

He got an arm around Caller's neck and dragged him back as a human shield. Fired wildly behind him and felt the distinct sounds of rounds slamming into the flesh of the fallen man. Brought the Glock up and trained them on the three hoods.

'Your call.' Calm voice. No panic or desperation. 'Let me go or he dies.'

The two hoods had their guns on him. The man he had shot gasped and shuddered. Caller swore and struggled and stilled when Cutter's arm tightened around his neck.

'You can't escape, pig,' one of the hoods called out. 'You'd better give up.'

He didn't reply. He backstepped, dragging his captive with him.

One step. Two steps.

He got closer to the mouth of the alley, where a bigger lane ran that led to other buildings. He could escape through the congestion of the housing project, which had enough nooks and twists and turns for cover. Provided more hoods weren't flooding the space. *And those two facing me stay where they are.*

The hoods didn't stay where they were. They spread out and came forward.

'Are you all from that gang? Rising Lions?'

Caller stiffened. 'Flack!' he wheezed.

One of the thugs fired.

Cutter reacted immediately. He pushed Caller at them and dived out of the alley. Something burned his shoulder. A round brushed his hair and then he was out, staggering, as shots reverberated in the confined space.

Go right!

He regained his balance and ran past a scared face in a window—a woman, pale, eyes wide in shock. Turned another corner. More densely packed buildings. No other person visible. Lights in various apartments. Clothing on lines, but no one showed themselves, as if shooting in the neighborhood was commonplace.

He leapt over a tricycle. Risked a glance back and spotted two hoods chasing him. No one else.

A growl escaped him.

Two against one.

Those were odds he could deal with, even if that shoulder throbbed insistently. He twisted and turned, changed direction unpredictably as they kept firing. A window shattered. A bullet clipped a metal door. A trash bin ahead. He grabbed its circular cover, spun on his heel and sent it flying toward the attackers. He heard one of them swear and fall, but he didn't stop to watch.

He resumed running. Long, ground-eating paces as he scanned his surroundings, swiftly looking for cover. He came out of the passage he was running through and faltered.

Open space ahead. A parking lot. Vehicles filling several spaces.

He dived to the ground when a shot rang out. Crawled quickly and ducked beneath an SUV. Peered from under. Another building behind him. One to the side, and to his right was a street. A feeder that went from the housing project to Livonia.

A line of cars ahead of him, blocking out the thugs.

No, he corrected himself as a heel scraped on concrete. *Can see their feet.* Just then, a pair came into sight.

One pair of feet visible, one car between him and the thug. No sign of the second shooter. He could guess where the other man would be, though. *Flanking wide, checking out the parked vehicles.*

One shooter not moving, deliberately making a noise to set himself as bait, the other crouching, ready to fire. The second gunman would be facing his gang member either fully or partially to get the best firing line. Which meant he would come up from Cutter's blind side on the left or right.

A trap in the urban jungle of a parking lot from which he wasn't sure he could escape, but there was no give in him. It was in his blood, in his genes, from when his ancestors had fought and died in distant lands, and Delta Force had shaped that animal instinct to the point of a spear. Without conscious thought, Cutter took the bait.

He slithered quietly, taking care not to brush his clothing against concrete. Moving on his toes and one hand, the other holding his Glock. Breathing shallowly, every sense firing. Open space between his SUV and the vehicles ahead of him. He peered cautiously around a tire. No sign of the second gunman.

A burst of speed, a fast crawl, his Glock ready, and then he was underneath a Cherokee. Next to it was the pickup truck beyond which Feet stood.

Cutter moved carefully, the smell of concrete and gas and burned rubber around him as a riff of air blew and cooled the sweat on him.

Under the truck. Recon to see if the second gunman was visible.

Nope. He's behind some vehicle, hidden by its wheel well.

Feet was there, however, right in front of him.

Standing too close to the pickup. An elementary mistake, the kind made by someone with no real combat experience.

Cutter's left arm shot out like a whip. Curled around the man's ankles and yanked hard. The thug fell with a startled grunt. His head crashed to concrete. A swift body drag forward, a vicious elbow to his throat, a shoulder roll despite the stinging burn from the injured joint, to get to his feet and go behind the truck's bed.

A whisper of movement a car away.

On his three o'clock, his blind side when he had been prone, just as he had guessed.

Cutter's body uncoiled like a spring being released. He rose in a controlled motion to let just his head show, and there the gunman was, his upper body exposed over the roof of a black sedan, his eyes searching where his friend had been. By the time he spotted the threat, it was too late.

Cutter triggered twice, ducked and fast-slapped a new magazine, ran around the truck, back to the line of cars where he had hidden, crouched behind a vehicle and snatched a look.

The thug was down.

He crab-walked, ready for a feint, but the man was sightless when he stood over him. Both rounds had taken his throat out and left nothing but flesh and blood and entrails on his neck.

Another crab-walk back to Feet, only to find that man was dead, too. It looked like his head had crashed so hard on the concrete that the fall had killed him, and if that hadn't, then the throat jab had finished him.

Cutter didn't let himself relax. He ghosted out of the parking lot, ready to take on more hostiles if they showed.

They didn't.

He went back into the maze of lanes. Circled and doubled back until he came into the dead-end alley.

Caller was dead, as was the other thug.

Both of them killed by their own men.

It was Sheller's code.

31

Cutter pocketed his spent brass wherever he could find it and got out of the housing project just as sirens wailed in the distance.

He got to Livonia as cruisers and emergency vehicles flooded the buildings and turned the evening into flashes of blue and red.

He walked without hurrying. Back to Mother Gaston, to check if Leader had returned. The strip of sidewalk where they hung out was empty. He went to his car and drove out of Brownsville as his blood cooled and the adrenaline spike diminished and the earth resumed spinning on its axis.

He shook his head, bemused at how he had survived the fight.

They were too eager, over-confident about their numbers. Still, he had pushed his luck when he charged at Caller. *Any of those rounds could have found me.* At the parking lot—that had been different. He had been in control.

He drove aimlessly, deliberately to let the endorphins dissipate.

What had he learned that evening?

That Davis had been replaced by someone called Nails. Serro was a gang member, as was Flack, but the latter was dead. He hadn't spotted the distinctive ink on the men he had killed, but that didn't mean anything. *They are Lions.*

Which brought him to Sheller.

And Joshua Gruber, an ADX inmate whom he had known before Horstman. An ascetic-looking prisoner who kept to himself and rarely opened up to anyone. Cutter and he had bonded over their love for chess. The men played whenever they could, quietly pondering their moves.

Gruber had killed his abusive parents in a fit of rage, and that had gotten him to Florence. Beneath the calm exterior was a killer capable of enormous violence, and his initial months in the penitentiary had taught other inmates to leave him alone.

He had given up violence. Had decided to go to college if he got parole.

And then Gunner had happened. He picked on Gruber to stamp his authority, to show the Lions were serious business. Kept taunting him, needling him, and Cutter wondered whether the prisoner finally broke and retaliated. He had found the inmate's body in the showers, stabbed several times. He had held him as his life bled away and had seen the triumphant scorn on Sheller's face at dinner.

Sheller had killed Gruber just because he was the wrong color.

It had become personal for Cutter from that day on. His hatred for Sheller.

He hadn't told any of this to Arnedra and Difiore and Quindica, because it hadn't been relevant. He had left that life behind him.

Until now.

A honk brought him back to the present. He startled when he realized he was now on the East Side, on Fifth Avenue. A couple of cruisers and a TV van marked Kevin Rubin's building. He drove past and thought of Darrell.

He had to question him, find out what his intentions were. If the boy had made his mind up to quit the gang, then his job was done.

What of Sheller?

He would leave the gang founder to Difiore and Quindica, he decided. It still was personal, but those two were more than capable of bringing the man down.

He would wait to hear from Horstman and present them with the intel, then watch from the sidelines.

Later, much later, he would wonder how events might have turned out if he had taken a different direction.

32

Cutter had one detour to make before he returned to his apartment: a metal shop in the Bronx that fabricated iron railings and decorative pieces for fancy apartments.

'Karim,' he said, hugging the elderly owner, whose balding head shone in the light. 'It's been a long time.'

'And whose fault is that?'

He winced when the man grabbed him by the shoulders, the burn reminding him that his wound needed attention.

'Look at you,' Karim said. 'Your skin's sticking to your bones. You need Nyla's cooking inside you.'

They laughed when Cutter's belly rumbled just then.

'You need something?'

'I need to be alone,' he told the owner, who nodded in understanding.

'Don't be a stranger.' Karim patted him on the back and led him to an inside workroom and left him alone.

Cutter donned a face mask and gloves. Brought out his Glock, bent over the gun and spent casings and cut them to small pieces. Tossed them into a ball mill, collected the fine powder and threw it into a small furnace. The holster, jacket, camera and gloves went into the fire, too.

He waved to the workshop's owner as he left, then drove back to his apartment, where he inspected his injury. It was a graze, as he had suspected. It would heal soon. *I got away easy*. Any lower and it would have been more serious. He washed his wound, showered, and prepared a simple dinner.

The TV news featured a rally in Arizona. Eric Tizzard, a prominent white nationalist, was spewing rhetoric at a crowd when someone pounded on Cutter's door.

He checked his phone. Nope, no one had called him.

Eight pm in his building, that required buzzer entry from the residents.

He sighed.

Who else could it be?

He opened the door and an angry-looking Difiore was there, along with Quindica.

'Your skin will sag and wrinkle,' he told the detective.

'What?' she ground out.

'That look on your face. It will age you.'

He thought he had gone too far. That she would pull out her service weapon and plug him on the spot. The SAC tugged her sleeve, and that seemed to dissipate the cop's fury.

'Where were you today?'

'Here and there,' he said. 'Why?'

'Where were you for the last few hours?'

'Driving all over the city.'

'There were several shootings in Brownsville.' Quindica intervened before the volcano-on-legs that was Difiore exploded. 'In a housing project. Two in an alley and two others in a parking lot.'

'What's that got to do with me?'

'All four were felons,' the detective seethed. 'They were in Davis's gang.'

'They're dead? Great. Fewer criminals in our city. I didn't kill them, however.'

'You got Davis arrested.'

'For which I deserve a medal, not an interrogation at night. Wait, how do you know they were in that gang?'

'You heard of CIs, dude? Informants? Snitches.'

'I haven't been near Brownsville,' he muted the TV when a roar came from the crowd.

His visitors looked at the screen. A fleeting expression of distaste crossed their faces.

'Your SUV's got a LoJack?'

'Disabled.'

'That's helpful,' Difiore snarled.

'Yeah, to me.'

'You own a Glock?' Quindica eyes roamed the living room.

'Yeah. They were killed by a nine mil?'

'Looks like it.'

'Let's see it,' the detective ordered.

'Nope.'

'We can come back,' the SAC said mildly, clearly playing the good-cop role, 'with a warrant. This will be easier and quicker. You know how it is. We need to cross every suspect off.'

'Since when have I become a suspect?'

'Since you turned into a vigilante,' the detective retorted.

'I am not—'

'Save it. Your choice. You can show us the gun or we can return later.'

He led them to his bedroom, saw them look at Riley's photograph but neither of them commented.

Difiore tested the spring-tight bed cover with a finger and nodded approvingly. 'Once in the military, always in the military.'

She crossed her arms and watched when he went to the wardrobe and opened the door wide. Blocked their view with his body and opened the rear wall, which swung away to reveal a gun cabinet.

Quindica whistled at his collection. 'Is that a Barrett ... and that one's an AWM?'

'Yeah. I have permits for all of them.' He addressed Difiore, who didn't repond.

Cutter reached inside and drew out a Glock from its holster and presented it to the cops. Quindica sniffed it. Broke it down and assembled it back expertly. 'This hasn't been fired.'

'Nope.'

'I bet these aren't the only weapons he has,' Difiore sniffed. 'Why do you need that many guns?'

'I don't,' he admitted. 'Many of those came with me from my time in Delta.'

He started to explain that he wasn't a gun enthusiast. His collection hadn't grown over time. Difiore was right. He had other weapons, stashed in caches all over the city, but that was only because of the business he was in. A gun was a tool, one he used as a last resort. He had even taken rounds because he had been late to fire.

Not the time for it.

'Will your phone back you up? That you weren't in Brownsville?'

He took them back to the living room, unlocked his cell and handed it over.

'You're not protesting,' Difiore said as she inspected its location history. 'I find that suspicious.'

'Suspect away all you want,' he growled. 'I don't care.'

He had anticipated such heat ever since the cops had appeared in his case. His cell phone was rigged to forward calls to burners that he carried with him. The throwaway that had been with him in Brownsville had gone in Karim's furnace as well.

'What's brought this on?' he asked his visitors when the detective tossed his phone back.

'Shit's hit the fan,' she said bitterly. 'Internal Affairs are looking into Davis's killing. That's muddied things for us. These

Brownsville killings ... looks like Sheller is tying up loose ends. Your friend the commish isn't happy. He wants results.'

'You're on the FBI's Task Force, right?'

'Yeah, but it's his city,' she flared. 'We've been chasing down every lead, tapping every snitch we have, and we've got squat. How can a gang operate so below the radar that no one, not even those in the street, know of it?'

'Dirty cops.' He raised his hand up to stop her outburst. 'Dirty judges, a lot of corruption everywhere. They're helping Sheller hide. And then he's got the loyalty.'

'He's a thug. How does he have that kind of reach?'

'Beats me.' Cutter shrugged. 'It's something I've been thinking about too.'

'How can we buck that?' She sounded defeated. 'Even with Peyton's resources, we haven't gotten anywhere.'

'You keep plugging away.' Cutter found it ironic that he was encouraging the detective, a cop who disliked him. 'You keep doing what you're doing. Someone, somewhere will give way. Not everyone will be as committed to him as he thinks or wants. Someone will open their mouth and—'

'Yeah, and he'll kill them before we get there. That's what has been happening all along.'

She flicked her hair back savagely and straightened her shoulders. The momentary flash of despair was gone. She was back to her in-your-face self. 'If we find you lied—'

'You'll nail my butt,' he completed for her.

Quindica's lips twitched. She put on a wooden façade swiftly when Difiore glowered at her.

'Never a dull moment,' he murmured to Quindica when the detective exited the apartment.

'Never,' she agreed.

He shut the door when they left and flopped on his couch. Checked his phone carefully. He wouldn't put it beyond the detective to insert some software in it. It looked clean, however. *Lucky for me, I deleted the recording when I returned home.* He removed the SIM card, cut it into small pieces and crushed the phone beneath his heel. It had outlived its usefulness. He unwrapped another burner from its plastic cover and set it up to take calls from his cell.

He frowned when he noticed the TV was still on and read the headlines.

Eric Tizzard's rally turns into a riot. Protesters fight with his supporters.

'Doofus,' he snorted when the state's governor came on and urged calm. 'What did you expect would happen?'

Cutter turned off the TV and yawned.

Just before he fell asleep, he wondered how Darrell was.

33

Darrell was thinking of Cutter.

He had told Manuel he was quitting.

'Man up,' his friend replied. 'Tell that to the boss.'

And that's why he had gone along to Mother Gaston. On arrival, however, Davis's replacement, someone called Nails, didn't even look at him. He was talking to the most senior members, getting a breakdown of the gang's activities and key people.

When one of the hoods yelled "COP," Darrell fled. He'd had enough. He wouldn't be returning to the gang.

Cutter was right. There was nothing for him in that group. It had been seductive initially. Being given responsibility, made to feel important. That hadn't lasted.

They'll kill me, he shivered. *They won't let anyone walk away.*

They might kill Mama, too. He sat up abruptly.

Did that mean he had to go back to the gang? Until he was killed or arrested? Because he knew those were the only two outcomes for him.

He racked his brains, scrunching his face in concentration. Surely there must be a way. Could he get witness protection? That's what happened on those TV shows.

Dumbass. That's only if I become a witness.

What did he know that was so important?

Nothing, he told himself bitterly. He could give up Manuel, who he was finding was not that much of a friend. He could tell the cops where Nails and his men hung out.

They'll know that. There are cruisers going up and down the street. They'll have noticed the gang.

He clutched the sheet hard as he tried to remember. There must be something. What about that bit about the Lions? He had heard one of the thugs talk softly, but Davis had shushed him immediately. *That was just a name. I didn't hear it again.*

Nope, nothing came to mind.

But the plan took root. Getting witness protection in return for snitching on the gang. That was the surest way to leave the gang safely.

He climbed out of bed and searched his school bag for Cutter's card. It was there, soiled and wrinkled, but readable. He memorized the number and scampered back into bed when he heard his mother enter the apartment.

He pretended to be asleep when she opened his door softly and peered in.

I'll find a way out, Mama. I won't let you down.

34

Steve 'Nails' Patchey tracked back several times until he was sure he was alone. He went to Mother Gaston and entered the developer's lot by climbing over the fence. Waited in the darkness until he heard footsteps.

Gunner came through the neighboring building. A large figure, looking ominous in the dark. Two figures with him, who stood back.

'What happened?' the Lions' founder growled.

'There was an undercover cop,' Nails told him. He had seen his boss snap the neck of a snitch. His large hands had gone around the man's throat and broken it with a mere twist. He wasn't scared, however. He was part of Gunner's inner circle, had been recruited personally by the man and had proven his loyalty and worth.

'Four of your men against him, and yet he got away?'

'They're dead, Gunner.'

'They might have snitched.'

'I know those men well. They wouldn't have. And even if they did, what did they know?

'Our name. We've kept it off the street so far.'

'There are enough gangs with similar names, Gunner,' he

scoffed. Took a step back when he saw the expression on his boss's face. 'I mean,' he said conciliatorily, 'it won't mean anything to the cops. Anyhow, I know they didn't talk. I got my people to question everyone in those neighboring buildings. A few residents watched what went down from their windows. No conversation.'

'You're sure?'

'Yeah.'

'Describe this cop.'

'I didn't see much, but Serro got a good look. He was tall, over six feet. Big nose, big everything. Bulky. But he could run.

'White?'

'Tanned. Won't the cops on our books know who he was?'

Gunner stared off in the distance and didn't reply.

'I'll find out,' he said.

'Any blowback from Davis getting killed?'

'None that you have to be worried about. Protect your turf, do your business, and you'll be fine.'

'Got it, Gunner.'

'You got any Jew shops here? Indian or Chinese takeouts?'

'There are a few.'

'Pick your best men. Attack them.'

'Just in Brownsville? I know several all over the city.'

'I don't care where. But let me know the stores. I'll run them past other cells so you're not stepping on someone else's territory.'

'There's a bodega in Brooklyn. Best cakes I've eaten. It's on Lafayette Street.'

'I'll check and get back to you. What's special about this one? Other than the cakes?'

'Owned by a Jew and a Chinese couple.'

Gunner stared at him.

'Jew *and* Chinese owners?'

'Yeah. I had the same reaction when I heard.'

'Hit it.'

'I'll do it myself.'

'This is urgent. Needs to go down in the next two days.'

'It will be done.'

'Use your senior men. No disposables.'

'They'll all be white, Gunner.'

'That's the point.'

'Understood.'

'Remind them of the code. If anyone's caught, they clam up and wait for help.'

Gunner departed as silently as he had arrived. No fist bumps or chest thumps. He wasn't into that.

Nails left the building and made a call.

'Serro,' he told his aide, 'get everyone together tomorrow. We've got work.'

35

Cutter was relaxing on his office couch the next evening. Of course, he didn't put it that way when Arnedra sniffed at him.

'I'm thinking,' he told her solemnly.

'I know,' she said snidely. 'Of food or sleep. Nothing else on your mind. You've closed the Darrell assignment?'

'That's what I'm working on. *Uninterrupted*,' he emphasized, hoping she got the hint.

If she did, she chose to ignore it.

She placed her hands on her hips and gave him an angry look.

'Cutter, if you don't get your ass—'

His phone rang. An unknown number.

'CUTTER!' a young voice panted.

'Yeah, who's this?'

'DARRELL. YOU'VE GOT TO DO SOMETHING. THEY'RE ATTACKING STORES. HURRY. CALL SOMEONE.'

'Whoa,' he sat up with a jerk. 'Back up a moment. Where are you? Are you safe?'

'Cutter, listen to me. I'm safe. I was with the gang in the evening. Just listening. Not doing anything. I swear. I swear on

Mama. Nails drew the hitters around him. Gave them instructions. They're supposed to hold up stores. Get their cash and run. He was going downtown himself. A bodega on Lafayette. I remembered. That's near Mama's office.' Words spilled out of him in a rush, like water from a broken dam.

'Where's this bodega? Did he say anything else?'

'He said something about cakes.'

Cutter was off his couch in an instant. He cupped the phone between shoulder and neck and jerked open his drawer to remove his Glock and holster.

'Do you know which other places will be hit?'

'No. When I heard about this one, I ran off to call you.'

'Nails said he was going there himself.'

'Yeah.'

'When?

'About half an hour ago.'

Cutter pictured the boy. Sweating. Frightened. But he had made the call.

'Darrell?'

'Yeah. Do something. Plea—'

'You did good.'

He hung up. Was out of the office in two strides. Heard Arnedra calling the emergency number. And then he was in the elevator, punching the button for ground. He tried Difiore. Got her voicemail.

'Several stores in Brownsville are going to be held up. About now,' he said tersely and hung up. Left a similar message for Quindica. Tried the bodega. Cursed loudly when he got nothing. Moshe didn't pick up his cell; neither did Chang or Lin Shun.

Cutter sprinted.

He zipped up his jacket when he saw a woman's eyes widen at the sight of his gun.

Half an hour. Enough time for Nails to have reached the convenience store. Was that why its owners weren't answering? Had something gone wrong?

He burst past a red light, threading through a narrowing gap between traffic. Got an earful of curses and snarls.

He tried the numbers again. The detective, the SAC, his friends. Jammed his cell in his pocket when no one answered.

Slowed when the bodega came into sight.

The warrior took over. Checking out the street. Everything looked normal. No. Those two men standing near the store, talking casually—they didn't belong. No one hung around like that. Not that near the entrance. The blinds were down, too.

He's here!

The animal took over.

36

'Got a light, bud?' Cutter used the timeworn trick to get close to the men. Left hand in his pocket, as if searching for a smoke, right hand near his jacket.

'Nope. Don't—'

He slashed the speaker across the temple with the barrel of his Glock. Brought the gun back and jammed it against the second thug's teeth.

'One word out of you and I'll spray you on the street.' He shoved the man ahead. Slammed him against the door so hard that it swung open and the bell rang.

Masked man with gun pointed at Chang and Lin Shun. Moshe by their side, as calm as ever. All of them behind the counter.

All of them turned toward the door when he and his captive crashed through the door.

Nails!

Cutter recognized the man's hair and build.

He sent his prisoner crashing against the display stand and dove to the floor when the thug fired. Bottles exploded behind him and showered him with liquid. He raised his Glock to fire a warning shot when the gangbanger reacted unexpectedly.

He jumped through the window, shattering the glass, bringing the blinds around him.

What the—

Cutter lunged out through the door, felt a shadow move. Ducked too late and caught a wicked blow on his temple. His head swam, his vision blinded for a moment. He reached out to his assailant, the second guard, caught his shirt with his free hand and tugged hard.

Felt movement. Nails, looking like a sci-fi movie character with the remains of the blinds around him. His scarf had slipped to reveal his snarl.

Cutter felt slow. His gun hand wasn't rising fast enough. His body felt sluggish. He took the only option he had. He bodyslammed the thug and sent him stumbling towards the leader. Got another blow to the back of his neck as reward and fell to the ground. Clawed desperately for his Glock, which had slipped out of his hand, and then a kick sent him into darkness.

'You were out just a few moments.' Moshe was swabbing his face with a paper towel. He handed him a bottle of water.

Cutter drank greedily and wiped his mouth with his sleeve. He winced at the movement. His body throbbed and his head felt tender. He was in the bodega, on the floor, back resting against a fridge. It felt cool and brought some relief to the burning inside him.

'What happened?' he said hoarsely.

'You got beat up,' Lin Shun said simply. 'That last kick knocked you out.'

'I'm disappointed,' Chang shook his head. 'There weren't six of them. Just two. You let them take you.'

Cutter flipped him the finger and let his eyes search the interior of the store. 'Where's the third man?'

The owner's face fell. 'He got away, too. We had him cornered, but we were distracted when we saw you outside.

What they were doing. He barged into Lin Shun and escaped through the window.'

'Did he hurt you?' he asked Lin Shun.

'Busted cheekbone,' her husband declared before she could respond. 'We'll have to X-ray it. It's a wonder she didn't break her neck.'

Cutter breathed a sigh of relief when she winked at him.

'We had them,' Chang continued. 'And then you had to show up.'

'You had them? That man had a gun on all of you!'

'We had it under control.'

'So, it's my fault?'

'Totally,' Moshe agreed and swabbed his face again.

Their eyes belied their words. Anxiety, concern, as they hovered around him.

'You got it on tape?' Cutter got to his feet with Moshe's help.

No swimming head. No dizziness. He took another long swallow, the water working its magic inside him.

'Tape? Who uses that?' Chang snorted. 'Yeah, cameras were recording. Here come your friends,' he broke off when cruisers rolled up.

'You're still alive?' Difiore greeted him.

37

Cutter raised his hands in resignation at her words and let Lin Shun brief the cops. The detective and the SAC recorded her statement on a phone while patrol cops checked out the store and questioned witnesses on the street. Tape barricaded the sidewalk, while another cop directed traffic.

'Now, you,' Difiore ordered, nothing on her face giving her thoughts away. Quindica watched silently, thumbs hooked in the pockets of her neatly cut trousers.

He went through it. How he had raced up, spotted the thugs outside and played himself in.

His eyebrows rose when she turned off the recording and pocketed the phone.

'How did you know this would go down?'

'I have a network on the streets too. One of my informants told me.'

'This snitch has a name?'

'Not to the cops.' *Why isn't she recording this?*

She didn't push him.

'Any of those assailants have a name?'

'Nails. He was the holdup man. The one with the gun.'

'How do you know him?'

'I don't. But I'm told he's taken over from Davis.'

The detective and the SAC pierced him with their eyes.

'Street talk,' he said helpfully. 'That's what my CI told me.'

'Cops have confidential informants,' Difiore said tightly. 'Not—'

'I do, too. How many stores were attacked?'

'Ten,' she growled. 'All over the city. Holdups. All in the last three hours.'

Cutter checked his watch. It was just past nine pm. Darrell had called him at six.

'You caught any perps?'

'They got away.' She looked accusingly at him. *As if I'm to blame for that, too*, he grouched inwardly.

Quindica straightened. The patrol cops left the store at a silent command from her.

'It seems to be coordinated. The attacks.' She fingered a broken blind and tossed it away. 'All the attackers were white. Young men. Late twenties or thirties.'

Cutter sensed it coming but still felt shock when he heard her.

'All the stores were minority-owned. People of color.'

'Any particular race targeted?'

'No.

'Lions behind it?'

'We don't know. We've asked our CIs too, but who knows what kind of word gets back?'

Cutter knew what she meant. *Dirty cops might not relay everything their snitches tell them*. His face turned bleak when another thought struck him.

Some of those cops will know who the perps are. They might be in contact with Gunner.

He was sure it was Sheller who was behind the attacks.

'Lions don't have a monopoly on race crimes,' Difiore channeled his thoughts. 'There are other gangs who could have committed these. Or all of them, copying one another.'

He nodded, unconvinced. 'You might get something from CCTV.'

'We'll be on it.'

'You're wondering why I didn't record your statement.' Difiore said it so softly that Cutter had to bend his head to catch it.

He followed her and the SAC when they went outside.

'I'm sure you can figure out why.'

'Your department is dirty.'

'Not every cop.'

'You don't want everything you see or hear going into your system. What about the Feds?'

Quindica gave him a wooden face.

'The FBI too?' he asked, shocked.

'We can't take anything for granted,' the detective responded.

'I know Bart and Bruce,' he replied heatedly. 'They—'

'Not them.'

'I'm on the side of angels now?' He grinned.

'No,' Difiore said flatly. 'But this ... your inside info, that's what we want from you. Nothing more. What I said earlier stands. Don't go rogue. Don't run your own investigation.'

He mock-saluted her, but that didn't bring any smiles.

These cops were hard.

He turned away from the gaggle of onlookers and reporters on the sidewalk being held back by tape and the cops.

'He'll know you're involved,' Difiore said in a parting shot.

Trust her to cheer him up.

He. Sheller. Who, if he watched TV, would see Cutter's face plastered on the local news.

38

Nails met Gunner at the same location on Mother Gaston, late at night. It was a low-risk location. They got a free pass since most of the cruisers that patrolled the area were in their pockets.

'This man ... any chance he was the same one?' the Lions' founder asked.

'Nope. This one was younger. Different features. Green eyes. Looked like a model.'

'A model,' his boss snorted, 'wouldn't take on armed men. You got any injuries?'

'A few glass splinters. Took 'em out. Nothing serious.'

'Your men?'

'They'll recover.'

'I'll check out who this man is, too. He might be a bystander, an off-duty cop, anyone.'

Gunner rarely watched TV; otherwise he would have known who the mystery man was.

'Fifth Avenue,' he told his driver as he buckled up.

All ten attacks had gone well. None of his people had been

apprehended. The cops would check security camera footage and would identify a few criminals, but they wouldn't find those men.

His Lions were good at operating beneath the radar. Right underneath everyone's noses, but unseen.

'Slow down,' he commanded when they were approaching the Frick Collection building. He searched the sidewalk and spotted a figure.

'Him,' he directed.

The SUV slowed enough for Sidewalk Man to get inside.

'I heard about it,' Mease, the arrival, congratulated him. 'Nothing else on TV but these attacks. *Disturbing rise of hate crimes*, one channel called it.'

'It would have been if we had killed anyone. I gave explicit instructions on that. No shooting.'

'Yeah, our supporters wouldn't have liked that either. It would have drawn too much heat.'

'How is he?' Gunner jerked his head in the direction of Central Park.

He. Rubin.

Mease knew who he meant. 'He's got interviews lined up tomorrow. Tizzard's rally, the riots, these attacks, he'll focus on those. Parsons and Farley both think we should get an uplift in the polls.'

'What do you think?'

'This alone won't be enough. The election's still several months away. We might need more *drastic* action.'

'From my people?'

'Yeah.'

'We're here to serve.' Gunner's smile was evil.

39

'That took courage.' Cutter patted Darrell on the back. 'Calling me.'

The boy didn't respond, didn't meet his eyes.

They were on Chester Playground.

He had followed the student after school; no Manuel, no joining the gang. The boy had flung his backpack on the grass and broken open a bag of chips when he approached.

'How did you find me?'

'I followed you after school.'

'Is that what you did earlier, too?'

'Nope. I told you about that.'

The boy emptied the bag and stuffed it into his pocket. Drank from a bottle of juice, which went back into his bag. Wiped his hands on his trousers.

'Why did you snitch on them?'

He took his time replying. 'It didn't feel right.'

Huh? And what you did before, with the gang, that was right?

Cutter didn't voice his thoughts, however.

'That number you called me from ... I didn't recognize it.'

'I used a stranger's. I told them mine ran out of juice. That it was an emergency. I couldn't risk calling from my phone. Nails might want to check all our phones later.'

'Smart,' Cutter said admiringly. He meant it.

'How does witness protection work?'

Cutter jerked his head up in surprise at the question.

'Why?'

'Answer me,' the boy replied stubbornly.

'You tell the cops or the Feds something. If it's important enough that it will lead to many arrests, they'll give you a new identity, a new life, and protect you.'

'Will they give it to Mama and me?'

'Darrell,' he said sharply. 'You took the first step in getting out of that gang by calling me. You need to end it with them. Stop going. Ditch Manuel.'

'You think it's that easy?'

'It is.'

'They won't let me quit like that. I know what they did to another kid. Leon, he cut his face up.'

That must be Davis.

'You saw that?'

'No, Manuel told me. He did it in front of the gang. As a lesson to them. You been in a gang before? It's not like just another job, where you go to your boss and tell him you're quitting.'

Anger in his voice, but also fear and the sheen of tears in his eyes.

'I have to do this my way.'

'Darrell—'

'No. Stop following me. Stop advising me.'

'You're a kid.' Cutter grabbed his elbow and jerked him around. 'You are way out of your league here. The smart thing to do is stop going. If they come to you, call me and call the cops.'

'What if they do something to Mama?'

'That's not how gangs work. They don't want heat.'

'You don't know this outfit.'

'Think of your mama.'

'I AM. I'M DOING THIS FOR HER.'

Darrell flushed when a few heads turned in their direction. He shrugged free, grabbed his backpack and ran away.

Turned back and pointed a finger at Cutter.

'And if you tell Mama, I'll—'

He raced away.

Cutter watched him till he disappeared from sight and then cursed himself.

Way to go, dude. You had him. You could have convinced him. No. You had to patronize him.

It was the surest way to alienate a youngster.

Was Darrell serious about witsec?

He pondered about it before shaking his head. The Federal witness program was the most secure one. Several states had their own versions, New York included. However, those programs were less extensive than the one operated by the Marshals.

Quindica can get him under the Federal program, but what does he have to offer? Nails? That wasn't good enough. The cops could get the leader on their own.

Cutter swore loudly again and got a reproving stare and a click of the tongue from a mom. He got to his feet and trudged back to his car.

He was back to square one. He would have to find a way to get Darrell out before he endangered himself.

I can't tell Carmel, either. She'll talk to him, and that will alienate him further.

He had to find another way.

Maybe I'll wipe out the gang myself.

It was a flippant thought, but it stayed in his mind.

40

Gunner did eventually turn on his TV.

He settled in on his couch and watched the candidate on various channels, expressing outrage at the spate of hate crimes.

'We need to come down hard on these criminals. Our cops are fighting a losing battle. The justice system is skewed in favor of thugs.' He passionately outlined how he would change the system. Provide law enforcement the tools to battle crime. The live studio audience clapped and cheered enthusiastically at his statements. If the elections had been held at that very moment, Rubin would have won.

The gang founder grunted in satisfaction. It looked like his people's actions had worked. However, he agreed with Mease. The attacks wouldn't be enough. The Veep and the other candidates would come back with policies and tangible proposals to address national issues. If Rubin had to ride a wave of emotion, there had to be something bigger happening.

More drastic than attacks, like Mease had said.

He reached for the remote to turn off the TV, then paused. An interview with someone who called himself The Fixer. Good-looking dude. He had stopped an attack on a convenience store in Lafayette two weeks ago.

His eyes sharpened. Hadn't Nails held up—? He snatched his phone and dialed a number.

'The Fixer—is that him?' he barked.

His aide, clearly thrown off by the abrupt question, took his time. 'You saw him on TV? His name's Cutter Grogan. I made the connection too, after we met. It was him.'

'You held up the same store that had been attacked just a couple of weeks ago? By our people?'

'I didn't know them, boss.'

Gunner clenched the phone so hard that the veins on his hands popped out. He forced himself to relax. It wasn't Nails' fault. That was how the gang worked. One cell didn't know what the other did. Only he and a very few trusted lieutenants could see the entire picture.

Boyce, Pupius and Tuttle were new entrants to the Queens chapter. They had been explicitly ordered not to get inked, but Boyce had gone ahead and done just that. They had been told to lie low and learn how the gang worked. They went and held up that bodega.

Gunner had gotten Mease to pull strings so they would get bail. He then arranged for their deaths. Those who dared disobey his orders found out quickly how harsh his sentences were.

'How did he come back to that same store?'

'Don't know, boss. Do you want me to find out?'

'No. Stay out of it.'

He dialed another number.

'Cray?'

'Yeah, Gunner.'

'I want you to find everything you can on The Fixer.'

'The one on TV?'

'Yeah.'

'On it.'

His tech specialist hung up.

Gunner had worked out early on that a computer whiz would be needed to support the Lions growth. Enter Cray. A hacker who had done time at Lompoc, who had heard of Gunner and the Lions through the prison grapevine. He shared the philosophy, was an enthusiastic member, and his skills were just what the gang needed.

Gunner called Mease. 'Do we have a heavyset cop on our side?' He described the undercover cop who had killed Nails' people, and what he had done.

'Our friends would have told me if there was any surveillance. I'll find out.'

MEASE HUNG UP. STRAIGHTENED THE TABLE LINEN WHILE HE scrolled through his mental list of contacts.

'It's me,' he told the same assistant chief he had called days ago. 'How's Martinelli holding up?'

'He's fine. Looks like the investigation will find some fault in his actions; however, he won't be fired or suspended. He'll be given light work. Admin stuff that cops hate, but he'll get away.'

'Great. He can expect a sizable bonus.'

'He knows that.'

'Do you have anyone undercover working in Brownsville?'

'Nope,' the chief replied categorically.

'Yeah. I would have known. Why do you ask?'

'Those killings in Brownsville—'

'Shooter got away. We're still hunting him.'

'Those men were ours.'

'I know.'

'We think he was a LEO.' Law Enforcement Officer.

'Not from the NYPD. Could be DEA or some other agency.'

Mease's brow wrinkled. Federal involvement was the last thing they wanted. He thanked the chief and called another number, this one in DC.

'Kosman,' he said and hung up.

Minutes later his phone rang. The Associate Deputy Administrator in the DEA's Intelligence Division called him back from his burner.

'Mease,' he hissed. 'We have a protocol. You can't call me at the office.'

'I wouldn't if it wasn't important. Do you have any undercover agents in Brooklyn?'

'This about those shootings? Nope. I would have given you a heads-up.'

'You sure?

'Of course, I am.' He hung up.

The strategist stroked his chin. He believed Kosman. The DEA official had too much to lose to lie. Mease had recorded him accepting bribes in return for intel. As if that wasn't enough, they had a recording revealing his white supremacy views.

His and Rubin's network of contacts was filled with believers. Blackmail helped, too.

GUNNER TOOK HIS CALL AN HOUR LATER.

'He isn't any kind of LEO.'

He thanked Mease and brewed himself coffee. The heavyset man wasn't a priority. However, he had come up from ADX, where any sign of weakness could be fatal. He applied the same philosophy to running the gang.

'Spread the word,' he told his cell leaders as he called each one. 'We need to find that shooter.'

41

Cutter was back at ADX Florence.

A hastily arranged visit, when the warden had called him and told him cryptically that a mutual friend needed to see him.

'Don't you have a message for me?' *That's what Jake and I agreed.*

'Just that you need to get your butt moving ASAP. Why the heck did I agree to be a postman?' He had slammed the phone down with that.

Which led to Cutter flying back, repeating his previous itinerary.

THE SAME MEETING ROOM AT THE PRISON. THE WARDEN conspicuous by his absence.

Horstman arrived with his retinue of guards, who waited outside the room.

'People will talk if we meet this often,' Cutter joked, but there was an underlying seriousness. Walls had ears, and the ones at prisons had sharp hearing.

'It couldn't wait. Bull and I talked. He was high. He had

gotten some weed, don't ask me how, you know how the trade is in here.'

Every prison had a strong smuggling operation and did brisk business in contraband items. Cigarettes, phones, food, anything was available for a price.

'Our friend's definitely alive.' Horstman lowered his voice. 'All I had to do was talk of a second life, and Bull started off.'

'He used Gunner's name?'

'No, but he described him. Who else looks like Sheller?'

Cutter agreed. He had been expecting such a revelation, but hearing it jolted him to alertness anyway.

'You didn't summon me to tell me just that.'

'He said Gunner had help in staging his death. External help. I took that to mean someone from outside ADX. And that'—he leaned forward—'he was working on something big. Very big.'

'What could be bigger than running a gang while the world thinks he's dead?'

'Beats me. I couldn't tell the warden to convey all that.'

'He say anything else?'

'He started rambling afterwards, and I didn't dare question him.'

'Don't bring it up again. Not by yourself. If he does, show that you aren't interested.'

'Yeah.'

'Do you know if Bull has any visitors?'

'Family. No one else.'

That didn't mean anything. A convict's loved ones usually doubled up as messengers. *He could be in active contact with Gunner that way.*

CUTTER LEFT ADX TROUBLED. HORSTMAN'S FINDINGS WERE useful, but how could he act on them?

How do I find a dead man?

Difiore and Quindica could help, but the ex-con had stayed off their radar too. What could they do?

He boarded his flight, still thinking furiously.

'You looked into Sheller's death?' he asked on a call to Difiore when he landed at Newark.

'Dead ends. Coroner's dead. Killed in a hunting accident. The detectives who had the case, two of them ... one's retired to Mexico, untraceable. The other's on some European cruise.'

'Their case notes?'

'Nothing there.'

'What about the body? The person who was killed?'

'Released to Sheller's distant family, who are—'

'Untraceable.'

'You got it. Four years is a long time, even in today's world with the internet and all that.'

'What about the man he had a fight with? I bet it was his body.'

'He's—'

'Disappeared, too.'

'Yeah,' Difiore said bitterly. 'And we can't re-open the case because that might alert Sheller. Why are you asking all this?'

'I met Jake today.' He broke it down for her swiftly. 'I've just landed, in fact.'

'Outside help could mean anything.'

'It means those who helped him had no prison connection. That's rare. Criminals and ex-cons move in a small circle. Civilian contact is usually friends and family or employers. No, this is different.'

'There's nothing to go on there.'

'Don't I know it,' he cursed.

He would blame himself for what happened next.

42

Prison walls *did* have ears.

They had eyes too, and ADX was no different.

The prison guard who had signed Cutter in had a sweet thing going. He got a cut of the prison's drug trade, several baggies each week that he sold outside for a hefty profit. All he had to do was call a certain number and feed some information.

Harmless intel, which was how he justified it to himself. Besides, many officials had side gigs going. His revealing some inside juice ... what harm did it do? Wasn't America the land of free enterprise?

'Yeah. Grogan. Cutter. C-U-T-T-E-R,' he spelled it out. 'Came down twice. Met just one prisoner. Ripper. Sorry, that's what we call him. Jake Horstman. Sure, will keep my eyes peeled.'

He hung up and returned to his station and checked out the visitor log on his screen. Were there any other names off whom he could make some profit?

His information reached the Colorado Lions cell leader, who passed it on straight up. It reached Gunner, who was touring the city in his darkened SUV. Checking out his cells, making sure that business was rolling smoothly.

The Lions' founder had just finished killing a defector, a gang member who had switched allegiance to a rival outfit.

'Bury him in that development lot,' he ordered as he wiped his hands on a rag, then set fire to it. 'The one with fresh concrete, by the river.'

He climbed into his vehicle, which creaked beneath his weight, and signaled his driver to leave. Looked back at his men, who were wrapping the dead thug in a tarp. There was no room for traitors, not in the Lions. The fool got what he deserved.

He reached into his pocket absently when his phone trilled. Recognized the burner.

'Yeah?'

He went still when a cell leader relayed him the ADX news.

'Grogan? Ripper? Yesterday? You're sure?' He bit back a curse. Of course, his man was sure. Everyone in his gang knew not to feed him false information.

'Do nothing for now. Keep an eye on who else visits him.'

He looked blindly out of the window when the call ended. It was the third time this Fixer dude had come up on his radar. How did he know Ripper? And what had the convict told him?

Gunner kept track of his enemies. Most of them were dead, and the few who were alive were in prison, which made it easy to keep tabs on them. His well-oiled network in ADX was his eyes and ears, his tripwire.

Perhaps it was time to change its function. Turn it into a weapon. However, he had to know more first.

'Cray?' he growled into his phone, 'What have you found on Grogan?'

'He's like a private investigator, boss. But without the license. He's based on Lafayette.'

'How big is his outfit?'

'Just him and his partner. A black woman.'

'Black?'

'Yeah.'

'Family? Girlfriends? Boyfriends?'

'None that I could find. No social media presence. He doesn't even own a credit card. Owns his apartment on Lafayette.'

'Owns it?

'Yeah.'

That meant the Fixer was loaded. Which also meant he might be well-connected. He had to find out more before deciding on a course of action.

Darrell was nervous. He looked back frequently, ignored Manuel's quizzical looks.

'We gotta be careful,' he told his friends. 'That hangout got attention.'

'Relax, bro,' his friend snorted. 'Nails has got it sorted out. We'll know if the cops come on to us.'

'We got friendly cops?'

'Yeah.'

'Who are they?'

'You don't want to know, bro. I thought you were leaving the gang.'

'What made you think that?'

'You hang back when we're with the dudes. You don't take the backpack anymore. People have noticed.'

'What are they saying?'

'This and that.' His friend didn't elaborate.

'I'm committed.'

'That's good, bro. That's our family.'

Darrell plastered on a smile and followed his friend to the gang's hangout on Mother Gaston.

He was seeing Manuel in a new light. His friend wasn't the same boy he had grown up with. He had become harder. Ruthless.

I don't want to be like him.

I want out.

Which meant he had to find something on the gang. Soon.

'I WAS WAITING TO HEAR FROM YOU.'

Cutter looked up to see Carmel Ward burst into his office, Arnedra behind her.

Afternoon. Rays of light coming through the windows, lighting up the hardwood floor. A floral arrangement that his partner had bought adding color to the room.

None of which distracted the mother. She shook her finger accusingly at him.

'I thought you would call and update me on what's happening. Darrell came home early a few nights. I thought that was it; I have my boy back. But he texted me today. Said he would be late. I checked with Manuel's mom. He's out, too. WHAT IS GOING ON? WHAT'S MY SON INVOLVED IN?'

'Bad company, ma'am,' Cutter said smoothly. 'Just like you suspected.'

His admission stopped her mid-tirade. She blindly reached for the back of a chair, maneuvered it and sat heavily.

'Like a gang?' she asked hollowly.

'I don't know, yet.' He hated himself for lying. 'I'm still figuring that out.'

'Can we go to the cops?'

'We can, ma'am. But Darrell might get into trouble too.'

She twisted her hands nervously as her lips trembled and her eyes filled. 'I thought I had my son back. When I got his text today ...' She sniffled, brushed her tears away and squared her shoulders.

'Mr. Grogan, please save my son.'

'Cutter, ma'am—'

'Everything I have is yours.' She brushed his words away. 'All I want is my son.'

He was brooding when Arnedra returned after seeing their visitor out.

'I thought you had a connection with Darrell. He called you to warn about the attack on that store.'

'I screwed up. I pushed him too far, too quickly.'

'Does he know how dangerous it is?' She sighed when he told her about his last meeting with the student.

'He thinks it's like how Hollywood shows it.'

'What are you going to do?'

'Follow him as much as I can. Be there for him.'

'You could go to the cops.'

'I will if I can't come up with another way. I'll see if I can get Difiore to go easy on him.'

'She just might. I mean, he's not gotten into anything more serious than storing drugs.'

'Yeah. It's not her I'm worried about.'

'The gang?'

'Yes.' He nodded soberly. 'The Lions will retaliate. With their network inside the NYPD, they'll know who's snitched on them.'

'And what Darrell tells them won't be important enough to afford protection.'

'Oh, they'll send a few cruisers, mount some vigilance, but what if those cops are dirty?'

'You're screwed.'

He grinned reluctantly. Arnedra had a way of cutting to the chase.

His smile disappeared when she went back to her desk.

He had completed every assignment they had taken satisfactorily. Sure, Carmel Ward hadn't paid him, but she was his client.

And it looked like he would fail her.

43

Terry Kobach was serving a life sentence for a string of offenses that had shocked the country.

He had raped an underaged girl in front of her parents and then murdered the entire family. He had escaped in their car and had shot up the neighborhood while being pursued by cops. Two more victims had died before he had been arrested.

He arrived at ADX with a rep. He got tested by other convicts. He smashed the skull of one prisoner against a wall and permanently maimed another. No one troubled him after that.

He had found a friend in Gunner. The Lions' man was as much a stone-cold killer as he was, and what was there to dislike about the white supremacy views?

He became the gang's enforcer in prison. A convict needed to be threatened, all Kobach had to do was look in that menacing way and most times that did the job. Sometimes he had to take more direct action. Like plunging a shiv between the ribs or in the jugular. In return, he got an unending supply of smokes, weed, and his choice of cell when he wasn't in solitary.

Violence and killing didn't bother him. He was already serving life. What else could they do to him?

The message came to him, words whispered hurriedly in his ears during dinner.

'YOU'RE A POPULAR MAN.'

Horstman turned in the yard to see Kobach leering at him. He put down the weights he was exercising with and wiped his sweat on his sleeve. The killer had been one of his attackers, along with Gunner, when Cutter had intervened. The two men had kept their distance when both Sheller and his friend had left prison.

'That so?'

'Yeah. I heard you got two visits in less than a week. The same person. Surprise, surprise, he isn't family.'

Horstman's skin prickled. How did the convict know of his visitors? Was he being watched?

'What's it to you?'

'Funny you ask me that. I was wondering who this man was and what he meant to you.'

Horstman realized with a shock that they were alone in the yard. No other prisoners, no guards, just him and one of the most dangerous men in ADX beneath the beating sun.

He raised a hand to wipe his brow, and that was his mistake. It left his chest exposed, enough of an opening for Kobach, who hit him with a clenched fist, the knuckles of his hand jabbing deep into his solar plexus.

Horstman doubled over. He reached out to stall his attacker's progress, but his hand was yanked and twisted so hard that a scream escaped him. It got cut off abruptly when Kobach's knee smashed into his jaw.

'Tell me, Ripper,' the man crooned in his ear. 'You know you want to.'

. . .

Cutter was driving to Brownsville when a pair of dumbbells crushed Horstman's ribs. He was adjusting his shades and following Darrell and Manuel when a weight fell on his friend's testicles.

He was crossing Mother Gaston, to the other side, when Horstman's ear was torn off.

Everyone breaks. Everyone has a point at which the brain shuts down the body to preserve its resources and decides to give in.

Horstman reached his when his tenth toe was broken.

He sobbed and confessed everything about Cutter to Kobach, who listened and left the yard when he ran out of words.

Only then did the guards rush in, along with paramedics.

44

Gunner got the news when he was having dinner in his Bronx apartment. He stopped eating and focused on the voice on the phone.

He was dimly aware of faint sounds from the outside, hushed noises of traffic, but they didn't break his concentration.

'Ripper said that? That Grogan was Farhaan Zaidi?'

'Yeah. He admitted to it.'

'He would have said anything to stop the torture.'

'There was no reason for him to say that name. I wasn't asking him about Zaidi.'

'Any problems with the guards?'

'No.'

'Where's Ripper now?'

'In an emergency room. You know where they are.'

'Keep track of him. I'll get back to you.'

Gunner pushed away his half-eaten meal and steepled his fingers.

Zaidi. The very same terrorist who had intervened and saved Ripper from the Lions. The same man who had protected the other terrorists from Gunner.

He didn't realize he was grinding his teeth until his mouth felt sore. He stopped himself and unclenched his fists.

Zaidi. The most bitter enemy Gunner had in ADX. The man he had vowed to kill, though he had failed to get the opportunity; the terrorist had simply vanished mysteriously one day.

Zaidi and Grogan were one and the same.

But why?

'Cray?' he barked into his phone. 'Can you match two people, see if they are the same? That facial recognition stuff?'

'Yeah, if I have images for the two men.'

'Grogan is one of them. The other is Farhaan Zaidi.'

A long pause. 'Zaidi? Wasn't he the terrorist who was in ADX with you?'

'The same person.'

'I'm not understanding, boss. The Fixer dude and this—'

'Cray,' Gunner snarled. 'I don't need you to understand. Find out if the two men are the same with that fancy software you have.'

He swore loudly and went to his computer. Searched for Grogan and watched several interview clips of him. He then searched for Zaidi. There had been some coverage of the terrorist when he had been captured. Nope. The Daesh man had a burn on his face. A thick beard. *He had an accent.* Only their heights were similar. But he could be in a disguise.

Another thought came to him. That heavyset man who had killed Nails' people. Could he be Grogan?

It was possible.

Did Zaidi, or the Fixer or whoever he really was, suspect Gunner was alive? Was that why he had targeted the Lions and gone to Ripper for information?

The gang founder's fists opened and closed repeatedly as he imagined they were around Grogan's neck. There was unfinished business between them, which he would end his way—by killing the man, slowly, painfully, and mercilessly.

But first he had to know more.

'Can you get to Ripper's room?' he asked Kobach. ADX might have been the most secure prison in America, but money talked there, too. Gunner's people had access to phones and contraband and could get special privileges for themselves.

'It will be difficult. More guards will have to be bribed. The medics, too.'

'I'll make arrangements. You'll have no trouble with them. Is he conscious?'

'I guess so. I didn't kill him.'

'Go to him. Ask him about Zaidi. Why was the man in prison?'

'He was a terrorist. Where else would he be?'

'Kobach,' Gunner thundered. Why did his people talk back? 'I don't need you to think. Leave that to me. Ask him that question. And once he answers, do what those terrorists do.'

45

Cutter returned from his recon without finding anything of substance.

He had tried following Nails after his meeting with his men, but the gang leader had a protective ring around him and he couldn't get close. Not without turning the street into a gunfight.

He had shadowed their vehicle but broke away when he found a second gang ride tailing Nails.

That's to spot tails and warn Nails.

Placing a tracker on his ride wouldn't have worked either. He had noticed how the thugs checked out their vehicle before climbing into it.

He was restless. Darrell had been with the gang, with Manuel. The teenager had headed home when the gang split up.

Cutter barely paid any attention to the news on TV, about the surge in the polls for Rubin. He paced his apartment and peered through the window. The sight of the city didn't calm him as it usually did. He punched his pillow into shape and tried to sleep. Nope, that didn't work either.

He got out of bed with a curse, slipped into his gym pants and headed out of his apartment for a late-night run.

He hoped some muggers would accost him; he was in that kind of dark mood.

It was when he had completed a fast ten miles that he realized what was bothering him.

A premonition.

His inner radar was pinging faintly.

Warning him of an incoming threat.

But from where and from whom?

KOBACH SLIPPED OUT OF HIS CELL AT TEN PM AND WENT DOWN the hallway. Sounds of snoring and mumbling. Someone crying. Another prisoner praying loudly. A voice angrily calling out for silence. Normal night sounds at ADX.

He tested the gate at the end of the corridor. It opened. No alarm went off, no guards came racing to put him down.

He went through more hallways and crossed a large reception area. Shook his head in admiration at Gunner's clout. Guards didn't look up from their screens when he passed. It looked like the security cameras had been turned off temporarily.

He entered the emergency medical section. No nurses or doctors. Bright fluorescent lights. Doors to various care rooms.

He entered the last one.

Ripper, on his bed, plugged into various pieces of equipment, with tubes running out of his hands and nose.

He went to his victim, who was breathing stertorously, and slapped him lightly on his cheek.

'Hey, Horstman? You awake?'

It wasn't tender, loving care, but Kobach wouldn't know what that was if it bit him in the butt.

'Ripper?' he growled, louder. Sure, he had free passage, but the guards couldn't turn a blind eye forever.

The prisoner's eyes flickered. He jerked and moaned when he recognized his attacker.

'No, no,' Kobach protested. 'No more beating, I promise. I need to know just this. Why was Zaidi in prison?'

He grabbed Ripper's chin and stopped him from looking away.

'Don't make me angry,' he said softly. 'Don't make me start again.'

He wrinkled his nose when the prisoner soiled himself.

'You're scared. That's good. Now, tell me what I asked. Be good.'

He coaxed and threatened and squeezed on the man's injuries until Jake Horstman gave up his last remaining secret.

And then Kobach removed the hacksaw blade from his sleeve and got to work, and when he had finished, he whistled as he returned to his cell. Several hours later he was beaten by the guards and sent to solitary, but by then it was too late.

He had what Gunner had wanted.

He had relayed the information.

And what could the authorities do?

Send him to death row?

He had no fear of that.

46

'Grogan!'

Cutter spun around, reaching for his gym bag, the previous night's unease still strong in him, until he recognized the voice and the two figures in the car park.

'Of all the places to meet, this is where ...' he trailed off when he read them. Difiore and Quindica, normally impassive, but something in the way they held themselves.

'Something's up? Darr—'

He cut himself off before he could complete the name. They didn't know of the boy. There was no need for his name to be mentioned.

'He doesn't know,' the detective said.

'Nope,' Quindica agreed. 'Inside.' She jerked a thumb in the building's direction.

'Hey,' he protested, 'you want my coffee, just ask!'

That didn't get a rise.

He ushered them inside and gestured at himself. 'Whatever you want to tell me can wait until I shower. You know where the kitchen is.'

A freshly brewed cup was waiting for him when he joined them in the living room. He nodded in thanks, took an appreciative sip when Difiore reached for the TV's remote and turned it on.

He was about to make a crack about her being at home in his apartment when the words died on his lips.

BRUTAL KILLING IN ADX FLORENCE.

PRISONER BEHEADED.

The banners cycled on repeat as the host broke the story of Jake Horstman's gruesome death. Someone exclaimed and moved. Quindica. Her words didn't register. She came to him and wiped his wrist with a towel, cleaning up the hot coffee he had spilled, the burn that he wasn't conscious of.

Horstman was dead. Killed in prison.

Little else registered.

The drink tasted like ash when he sipped it unconsciously. He put it down and moved away from the cops. Crossed his arms across his chest and watched the report over and over again until Difiore switched off the TV.

'We thought you would know.'

He didn't respond.

Now he knew what that premonition had been about. He welcomed the coldness, the distant feeling that swept over him.

'I didn't. I rarely watch the news.' He was conscious of the sharp glance she threw.

He was grateful for their silence. That they didn't offer meaningless platitudes. His friend wouldn't come back. His death wouldn't be lessened by any words.

'The reports are of a prison fight,' Quindica briefed him impassively. 'Horstman was in emergency care after being brutally beaten.' She described what had been done to his friend. Waited for his reaction and, when he didn't respond, continued. 'He survived that attack. A prisoner got to him at night and did that.'

'Kobach.' Difiore added. 'That's his name. The perp. His name's not yet released, but it will come out. He'll face charges—'

'I know him. It won't matter to him.'

'You know why?'

'Sheller. It's his doing.'

'That's a leap. We spoke to the warden and the various authorities. Kobach is suspected of killing other prisoners. He and your friend had several run-ins.'

'He's behind it. He's sending me a message.'

'How do you figure that?' Quindica frowned.

He didn't elaborate.

Difiore sucked her breath sharply. 'Zaidi!'

'Yes,' he smiled bitterly. 'Sheller found out I had met Jake. He wanted to know who I was. He sent his enforcer to ask questions.'

'The beheading.' The detective paled. 'He knows you were impersonating a terrorist. He might come after you. I'll arrange protection. Patrol cars—'

'You'll do no such thing,' he cut her off savagely.

'Grogan,' she replied heatedly. 'This isn't Syria. It isn't the Wild West. You'll take our protection.'

'I don't need it.'

'You want him to come after you,' Quindica guessed.

'You,' Difiore jabbed his chest with her forefinger, 'will not do anything that will risk our investigation. I don't care how personal this is for you. DO YOU UNDERSTAND?' she bellowed.

He couldn't help smiling despite the circumstances. 'Yes, ma'am.'

She was right. Their investigation couldn't be jeopardized. But that didn't mean he couldn't help them.

47

'We need to meet,' Gunner called Mease.

'Come to the parking lot.'

'No. Our friend needs to be there, too.'

'That will be harder to arrange.'

'Make it happen.'

'It's that important?'

'Yeah.'

THEY MET IN A PRIVATE CLUB IN THE BRONX THAT WAS OWNED by a Lion.

Rubin was in the neighborhood to make a speech, and after he glad-handed supporters, his team drove Mease and him to the establishment.

He met more fans there, smiled for the cameras, thanked people for their support and signed ballcaps and shirts.

He went to the bathroom with Mease while his bodyguards waited outside.

'This had better be important,' he told Gunner when the Lions' leader came out of a stall.

'It is. You heard about the killing in ADX?'

'Yeah.' Mease looked at him curiously. 'You knew the victim?'

'I tried to kill him. He was saved by another prisoner.'

'Where's this going?' Rubin glanced at his watch impatiently. 'What's a prison fight got to do with us?'

'You'll find out if you listen.'

The candidate flushed at the menace in Gunner's tone. He was no stranger to violence, and the gangster didn't scare him.

He's an ally, he reminded himself, nodding imperceptibly at Mease's warning glance.

'The floor's yours,' he smiled winningly.

'Ripper, the dead man, said something interesting. There was a prisoner in ADX, Farhaan Zaidi, a terrorist, who he was close to.'

'Huh?' Rubin gestured, puzzled. 'A terrorist and a criminal were friends?'

'Unusual,' Gunner agreed, 'but it happened. Anyhow, it turns out Zaidi wasn't who he was. He wasn't a terrorist.'

'Who was he, then?'

'He was a plant. An undercover agent.'

'A cop?'

'No. Military. Some kind of covert operative.'

'Why?'

'He was in ADX to get inside intel from the other terrorists there.'

'Got it. Undercover operations happen,' Mease said. 'What's special about this?'

'You've heard of Tayyib Mansoor?'

'Who hasn't?' the strategist grunted. 'There was a lot of publicity when he was captured.'

'Mansoor was at ADX too.'

'*Was?*'

Gunner grinned.

'Yeah. This undercover dude, posing as a terrorist, killed him.'

His smile widened at their stunned expressions.

'This was a hit sanctioned by our government?'

'Looks like it. And there's more.'

He paused dramatically.

'That man, the military operative, is in New York,' he said triumphantly. 'He's some kind of celebrity himself. He calls himself a Fixer. Someone who gets things done. He was on TV recently. His name is Cutter Grogan.'

48

'We can use this.' Rubin stroked his chin thoughtfully as Gunner answered Mease and his rapid-fire questions. 'This must have been a Defense Intelligence Agency mission, or some other covert agency. Sanctioned at the very top. Sec Def would have signed off on it. President Morgan might have been involved too.'

'Nope, we can't use it. Not right away.' Mease waved in the air.

'What?' Gunner stared at the strategist. 'Why not? Everyone believes Mansoor is still alive. Imagine the headlines, the demands on the politicians to explain this. There will be a public Senate hearing, at the very least.'

'It will hurt President Morgan,' Rubin agreed, 'and the Veep too. We can drag him into the controversy. However, we are doing well at the moment. This is our secret weapon. We reveal it at the right moment, which isn't now.'

He clapped Gunner on the shoulder and smiled genuinely at him. 'Great work.' They had come a long way from that first meeting in Florida. There was mutual trust and respect.

'Who else knows about this?'

'My computer specialist,' Gunner answered Mease. 'Just him and me.'

'Cray?'

'Yeah. He can be trusted.'

'Everything good on the street?'

'What is it?' Rubin asked sharply when the Lions' man hesitated.

'Grogan. He might suspect I'm alive.'

'What do you mean? How?'

Gunner told them about the bodega holdups and Nails' gang.

'That shooter could have been anyone,' Rubin objected. 'You have nothing to link him to Grogan.'

'Yeah. But Mease checked with NYPD and the DEA. They haven't deployed anyone undercover.'

'That doesn't mean anything. Our people in there might not know of the operation.'

'Why is Grogan interested in you? If it's him?' Mease jammed his hands in his pockets and rocked on his heels.

'We have history, from ADX.'

Rubin brooded for several moments when Gunner finished his story. His mind raced as he thought of the campaign implications. Mease was similarly occupied when he looked at his strategist.

'Why now?' the former accountant asked finally. 'What's made him suspicious? You've been dead a very long time. A good few years. He was out of prison before you.'

'I know where he works, where he lives. I can get Cray to do some digging.'

'Find out,' Rubin nodded. 'Discreetly, without exposing yourself. For all we know, his appearances at that store were coincidental and that undercover man is from some agency.'

'That's the most likely explanation.' Mease glanced at his watch and straightened. 'We've been here too long. Stick to the script,' he warned the Lion. 'No vengeance run on Grogan. The past is behind us. Information only—that's what we need on him.'

'What if he's coming for me?'

'If he was, do you think we would be here? He's got nothing. Stay low. Don't go after him. It'll risk everything we've been working on.'

RUBIN SHOOK GUNNER'S HAND WARMLY, PUT ON HIS campaign face, and left the bathroom with his strategist in wake.

'What do you think?' he whispered when they were in his car.

'Let's see what he comes up with. I don't think we have anything to worry about.'

'Will Gunner go off the rails?'

'No. He's too disciplined for that. He's with us all the way. Even if he does ...'

Rubin nodded in understanding. They wouldn't have come that far in the campaign without the Lions. However, everyone was expendable, and if push came to shove, even Gunner could be dealt with.

He's not the only gang leader we know.

GUNNER WAITED UNTIL HE HEARD A DISCREET KNOCK ON THE bathroom door. One of his hitters opened it and nodded, indicating the coast was clear.

He went out through the rear entrance and climbed into his vehicle.

'Lafayette Street,' he told his driver.

He wanted to check his enemy out. See where he lived.

Mease had warned him to back off, but what did the accountant know? He had done time in a cushy prison. Gunner snorted in disgust. The strategist and Rubin, they hadn't been through what he had.

Cutter Grogan was the only man who had stood up to him. Had diminished him in ADX.

The Lion hadn't forgotten that. He had a code to live up to: destroy enemies.

Nope. The Fixer wasn't off-limits, whatever Mease and Rubin said.

However, he wouldn't hurry to deliver punishment.

I'll find out what he's up to. Then take him down.

49

Pete Martinelli, Cutter decided.

The cop was the one to look into. If he was a Lions supporter, a white nationalist, then he would have received orders in some way. Find out who had given him the word.

Track back from there, and it would lead to Sheller.

He could go after Nails too, since he knew where his gang hung out. *I got nowhere when I followed him. And they'll be prepared now. They'll be alert for strangers, tails. They've lost Davis and several men. They think someone's undercover and looking into them. Nope, the cop's easier to go after.*

He wasn't home when Sheller's vehicle swept past his building. He was in a Columbus Avenue highrise, jabbing the elevator button, when the Lion looked out of his vehicle at Cutter's darkened apartment and signaled his driver to take him home.

Cutter got out at his floor; used a swipe card to enter a darkened office. Motion sensors turned on lights as he progressed. Warm-colored throws on the couches, rugs on the floor. A golfing strip by the floor-to-ceiling windows overlooking the street. A basketball hoop on a wall; baseball bats, balls and gloves; a snooker table.

It was unlike any office he had visited.

He went to the pantry and brewed himself a cup of Jamaican and went to a desk. Pressed the keyboard to bring the screen to life and typed in his password.

Scratched his head when it was accepted but the screen remained blank. A wall of blue with the cursor in the center. No directories, folders or menu of any kind.

He jabbed several keys. Nothing happened. Looked beneath the desk. Nope, no tower drive. Surely there was a way to access the computer's secrets, but he couldn't find it.

He was hunched over the keyboard when his radar warned him. He wasn't alone. The screen was the non-reflective kind that didn't show him who or what was behind him.

Cutter slid his chair back on its wheels, kept his hands down to indicate he was no threat and turned slowly.

A large man watching him impassively. Skin gleaming underneath the lights, biceps bulging beneath his sleeves, Tee stretched tight across his chest. He was motionless, an air of menace around him.

'I wasn't stealing anything.' Cutter didn't make any sudden moves.

No response. Another man came up and stood beside him. Equally large and muscled. Neatly trimmed beard. Hard-faced. Neither of them sporting any weapons. *Heck, with their size, why would they need guns?*

Two more men came up. Good-looking, smartly dressed, as if returning from a photo shoot. One older than the other.

A fifth person joined them. Dark brown hair, clean-shaven, lithe and panther-like as he approached.

'What's up?' a woman's voice came from behind them.

'He steals our coffee,' the first entrant said.

Cutter thought he heard the windows reverberate at his growl.

'Then he steals our computer time.'

'Computer time?' he protested. 'Is that even a thing?'

None of the men smiled.

Three women came up. One of them petite, the others identical-looking twins.

One of the sisters looked at him, then the screen, and read the scene instantly. 'Didn't get anywhere, huh?'

'It isn't working,' he said defensively.

'Shall I throw him out?' the first speaker glowered.

Cutter got to his feet. It looked like things would turn ugly. 'About that coffee,' he tried placatingly, 'I was thirsty.'

'You could drink water.'

'Why would I, when there was coffee?'

The speaker had no comeback. His face broke into a wide smile. He came forward and grabbed Cutter in a bone-crushing hug. The second man thumped his back so hard he thought his ribs cracked.

'Move,' Beth, the woman who had spoken, ordered.

He gave way for her to occupy his seat while Zeb, the lean operative, shook his hands.

'You've become a stranger,' said Chloe, the petite woman, and she kissed his cheeks.

'I was traveling.'

'Colombia,' said Roger, the younger of the two men who looked like models, as he fist-bumped him. 'Broker'—he nodded at the older man—'and I were talking about it. That was some mission.'

'I was lucky to get away alive.' He tested his shoulders. They worked, despite Bwana's hug. He felt his ribs discreetly. Bear's back-thumps hadn't cracked any.

'So,' Meghan, the elder twin, surveyed him quizzically. 'Why are you stealing our computer time, as Bwana put it?'

Cutter took them in. Zeb's team. The most lethal covert operatives he had come across. All of them lounging casually, but he knew those looks were deceptive. They could go from zero to action in the blink of an eye.

'It's something I've been working on.' He was deliberately

vague. *They have their own missions. No point in dragging them into my problems*.

'And you thought you could come here, check out whatever you were looking for and leave?' Beth said scornfully.

'Something like that,' he admitted sheepishly.

'We were out for dinner. We had just finished when the alarms chimed on our cell phones. It wasn't hard to figure out who had broken in.'

'Break in?' he protested. 'You gave me access.'

He knew if he had been a perp, the reception would have been very different. Bwana wouldn't have stood there, giving him the hard eye. He would have taken direct action.

'What are you looking for?' Meghan, to the point.

He hesitated.

'You're among friends,' Zeb told him mildly.

Cutter looked at them searchingly and then decided. *Heck, they deal with classified intel all day. They meet President Morgan regularly.* He could confide in them.

'I'm looking for a cop. Pete Martinelli.'

'This is related to why you were on TV?' Chloe guessed.

'Sort of,' and he launched into an explanation of everything that had happened.

'Hard to imagine someone could carry that out for so long. Playing dead.' Roger picked up the basketball and twirled it on his forefinger.

'Sheller is no ordinary criminal.' Cutter turned when a chair squeaked. Beth, rolling herself forward to her screen. Her fingers flew rapidly over the keyboard and a program appeared on the screen.

'How did you do that?'

'We gave you access to the office,' she smirked, 'not to Werner.'

Werner, their Artificial Intelligence program that seemed to be hooked into every national and international database and could perform wonders, according to the twins' description.

'Martinelli,' she mumbled to herself as she typed rapidly.

'This him?' She pointed at the picture of a cop on the screen. In his forties, thinning hair, leathery face, hands hooked into his belt, swaggering for the camera.

'Yeah.'

She looked up another file, checked out a few media articles and nodded to herself. 'That's him. Seventy-Third Precinct.' Her fingers danced. Another file came up. 'Bayside, Queens.' She wrote down his address and passed him the note. 'Lives alone in a two-bed. Divorced. His wife's got custody of his kids. Teenagers, a daughter and son. Doesn't look like there's any love there.'

'You got that from his file?' he gaped at her.

'Ex is in Hempstead. His phone hasn't traveled to her house in years. Which means he hasn't visited them.' She shrugged, as if anyone could have made the deduction. 'Credit rating is fine. Doesn't save much. Is on top of the alimony payments to his wife. No unusual transactions in his bank account. No big purchases on his cards either. That's all you wanted?'

'Yeah,' he said with feeling. 'That was like magic.'

'That's what we do every day.' She grinned cheekily. 'Doesn't look like he's dirty. Not from his financials.'

'If he's into white nationalism, it isn't about money.'

'Yeah,' Zeb agreed from the couch where he was sprawled, deceptively still. 'Why would Sheller go to all that trouble? Why fake his own death?'

'Beats me.'

'You need backup, bud?' Bear asked him.

'I'm going to check Martinelli out. Nothing more.'

'Not for him. With Darrell and this Nails and his dudes and the Lions.'

'Nope,' he grinned. 'Not looking to raze the city to the ground.'

He chuckled when Bwana gave him a look of mock disappointment, hugged them, and made to leave.

Stopped before he reached the door.

'Forgot something,' he told them and went to the kitchen. Stuffed two coffee bags into his pockets and left.

'Hey, we don't own the plantations!' Broker yelled at his back.

'It's for Arnedra,' he explained to sarcastic laughter.

'You think he needs help?' Chloe looked at Zeb.

'Cutter? Help? He's a one-person wrecking team.'

'How's he holding up?' Meghan pursed her lips thoughtfully.

'It doesn't go away.' Zeb knew she was referring to Riley's death. 'You get better at dealing with it, that's all.'

They nodded, knowing he was speaking from experience.

'It would've been good to have him.' Bear went to the window to look down the avenue. People were ant-sized figures from this height, making it impossible to recognize anyone.

'I offered. He declined. He's a loner.'

'Takes one to recognize another.' Beth smirked.

Zeb raised his hands. 'Hey, I'm here with you all, aren't I?'

The subject of their discussion was having a similar conversation with himself. That office, the team—it brought back good memories. On top of that, Zeb, the twins, all those operatives, they were good friends.

Did I make a mistake in turning him down?

He pondered this as he crossed at a light and got to his vehicle.

He shook his head unconsciously. He had quit the military because he wanted to get away from the order. From others planning his life.

This is how I want it. Just me.

50

Pete Martinelli lived in a quiet neighborhood. Very little traffic on his street. Kids going to school early in the morning. Moms and dads rushing to their workplaces. No hoods hanging around, no loud beats thumping from passing vehicles.

Seven am the next day. Cutter in his SUV, drinking store-bought coffee and biting into a croissant, a newspaper unrolled on the wheel, giving the impression he was reading it.

Life in the fast lane for the intrepid Fixer.

Martinelli came out of his building and nodded to a neighbor. The officer was in plain clothes and lit up the lights of a sedan with his key fob.

So far, so good. No secret handshakes or gestures with anyone. Which didn't mean anything. Difiore hadn't confirmed that the cop was dirty, nor had she told him how the internal investigation had progressed.

He snorted in his coffee. *As if she reveals anything!* He placed the cup in its holder and keyed the engine and set out to follow the cop.

Martinelli drove to the precinct without any stops or

detours. He disappeared inside the building and didn't return until the evening.

Cutter slept.

Rest and food. It was drilled into him during his training and reinforced at Fort Bragg. Eat and sleep whenever the opportunity came up.

He wasn't in deep slumber. He was conscious of his surroundings and passing traffic. However, he wasn't alert enough to notice the brown Ford that passed him twice and the curious eyes that looked at him from the rolled-down window on its second pass.

He woke up instinctively when Martinelli's car nosed out of the precinct's lot. He followed the cop to a takeout, grabbed a bag of food and shadowed him home.

By nine pm, Cutter had had enough. He wasn't going to get anywhere with the shadowing. He stuffed a bandana into his pocket and strapped on his shoulder holster. Covered it with a dark jacket and stepped out of his vehicle.

Waited for a resident to card the keypad, made a show of patting his pockets, shrugged and rushed inside before the door closed. He went to the mailboxes and pretended to check for letters while the resident waited for the elevator. He raced up the stairs as soon as the man disappeared into the car.

Martinelli was on the sixth floor. His apartment the third door from the stairway entrance. Muted sounds of conversation behind one door, a TV playing in another.

Cutter checked the ceiling. No cameras. He bent his head and tied the bandana across his face. Slipped on a pair of gloves, buzzed the cop's apartment and moved away from the peephole.

Muffled footsteps. A faint 'Who's there?'

The footsteps faded.

He pressed the bell again.

The cop returned. He seemed to curse and unlatched the door, at which moment Cutter shouldered it; he heard it slam against Martinelli, who grunted, but by then he was inside, his Glock trained on the cop.

51

Martinelli's eyes widened at his sight.

'What—'

Cutter jabbed the gun against his chest and pushed him deeper inside the apartment. Alcohol on the man's breath. The source was a half-empty bottle on a table in the living room. A glass beside it.

'Anyone else?' he growled in a deep voice.

'Who are you?' Martinelli lunged toward his cell phone and went sprawling on the floor when Cutter kicked him.

He grabbed the cop by his collar and flung him onto a couch, which protested against the sudden impact.

'Who else is here?' he grated.

'NO ONE! DO YOU KNOW WHO I AM? I'M A COP—'

Cutter slapped him hard, a blow that split the officer's lips.

'I ask the questions. We heard you've been talking. We warned you.'

'WHO ARE YOU? WHO TOLD YOU THAT? WHAT ARE YOU TALKING ABOUT?'

Martinelli cowered when he raised the Glock threateningly.

'Pipe down,' Cutter warned him. 'You know what this is about.'

The cop took in the dark, menacing figure, felt his mouth with trembling fingers and stared at the blood on them.

'Davis?' he shuddered. 'Crump sent you?'

'You've been talking too much. Making threats. Demands.'

'NO! I'VE KEPT QUIET. I'VE SPOKEN TO NO ONE BUT THE INVESTIGATORS. I STUCK TO THE STORY. I TOLD CRUMP. I KNOW OUR CODE. I'M A LION MYSELF. I HAVEN'T—'

Pounding footsteps outside the door.

The animal took over.

'You said you were alone!' Cutter looked up, whirled toward Martinelli and slapped him again to keep up the pressure. He darted to the window. Backyard. Steep drop.

The door crashed open. Two hoods shouting, yelling, their faces masked, their guns rising.

Cutter didn't stop to talk about the weather.

He threw himself out of the window just as two rounds blew past him and shattered the glass.

Wind rushed past him as he fell with his left arm outstretched. It caught the sill of the window beneath Martinelli's and broke his fall with a jarring shock to his shoulders.

He dropped again as a head appeared and shot at him wildly. Another ledge to break his fall. Desperate twists to shake the thug's aim, and then he was on the ground, rolling, stumbling to his feet.

He ran around the building's corner. Got to the front. A quiet street. A brown Ford that was half on the sidewalk. No heads peering out of windows. The sounds of shots hadn't registered on residents yet.

He hurried to his SUV, thankful that he'd had the presence of mind to slap false plates on it. Got inside his vehicle and tore away. Memorized the Ford's number as he drove past.

. . .

'Who was that? What did you tell him?' Nails asked the cowering cop.

'I DON'T KNOW! WHO ARE YOU?'

The gang leader reached forward almost lazily, caught Martinelli by his shoulders and lifted him effortlessly.

'What did you tell him?' he hissed.

'NOTHING, I—'

The officer choked when Nails punched him in the throat. He fell to the couch and wheezed desperately. Tears ran down his cheeks as his hands shook and his body trembled.

'He had a few minutes with you. Surely you told him something.'

'I swear. I don't know who he was. I asked him if Crump had sent him—'

Nails stiffened. 'You used his name?'

'WHO THE HELL ARE YOU?'

The gang leader shot him in the forehead.

'Put it across his body,' he snapped at his thug, who was pulling a note out of his pocket.

He tied a scarf across his face and brandished his weapon as his men joined him outside. Neighbors scrambled into their apartments at the sight of them, and by the time the cops were called, Nails and his men were away.

Cutter drove to the nearest fast food joint. He parked in its lot and hurried to the restroom. He checked that he was alone and washed his Glock in the sink. Dried it against his jacket and holstered it.

Returned to his car and drove back to Martinelli's building, to find it was flooded with cruisers and FDNY vehicles.

He nosed into a space, grabbed his now-cold cup of coffee and joined a bunch of onlookers.

'What's up?' he asked a bystander.

'Neighbors heard shots.'

'That happen often here?'

'Nope. You're new?'

'Just moved in across the street. Wondering if I made a mistake. Wife will be joining me in two days. She'll give me hell when she finds out about the shootings. Find a quiet place, she told me.'

'Buddy, this is New York. Shootings happen everywhere here. You wanted quiet, you should have stayed in—'

'Missouri.'

'Yeah, there. Wherever it is.'

New Yorkers. They had that welcoming attitude.

Cutter's eyes narrowed when he overheard a soft conversation nearby. A woman talking with her friends.

'Yeah, I knew him. Martinelli. Same floor. I heard the shooting. Called the cops. Looked out to see these men with masks. Went out when they had gone. His door was open. I called for him. Went inside and saw he was dead.'

'You should go to the cops,' one friend urged. 'Give your statement.'

'No way.' She shook her head stubbornly. 'I'm not getting involved in whatever went down. Those men looked like gangbangers.'

Cutter drifted away and dumped his cup in a trash bin.

Martinelli was alive when I jumped out. Those hoods must have killed him. Why? How did they arrive just then?

Was he being followed?

No. Checking for tails came naturally to him, and he would have gotten that warning feeling.

Martinelli. They were watching him.

How did they know I was with him?

He thought about it as more cops filled the street.

They didn't, he concluded. *They must've known who the residents are. Saw I was a stranger. Decided to check on Martinelli.*

It was how he would have played it.

. . .

DIFIORE AND QUINDICA ARRIVED AT TEN-THIRTY PM IN THE detective's unmarked vehicle.

He watched them as they conferred with the cops and went into the building. He was still there when they returned forty-five minutes later.

He moved deeper into the darkness, using other bystanders as cover when the detective searched the street with a hard glance. She nodded at a cop, spoke to Quindica, and the two returned to her car and drove away.

Eleven-thirty pm, driving to Manhattan, when his phone rang.

He didn't pick it up.

Difiore left a message.

Grogan, I know you are involved. Call me!

He shook his head. There was no way the cops could place him at the scene. They would have tracked him down if they knew. The detective was playing her usual hard self.

His smile disappeared when he recalled what Martinelli had told him.

Crump.

He had a name to check out.

52

'No way of knowing who that man was?' Gunner mused when Nails called and briefed him.

'No, boss.'

'You say your men saw him and followed him to the precinct?'

'Yeah. But he's got dark windows. They couldn't make out who he was. They didn't get a good look at him on the street.'

The stranger had jumped out of Martinelli's window. That showed quick thinking. He hadn't fired back, even though he had a gun. That showed control.

Was it Grogan?

He ended the call and dialed his tech wizard. Twelve am. It wasn't too late for the geek. The night was when he was most active.

'Yeah?' Cray mumbled.

'You know that building where Martinelli lived?'

'What about it?'

'Check if there are any security cameras. Find out who entered the building tonight.'

'Why?'

'Martinelli's dead.'

'Who killed him?'

'We did.

'Why?'

'He was a liability, Cray. Stop asking questions and get to work.'

Crump.

He fired off a text, and a moment later his phone buzzed.

'You heard what went down?'

'YOU KILLED A COP!' Despite the late hour, the assistant chief of the NYPD sounded awake and alert. And furious.

'How do you know that?'

'WHO ELSE WOULD? YOUR GOONS SHOT HIM AND MADE IT LOOK LIKE A REVENGE KILLING.'

'What have the detectives found?'

Crump seethed and raged for a minute before he got hold of himself. 'They're treating it like a gang killing because of that note. Doesn't look like they have much to go on. No witnesses, at least none who'll come forward. No camera evidence, nothing. Difiore's the detective. She's smart, tough, won't back off for anyone.'

'She won't get anything. It was a clean kill.'

'I hope so, for your shooters' sake. Something's a little off. There's a Fed hanging out with her.'

'An FBI agent?' Gunner looked up and stared blankly at the TV, which was muted and playing reports of the shooting.

'Yeah.'

'Who is he?'

'*She*. I don't know. No one knows. She wasn't introduced. She flashed her badge at the scene and that's how we know.'

'Nothing about her in the system?'

'No. She's got no role in the investigation.'

'It could be anything.'

'Yeah. That's what I'm assuming. Not everything's related to us. BUT WHY DID YOU SHOOT HIM?' The cop exploded. 'I CALLED HIM PERSONALLY. HE WAS GOING TO

KEEP HIS MOUTH SHUT. MARTINELLI WAS A GOOD OFFICER. HE WAS A LION. HE WAS ONE OF US.'

'There were complications,' the Lions' founder told him coldly. The assistant chief needed reminding who was in charge. 'Nothing can get in our way.'

'OUR WAY? IT LOOKS LIKE YOUR WAY. You could have told me. I could have done something. But you had to act bull—'

'STOP!' Gunner roared. 'Don't forget your place.'

'YEAH? YOU DON'T FORGET WHO YOU'RE TALKING TO. I'M AN ASSISTANT CHIEF IN THE NEW YORK POLICE DEPARTMENT.'

'You're a Lion first.'

'I'm wondering how that helps me in any way,' the cop said bitterly. 'Killing a cop is a big deal. What was the complication? I could have helped with it.'

'There's a stranger nosing around in our business.' Gunner gave it to him. 'He was in Martinelli's apartment, who mentioned you. By name.'

He grinned evilly at Crump's sharp suck of air. *You're not yelling now, are you?*

'How do you know?'

'We were watching Martinelli. We thought this dude would approach him. My suspicion was right.'

'That's why you killed him.'

'Yeah. We did it to protect you.'

'The window ... it was broken. I read Difiore's initial report.'

'That's how that man escaped when our people entered.'

'NYPD doesn't know about this person.'

'Keep it that way.'

'Why?'

Because Grogan, if arrested, could reveal his suspicions. If Difiore was as smart as Crump made her out to be, she would pursue that angle. And that Fed with her might get involved, too.

'I'm dealing with it.'

'Can I do anything?' Crump turned conciliatory. 'Who is this man? Is he a journalist?'

'No. NYPD knows him well. Cutter Grogan. He works out of Lafayette—'

'The Fixer. He intervened in those bodega attacks. Yeah, we know him.'

'He's got a record?' *Why hadn't Cray let him know about that?*

'No,' Crump corrected him. 'In fact, he's helped out in a few cases. I know some detectives farm out cases to him, where we can't help. And then, he's been at the scene of some attacks. Randomly, like at that store.'

Was that by chance? Cray was looking into it.

'You'll handle it?'

'I will,' Gunner promised.

He called another number when the cop ended the call.

'Clint,' he told another of his Brooklyn cell leaders. 'We have a problem. I need you to take care of it. Personally. Take your best men.'

He gave instructions and went to bed satisfied.

It looked like the thorn in his side would be pulled out soon enough.

53

The TV was all over it the next day.

REVENGE KILLING.

DRUG GANG HITS BACK.

The banners rolled on as reporters and talking heads covered the story breathlessly.

Commissioner Rolando came on and warned the public not to leap to conclusions. It was an active investigation, he said.

His words had no effect.

The killers had left a note on Martinelli's chest. One word scrawled on it.

PIG!

That was enough for journalists to draw conclusions. Davis's gang had retaliated. Since the outfit had no official name, the media had dubbed it the Brownsville gang.

That'll help Sheller, Cutter thought sourly. A different identity meant any link to the Rising Lions would get buried even deeper.

He was surprised Difiore and Quindica hadn't pounded on his door yet.

I left no trail. Even if street cameras captured me, I was unidentifiable.

He thought he had recognized one of the shooters from his hair, a criminal who hung close to Nails. But he wasn't sure. It had been no time to stop and ask for identification. And he wasn't going to volunteer information to the detective.

Not unless I want my butt in prison, he smiled as he washed his breakfast dishes and wiped his hands.

Crump. He had a name. It was unusual enough that he could narrow down who Martinelli had been referring to.

He went to his computer and searched for the name. A real estate agent. A finance company. An insurance salesman in New Jersey. A few political connections came up. The opposition party's spokesperson was a Crump. A lobbyist in DC had the name.

Cutter tossed a tennis ball high in the air and caught it as he leaned back in his swivel chair. He couldn't track all those people down and check them out.

Perhaps there was an easier way.

'How can I be of service?' Beth asked him sweetly when he called.

He stared at his phone suspiciously. Had he dialed the right number? That response was too saccharine.

'Uh—'

'Your personal secretary is awaiting your instructions, Cutter,' she told him.

That snarky attitude was more like it.

'That software you have—'

'Werner. It's got a name.'

'Yeah, Werner. It's AI, right?'

'Not just AI, Cutter. It's the best in the world.'

'Got it. Can it make correlations—'

'There's not much it can't.'

Sarcasm, he decided. He would take the twins' attitude any day over this overly sweet and helpful approach. He hoped this was a passing phase, but he didn't tell her that.

'If I give a name—'

'Yes, Cutter. Werner can tell the probability of such a name connected with a particular case.'

He nodded and then realized she couldn't see him.

'Who is it? I don't have all day,' she told him. The slightest trace of impatience in her voice.

'Crump.'

'Is that the first name or second?'

'No clue.'

Do I hang up and wait for her to get back?

He was still thinking about it when she spoke. No sweetness, no sarcasm.

'Cutter,' she breathed, 'this feels ugly.'

'Why? Who is it?'

'Dennis Crump is who it is. Assistant chief in the NYPD.'

It made sense, Cutter mused.

Sheller was into details, a micromanager, but he wouldn't communicate with Martinelli directly. That would be someone else. Who better than a senior cop in the department?

Crump was the Assistant Chief of Crime Control Strategies, a rung away from the head of the department. He had power, access to intelligence on operations across the NYPD. He wouldn't have interfered in Martinelli's investigation, but he could have subtly influenced it.

How high do the Lions go? Cutter thought bleakly. *Do I tell Bruce?*

What could the commish do, however? *It's just my word, and I was present at a crime scene. They'll treat me as a suspect.*

Going to his friend wasn't an option. He would have to tackle Crump.

Hard, fast, give him no time to react. That was the quickest way to get answers and find out where Sheller was.

. . .

New false plates on his SUV, which was an anonymous gray color. A fake nose, brown contacts in his eyes, and blond streaks in his hair. Body armor beneath his Tee and jacket, giving him a bigger appearance, and gloves over his hands.

It was late evening when Cutter drove out of his building to Brooklyn, to the address Beth had given him.

A rowhouse on Linden Boulevard.

He parked his vehicle a block away and walked as night fell. Checked every parked car on the street. There was no way he was going to be caught unawares again.

No figures in any of the vehicles, no suspicious-looking men.

Crump's house was the first in the line, to the right. A high wall separating it from the next block of residences. A small front yard with a waist-level gate. Red-brick wall at the front that looked brown under the street lighting. Dark windows at the front.

Cutter passed it once. Saw nothing out of the ordinary and returned for another recon run.

The cop lived with his family, he recalled from Beth's info. Wife, two school-age daughters. Clean financials.

It was on the third pass that it came to him.

54

Crump's driveway was empty, which was odd given that he had left OnePP. A call to one of Cutter's NYPD's contacts had confirmed that. Had also affirmed that the assistant chief was very much a family man. He went home straight after work; no deviation from his routine, which was the subject of many stale jokes.

That door and gate.

Both were open a crack. A dark line at the jamb where the former would have sealed shut normally. There could be any explanation for the wrought-iron entrance to the yard, but the main entrance?

He carried on walking, checking everything out with a heightened awareness.

He circled back when nothing triggered his animal sense, reached into a pocket as if checking an address, and slipped inside the gate.

No outcry of alarm. Floodlights didn't turn on to pin him down.

Cutter went down the side path that ran parallel to the boundary wall, which was so close he could stretch out his arms and touch it as well as the outer wall of Crump's house.

Windows at eye level. He could make out the dim outline of the entrance hallway. The next room seemed to be the living room. He squinted to see past the reflection. That flat shape was a TV. A couch, another long seater. Some shapes on them. He cupped his hands to the glass to see better.

Stumbled back in shock at what he saw.

'YOU!'

Two men came from behind the house, down the path he was on. Three others emerged from behind him.

They were in the house. Waiting for me.

He was trapped between two groups of masked men, all armed but with guns pointing downwards, so sure were they of his surrender.

Don't bet on it.

Cutter drew and fired, at the two men and then at the three behind him. Shooting deliberately wide, over their heads, making some of them drop, the others dive for cover.

A slim opportunity for escape that he grabbed with both hands.

He went up.

He jumped high in the air, braced his legs against the partition wall and the house, Jackie-Channed up the sides of the house using his legs and hands to spider climb swiftly.

Got both feet on top of the concrete separation, where he paused briefly and fired at the hoods to keep them at bay.

He got a few shots in return as they yelled in startled surprise at his move. That turned to anger quickly, but by then he had leapt high in the air to grab the frame of a satellite dish that was fastened to the building's side, which took his weight, and heaved himself to the roof.

A shot slammed into his side just before he reached the top, making him gasp for breath, while another tore the heel of his shoe, and then he was over the side, safe. He lay panting for a moment, and that's when he heard sirens, approaching fast.

His side felt like a tree trunk had crashed into the side of his body. The body armor had stopped the round, however, and it didn't seem like any rib was broken. He peered cautiously over the roof's edge and reared back instantly when he spotted some of the shooters climbing up.

He got to his feet and ducked low, breathing harshly as he drew air into his lungs, his chest hurting with every heave. He lumbered over the roof toward the end of the houses. The sirens grew closer as his ribs got used to his rapid inhales and exhales. They still hurt, but he ignored the dull burn. It wasn't the first time he'd been shot in his armor, and it wouldn't be the last. The night lit up with flashes of blue and red as voices and the sound of doors and windows being slammed floated up to him.

A shout from behind him.

Two men, silhouetted in the dark. He shot at them swiftly, making them duck, and zigged and zagged as he leapt over piping and trash and circled cooling fans on the roof.

He reached the end of the long stretch of residences and snapped a glance back. No pursuers. It seemed they had fled, gotten away before the cops had sealed all exits.

He could hear the growing presence of police on the street. *Neighbors will tell them of shots on the roof. That'll get them to seal the entire block.* He'd have to go into flight mode. The narrow alley between his row of houses and the next was a steep drop. He couldn't climb down the way he had come up. The next line of houses wasn't close enough. What was that dark line, though?

He hurried to the rear of the roof and thanked his luck when he found it was a drainpipe.

Held his breath when he grabbed it with his hands and let his body swing down and slam against the side of the house. That sent a fiery jolt of pain through his chest, but the drainpipe held. It creaked ominously on its fastenings but didn't collapse.

He slithered down as fast as he could, gritting his teeth against the burning of his palms, and after what felt like an eternity, dropped to the ground.

Cutter cursed when a dog barked somewhere. He blindly ran

down the alley, away from Linden Boulevard, thanking his luck again that the cops hadn't reached its mouth yet. It would only be a matter of time, however.

He swore to himself when he reached a wall. Ran at it and scaled it, dropped into a garden. Another dog joined the chorus. He heard voices. Lights turned on in the backyard. He didn't dare look behind him, lest his face be illuminated. He was disguised, but why take the risk?

He raced to the end of the yard, leapt over another fence to land in a narrow passage between another line of row houses. He squeezed through the slimmest opening between two walls and almost sobbed in relief when it opened into Caton Avenue.

No cops there.

He dusted off his clothing and straightened his walk as much as he could despite the torn heel in his shoe.

His body cooled, the sweat on his face started drying slowly, and his ribs settled into an angry twinge. He fished out his cell.

'Karim,' he said when the metal shop owner answered after several rings. 'Can you open up for me?'

'Of course,' the owner replied. He didn't complain, didn't ask why; nothing in his voice but ready agreement. Their shared history was such that no explanations or questions were needed.

'I also need some clothing.'

'They'll be a tight fit, my friend.'

'I need them just for the night.'

'Anything I have is yours. Even my life.'

Cutter grinned in the darkness.

Melodrama. No one could top Karim when it came to that.

He means it, though.

55

Cutter circled back to his parked SUV. No cops near it. The boulevard was blocked: cruisers, command vehicles, FDNY, forensic technicians and the inevitable TV vans.

He navigated out with difficulty and exhaled in relief when no one stopped him. He drove to the metal shop and parked in its front yard. A line of light beneath its shutters.

He raised them a crack to roll beneath them and was greeted by a beaming Karim, holding a steaming cup of coffee.

'I knew you would need this.'

Cutter nodded gratefully. Slipped out of his clothes, then picked them up and stuffed them into the furnace. Broke his cell phone and tossed its remains into the heat.

He dressed in the owner's clothes—a close fit, but that was okay. *I need them just for the drive back.*

He ground his Glock into powder and followed it up with his ammo.

He held his armor speculatively and looked up when he felt a hand on his shoulder.

'I'll take care of that.'

'Karim—'

'I'll take care of that,' the owner repeated and thrust the cup of coffee at him.

Cutter sipped and closed his eyes at the warmth that seeped through him. He sat down in a leather chair in the corner of the shop and let his body relax. Karim returned presently, wiping his hands on his apron.

'Done,' he said simply. 'No trace of your clothing.'

Machinery and tools behind him, brightly lit. A photograph discreetly hanging from a wall: a woman laughing as if the world was hers.

Karim's daughter, whom Cutter had rescued from a prostitution ring. She was a mom of two kids, enjoying her life on the west coast. His only child, whom he had reared as a single parent.

The owner followed his eyes and smiled gently.

'Even my life will not be enough—'

'Stop.' Cutter heaved himself up and hugged his friend. Headed out and replaced the false plates on his SUV with spare ones in his vehicle. Handed the old ones to his friend, who took them.

An hour later, he was back home, with a new burner phone, a new Glock in his holster.

He didn't sleep for a long while. What he had seen through the window played over and over again in his mind.

Crump, his wife and kids on the couch. Staring sightlessly. Dead.

Sheller had acted faster than he had and had tied up all loose ends.

I'm no closer to getting to him.

56

Attack was the best defense.

Cutter was confident there was no way the cops could link him to Martinelli's and Crump's homes and deaths, but he decided to take the bull by its horns.

He would confront the cops.

He steamed onto the eighth floor of OnePP using a visitor pass that a friend had arranged. Stood outside a glass-walled office until he got the attention of its occupants.

'What're you doing here?' Difiore greeted him furiously when she opened the door.

He barged past her, nodded shortly at Quindica, whose only reaction was a twitch of her lips and a dancing light in her eyes.

'Out,' the detective barked, jerking her thumb at the room's other occupants.

'Sorry, folks,' Cutter told them as the cops streamed out. He had interrupted a briefing in a meeting room.

He helped himself to the coffee on the side table and munched on a biscuit. They had nothing on Beth's beverage and cookies, but he wasn't complaining.

'We're waiting,' Difiore told him icily. She and the FBI SAC, their arms crossed against their chests, leaning against a wall, a whiteboard behind them with names and dates and several details scribbled on it.

'I'm waiting, too.'

'This isn't some game, Grogan,' she hissed. If a voice could freeze, he would have turned into a life-sized block of ice. 'You burst into our office, interrupt us—'

'Because Martinelli is dead,' he interrupted her. 'And this assistant chief in Brooklyn. What was his name? Crump? He and his family were killed. Did he have any connection to the officer? WHAT'S GOING ON?'

It was difficult to thunder with a mouthful of biscuit, but he managed to pull it off.

It didn't have the result he wanted.

'We don't answer to you,' Quindica said frostily. Her amusement at his arrival had disappeared.

'You don't, but I'm involved.'

'Your only involvement is to follow the news and our press statements, like any other New Yorker.'

He made to rise but sat down when Difiore wagged a finger at him.

'Can you read the room?'

The sense of urgency was unmistakable when he looked through the glass. Tense faces as cops worked the phones or sat at their screens. No smiles, no jokes, no watercooler or hallway conversations.

'That's our task force. How you got on this floor I've no idea. Can you see anyone idling?'

He couldn't.

'That's our answer. We are working our butts off, and thank you for visiting us, but we can't help you.'

'Why was Martinelli killed?' he asked stubbornly.

'He won't go,' Quindica said.

'No. Not unless we throw him out,' Difiore agreed.

'That would make a scene. Our team would wonder who he was.'

'They must be thinking that already, the way he entered.'

'I'm right here.' Cutter waved a hand, but they ignored him.

Something unreadable passed between the women, who pulled out two chairs and sat across from him.

'What do you want to know?' the detective asked.

'Martinelli's death. Crump's killing. A day apart. That can't be a coincidence.'

'We're pursuing all leads.'

'Don't give me that,' he exploded. 'I deserve to know more.'

'You deserve nothing,' she said flatly. Her hostile gaze flickered to Quindica's, and that same unreadable look passed between them. 'The gang killed Martinelli. That seems to be obvious, going by our investigations.'

'Sheller's tying up loose ends,' he guessed.

She nodded.

'But why now?' the SAC thought aloud. 'Why wait all this time? Why plug him that night and not before?'

'There was someone with him in his apartment,' the detective took over. 'Someone escaped through his window.'

Cutter congratulated himself on his poker face. 'Neighbors saw this person?'

'No.' Her hair flew out in a circle when she shook her head. 'No cameras, either. There's no other explanation for the broken window—' She caught herself before she revealed too much. 'We've canvassed the street, sought out information, but ...'

He nodded. Crank calls would have flooded their system. *Besides, I was careful. They've got nothing to go on.*

'Crump?' he reminded them.

'We don't know,' she said slowly. 'Like you said, it's coincidental. But there was no note on the body, nothing to link it to a gang killing.'

'White supremacist?'

'We're looking into it, but so far, nothing.'

'They don't advertise themselves,' he said bitterly. 'Not the ones that senior. That's your case too?'

'Yeah. Commish and her boss'—she nodded at her partner —'want daily updates.'

'What do you have for us, Grogan?' The SAC pinned him down with her dark eyes. 'We told you what we got. It's your turn.'

You'll throw me into prison if I tell you anything.

'Street's quiet. Too quiet.' He shrugged. 'My snitches have clammed up.'

'Tell us something new.'

'I don't have anything.'

Other than the fact that I know for sure Crump was a Lion. However, there was no way he could admit that.

'I'm sure the assistant chief *was* in Sheller's gang,' he said carefully.

'How do you figure that?' Quindica and Difiore's poker faces were as good as his.

'If there was a stranger in Martinelli's apartment—'

'There was,' the SAC interjected flatly.

'He might have fingered Crump to this intruder. Sheller's men must have arrived as he was interrogating Martinelli. Which was why he had to escape through the window. The shooters questioned the cop, who confessed he mentioned Crump. They killed him. Sheller then ordered the hit on the assistant chief.'

He paused as if to ask: How am I doing?

They didn't reply, but neither did they contradict him. *They must have worked it out the same way.*

'Why did they kill his wife and kids?' Quindica's rage cracked through her stone visage. 'They had nothing to do with whatever went down.'

'That's how he works. He demands utter loyalty and enforces it with extreme violence.'

'Crump hadn't exposed him.'

'He could have. Sheller acted preemptively and decided to send a message at the same time. His gang isn't like the others.

Families aren't off-limits.'

He ran his fingers through his hair restlessly. 'We're missing something. Jake, my friend in ADX. Remember what he said? That Sheller was working on something big.'

'Killing an assistant chief, executing his entire family is big enough,' Difiore snarled.

'Nope. That was him covering his ass, there. There's got to be something else.'

'If you find out, you'll let us know.'

'Don't you think you're forgetting something?'

'What's that?' he asked Quindica.

'Sheller knows that intruder escaped with Crump's name.'

'What can that man do?' Cutter challenged her. 'Go to the press and say Crump got Martinelli to shoot Davis? He has no proof. Just his word. And,' he smiled wickedly, 'I guess he would be a suspect for you, too.'

Difiore stirred after a short silence. 'It just struck me.'

'What's that?'

'Every Lion in the city—heck, all white supremacists, every one of Sheller's cops—will be looking for that person. How long can he hide?'

CUTTER LEFT THEM ON THAT UPBEAT NOTE.

He put on his shades as he exited OnePP. *At least they didn't arrest me*, he told himself. *That was a win.*

Quindica's right. Sheller will have everyone looking for me.

He stopped so abruptly that someone bumped into him from behind and cursed. He didn't pay heed.

Sheller knows I am Zaidi. That's why he got Kobach to kill Jake that way. He might suspect I was the person at Martinelli's. Which is why his hitters were at Crump's.

Why hadn't the gang leader come after him? *He can easily find out where I live and work.*

It had to be that project he was working on. It's why he's holding back from an all-out attack. Cutter couldn't think of any other explanation.

However, the Sheller he knew wouldn't let anything stand in his way to get to his enemies.

He'll still come after me. Sneakily. He won't rest until he's killed me.

'Nope,' Arnedra huffed. 'No thug's going to stop me from coming to our office.'

'This is no ordinary gangster,' Cutter fumed. 'He's the most dangerous man I know.'

'Even more than that terrorist? Mansoor?'

'Yeah. Listen to me,' he urged. 'This will be temporary. Until the cops find out where he is.'

'It's okay for you to come here,' she glared at him, 'but not for me?'

'Arnedra, he's after me!'

'And you'll expose yourself, set yourself as bait. I know you. Nope, I'm not running away. I'll be right here.'

She jumped when he slammed his palm on her table.

'Yes,' he told her ominously, 'I want to set him up, but I can't do that if I am constantly worrying about you.'

'He doesn't want me. Heck, I bet he doesn't even know of me.'

'He knows. He's smart. He's evil. He knows about this place, where I live, where you live. He works like that.'

'I don't believe you—'

'He cut off Jake Horstman's head,' he yelled. 'Isn't that warning enough for you? That was his doing. You must have heard it on TV.'

Her eyes widened. Her shoulders sagged.

'They said it was a prison fight,' she whispered. 'The killer wanted revenge.'

'Yeah, Sheller got his killer to make it look like that. *He* ordered the hit.'

She wet her lips and looked away from his stare.

'I can't risk you,' he said gently. 'Did you hear about that cop and his family? In Brooklyn? He's behind that, too.'

He brought her up to speed on all the incidents and his findings since their last meeting. 'He didn't have to kill Crump's family. Sheller ... he's the most vicious and brutal man I've ever known.'

'You've convinced me,' she laughed shakily. 'I'll go.'

'No, don't go to your Bronx apartment. Your sister, she's in California, isn't she?'

'Yeah. But—'

'Visit her. I know you have a standing invitation from her. Take her up on it.'

'I'm not sure.'

'Arnedra,' he said savagely, 'I don't want to come to the office one day and find your head on the floor.'

That clinched it.

57

Cutter mounted more cameras in the office once Arnedra had hugged him tight and left him. He installed pressure pads at the entrance and near the windows.

There were two escape routes for quick getaways. One was through the bathroom window, down the drainpipe, into the bathroom of an office two floors below. That property was rented by him on a long-term lease.

The other was through the kitchen. He could jump up and grab the sill of the window above that opened into an office on the upper floor. That space was also leased by him.

He had similar escape routes at his apartment building. It was standard operating practice for him. There had to be multiple ingress and egress options wherever he spent considerable time.

He surveyed his installations, tested them to check that they sent alerts to his cell and burner phones.

He washed his hands at the kitchen sink and went down to the parking lot.

. . .

BACK TO DARRELL'S SCHOOL IN THE EVENING, BECAUSE THERE was no other way to find out about Sheller.

Shadowing him with custom-built Ray-Bans over his eyes. Provided by Meghan. Their stems were bored out and miniature cameras fitted into the hollows. They projected the rear views on a small portion of their lenses, turning the upscale eyewear into a counter-surveillance device that let him monitor his six.

The school boy was with Manuel, but even from a distance it was apparent the previous camaraderie was absent. The students didn't joke with each other, didn't high-five or fist-bump the other. They seemed to speak in monosyllables and rarely looked each other in the eye.

They didn't go to Mother Gaston. They cut down to Rockaway Avenue and continued down it, all the way to Hegeman.

They leapt over a chain fence that had a *Keep Out, Private Property* sign on it.

Cutter checked it out on his first pass. The remains of a garage, by the looks of it. The crumbling building was leaning against a line of stores and shops. The rusting hulks of vehicles in its yard. A car wash standing forlornly in the corner.

Some developer must have bought the plot to rebuild it, which never happened. An island of desolation in the neighborhood that the Lions had taken over.

Their presence was visible. Hard-faced men and youngsters huddled around a central figure. Nails, he recognized on his second pass. Giving out instructions to his people while Darrell stood at a distance.

Nothing of significance happened. *They're right in the open. Any passing cruiser can see them.* It spoke of the clout the Lions had that they could flaunt themselves so openly. *They've posted sentries in any case. That thug at the light, the one on my side of the street, they're gang members. There'll be more that I can't see.*

Their job would be to keep away inquisitive people and warn if any cops arrived.

Cutter sat at a juice bar on the opposite sidewalk and

ordered a drink. Some of the hoods glanced his way, but his old-man getup didn't seem to arouse any suspicion.

He heaved himself up when night was falling, crossed at a light and hobbled past the chain fence.

Nails was crouching in front of Darrell. Wagging his finger furiously at the boy, who was shaking his head. He went to the end of the street and leaned against a store wall drunkenly. Sang aloud as he waited for the gang to disperse. Nails came out of the lot, surrounded by his men. He got into his vehicle, which tore away. Two other rides followed at a distance.

Nope. Can't risk following him. Not when I'm alone.

But he had an idea.

'THIS IS A PIECE OF JUNK.' MEGHAN SNIFFED IN DISGUST AS SHE examined the burner.

'You think I'm going to use a three-hundred-dollar phone for surveillance?' Cutter demanded.

'He's got a point,' Beth nodded sagely. 'So, you want us to install cloning software on your device so that you can transfer it to another phone, and that second phone—'

'Will clone a third phone when it's close to another one. I am interested in cell number three.'

Nine pm in the Agency's Columbus Avenue office. Just him and the twins, who had stayed back to work on some mission's opsec. They had invited him when he called to see if they were around.

'You'll have to explain better,' Meghan frowned when he finished.

He studied them. Nope, he couldn't see past their bland faces, didn't know if they were pulling his leg. Nevertheless, he launched into what he wanted.

'It's Darrell. He hangs out with the—'

'We know. You told us,' Beth interrupted.

'I want his phone to clone Nails' cell when they're close. But first, I'll have to clone his device.'

'Yeah, but he'll be close to so many others as well. His classmates, his teachers—heck, his mom. The software isn't intelligent enough to know which device should be copied.'

That floored him. 'Why do you think I came here?' he yelped.

'What you're asking is science fiction,' Meghan told him solemnly.

Cutter's face fell. He tried to keep the disappointment off his face and made to rise.

'Lucky for you,' Beth cracked, 'we can do the impossible.'

'We'll get the software to activate at a certain time only,' Meghan explained. 'After school and until midnight. We'll program it to ignore his mom's phone.'

'He spends time with Manuel, his friend.'

'We'll get his number,' she said patiently. 'Block that, too.'

'I might have to ditch that burner.'

'Your main phone will have that program. It will connect to a cloud account that will deploy the software to all the burners connected to it. All the data from all the cloned phones will get backed up there.'

'The cops are nosy. Difiore—'

He stopped when the twins turned their backs on him and typed away on their keyboards.

'Gina Difiore and Peyton Quindica?' Meghan asked.

'Yeah.'

'Tough cops, both of them,' the elder twin murmured.

'Yep, you sure hit the jackpot there.' Beth smirked as she turned back to him. 'They're trouble for the likes of you.'

'Don't I know it. What if they find that software on my phone?'

'They won't. You know, Nails has a real name. Steve Patchey.'

He leaned forward, intrigued. No, he didn't know. 'He's got a record?'

'Yeah.' Her fingers performed some magic, and an NYPD file came up. 'Don't ask how we can access that. You wouldn't understand,' she told him pityingly.

He read it swiftly. Burglary. Assault. Kidnapping. All of them on black and other minority victims.

No wonder Sheller's appointed him as leader. He's a Lion even if he has no tattoo.

'Now, make yourself useful.' She shooed him away when he had finished. 'Make us some coffee and let the adults work.'

Lines of code were flying on their screens when he returned with their steaming cups. Neither of them looked at him as they reached out blindly and sipped.

'Good,' Beth grunted. 'You want to come work here as our chef?'

He hurried to the couch before they got any more employment ideas for him. Plopped himself on it and flipped through a magazine as he bit into a cookie.

He was snoozing when a throat cleared beside him. 'Resting my eyes.' He sprang to his feet.

'We didn't say anything.' Meghan chuckled and handed him the phone. 'You'll have to hook this to Darrell's cell. We couldn't work around that. Then, the software will do its job.'

'It will upload everything from all devices to that cloud account you gave us,' Beth told him as he pocketed the device. 'A file for every device.'

He thanked them and cocked his head toward the ceiling.

'Rest of the crew are sleeping?'

He knew each one of them had apartments above the office.

'Nope,' Beth replied. 'Recon run. You don't need to know anything more.'

Cutter left into the night.

He had a reconnaissance mission himself.

. . .

'YOU THINK HE'LL FIND OUT?' BETH ASKED HER SISTER AS THEY turned off the lights and headed to the elevator.

'That we cloned *his* phone? Nope.'

It was a protective measure. They now had eyes and ears on their friend.

Werner would alert them if Cutter was in danger.

58

Saratoga Avenue was dark when he reached it at two am. There were street lights but only a few of them worked, casting a dim glow around their immediate vicinity.

Carmel's building had a motion-sensor front light over the keypad. He knew from his previous visit that there were no cameras. He went down the length of the street to check the parked vehicles, and on his return pulled a balaclava mask over his face and gloves on his hands. Tested the backpack and ensured it was securely fastened, with straps running across his chest.

He took a running leap and pivoted off a ground-floor apartment's windowsill, jumped higher, caught hold of another ledge, and climbed his way up to Carmel's living room window.

He tried it gently. It was fastened from the inside.

That wasn't a deal breaker.

He had automatically checked out the window during his visit to the apartment. *Old, wood frame. Simple latch on the inside. No wiring for any alarm.*

He hung off the sill with his left hand while his right came up with his Benchmade. He jammed its point into the soft wood and sliced away a sliver of frame. That made room for his blade to go deeper inside. Rinse and repeat until he connected its point to the latch, jimmied it free.

He held his breath when the window creaked as it swung open. No one stirred, however. He clambered in swiftly and closed the window. Breathed shallowly and lowered his *chi,* his inner energy, and felt things out with his senses. The apartment was warm and had the lived-in feeling that empty ones didn't.

He skirted the center table and padded through the hallway. Carmel's bedroom door was closed. No light showing through.

A dim light in the kitchen illuminated the passage as he went to Darrell's door and tried the knob. He ghosted inside when it turned easily.

The sounds of breathing. A shapeless lump on the bed, beneath the duvet.

He went over to Darrell and peered over his body. Nope, no phone. He slid a hand gingerly beneath the pillow. Still nothing. He moved the hand beneath his shoulders. The boy twitched but didn't turn. His fingers touched the hard shape after several seconds of probing. He fist-pumped mentally when he extracted the phone with two fingers and cable-connected to his phone.

Beth's instructions had been clear. He had to do nothing else. There would be a warning beep when the software was uploaded, which would be his cue to disconnect the phones.

He brought out a business card from his backpack, scribbled on it, and placed it on top of Darrell's school bag. Removed the cable and powered Darrell's phone off and on when the warning sound came on.

Its screen glowed to life, looking no different.

He shrugged in the darkness. The twins had promised him the software would work. He trusted them.

'I still think you should quit the gang, bud,' he murmured softly. 'Call me if you're in trouble.'

No reaction from Darrell.

Cutter exited the apartment the way he had arrived. He was

counting on Carmel not noticing the slashed window. Even if she did, what would she do? Nothing was stolen.

She'll suspect someone tried to break in but won't call the cops.

People of color rarely did, he thought bleakly. Not when the crimes seemed insignificant. There wasn't a great deal of trust in the police.

59

Darrell woke up at eight am and stumbled sleepily to the bathroom. By the time he had freshened up, his mom was ready for work.

She hugged him hard, enveloping him in her unique scent that was all mother. He resisted and grumbled because that's what teenagers did, but secretly reveled in the contact. She ruffled his hair and told him breakfast was ready and warned him not to be late.

His eyes fell away guiltily when she sighed and marched out of the apartment.

There was no way he could tell her he was involved with a gang. *I'll get out of it, Mama. My way, and we'll be safe.*

While dressing for school, he remembered the previous night. He thought he had heard Cutter's voice asking him to leave the gang, but that wasn't possible. It must have been a dream.

He froze when he saw the card on his backpack.

Cutter was here!

He looked around wildly, as if the Fixer was still in his room.

How did he get inside? Did he steal anything?

No. He isn't a burglar. He came to warn me.

Darrell's lips jutted out stubbornly. No one was going to tell him what to do. That reminded him. He checked his phone. Yep, full charge. He checked his Bluetooth earbuds. Those were juiced up, too.

He raised his shirt and taped his phone to his bare chest. Practiced turning on the voice-recording app he had downloaded. Lowered his shirt and finished dressing. Stood in front of the mirror and practiced until his hands found their way automatically to the right spot on his phone.

He was ready to record his gang.

He had one last detail to check out before leaving for school.

How did Cutter get inside?

He found the window and grinned to himself. *That's how.*

He wouldn't tell Mama, and if she discovered it, he would confess that it was he who had slashed the window.

Cutter's entry route would be of use to him.

60

'Tell me,' Gunner commanded.

Cray bobbed his head and spread several printouts out on the table.

Eleven am in a Lions-owned bar in Harlem. Just the two of them, with a protective ring of hitters outside the room.

'That bodega Boyce and his friends held up,' the tech expert began as he held up a photograph of the store, 'its owners are Grogan's friends.'

Gunner nodded. He had been expecting something like that. 'How did that happen? The Jew getting together with the Chinese?'

'I had to dig into police records for that. Relax. I left no trail. I'm one of the best hackers in the country.' He said it like it was fact, not a boast.

The Lions' founder believed him. The National Security Agency's cryptoanalysts had rated Cray's skills highly and had declared him to be a security threat.

'Grogan saved Chang and Lin Shun, the Chinese owners, from a mugging a few years ago. Moshe Sternberg was passing by as well. He helped too. That's how the four of them met. The

Chinese lost their son in that incident. I suspect that got the Jew close to them.'

Gunner drummed his fingers, stopped when Cray noticed. He didn't like to show any mannerisms in front of his people. They were a sign of weakness. He glanced at the images of Sternberg and the couple.

'Is Grogan an owner too?'

'Nope. Those three are equal owners.'

'Jews,' the felon spat. 'They control everything.'

'He's one-third—' Cray subsided when Gunner glared at him. Jews were responsible for many of the world's problems. It didn't matter how large a piece Sternberg owned. 'From the police records, Grogan was heading to the store when Boyce and his pals held it up.'

'What about the second time? How did he get there? He almost got Nails.'

'That's the troublesome bit. The owners said they didn't call Grogan. He sticks to a schedule when visiting the store. The holdup was outside his window. He said he was passing by.'

'You don't believe him?'

'It's too coincidental. If I can track his movements, I'll know for sure. If I can get his phone records, that will even be better. I'm working on those.'

'What about Martinelli and Crump? Was he the man at their places?'

'No cameras, boss, so can't be sure. But the height fits. The stranger was stocky at both places and Grogan is lean ... but he could be wearing a disguise.'

Gunner didn't need any video confirmation. He was sure the intruder at both places was the Fixer. His fingers started to curl into fists before he stopped himself. He straightened them consciously and wiped his palms against his jeans.

'Who's his partner?'

'A black woman.'

'Black.'

'Yeah. She and her husband ran a PI business from that address. They were doing well until he died of an illness. Grogan saved her from a mugging in Central Park. He seems to have a habit for that. He bought into her business after that.'

'He's a PI too?'

'Nope. Never applied for a license.'

'Because of his time in ADX?'

'No one knows about that, though, boss. He was using a different identity.'

'He didn't want attention.'

'Well, he's not shy about giving TV interviews. Arnedra Jones, his partner, is the one who runs the office while Grogan does the field work. But,' Cray paused dramatically, 'there's no one at their office today. Calls go to a recorded voicemail. That they will get back.'

'Where does she live?'

'Bronx. Three blocks from where Warren hangs out.'

Warren, one of their cell leaders in that borough.

'Get him to check out her building.'

'Ahead of you, boss. Her apartment's empty. I got her phone, tried it, no response. I got Warren to send some of his men to look it up. They posed as construction people she had booked a job with. Neighbors said she left in a hurry yesterday. They don't know where. I hacked into a few airline manifests, but no record of her.'

Grogan's taking precautions.

'Ripper—maybe we shouldn't have killed him in that manner, boss. Looks like he knows you're alive.'

Gunner's eyes blazed. '*If* I want advice, I'll ask for it,' he rapped out.

Cray raised his hands in a whatever-you-say gesture. 'I found something else about him. I told you he was Delta—'

'Yeah, tell me something new.'

'His file, the one I could hack into, was redacted.'

'So? That's common. They do that to hide the operations.'

'I know that. But I got a trail of who else handled that file electronically. It was most recently looked at by the FBI Director. Just over two weeks ago.'

Gunner stared at his man. 'FBI?' he repeated.

'Yeah.'

'Why would they be interested in him?'

'Beats me. I would have hacked into the FBI's systems, but that takes time and it might set off alarms.'

The Lions' boss looked at the photographs absentmindedly as his mind raced. Crump had told him something about an FBI agent tagging along with the NYPD detective. What was her name? Some Italian ... *Difiore*, that was it.

'Give me ten,' he ordered his man.

He waited till Cray went outside and joined the ring of hitters, one of whom passed a joint.

Gunner opened his mouth to yell at them. Everyone in his senior ranks was to stay clean. No drugs, no joints, no heavy drinking. He stopped himself from shouting. He had to cut his men some slack.

He brought out his burner phone and called another number. Crump wasn't the only senior cop he or Mease knew. There were several others.

'Yeah,' a deputy chief answered in a low voice, after both men had gone through the security protocol.

'There's this detective, Difiore, who's investigating several cases. I heard there's an FBI agent with her. What's that about?'

'Quindica, that's her name. She isn't an ordinary agent. She heads the New York office. Special Agent in Charge. She's leading a joint task force, which Difiore is part of.'

Gunner stilled. 'Task force? What are they looking into?'

'Cartels. The FBI thinks the Mexican gangs are muscling into every other gang's activities. Even low-level ones, such as burglaries, holdups. As if they want to *own* the city.'

'You're sure? Crump didn't mention this.'

'Yeah. Commish called a meeting of all chiefs after his killing.

Announced that the task force would no longer share information with all of us.'

'Why's Difiore still investigating those holdups? And why does she have the Martinelli and Crump cases?'

'Possible cartel connection is what I've heard.'

Gunner breathed easier at the news. *Cops are going down a false trail.*

'What about Grogan, that dude who calls himself the Fixer? Is he involved in any way?'

'Him? The task force looked into him because he was present at those holdups. But he's clean.'

That's why the FBI requested his file.

He thanked the cop and hung up. It made sense, but still, it didn't hurt to confirm. He dialed a DC number and instructed an FBI contact to look into it.

'Cray,' he called out when he had finished.

'That FBI woman got his file,' he told the hacker, 'to clear him off. Nothing more to it. I've got someone to double-check, however. You keep digging, see if you can get Grogan's phone records.'

'Will do, boss.'

Gunner dismissed him and called Nails.

'I've got a job for you. This one needs to be handled by your disposables.'

It was time to test his enemy.

61

'Nothing on him?' NYPD Commissioner Bruce Rolando looked piercingly at Difiore and Quindica.

His office, late evening, the task force leaders briefing him and FBI Director Bart Jamison, who was on video.

'No, sir,' the detective confessed. 'The few witnesses we have at Martinelli's said he was tall, heavily built and had an SUV. No one saw his face.'

'That description could fit a few million people, sir,' Quindica offered.

'What about the scene at Crump's building?'

'Our technicians pieced together the shooting, sir. Looks like several gunmen were hiding in his house. They fired on an unknown person, who escaped over the roof. We found several casings from different guns. Ballistics is trying to match those to previous shootings.'

They looked at the TV screen as Jamison's chair creaked. 'I've looked at the photographs you shared. The side of the building is steep. Going up that way takes great skill. You think it was the same man who showed up at Martinelli's?'

'It feels logical, sir,' the SAC admitted. 'The cop told him about Crump. He went to question the assistant chief. There's a layer of dust in that side alley. We have some shoeprints. We worked it out that he went to the side windows and looked inside. That's when the shooters showed up.'

'Crump was dirty?'

She hesitated and glanced at Rolando, who nodded impassively.

'Yes, sir. He and Martinelli. But we have no proof. We suspect there are many cops and FBI agents who are white nationalists. Which is why we requested for you and the commish to go public about what the task force was investigating. To throw a false scent.'

Jamison waggled his fingers acknowledging the implied thanks in her words. 'And all this ties back to this secretive gang, the Rising Lions?'

Quindica didn't show any irritation or impatience at covering the same ground. Her boss, as well as the commissioner, were clued in from day one of their task force. The director repeating the questions didn't mean anything other than that he was thinking aloud.

'Yes, sir.' She briefed them all over again and waited while two of the most powerful law enforcement chiefs in the country pondered silently.

'You didn't know of this gang before?'

'No, sir,' Difiore said, backing up her partner. 'We still don't. Cutter Grogan told us about it. Until then, all we had were the tattoos on several perps who had gang connections, but none of them bore that name.'

'Was it Cutter at Martinelli's and Crump's places? He's capable of escaping that way. He prefers a Glock.'

'We checked his gun, sir, after the Brownsville shooting. We've checked his movements, too. He wasn't near the cops' houses.'

'A man of his capabilities and connections,' Rolando mused, 'it wouldn't be difficult to fake all that. What do you two think?'

'I don't like what he does, sir,' Difiore admitted.

'That's no secret, Gina,' the commissioner chuckled, momentarily lifting the tone of the meeting.

'Yes, sir. Vigilante behavior and all that. But I don't think he killed Martinelli or Crump. That's not who he is.'

'He's helping you, isn't he?'

'Without him, we wouldn't have known of Sheller, sir.'

'There's no proof. All this is speculation,' Jamison reminded her.

'Yes, sir.' She didn't take it as a rebuke. The director was stating a fact. 'It would help if one of you called Grogan and asked him outright. You have history with him. He wouldn't lie to either of you. We could then eliminate him as a person of interest for good.'

Cutter was at the window, looking down at Lafayette, when the call came.

'Sir?' he asked, surprised that the caller was Jamison.

'Cutter, you've been busy,' his former CO said. 'Going on a shooting spree.'

'Yes, sir, at the range. Got to stay in practice.'

A pause.

'I'm on a conference call with Commissioner Rolando, Detective Gina Difiore, and my New York SAC, Peyton Quindica. You've met them.'

'I've had the pleasure, yes, sir.'

'Cutter, I'm going to ask you a question. You need to answer truthfully. Know that this is being recorded.'

'Yes, sir.'

'Did you kill Martinelli and Crump?'

'No, sir.'

'Were you at their residences?'

'No, sir.'

'Will you take a lie-detector test?' Difiore fired.

'Yes, ma'am. Any time.'

'Thank you, Cutter,' Jamison said formally. 'I don't need to remind you of your security status—'

'I'm aware, sir. This call, all my discussions with Detective Difiore and SAC Quindica will remain confidential.'

'Have a good night, Cutter.'

'To all of you, as well.'

He grinned when he hung up. *I bet Difiore instigated him to do that.*

He wasn't worried about the lie-detector test. Controlling his mind and body had been an essential part of his training. A vital skill that had helped him survive in numerous missions as a covert operative.

He would ace whatever test the FBI or the NYPD threw at him.

62

'You didn't think of asking me or our friend before acting?' Mease raged at Gunner.

The Lions' founder had finally responded to his calls and messages and had arrived at their rendezvous, the Melrose building parking lot.

'There was no time. My men found Martinelli had mentioned Crump. I had to act.'

'You could have told me,' the strategist fumed.

'Yeah? What would you have done?'

'I would have spoken to him.'

'Did your contacts in the NYPD tell you there was a stranger in Martinelli's apartment? He got away. It's likely he knows about Crump. Nope, I did the right thing.'

'You can't kill cops—'

'He was a Lion. Both of them,' Gunner replied fiercely. 'They knew the risks they took when they signed up to the gang. They're not like your white nationalist friends. We take our oaths seriously.'

Mease jammed his hands in his pockets and kicked furiously at a nonexistent pebble on the concrete. 'What's the blowback?' he growled. 'Have you thought of that?'

'There's none. Cops are going around chasing false leads.'

Mease brooded for a moment and then shrugged dismissively. 'You heard about Tizzard? About his rally in the city? You set him up for that?'

'Nope. You want us to get involved?'

'I'll come back to you on that. A repeat of Arizona may not help us much ... but this will be too good to pass up.'

'Let me know,' Gunner replied and walked away.

Mease thought of calling him back, of patting him on the shoulder, making friendly with him, but the Lions' ride was disappearing before he could react.

Let him go. The closer the elections get, the more frayed our nerves will be. Tempers flaring occasionally wasn't something to be worried about.

Will he go rogue?

That was something he was worried about.

Gunner going off-script could wreck the campaign.

No, he decided. *He's got as much to lose as us. In any case, he did the right thing in killing Martinelli and Crump. And in not telling us. We have to keep our distance.*

He walked out of the parking lot and put the Lions out of his mind. He had a bigger problem to deal with.

Could they carry off the campaign on their own? Did they need to have support from big hitters from either of the other parties, and if so, which one? If they went down that route, they would have to choose which party to court. That would be a difficult choice to make.

Mease walked a long time in the night as his accountant brain coldly looked at the facts and weighed the pros and cons, unaware of what his Lions' ally had started.

63

The alarm sounded at three am.

In a Hollywood movie, it would have sounded a few times and Cutter would have thrown off his sheet to reveal a woman next to him. He would have rubbed his eyes and searched for his phone.

He wasn't in a movie.

He woke, instantly alert, the animal inside him going into fight mode in a heartbeat. He thumbed his phone and brought up the camera feed he had set up in his apartment.

Three hooded figures at his door, their bodies hiding what they were doing. No one else visible in the hallway or stairs.

He moved quickly as he watched. Slipped into his combat trousers and strapped his armor over his vest. The Glock went into his shoulder holster, Benchmade into his thigh strap. A baton went into a sheath on his other leg.

He slipped out of the apartment he was sleeping in, the one above his residence, just as the thugs picked the door to his home.

He was impressed. *That's a high-security lock.*

He took the stairs carefully, encountering no one. No sentry on his floor. He went down one level to check. No watchers.

One last check on his phone to see the thugs had spread out in his living room, holding dimmed flashlights, unaware of the infrared cameras capturing their every move.

All of them with masks, gloves and guns, ten feet from the door.

Cutter slid the phone into his pocket, unlocked his door and burst inside.

His left hand reached out to flick on a switch that turned on intense halogen lights, as he let out a roar for added effect.

Shock in their postures. The nearest man stiffened as he started turning. The others were slower to react.

'WHO ARE YOU?'

Two long strides to First Man, his baton coming up in a slashing blow to knock the man's gun from his hand. A long side-step to hit Second Man in the neck in the same motion and kick him in the groin. Third Man was quick. He leapt back and brought up his gun arm and triggered, but Cutter had dived low and, with a loud yell, bodyslammed and crashed him against the wall.

Need them alive!

He headbutted the man, felt the spray of blood on his face as the thug's nose and lips split, felt a shout behind him, twisted desperately and sent the attacker heaving towards First Man, who was lunging toward them.

The rushing man turned at the last second, but not before both the hoods crashed and were off-balance. He placed Second Man automatically, still out of commission, groaning, doubled up and clutching his groin. Cutter grabbed a chair and threw it at the other attackers, followed that up with a vase as the first missile struck and a thug yelped. He was reaching for another chair when someone staggered inside the apartment and yelled.

'COPS!'

That voice!

He turned to the door, stunned to see Darrell, whose face twisted in shocked recognition.

MOVE, the animal warned him, but he had given away his advantage with the split-second pause.

A blow to his back sent him stumbling. Someone swore and a gun crashed into his temple. Cutter reeled and was clawing for his Glock when a shot punched into his belly. He fell to the floor, the world swimming around him, his vision dimming.

'LET'S GO. THEY'RE HERE!' Darrell screamed.

Cutter thought he heard pounding footsteps and raised his head drunkenly; then a kick to the head knocked him out.

'YOU WERE OUT ABOUT FIFTEEN MINUTES,' THE EMT NURSE told him. 'Maybe a few more, but there's no way of knowing. Neighbor called the cops when she heard shouting.'

Cutter peered over her shoulder and smiled tiredly at Ellen Konta, who lived in the other apartment on the floor.

'Thank you,' he mouthed and got a worried nod from her. He sagged back against the wall as the medic cleaned the cut on his temple and surveyed him critically. 'You got lucky. No broken ribs. Limbs and joints seem to be intact. We'll need to take you in for a checkup. You might have a concussion.'

Her eyes lingered on his armor, but she didn't comment. She and the cops had been surrounding him when he came back to consciousness. He was still groggy but cooperated with them as they removed his protective vest and cut his Tee.

They had taken his statement when he regained his faculties. A sergeant arrived soon after and supervised grimly.

'No hospital,' he protested.

'Mr. Grogan,' DeSanto, the senior officer, growled as politely as he could. 'That's not an option. We haven't finished with you, but you need to get attended to, first.'

He jerked his head at the armor. 'That's different from what we have in the NYPD. Even our ESU teams don't have those.'

ESU. Emergency Service Unit, which performed SWAT operations in addition to other duties.

'I was in the military,' Cutter said, gritting his teeth and fighting a wave of dizziness as he got to his feet. 'A leftover from those times.'

It took two more hours for Cutter to clear his hospital scans—no concussion—and finish the NYPD's questioning. He produced his gun permit, gave them a copy of his camera footage and produced a copy of the rented apartment's lease.

'I've always had it,' he told the skeptical cops. 'The kind of work I do ... I get a lot of threats. I moved to that apartment the day after I tangled with those thugs at the convenience store. The ones who escaped.'

They probed and questioned, but he wasn't giving anything more away. Finally, he put on an exasperated look. 'I'm the injured party here. Shouldn't you be focusing on my attackers?'

He dragged himself out of bed at eight am, and after freshening up and feeling human again, he went to Ellen and thanked her for her help.

'I didn't know what to do,' she said, clutching his arm. 'You lay still and there was blood on your face.'

She was seventy years old and baked him a Christmas cake each year. Flippancy wasn't the tone to take with her. He thanked her again.

He was biting into his toast when there was a pounding at his door.

'You're alive,' Difiore said, greeting him with her customary warmth and concern as she swept in, along with Quindica.

Someday I'll ask her who buzzes her in.

He ignored them and finished his breakfast as they checked out his living room. He had cleaned up on his return from the hospital, but there were scuff marks on the wall, and the remains of the chair and the vase were still in a corner.

'Show us the one above,' she demanded when he was pouring coffee into three cups.

He took them up wordlessly and stood aside while they inspected the rental apartment. Their eyes swept over its barren interior, skimmed over the mattress and the sheet. Quindica nodded imperceptibly at the detective, who led them out and back to his apartment.

He handed them their mugs and took his first sip of the day. His head throbbed and his body ached, but it was better than the alternative.

'Walk us through it. Everything.' Clearly his beverage hadn't softened the cop.

He thought of protesting but rejected the idea immediately. *She's persistent. Won't give up.*

'Why did they escape? They could have killed you,' Quindica asked when he had finished.

'Don't know,' he shrugged. He wasn't going to mention Darrell or his intervention.

'Sheller?'

'Who else?'

'I didn't think killing you like that was his style.'

He peered at her over the rim of his cup. The FBI SAC was her usual stoic self, letting the detective do the talking. Her silence didn't fool Cutter. *She's as sharp as Difiore.*

'I think it was a grab operation,' he admitted. 'You're right. Finishing me like this would give him no joy. He'll want his hands on me.'

'Is that why your office is closed?'

'Yeah. I persuaded Arnedra to go to a secure location. Somewhere far off.'

'Blood results came back. Yeah,' she chuckled mirthlessly, 'your friend, the commish, expedited the tests once he heard it was you.'

The cops had swabbed his face when he had told them some of the blood on him was from one of the attackers.

'Nothing,' she said bitterly. 'He isn't in the system. No prints. They were careful.'

'And good,' he pointed out. 'That's one of the best locks on my door. They picked it just like that.'

'You could have shot them,' Quindica said. 'We saw the video. You had them. You had your Glock on you.'

'He wanted them alive,' her partner interjected. 'He would have questioned them, tracked back to Sheller.'

'Would you have shared his deets with us?' the SAC queried.

'Of course.' He spread his hands widely.

After killing him.

64

Darrell was distracted the whole day.

He had crept back into the house late at night and crawled into bed, shivering with fear.

He had slept fitfully, waking up every now and then to check the news on his phone. Cutter's face haunted him. The shock at his arrival, the blood on it, the way he had fallen when shot.

The media picked up the story at nine am, that the Fixer had been attacked at his home. The crushing weight on him lifted when he read the NYPD statement, that Cutter Grogan was injured, but not seriously.

He went through the motions of the day, and when Manuel nodded discreetly at him in the evening, he joined his friend with almost a skip in his step.

Nails was furious when they arrived at the Rockaway meeting point, but that anger wasn't directed at him. In fact, he patted Darrell on the back. 'That was good work,' he complimented. 'Without your warning, these—' he turned scornfully at the three perps, '—would've been arrested. You couldn't take down one person,' he spat at them. But surprisingly, he said nothing more about it. He discussed gang activities, distribution and the daily take, and then dismissed them.

Darrell split from Manuel and hurried back home. He checked his phone discreetly when he was away from the gang. Yeah, everything was recorded. However, it still wasn't valuable enough to grant him and Mama witness protection.

I need to give them Nails in action, or his boss. He had tried to find out who that mysterious figure was, but Manuel had shut him down every time. *He pretends to know who that is, but I think he doesn't know either.* Only the senior, white hitters knew, and they wouldn't give him the time of the day.

The fifteen-year-old sighed and turned the corner to Sutter Avenue and yelped when a shadow crossed the street to meet him.

Cutter!

He took Darrell's arm and marched him to his SUV. Went around the hood and climbed into the driver's seat.

'I didn't know it was your house. They weren't going to kill you. I swear. I would have warned you if I had known. I shouted when I saw Duke—'

'Duke, is that the one who shot me?' Darrell shivered at the way Cutter's voice had gone soft. Like a panther going into stealth mode before pouncing.

'I can't give their names.' He looked away from the intense green eyes and the bruised face.

'You're in deep trouble. I kept your name from the cops, but how long do you think it'll take them to piece it together? That a boy was there, too? They'll check out security cameras, ask neighbors. The detective who's in charge, she's very good.'

'There are no cameras there. Nails confirmed that. We got away clean.'

'Why were you there?'

'I told you. They wanted to get you and bring you to Nails.'

'Why?'

'I don't know. I swear,' he said, his voice rising when Cutter looked at him in disbelief.

'To kill me?'

'No! He was clear on that. No guns, no knives. They were going to knock you out. Duke,'—he had already blurted the name; no point hiding it anymore—'he said, you attacked them, they acted in self-defense. They didn't know you were wearing armor.'

'So, they would have killed me if you hadn't arrived?'

Darrell looked away in shame.

'You didn't answer my question. Why were you there? Why did Nails send you and not anyone else?'

He looked at Cutter in surprise. 'Because we're disposable.'

'Disposable? What does that mean?'

'Only white hitters go on important jobs,' Darrell explained. Didn't Cutter get it? 'Duke, Trigger, Kelly, they're like ...' he gestured at himself.

'Is that the word they use?'

That soft voice again. Darrell shifted uneasily on his seat. He didn't like the way Cutter's eyes had gone flat and hard.

'Yes,' he mumbled. 'Manuel explained it to me. We don't know much about the way the gang works. There's no big loss to the gang if we get caught. If Marv, Chino, some of the others, or even Nails—if they're arrested, then the gang goes bust. They know a lot more than we do, and the cops can make them talk.'

'And you still want to be with them.'

Darrell flushed and looked away. 'Not anymore.'

'You were on a grab mission. That doesn't feel like you want to quit.'

'I HAVE TO GET ENOUGH INFORMATION.' His shame turned to anger. 'UNTIL THEN, I HAVE TO GO ALONG WITH THEM.'

'It will get you arrested or killed. Your mother ... what will she do then?'

Darrell's rage exploded. 'I DON'T HAVE TO LISTEN TO YOU.' He escaped out of the vehicle before Cutter could react and slammed the door hard. He raced away and slowed down only when the Fixer wasn't following him.

. . .

CUTTER CLOSED HIS EYES TIREDLY AS THE TEENAGER RAN away. He had flubbed it again. He should have taken a more understanding approach.

He was on a kidnapping attempt, he flared at himself. *Doesn't he get how serious that is?*

He does. He thinks he can work out his exit.

I should go to Carmel, tell her everything.

Really? That will fix everything? She'll confront him, drag him to the cops. The Lions will find out and send shooters and no cop will be able to save them. Or, Darrell might run from home. That will be worse.

He had no choice. He had to let the teenager ferret out whatever information he could.

He checked his cloud account and grimaced when he found Darrell's phone hadn't turned up anything useful. It had cloned with the three kidnappers' devices.

Nothing useful on them, he thought as he went through the messages and calls. Talk about the kidnapping incident. Drug deals. There was an upcoming one in the neighborhood.

He created an anonymous email account and emailed the details to Difiore. *She won't know it's from me.* He was connected securely to the internet, and the email provider bounced the message off several servers before delivering it.

Kelly, Trigger and Duke. He could go for them. They were older and might know where Nails hung out.

He gunned his engine and drove out, his lips tight as Darrell's description came back to him.

Disposable.

65

Gunner met Nails in the Harlem bar with Cray by his side.

'The cops don't have anything,' the Brownsville leader said as he finished his narration. 'No description of our men, no witnesses, nothing. He had cameras. No other explanation for how he got there.'

'I thought you checked out Grogan's apartment,' the Lions' boss addressed the hacker.

'I didn't go there. I would have spotted his security setup if I had visited.'

'How badly is he hurt?' Nails asked. 'TV says he's recovering, no other details.'

'I called a few contacts.' Gunner sipped his beer and wiped the foam from his lips. 'He was wearing armor. Nothing broken. Just a cut or two.'

'We can go again. I can send better hitters.'

'No. He'll be alert. Cops could have a protection detail.'

'I've got something,' Cray announced and turned his laptop screen toward them. He played a video clip that showed Grogan running down Lafayette, his phone to his ear. 'That was over a block away from the bodega.'

'When was this?'

'Nails' holdup. That day.'

'What am I looking at?' Gunner growled, even though he had worked it out.

'Police reports say he was passing by when he sensed something off and confronted Nails' watchers. This video doesn't back him up. He's running to the store. He's making calls—'

'You hacked his phone?'

'No, but I've got the store's records. Their line was busy. Grogan didn't get through, if that's who he was trying. That video ... he wasn't passing by. He knew there was a holdup going down.'

'How did you get this video?'

Cray smiled slyly. 'There's an amateur photographer and blogger on Lafayette. He's writing about life in the city. I tracked him down and found he's got a video camera pointed at the street. Twenty-four/seven, throughout the year. That clip is from his feed.'

'Cops don't have it?'

'Nah,' he snorted. 'This dude's got history with them. He's not going to help them.'

'You know what this means?' Gunner turned to Nails.

'You have a snitch,' Cray cut in.

'You're reaching,' the Brownsville leader protested. 'He could be running for any reason. Heck, he could be going to the bodega for a cake. We know he's friendly with the ...' His voice trailed off under the founder's slitted-eye glare.

'My gang isn't the only one that held up stores that day,' he tried again. 'All the Lions' cells did that.'

'No. But you got interrupted. No one else did.'

'Boss—'

'I agree with Cray. You have a snitch. Find him. Bring him to me.'

Nails swallowed and got to his feet. No one challenged Gunner, especially when he was in this kind of a mood.

'And deal with those three hitters, the ones who failed to get Grogan.'

The Brownsville man nodded stiffly and went out of the bar.

'You really want to do this, boss?' Cray asked when they were alone.

'Do what?'

'Get rid of Duke, Trigger and Kelly? They're the men who went for Grogan,' he added when Gunner gave him a mystified look.

'We don't tolerate failure in the Lions.'

'But this was a test, boss. You said it yourself. You wanted to see how alert the Fixer was.'

'I wanted him captured as well. They're black, aren't they?'

'Yes, boss.'

'What are you complaining about, then?'

'I'm not.' Cray backed off. 'Too many bodies. That's what I am worried about.'

'No one will worry about them,' Gunner said dismissively. 'About this snitch—'

'He's low-level, I'm sure of that,' the hacker said quickly, eager to move on. 'Otherwise, Nails himself would have been arrested by now.'

'That's what I figure, too.'

'We can set a trap, however.'

Gunner, interested, made a tell-me-more gesture.

'Tizzard's rally here. We could let our gang know that you'll be there, making a brief appearance.'

'It'll get back to Grogan,' Gunner mused. 'But he may not turn up. He knows the kind of people who turn up. The event can turn hostile, violent. Anyone could get hurt.'

'He will, boss. I've studied him. I have created a psychological profile for him. It's too big a bait for him to pass on.'

'He won't be alone. He might come with cops.'

'Doesn't matter who he comes with. We'll let him get away.

Snatching him in front of hundreds of people, even if they are supporters, isn't safe.'

'We'll get proof of a snitch, however.'

'That's right, boss.'

'Do it. And check out Nails' people too. Everything about them. Where they live, who they hang out with, their phones.'

'On it, boss.'

Gunner went out and made a call from his vehicle.

'That rally,' he told Mease when the strategist answered. 'It's going to get violent.'

'I said I would get back to you on that. We haven't decided—'

'I have. My men need some action,' he replied peremptorily and hung up.

Grogan would escape, but not before he got roughed up.

Gunner smiled to himself. He was toying with the Fixer. Testing him, probing, landing a soft punch occasionally.

Preparing him for the finish, which he would deliver in person.

66

'What is it?' Rubin asked when Mease had hung up.

'It's Gunner.' The strategist helped himself to coffee and stood at a window admiring the Central Park view. 'He's decided his men are going to be present at Tizzard's rally. I told him we were still thinking about it, but he said they would be there.

'It's the way he said it.' He turned to the candidate with his cup in hand.

'He and Tizzard go a long way back,' Rubin shrugged. 'He's got to support his friend.'

'Yeah, but ...'

'You think he's getting out of control?'

'Out of *our* control,' Mease corrected him.

'From a campaign point of view, any violence is good. It'll play into our hands. If he wants to break away from us, what's our loss?'

'We lose muscle.'

'We can get that from other gangs.'

'Not many of them share our views. What we really think.'

'I worry he'll go after Grogan.'

'We've told him to back off.'

'Gunner is his own man.'

'Let's cut him some slack, see how he behaves.'

Mease nodded. Rubin had a point. They were too far into the campaign for them to make any changes.

'Besides,' the candidate reminded him, 'he's got as much as us to lose. You've recorded all our conversations with him.'

'Yeah,' Mease brightened at that. Mutually assured destruction was great at controlling people.

CUTTER DECIDED TO GO AFTER DUKE.

Not because he shot me, he assured himself, but because he was the eldest. He might have some seniority in the gang and just might know more of its operations and who Nails reported to.

The hitter lived in a public housing project on the outskirts of Brownsville, between Atlantic Avenue and Fulton Street.

Red-brick buildings, small parks, waist-high metal fences, children playing under the watchful eyes of parents and relatives.

Cutter parked his SUV two blocks away and walked down Herkimer Street. The program the twins had uploaded didn't just clone the phones. It also tracked them, letting him know where they were at any point in time.

At eight pm, the day after his confrontation with Nails' men, the hitter was in his apartment on the sixth floor.

It looked like he was alone, because his phone hadn't interacted with any other. He had been worried the cloning software would duplicate any random device it came into contact with, but that hadn't happened. *Beth and Meg did some fancy programming.* They hadn't explained it to him, and he hadn't asked.

'Ma'am,' he smiled and held the door open for a mom who was leading her daughter into the building. 'This where Duke lives? A little shorter than me. Tatts all over him—'

'Duke Posey? Yeah, sixth floor,' she replied, sounding harried as she dealt with a restless child.

'Thank you, ma'am.' *I've got a second name for him now.* 'I'm a friend of his. Visiting the city. Thought of surprising him.'

'You don't look like any of his buddies.' Her opinion of Duke's visitors was clear from the way she sniffed. 'I've seen some of them.'

'We took different paths in life, ma'am. I haven't been in touch with him for a long time. Now I'm wondering if I should have let him know.'

'You're here,' she said grudgingly. 'Just know that people change. What you know of him might be different to what you make of him now.'

He checked her out as they went into the elevator and noticed her punch the sixth-floor button.

'Ma'am, if you don't mind being honest, has he fallen into bad company?'

'Hell, yeah. He runs with a gang.' She clamped her lips tight as if she had realized she had said too much.

'I understand, ma'am. I'll knock on his door. If he recognizes me, great, we'll shoot the breeze for a few minutes, and then I'm gone. If he doesn't, I'll get out fast.'

She looked at the door, clearly not wanting to engage anymore.

Can't blame her. I'm just a stranger to her. Must be thinking I'm with a gang as well.

He had dressed down. A hoodie, loose Tee, torn jeans, scuffed shoes. Tattoos that he had painted on his neck with washable ink. No other disguise, because he wanted Posey to recognize him. His Glock was hidden beneath the outer layer, not visible to the practiced eye.

He waited for her to exit when the car arrived at their floor.

'That's his.' She jerked her head left, toward the last apartment on the floor.

Dim lighting, concrete floor, stale air, trash outside a few doors.

'Thank you, ma'am. I'll try his phone, first,' he said and

exhaled in relief when she turned right, down the hallway to another apartment. He waited for her to disappear into her residence, then swiftly removed a thin cable that was fastened to his trouser leg. Inserted one end of it to his cell phone and then sent the other beneath the door, through the narrow gap between its edge and the floor. It was a cable camera that drew its power from the phone and fed back images in high definition.

A darkened living room, which was empty. Beats playing on a soundbox. A hallway beyond, which had light dappling on it. A shadow crossed it. *Is that the kitchen? Is he there?*

There was only one way to know.

He knocked on the door.

The shadow moved again and a head cocked out into the hallway. Yeah, that was Duke Posey, alright.

He pounded the door again, and that got the thug to come into the hallway, wiping his hands on his jeans.

'Who is it?'

'Open the door, man. Can't hear you. Got a thing going down.' He roughened his voice and stayed out of the peephole's vision.

'Trigger? That you?'

A latch clicked. The door opened a sliver and swung back with force when Cutter shoved against it with his shoulder.

'Hey! That hurt. Why did you—' Duke trailed off when he recognized his visitor. His eyes widened, fear in them warring with anger. He jumped back and looked around wildly. Dived to a couch, clawed beneath its cushion, and came up with a gun when Cutter crashed into him.

Can't let him use it.

That would alert the entire floor. Nor did he want to kill the thug. He wanted answers, not a dead body.

Duke was wiry and slippery. He twisted and turned as he tried to escape from Cutter's grip, kept cursing and snarling and kicking up with his knees in an attempt to dislodge his attacker.

'I. Don't. Want. To. Hurt. You.'

The gangbanger wasn't listening. His neck muscles bulged as he tried to straighten his gun arm and bring it to bear on Cutter, who had one hand clamped around his wrist, forcing it away from him, and the other jammed on the thug's chest. He was forcing him down on the floor when the hood heaved up suddenly with all his strength.

Cutter slipped. His feet skidded and he lost his leverage. He ducked as Duke's elbow came up towards his throat. It grazed his neck in a stinging blow, and when the thug reared up for a head blow, he let go to scramble away.

The gangster pushed the couch away, roared in rage and powered up off the floor to attack—just as footsteps thundered to the door.

Didn't shut it.

Cutter sensed the new threat and rolled away desperately on the floor to come up against the wall.

At the doorway, a figure appeared, took in the scene with an exclamation, and fired three times, hitting Duke in the chest and sending him staggering back.

Cutter dived behind the couch frantically when the newcomer turned in his direction. Rounds thudded into the wall, spraying concrete chips. He drew his Glock and was at the point of firing back when the shooter fled.

Why didn't he shoot?

The reason became apparent instantly when the hallway exploded in noise. Voices sounded in alarm.

'GO SHOOT SOMEWHERE ELSE!' someone raged.

'Who is Nails' boss?' Cutter asked urgently as he bent over Duke, conscious of time slipping away.

All he got was blank eyes, as the light faded in them.

He moved quickly. Checked out the window. No escape from there. Bathroom, kitchen, same result.

Untidy bedroom. Window wide open to let air in.

Yes, that was a possibility.

Thought turned to action. He climbed out and let himself fall as more shouts sounded in the hallway.

Grabbed a lower ledge. Let himself go again, repeating the same escape trick that got him away from Martinelli's.

He fell on an uneven patch of yard and took stock of his surroundings. He was on the side of the building that faced a children's park.

He counted back from the time the killer had shot Duke. The shooter had three, maybe four seconds of lead.

He burst into a sprint, crouching low, beneath the line of windows. He ran around the side of the building and slowed when he came to the front. No shooter, no other person visible, though all the windows in the building had lit up and he could hear alarmed cries.

Cutter cut across the small lawn and leapt over the fence, Glock in one hand. Landed on sidewalk. Peered cautiously over a line of parked vehicles.

There!

That was the shooter, walking swiftly, seemingly headed toward a vehicle.

Cutter thought he recognized him from the doorway. He got further confirmation from the way the man held himself, and his gait.

It was Nails!

67

Cutter crouched and ran, using the vehicles as cover. The gangbanger was on the road, a good tactic since that gave him more space to escape. He wasn't looking left or right, nor was he checking his six.

He's focused on getting away. Not letting him do that.

He gritted his teeth as he checked through the windows of the cars to place the thug. An SUV seemed to be the Brownsville leader's target. No shadows moving inside.

He came alone?

The distant wail of sirens.

No time to lose.

Cutter powered off the roof of a low slung car, using his left hand for leverage, his body swinging up and over it in a tight arc, right hand down his side holding the Glock.

His move alerted Nails, who whirled around, his hand reaching inside his jacket.

Cutter landed smoothly.

He lunged forward as the killer's gun came out.

His shoulder fell as the barrel turned towards him.

With a roar he crashed into Nails, sending him flailing back. He chopped up with his Glock against the gangster's wrist, sending his weapon clattering to the ground. But the blow and his uneven stance made him lose his gun, too.

Furious with himself, he slammed the man against the nearest vehicle. They struggled—punching, grappling, each trying to gain dominance.

A pair of headlights turned on and an engine whined, warning of a vehicle's approach. Cutter looked up momentarily. The dark shape of a car. A shooter lining up through a window.

He reared back and grabbed Nails by his collar, ignoring the neck and belly punches. He swiveled awkwardly and flung the thug in front of the approaching car. Tires squealed as brakes slammed, but he didn't hang around to watch. He dived over the roof of the car and fell on the sidewalk just as the first round smashed into its side.

He crawled behind the wheel well, swiftly, getting out of the way as more bullets searched for him. There was a protective shield of metal, carbon and rubber between him and the shooters as the line of vehicles gave him cover, and then the shooters were gone after another fusillade of shots.

He scrambled back, slumped against a lamp post and caught his breath. Felt something warm and wet against his cheek and fingered his face. The cut in his temple had opened up.

He looked up when a dog barked. Its owners, a couple, stood at a distance, shocked.

'Stay back,' he told them tiredly as the first cruiser rolled up.

68

'It wasn't me,' Cutter told the stoic-looking Difiore and Quindica.

He had already surrendered himself to the cops and had given his initial statement when the two arrived. The detective nodded to the officers and took charge.

She led him to the children's park, where he sat on a bench and answered her questions.

'Witnesses placed you in the apartment,' the SAC said coldly.

'Yeah, that was me. I went up the elevator. I was in Duke Posey's apartment, but I didn't kill him.'

'How did you know his name? Where he lived? Why didn't you call me?' A staccato burst of questions from Difiore.

'My street snitch, he told me about him. That he was one of the thugs who invaded my apartment. Calling you? Why should I trust the NYPD? You know you've got dirty cops.'

Her rage was so palpable that he thought she would strike him. Quindica placed a hand on the detective's shoulder, and that seemed to have an effect. Difiore's face turned wooden. She shrugged off the SAC's hand and looped her thumbs in her belt.

That's some control. I would have lashed out in her place.

'Your gun?' she demanded.

'Your people have taken it. They'll find I didn't shoot. The bullets in his body won't match my gun.'

'Walk us through it again.'

'I've done that three times now.'

'Once again won't hurt.'

He sighed theatrically and launched into his recital, describing what happened from the time he had approached the building to the arrival of the cruisers.

'None of the bullets on the street are from my gun. You could match them to other crimes—'

'You're teaching me how to detective?'

That's not a verb. Going by her expression, the finer points of language wouldn't interest her or the SAC.

Quindica broke away from her hostile stare and looked up the side of the building.

'You want us to believe you jumped out of the sixth floor and landed without a scratch?'

'Believe what you want. Your technicians will find glove marks on those ledges. They will match these.' He held up his tactical mitts.

Difiore bagged them and handed them over to an officer.

'Is this the shooter?' She scrolled through her screen and showed him a photograph.

'Yeah,' he recognized it. 'That's Nails. He's taken over the Brownsville gang. I told you about him.'

'AKA Steve Patchey. He's got a record. Served several years for assault, burglary—a nasty, vicious piece of work.'

'Tell me about it,' he replied with feeling as he kept a straight face. *No need to let on I knew who he was.* The walking volcano that was Difiore would explode at that.

'Something funny?' the detective fumed when his lips twitched.

He summoned anger and glared back at her. 'You know him, and yet he's out there on the street.'

She let his comment slide. Looked away broodingly and then turned back to him.

'What were you really doing there?'

'I told you. My informant found out about Posey. That he was one of the attackers in my apartment. I wanted to question him. Find out who had sent him and his men.'

'You get any answers?'

'Nope,' he admitted truthfully. 'He recognized me and went into fight mode. That was when Patchey showed up. Have you placed the other attackers? The ones in my building?'

'No.'

'No hurry, now.'

'What do you mean?' Quindica asked sharply.

'Why do you think Patchey came here? He would have killed Posey even if I wasn't there. Any guesses where he is right now?'

69

'Yeah, that was Grogan.' Nails winced and rubbed his neck as he squinted to see the photograph Gunner presented. 'I recognized him.'

'He can hit. You should know that by now.'

The founder chewed on a toothpick as he looked at the night over Brownsville. They were in their usual rendezvous, with a security perimeter on the outside.

'Who jumps out of the sixth floor?' he snorted.

'You sound as if you admire him, boss.'

'I hate his guts. I want to pound his face into pulp. I want to see his eyes as I cut his belly and his intestines flop out,' Gunner said viciously. 'But he's got steel in him. I'll give him that.'

He straightened, and his command voice came back on. 'How bad is our exposure?'

'Grogan will have told the cops about me. I don't think he saw Marv and Chino. They were in the getaway car and things happened quickly. In any case, they were masked.'

'Why didn't you wear one?'

'Boss, I would have been noticed. And Duke wouldn't have opened the door if I had my face covered.'

'Did he talk to Grogan?'

'No. They were fighting when I arrived.'

'What about the others?'

'Kelly and Trigger? The ones who were with Duke at Grogan's? Dead. I killed them.'

Gunner nodded thoughtfully. Nails had acted swiftly and decisively, and no damage had been done.

'What about your snitch?'

'I'm working on it, boss,' his man said defensively. 'But I'm not sure if we have one—'

He broke off when Gunner glared at him.

'I'm investigating,' he mumbled. 'It'll take time.'

Let him do that, but I bet Cray will find out quicker. Then I'll decide what to do.

He squeezed Nails' shoulder hard enough to draw a yelp. He was the boss. He had to show it.

'Make sure the message spreads. Those who screw up, die.'

'No need for that, boss,' his man panted. 'They know it, and when they see we're short three disposables, that will hammer the message home.'

'GROGAN WAS RIGHT,' DIFIORE SAID DULLY AS THEY STOOD outside the Williamsbridge building and watched the technicians load two bodies into their vehicles. 'Patchey cleaned up.'

Neighbors had reported gunshots and summoned the cops. They found two dead men in the apartment. Residents said the men went by the street names of Trigger and Kelly, who turned out to have records. Yeah, some of the occupants confirmed, they had seen Posey visit and hang out with the men on occasion.

No further confirmation was needed when the detective and the SAC arrived and matched the faces to the ones from Cutter's security cameras.

'We're too late. Every time,' she raged beneath her breath.

'You know what hurts more?' She turned to Quindica. 'It's Grogan. He's ahead of us—'

'You think so? He hasn't gotten any leads, has he?'

'He isn't passing them on to us.'

'Someone sent me that email. About the drug deals in the city. We busted them.'

'You think that was him? Not his style. He would have called us. In any case, those were small busts. Sure, we got a few street dealers and stopped some powder going out, but nothing more. I'm sure he's as much in the dark as us. It's just that he's able to move quicker than we can because of his ... unorthodox ways.'

'Don't defend him,' she fumed.

'I'm not. But you know he's our ally.'

Difiore turned away, not wanting to acknowledge that the SAC was right.

'Check out cameras,' she snapped at the cops. 'Go door to door and see if anyone saw Patchey.'

No one will come forward, she thought bleakly. *Sheller's always several steps ahead of us.*

70

'His phone wasn't on him,' Beth told Cutter when he called the twins the next day.

He had wondered why his phone hadn't cloned with Posey's during that fight, then decided to give his gray cells a rest and reached out to the Petersens.

'How do you know that?'

'Check your phone.'

He tapped his screen to bring it to life and saw a photograph of a room. *Posey's bedroom*. A side table had the phone, as well as a gun beside it.

'You got this from the police reports?'

'Phones can't clone at that distance,' she said, evading his question. 'On top of that, those walls, the hallway—there's too much obstruction for the program to work.'

'Darrell's phone has cloned just one more device other than those kidnappers, Manuel's,' he said in frustration. 'By now, we should have gotten more.'

'They might be switching their cells off when they meet. You thought of that?'

'Guess not.' Meghan smirked at his silence.

. . .

DARRELL'S PHONE FINALLY YIELDED SOMETHING LATER IN the day.

Cutter frowned when he played back the recording of the incoming call on the boy's phone.

'Manuel?'

'Chin—'

'No names, bro. I thought you knew that.'

'Yeah, sorry. What's up?'

'You and the new one, what's his name?'

'Darrell.'

'Yeah, him. You both will be required at The Elitist in two days' time.'

'What's that?'

'A private club on 45th West. Between Fifth and Sixth Avenue. A big speech by Eric Tizzard. You heard of him?'

'Yeah. Isn't he the—'

'That's who he is. Darrell and you, heck, every one of us has to be there. Orders of the boss.'

'Nails? We were at the hangout today. He didn't say anything.'

'His boss. Nails heard it just now. I'm calling everyone.'

'What do we need to do there?'

'Help out. Whatever's required. There's going to be a big crowd. A surprise guest.'

'Who is that?'

'It wouldn't be a surprise if I told you,' the caller chuckled. *'It's someone who has come back from the ... nah, that would be giving it away. Be there with the other kid, too.'* He issued a few more instructions before hanging up.

Cutter played back the call again and steepled his fingers when it ended.

The caller was Chino. *Who else could it be?* Manuel had all but blurted his name.

He looked up The Elitist and found it was an exclusive, men-only private club. Founded a century ago by a wealthy banker, it carefully screened members, who paid thirty grand to join and signed non-disclosure agreements.

He dug deeper in the internet and found a few mentions of the club being a white men's outfit. *If Tizzard's speaking there, he's got to have supporters there. Heck, all its members could be white nationalists.*

It wasn't the club's composition or the fact the supremacist was speaking there that interested him.

It was Chino's line. Where he had cut himself off.

Someone who has come back from ... the dead?

Would that be Sheller? Would he show himself at the rally?

71

Gunner had come up with the idea after meeting Mease that morning. The strategist had briefed him on how the campaign was doing.

'Everything's heading in the right direction,' he declared. 'Rubin's got a few TV appearances, town halls, all over the country. He'll consolidate his lead over his opponents. That's what our pollsters say. That leaves just him and Thyssen.'

'I'm hearing rumors of his getting support from other parties.'

'Several politicians have reached out discreetly. Big names. We've discussed that possibility. We won't make any decision until just before the elections.'

'That will give us maximum leverage?'

'Yeah.' Mease smiled at the felon's use of *us*.

'Tizzard's speech is going to turn violent.'

'I thought he was supposed to be at a private club.'

'We're going to allow a few protesters to enter. That will trigger the action.'

'I'll get Farley and Parsons to book TV interviews soon after it's over. He can get some good soundbites out of it. What about Grogan?'

'I'll deal with him.'

'We told you to—'

'There will be no blowback. I'm going to sucker him into a trap. You'll have to trust me on that.'

'Spread it around that I might show up,' he instructed Nails. 'Don't mention my name, however.' He repeated the message that Cray had crafted. 'Use that line, exactly in that manner.'

'I'm working on the snitch, boss,' his man protested. 'There's no need to do it this way. If there's a snitch, he might suspect he's being set up.'

'Nails,' Gunner said softly, in the way his people had grown to fear. 'I am not asking. I'm telling.'

And that had resulted in Chino's call to Manuel.

Cutter learned that Eric Tizzard's rally at the private club was no secret. Many media outlets were talking about it, and the dark corners of the internet where racists and haters gathered had a field day.

Chino's right. It looks like there'll be a big turnout.

Cutter cleaned his Glock as he thought of his options. Going to Difiore wasn't one of them. *Should I go? Would Sheller expose himself? Why would he do that after playing dead all these years? Why now?*

It could be a trap, he answered himself. *He's tried to get me before, and failed. He figures I'll take this bait.*

He assembled his weapon and wiped it a last time with a clean flannel. He slipped it into its holster and stretched.

Decision made.

If there was even a remote possibility that Sheller would be there, he would be, too.

72

'I feel like I'm imposing on you,' he told Meghan the next day when he arrived at the Columbus Avenue office.

'We'll tell you when you're a pain in the butt, hotshot,' Beth grinned.

Her smile faded as she checked him out. 'What you're planning is madness. None of us would go alone in such a setup.'

'I don't have a choice,' he threw his hands up. 'If Sheller does come there, I can alert the cops. If he doesn't, there's nothing lost.'

'Except maybe your life.'

'Which is why I've come to you. How can I get out of there alive?'

Three hours later, after poring over building plans and the club's layout—items not available to the general public—he had mapped out three escape routes.

One was straightforward: through the basement kitchen and out the service door.

The other was through the laundry room, hidden in one of the automated trolleys that rolled beneath a drying window, from which he could climb out.

The last was through the air-con ducting.

'First is obvious.' Meghan tapped her pen against her teeth. 'They'll block that off. The other two they might disregard because of your size. You'll be a tight fit for either of those routes, but you will get away.'

'There's a fourth.' He leaned over their shoulder and toggled the touchpad to bring up the roof. 'I can go up to that balcony, climb to that window that overlooks the roof.'

'And then?'

'Break through the glass and escape.'

'Escape how? That's a hundred-and-fifty-foot drop. That building is tall. No drainpipes, no window ledges, which seem to be your preferred mode these days,' she snickered.

'I know how you got away in Tehran.' It was his turn to smirk at the look on their faces as he referred to the covert mission they had carried out in Iran.

THE DELIVERY MAN HAD HIS HEAD DOWN AS HIS FOREMAN yelled orders. It was a white-glove service that brought the best ingredients from select food retailers to The Elitist. Chicken breasts, pork chops, spices, organic veggies, butter and spreads—whatever the club needed, the firm provided.

The delivery man was a last-minute replacement, since one of his regular employees had fallen ill. The foreman had a list of manpower providers to address such a contingency, and the newcomer had come from such a company.

'Don't look in anyone's eyes. Don't talk,' he shouted at his assembled men. 'Don't remove your gloves, ever. Take those crates and stock them where you are told. Go!'

The men got to work like a well-oiled machine. They went to the rear of the truck, collected the deliveries and went to the service entrance, where a uniformed man stood aside to let them through. An assistant manager directed them inside the club to place the stock.

Cutter, the delivery man, stacked several crates of ingredients in the storeroom over multiple rounds. On his last trip, he went to the club official and showed him the label on the crate.

Window Wipes and Cleaners.

'Put that in the storage room as well. Separately from the food.'

'This goes up, usually. On the balcony.' He spoke softly. Meghan had checked out the staff in the club and found that the assistant manager was new. He wouldn't know much about its operations. *I hope*, Cutter thought, crossing his fingers mentally. 'I place it there each time. Makes it easy for the cleaners. They start from the top windows and work their way down.'

'You know your way up?'

'Yes, sir.'

'Go quickly.'

Cutter hurried away before the man changed his mind. He wasn't worried about the cameras. The twins had arrived earlier and flown a drone near the club, which had EMP-blasted the security devices. He could see uniformed technicians from a well-known protection services firm checking them out.

He climbed the grand stairs that ascended from the side of the central room to the balcony that ran around the top. He checked out the various windows quickly and found one that opened to the sloping roof. The city's skyline was visible through the clear glass. He placed the crate beneath it and wiped his hands. Looked around to check that no one was watching him.

He went to the nearest curtain and slashed with his knife to tear away a large chunk of its inner lining. Repeated the act until he had a substantial pile of fabric. He bundled it up and stuffed it in the crate. Checked that he had everything he needed in it. Glock, magazines, the Benchmade that he tossed in it, and a bottle of lighter fluid.

He paused a moment to admire the inside of the club. A transparent cupola of colored glass at the top, admitting natural light. Chandeliers dangling from a high ceiling, paintings on the wall and artwork on display stands. A polished wooden floor, a small stage for intimate performances. The club could easily hold five hundred people, standing.

Cutter returned the way he had come to find the foreman glaring at him.

'You're late!' the man stormed. 'We've got more deliveries to make.'

He climbed inside the van silently and joined the other stockers on a bench. He smiled to himself as it drove away.

His getaway mode was in position.

73

'Circulate these to all your men,' Gunner told his assembled cell leaders. It was a rare moment, his meeting all of them in person, in the Harlem bar. The more people who knew he was alive, the harder it was to maintain his cover. But there were times when he had to show himself. He was confident his personality and their fear of him would ensure their silence.

He handed a set of printouts to each leader. 'Some of you might have seen him on TV. Cutter Grogan. Calls himself a Fixer. Claims to help people—'

'What's he done, boss?' his Queens man inspected the first photograph.

'Nails knows what he's done. He's been interfering in our Brownsville operations.' He didn't tell them about Martinelli. Other cells didn't need to know that. 'The first few pictures are of how he looks. The heavyset man in the other drawings, that's him, too. In disguise.'

'We grab him?' Nails eagerly asked.

'Yes, if your men see him at The Elitist.'

'He'll be there?'

'He might.'

'Why will he come there, boss?' Nails drew back when Gunner glowered at him.

'He's smart, very capable—some kind of special- ops soldier previously. He's violent. Try not to get hurt. And don't kill him. I want him alive.'

He waved at them dismissively and returned to the counter to join Cray as they filed out of the bar.

Clint didn't leave. He hung around until the other leaders had left and went to Gunner.

'That was him, boss? At Crump's house? We didn't get a good look. All we could make out was that he was big.'

'Yeah.'

'He's got some skills. The way he got away from us—'

'I told you all. He's a soldier. Don't underestimate him.'

'We won't, boss.'

DARRELL TRIED HARD NOT TO TREMBLE WHEN NAILS HANDED him the photographs.

Cutter's pictures!

'You're Darrell, right? Manuel's friend?' The leader's eyes were sharp, probing, as they sized him up.

'Yes, boss,' he whispered.

'I have my eyes on you.'

The teenager froze at that.

The gangster smiled. 'You've been doing well.'

'Thank you, boss. What are these about? Who's he?' Darrell congratulated himself on his steady voice.

'You'll find out in a moment.' Nails straightened. 'Listen up,' he called out his men to gather them close.

'We got our orders.' He held up the images. 'There will be protesters at The Elitist tomorrow. We rough them up, but not so much that we start a riot. No, sir. The good people there, they came for a nice evening. Can't spoil their dinners.' He got a laugh at that. 'This dude might turn up as well. Him, we can rough up as much as we want. But we got to take him alive.'

DARRELL RACED BACK TO HIS APARTMENT AS SOON AS HE GOT free. Checked his phone. Yeah, it had recorded everything. He emailed the recording to himself and deleted it from the phone. His insides clenched when he glanced at the photographs. He could warn Cutter. He had to. He was reaching for his cell when something stopped him.

That's the only time Nails has spoken to me. There was that one moment when the cell leader had patted him, but it had been a fleeting gesture.

Does he suspect me?

He shivered in fear. Sweat popped up on his forehead. He forced himself to get up and checked out the street-facing windows. He couldn't see any watchers.

Nails would have done something if he knew, he reassured himself. No. There was no deeper meaning in the leader's talking to him. Still, he had to be careful.

Which meant he couldn't warn Cutter.

He went to bed uneasily and hoped the Fixer wouldn't show up at the club. Because if he did, there was no way he could escape from the gang.

CUTTER STIFFENED WHEN HE SAW DARRELL'S CELL HAD cloned a phone and there was a recording.

He played it.

'Clint?'

He recognized the caller's voice. Nails.

'Bro, what's up?'

'What did the boss say? I saw you went back, at the bar.'

'I can't tell you, dude. You know how we work.'

'Come on, Clint. We've been thick all these years.'

'It's nothing to do with you or your gang.'

A long silence.

'Alright,' Clint sighed. *'But you can't leak this. Ever, to anyone.'*

'I won't.'

'Crump. I took him out. This dude Grogan was at the scene. We didn't recognize him. It was dark. He was big, though. The boss confirmed that it was him.'

'That was some shooting, bro.'

'Nothing to it. You would have killed them if the boss had told you to.'

'Yeah. I was wondering who he gave the order to.'

'This stays between us.'

'Of course, bro. See you tomorrow.'

'We'll get him at the club.'

'I hope so. I want to get my hands on him.'

CUTTER KEPT STARING AT THE PHONE WHEN THE CALL ENDED. He roused himself finally and called Beth.

'Can you run a recording for me? See if your—'

'Werner.'

'Yeah, see if it can identify a voice.'

She seemed to sense something in his voice when she replied, business-like. No teasing, no yanking his chain.

'Send it over.'

'Uploaded to my cloud account.'

'I'll call you back.'

CUTTER PREPARED DINNER WITHOUT CONSCIOUS THOUGHT. His mind was racing as the call played in his mind.

He knew Crump's killer. He could pass that on to Difiore and Quindica. It was a big break.

Is it, though?

There's still no link to Sheller. They referred to some boss.

It proves these cells aren't the independent gangs the NYPD thinks they are.

So what? What can they do? There might be other dirty, senior, cops who might alert the Lions.

No, it was better he kept the call to himself. The last part of the conversation returned to him. They were talking about him. His guess had been right. Sheller had set a trap.

Does that mean he won't turn up?

He thought about it as he ate hastily and cleaned up.

The Sheller he knew from his ADX days wouldn't back out of a challenge.

He will show up. Briefly. Disguised, maybe, but he'll be there. He'll want to see me captured.

'CLINT KNOWLES,' BETH CALLED HIM. 'HE'S GOT A POLICE record. Voice analysis on his NYPD interview.' She sensed the question in his silence. 'I've sent you a package. His photograph, his cop file, the works. He hangs out in Brooklyn but is no longer at the address the NYPD have for him.'

'You can place the locations of those two phones? Nails and Knowles?'

'Nope. I looked up the cloned data. Nails' phone went offline the moment after this call. Knowles's too.'

'You know where they were before? They mentioned a bar.'

'I checked that out. Nada. These dudes are smart. They turn on their devices briefly. They seem to switch burners frequently.'

'They can't keep using a new throwaway phone each day.'

'Yeah, no one can.' She pondered that for a moment. 'The way I see it, this was a new burner for Nails. That's why the software got only this call and it was so important that he junked it and used another one.'

He heard an indistinct conversation at her end before she returned. 'Sis thinks the same.'

Sis. Meghan. Elder by a few minutes. Who came on the call, her voice sharp. 'Cutter, they refer to some boss. Is that Sheller?'

'I think so.'

'We'll keep trying, but I don't think we'll get anything more. These people have some smarts. Way beyond an ordinary street gang.'

'Want us to send this to your cop friends?' Beth asked slyly.

'How?' he growled frustratedly.

'Leave that to us,' she said sweetly. 'It could be an anonymous tip.'

'Do it.'

'They might figure out it's you they're talking about.'

'If that brings them to the club, great. They'll get Sheller.'

'If he shows up.'

'I'm counting on it.'

74

Cutter went as an elderly man, using an invite the twins had conjured up for him.

'It's legit,' Beth told him. 'We hacked into the club's member directory and found him. Old man, as you wanted.'

Vance Trent, the member he was impersonating, had made his money in banking, back in the days when Wall Street was like the Wild West. He was a reclusive millionaire and seldom turned up at The Elitist's events.

Silvery hair, leathery cheeks, black eyes, a cane for walking, a smart-suit—that was his getup. No Glock, Benchmade or any other weapon. He couldn't risk their being discovered at the club's entrance.

I've got backup weapons in that crate. Whether I'll be able to get to them ... he grinned sardonically as he exited the limo he had hired for the evening and ascended the stairs to The Elitist's entrance.

Several hard-faced men at the door, along with the uniformed usher. One of them took his invite and ran it through a bar-code reader. Another man wanded him, while a third patted him down.

'Your phone, sir,' the usher said, presenting a tray. 'You can collect it as you leave.'

Cutter placed his throwaway in it and went inside the club. He nodded to a few other members and headed to the bar. Ordered a drink and made a pretense of drinking it while he checked out The Elitist.

There were already more than a hundred people, and it wasn't even six pm. All of them white, ranging from the young to the old. A few women, but the crowd was predominantly male. The event wasn't free. Each attendee had to shell out three hundred dollars. *Tizzard's got appeal and a fan following who will pay*. A range of attire was on display, from the formal to Tees and jeans. Fancy tattoos and haircuts proudly displayed, along with a few flags. *No Lions ink, but they'll be here.* He peered over the heads of those around him to see if he could detect Nails or Knowles, but there were too many people.

At seven pm the chandeliers lit up and a gasp swept through the room at their majestic glow.

Cutter took his seat to the side of the crowd as the host appeared. He checked out the staircase, just behind him. It was cordoned off, a security guard watching impassively. The balcony was dark and empty. *Escape route's clear.*

A drumroll from the band on the stage and the program began. A comedian took the spotlight and soon had the crowd in stitches. Cutter couldn't help grinning at some of the gags. *None of them are racist. So far.*

The band played light music at the change of program. Several attendees went to the bar and helped themselves to drinks. The lights dimmed again and another speaker came up. A well-known nationalist, not as prominent as Tizzard. *The smaller guns are coming out to warm up the crowd.* Cutter clapped and got a grin from the man beside him.

'Quite a show, huh?'

'Yeah.'

'You been to any of these before?'

'A couple of Tizzard's rallies.'

It was true. He had attended some of the man's speeches around the country. Once was out of curiosity, to see what his appeal was, the other was during an assignment.

The back of his neck prickled when a shadow drifted up his side. He recognized the man immediately. A hitter who hung out with Nails, one of his trusted men. The thug wore a loose jacket as he checked out the seated attendees. He met Cutter's eyes, nodded politely and moved on.

They're looking for me.

He searched the hall and found more men around the hall, making their way up and down the edges of the room, sizing up the attendees. Many had cell phones cupped to their ears. None of the security guards challenged them, and participants seemed to take them for organizers.

At nine pm, the main act arrived, to loud cheers and applause.

Eric Tizzard cocked his head and mock-frowned. 'Is that all you got? Are you being politically correct?'

The accompanying roar and clapping were thunderous.

He's a good speaker. Reads a crowd well. It showed, as the supremacist soon had the attendees eating out of his hand. He trotted out familiar tropes and sound bites, none of them new, but that didn't matter to the crowd. They cheered and yelled their support at every punchline.

Dinner break. Cutter joined the line for the side tables, made casual conversation with those around him. More thugs passed him, standing out easily from the way they dressed and carried themselves. None recognized him.

He didn't see Sheller. *He'll be in disguise as well, though there's nothing he can do about his size.* But he didn't see anyone who came close to the Lions' founder's shape. There were large men, bald heads, pink and sweaty faces, eyes gleaming in excitement, but none was the ruthless killer from ADX.

It happened as Tizzard was winding down his second act.

75

A commotion at their backs, where the entrance was located. Loud voices burst out, and a ripple swept through the crowd as a scuffle broke out.

Cutter turned to see several protesters, young men and women, holding placards and banners, resisting the security guards.

'Here come the do-gooders,' Tizzard sneered. 'They can't hold their own rallies. The food's over there!' he shouted, to loud laughter.

The fights should have been subdued quickly when the thugs joined the guards, but men rose suddenly from their chairs, and several whipped out placards, revealing who they were. Protesters masquerading as attendees.

Their presence among the seated crowd lit a fuse. A burly man threw a punch. His target ducked and flung his chair. A woman screamed as brawls broke out.

'That's it for the night, folks,' Tizzard called out hurriedly as a bunch of men swarmed around him and took him away.

Cutter edged to the side and watched in amazement as a free-for-all broke out in the hall. He ducked when a missile, a fork, came his way and disappeared behind him.

'You're on which side?' a sneering face challenged him, with fist cocked.

'Mine.' He took out the man with the hard edge of his palm and followed it up by jabbing hard with his cane in the man's belly. The attacker wheezed as he went down and was in danger of being trampled as the fight swept across the hall.

Cutter yanked the man assaulting him and shoved him to the sidelines, to safety. He stepped back as men and women flailed with the protesters, whose numbers seemed to have taken the organizers and the Lions by surprise.

But the nationalists prevailed, and in a matter of minutes, the intruders were bundled out. Excited chatter burst out as the attendees mopped their faces.

Why hadn't the cops come in? Did the Lions block their way?

That couldn't be it. Maybe the fight was over faster than they could respond. *Or,* he thought bleakly, *Tizzard and the Lions had an agreement with the dirty cops. The supremacists would deal with the protesters themselves.*

'That was the icing!' a man exclaimed. 'I'd heard Tizzard's rallies turned violent. I was hoping something like that would happen here, too.'

Cutter looked contemptuously at him. Checked the hall again, his eyes sweeping it in tight sections. Nope. There was no one who looked like Sheller.

A trap for me, but he didn't show up.

He was sure that if he had appeared as himself or in his heavyset disguise, he would have been captured.

He headed to the bathroom at the far end.

A long line of porcelain sinks in front of a large mirror. A row of stalls behind. A bunch of people, talking, laughing.

Gangbangers, judging by their outfits. He recognized a few from before, when they had been checking the crowd from the sides. *They must be from other cells. Haven't seen any of them with Nails.*

He didn't miss a step. Put on a polite smile and went to the far stall. The thugs made way for him. An old man with a cane? No threat.

He emerged from the stall and went to the sink. Was washing his hands when a large man came up on his left. The stranger bent his face to the tap and pushed back the cap on his head.

Cutter froze inside.

That's Sheller.

76

The stranger had a jowly face and a broken nose, but Cutter made him out from the way he moved. There was no mistaking the man's powerful build, the way he cocked his head, the sheer menace he exuded, for anyone else. His time at ADX had imprinted every aspect of the killer in his brain.

Jeff Sheller was beside him. And he had showed himself!

He was at the back of the stage during the change of sets! Moving furniture, Cutter realized.

He had appeared and disappeared so fast, his presence hadn't registered.

'You had a good evening?' The convict seemed to sense his scrutiny.

'Got my money's worth.' Cutter chuckled as he wiped his face with a soft towel.

The Lions' man patted him on the back and went to the exit.

Take him down?

How?

He's got his men. I'm alone; don't even have my Glock.

And by the time he had finished arguing with himself, the ex-con had left the room and was surrounded by his men in the hallway.

All but one of them.

Clint Knowles stood near the door, smiling at him.

Cutter recognized the hood immediately from the file Meghan had sent him.

'That a lion?'

'Huh?' he asked, nonplussed.

'That tatt on your neck?

'That? Yeah.' It appeared his collar had slid back to reveal the ink he had drawn on himself.

'Lions,' Knowles grinned. 'They're everywhere.'

'Common enough drawing.'

'That's all it is to you? An animal?'

Cutter faced him squarely, his cane in his left hand. 'Depends on who's asking. To many, they are just that. To some, they're a sign.'

'A sign?'

'Of a return?'

'Like a rising?'

He's verifying me. To see if I've heard of the gang.

'That's right.'

'I didn't know they were around in your time.'

'Son,' Cutter said contemptuously, 'You weren't born when I performed my first ... what do they call it now? Hate crime? Yeah. That. I beat up—'

'You are one of us,' Knowles breathed.

'I don't know what you're talking about.'

'You don't know who was here, do you? That man next to you?'

'A Tizzard fan, like me?'

'Tizzard fan? Heck, Tizzard is a fan of *him*! That was Gunn—say, who initiated you?'

'That was Gunner?' Cutter asked in awe. He took a step forward.

'Who inducted you into the gang?'

'I've always wanted to meet him.' He frowned and took another step. 'But I thought he died.'

'I'm asking you—'

Cutter punched him savagely in the throat.

Knowles's eyes went wide, and then he wheezed and gasped and groaned as he doubled over.

Have just a few seconds before someone comes in.

It was a big risk, questioning the hitter in the bathroom. He couldn't escape if more thugs arrived through the door. He had to grab the opportunity, however.

Cutter grabbed him by his Tee and hauled him up. Jabbed the point of his cane in the thug's belly.

'Where's Gunner?' he whispered. 'Where does he hang out?'

Knowles shook his head, blindly clawing at his throat, wheezing.

'WHERE IS HE?' Cutter shook the thug, but the man was panting for breath.

He swore and dragged him to the farthest stall and shoved him inside. Searching the thug, found his gun, a Sig Sauer, and pocketed it. Straightened his clothing, patted his hair into place and went out of the bathroom.

Spotted some of the thugs hurrying back.

They're looking for him.

Cutter sped up, his cane clacking on the floor as he headed towards the staircase. The hall was emptying as attendees went for the exit. Chairs tipped over, placards trampled, broken china —all the signs of a fight, but no sign of Sheller.

'HEY! YOU!'

Cutter didn't turn around at the shout.

They found Knowles.

'IT'S HIM!'

He glanced back. Four men, one of them pointing at him, a good thirty feet away. Several attendees between them and him. To his left was the staircase.

'THAT'S HIM. THE OLD GUY.'

Cutter drew the gun at their approach and fired over their heads.

Screams burst out. The orderly exit turned into a stampede. The rushing thugs were blocked by the fleeing attendees.

He fired at the chandeliers. The largest one exploded and showered glass and crystal onto the floor. Cutter flung his cane away and sprinted. Whirled for an instant when he reached the steps and emptied the magazine at the lighting and then over the heads of the fleeing people. The Lions who had spotted him were trapped between the bathroom and the mass of people. Other thugs were jammed at the entrance. A gun went off wildly.

Cutter raced up and went to the crate he had stored earlier.

He had planned for buying some time and hoped his methods would work.

He opened the box and brought out several smoke bombs and fake grenades. He tossed them into the hall and down the stairway, where they detonated satisfyingly and added to the chaos.

He removed the bundle of fabric next, and emptied the bottle of lighter fluid over it. He lit one end of it, and as it whooshed into flame he ran to the edge of the stairs and threw it down the steps. The curtain lining burst into flame and burned brightly as it rolled down and settled over the lower steps.

Panic, smoke and fire.

That got him the time he needed.

He went to the crate and extracted the last item he would need for his escape.

A base-jumping wingsuit.

He climbed into it, conscious of the passing seconds. Several stray shots came his way as the thugs sought cover from the explosions and the thick smoke. No shooter had a clear line of fire at him, and all their rounds went wide.

They'll soon find out that isn't tear gas and those aren't grenades.

They would surge forward then, and the fire wouldn't be a significant obstacle.

He shattered the window with Knowles's gun barrel and grabbed the Glock he had stowed in the crate. He threw the thug's weapon as far as he could in the general direction of the bathroom and turned to the window.

It was a tight fit, but he managed to squeeze through without ripping his suit. Cool air bathed him. The loud sound of sirens on the street and escaping attendees shouting.

He ran down the sloping roof and launched himself from its edge just as he heard thugs shouting and yelling from the stairs.

A shot sounded, but the bullet came nowhere near him, and then he was away, flying over the streets of the city, navigating between highrises and office buildings.

There was the taste of sour ash in his mouth as he escaped.

He had gotten away, but so had Sheller.

I didn't recognize him when he came on stage.

77

'Where are you?' Difiore called him at three am, her voice tight, clipped.

'Central Park,' he told her.

He had landed near Grand Central, and while he had drawn a few strange looks from passersby, no one commented. Even the sight of someone base-jumping and landing near one of the busiest train stations in the city didn't faze New Yorkers.

He had ducked into an alley and shrugged out of his wing-suit, which he stuffed into a trashcan. He went to a hotel in his elderly person disguise and checked into the room he had rented previously.

'What are you doing there? This time of night?' Difiore asked.

'Running.'

That was true. He had left the hotel in his running gear and backpack and was cooling down when she called.

'Come to Columbus Circle. We'll meet you there.'

They drove up in her Chevy, came out and leaned against the car while he leapt over the railing and joined them.

Quindica and the detective in their suits. No creases in their clothing, nothing astray, despite the late hour. Only a faint shadow beneath their eyes revealed their tiredness.

'What's up?' he asked. Casual. Friendly. Like he always was with cops.

'Where were you this evening?' Difiore asked peremptorily. As she always was with him.

'Hanging out with some friends, not far from here.'

Beth and Meghan had worked their magic to show his phone was in their office. They said they would back him up if they were questioned. He had frowned at that, but they had waved his protests down. 'It's nothing,' the elder twin had assured him. 'We'll be your alibis.'

'Don't get killed,' Beth had warned him.

'All night?' the cop asked him suspiciously.

He uncapped a bottle of water and took a generous swallow. 'What's this about?' He wiped his mouth. 'I'm sure you've checked my phone, placed its location.'

'Heard of The Elitist?' Quindica looked at a cruiser which raced past, siren wailing.

'Nope. What's that?'

'A private club on West 45th.'

'Never heard of it. The only clubs I go to are gyms, and those rarely.'

'It's a men-only establishment. For the super-rich and connected.'

'Is this going somewhere?'

'Eric Tizzard gave a speech last night,'—she glanced at her watch—'nine pm. Protesters burst into the building, heckled him, fights broke out.'

'That's standard for his rallies, isn't it?'

'There were shots this time. The club nearly burned down.'

'And I am involved, how?'

'Grogan,' Difiore broke in before the SAC could speak. 'You know a lot more than you let on. You've got some contacts we would love to talk to. WHAT THE HECK'S GOING ON?'

He shrugged helplessly and looked at Quindica with a *what's she talking about* expression.

'We found the gun that killed Crump. It was in the club,' the FBI agent explained. 'We also found a body. Clint Knowles. His throat was crushed. He was a hardened criminal; his prints were on the gun. We think he was the shooter.'

He's dead? Did I punch him that hard?

'You got Crump's killer? That's great. Why the long faces?'

'We think Sheller was there. Witnesses say an elderly man was in the bathroom with Knowles. He came out shooting—grenades, tear gas, fire, the works.'

'Sounds like he started a war,' Cutter grinned and immediately wiped the smile from his face when the detective glared at him.

'That's what witnesses say. The grenades were dummies. They gave off a loud bang. The smoke was just that. Not tear gas. The fire was real, though.'

'I wasn't there, if that's what you're thinking. I was with my friends. Beth and Meghan Petersen, at their office on Columbus Avenue.'

'Give me their details.'

He recited their numbers and address.

'Why do you think I would be there? You think I was that man? Do I look elderly to you?'

'Have you heard of disguises? That man escaped in a wingsuit. Base-jumped, from what we can work out. That sounds just like you.'

'Search me.' He held his hands up. 'No wingsuit on me. That club will have cameras. You can run your facial recognition program and see if that man's me. I'm sure the tech you've got can see past disguises.'

'Their cameras were down,' Quindica spat in disgust. 'Very conveniently, don't you think? Several people saw him fly, and there are a few videos floating on the internet. But they're too dark or blurry.'

'Cops are searching for anyone who looks like him and his wingsuit,' the detective glowered at him. 'He couldn't have been carrying it around with him. Too noticeable.'

They haven't found it yet. Nor the hotel, either.

'Base-jumping. Grenades. This dude must be a Hollywood stuntman,' Cutter chuckled.

'Grogan,' Difiore warned him, low and fierce. 'This has become personal for you. With Sheller. Back off. Let us do our job. We'll bring him down.'

No, you can't. He bit his lip before the words escaped him. *Not without help.*

78

'Describe him,' Gunner commanded the men facing him. 'Again.'

To his left was Cray. Nails and some of his crew were on the right. Standing in front of him were five men, the senior hitters in Knowles' cell.

'He was tall, boss,' a thug named Crebs responded. 'White hair. Cane. He was a member.' He shifted his feet uneasily. 'He was in the bathroom when you were washing up. You spoke to him. He didn't look like Grogan.'

The Lions' founder raged inwardly, though he didn't let his anger show.

It was Grogan. No one else. He was that close to me. I could have snapped his neck right there.

He hadn't been paying attention. That was the only excuse he could come up with. Knowles had checked out the bathroom and had assured him it was empty. He and his men were joking about how they had crushed the protesters when the old man entered. No one took a second look at him. Not even Gunner. They were all on an adrenaline high after the fight.

The Lions' founder had worked it out with Tizzard that he

would appear in a disguise, briefly, and then go into the security room to watch the proceedings.

He hadn't spotted Grogan.

Nails had been with him and relayed everything to him, while Knowles and the other cell leaders spread out their men and checked out the crowd.

None of them had seen the Fixer.

And then the cameras had gone down when the protesters burst in.

A glitch, the head of security informed Tizzard's team.

Grogan did that, Gunner swore at himself.

'Was he alone?' he asked coldly.

'Yes, boss.'

'Those weren't grenades or tear gas.' His cop contacts had confirmed that.

'We didn't know that at the time, boss.' Sweat broke out on Crebs' forehead. 'There were a lot of people. It wasn't easy to get to him.'

'He was on the balcony. All of you were armed. How hard was it to shoot him?'

'Not easy, boss,' another hitter spoke up. 'He was in the shadows. We couldn't see him clearly—'

Gunner drew his Sig Sauer from his pocket and shot the hitter between the eyes and blew Crebs' head off in one move.

His harsh breathing was punctuated by the sound of falling bodies.

'What are we?'

No one answered.

'WHAT ARE WE?'

'WE ARE THE RISING LIONS,' his men thundered back.

'That's right,' He glowered at the remaining men in front of him. 'We have survived and grown, despite no one knowing who I am. The world thinks I'm dead. We run drugs all over the country. We own cops and lawyers and bankers and politicians. AND YET WE COULDN'T CAPTURE ONE MAN?'

'GO!' he yelled at them, his face red. 'Find that man.'

The remaining members of Knowles' gang scampered out.

'Cray?'

'Yes, boss.'

'Give me a list of five men. I'll select one of them to replace Knowles.'

'Yes, boss.'

'Have you spoken to our NYPD friends?'

'Nothing there, boss. They're looking for this man, too. They don't have any connection to Grogan.'

I'll have to plant that suggestion.

'Their investigation is all over the place, boss. The protesters, how they got inside, the fights, this old man ... they haven't had time to make any progress. The lack of camera footage is stalling them.'

'Grogan's working with anyone?'

'He's a loner. Other than that woman—'

'Have you found anything on her?'

'No, boss.'

'Nails, anything on your snitch?'

'No, boss. I spread the word around, like you said, but I don't know who might have leaked it. It got complicated. There were rumors on social media. Grogan might have seen those and come to the club. I don't think I have a snitch.'

'You have. Cray,' Gunner turned to the hacker. 'You told me Grogan was friendly with that bodega's owners?'

'Yes, boss.'

'Nails?'

The Brownsville leader raised his head.

'Spread the word that you're going to kill them.'

'Yes, boss.'

'And do it.'

There was more than one way to draw Grogan out of hiding.

And hurt him.

79

'Have you seen him?'

'No.'

'Keep looking.'

Cutter kept playing the three lines over and over again. His phone had gotten them from Knowles', which had more calls and messages on it, none of which were related to Gunner.

That first speaker sounded like Nails. There was some background noise, however, as if Patchey was relaying the info to someone else.

Cutter inserted the voice file into an audio-editing program and played around with various filters and eliminators. The crease in his forehead smoothed when he heard a voice just before Nails' last command.

'Tell him to keep looking.'

That sounded like Sheller. It had been a long time since he had heard the ex-con, but the voice of authority in that order sounded just like him.

He sighed and slid back from his chair. He was in his office, alone, his security set up to warn him of any intruders.

'Why didn't I recognize him quickly?' he asked himself aloud.

Those jowls were as fake as my silver hair. That broken nose as well.

He hadn't been looking for the killer in the bathroom. He hadn't anticipated that, which was why his radar hadn't been working.

'That's how you get killed,' he swore at himself. 'By being careless.'

He had nothing. No way of discovering where Sheller had gotten to. The cloning software hadn't provided anything useful.

He crashed his bunched fist on his desk and got to his feet.

What would Sheller do next?

The answer was obvious.

'Arnedra?' he rapped out when he got his friend and business partner on the call. 'Are you safe?'

'Yeah, why?'

'Just checking. How is it over there?'

'There's so much sun here,' she gushed. 'I might stay longer.'

'Take all the time you want. I'll let you know when it's all over here.'

'How are you?'

'Could be better,' he admitted and gave her the bare outlines of what had gone down since her departure.

'I need to be with you,' she said.

'You need to go where I know you're safe,' he told her firmly. 'Which is with your sister.'

He threw the phone on the desk, jammed his hands in his pockets and paced.

There had to be a way to bring Sheller out of hiding.

'Difiore?' he reached for his phone and dialed another number.

'Yeah.'

He glanced at it. None of the usual rudeness in her voice. She sounded flat, exhausted.

'I want to set myself up.'

No response.

'Are you there?'

'Yeah. What do you mean?'

'Let it be known that I'm planning to cooperate with you. That I've got info that's so explosive that the NYPD will take formal statements from me under tight protection.'

'The Lions will come for you.' Interest in her voice.

'They already are looking for me.'

'Was that you at The Elitist?'

'Yes or no, Difiore?'

'Be on your number. I'll need to check with Peyton, the commish and her boss, Jamison.'

RUBIN WAS BEAMING WHEN MEASE MET HIM.

'I just finished with Farley, Parsons, the pollsters ... we're getting there.'

He had gone in front of the cameras in the immediate aftermath of the fights in The Elitist. Those interviews had resumed in the morning when more details emerged of the fire. The base-jumping escape dominated the headlines, which the candidate made full use of.

'Vigilantes running loose in the city,' he thundered. 'Because the police are toothless and powerless.'

Judging by the opinion polls, he had done a great job of presenting himself, and his message was resonating across the country. He still trailed the Veep, but the gap had been reduced to low double-digit points.

'Let's not get ahead of ourselves,' Mease warned him. 'We've got a long way to go.'

'I know.' Rubin hadn't stopped smiling. 'Look.' He picked up a few sheets of paper. 'This is what I've been working on.'

The strategist scanned the bulleted lines quickly and looked up in amazement when he had finished.

'These points are going to be your first legislation?' he asked in awe.

'Yeah. Stop *all* immigration unless it's to join families. Roll back anti-discrimination laws. Employers should be free to choose who they hire. If bosses don't like blacks or Jews, they shouldn't be forced to even consider those candidates. Abortion, gone! None of that women's-right-to-decide nonsense.'

He chuckled when he noticed the strategist's fingers tremble in excitement. 'You should have seen our meeting. We can smell the victory. Calls have been pouring in from all over the country. Donors wanting to contribute. People want to start new PACs and super PACS.'

'The main parties?'

'More calls from their Senators and House Representatives from both parties. I took some of them myself. Told them we wouldn't dilute any of our policies if they came out to support us. All of them agreed.'

'They want to latch on to our ride. Get positions within government if we win.'

'Yeah, we're there, Doug. I can smell it.'

'Slow down, hotshot. Anything can still happen,' Mease cautioned him. 'Go around the country. Capitalize on this wave of support. Speak to small and large crowds. Go, be seen.'

'That's what we agreed on,' Rubin nodded. A far-away look entered his eyes. 'When you approached me in Otisville, is this what you thought would happen?'

'No,' Mease admitted. 'I thought we would make some waves, become more powerful and influential—'

'I didn't dream I had a good shot at becoming president.'

'Go, make it happen.'

Rubin left the meeting with a spring in his step and a grin on his face.

'That worked out better than we expected,' Mease said as he briefed Gunner later in the day. 'What your men did at the club was explosive.' He chuckled at his own joke.

'We had help,' the Lions' founder rumbled. 'Grogan—'

'That was him?' The strategist whipped his head up. 'The base-jumper?'

'We set a trap for him. He walked right into it. But he escaped.'

Mease stared at him as his excitement drained away. 'We told you to—'

'You don't tell me to do anything. I've brought the campaign to where it is now. Without me, Rubin would be just another no-hope candidate appearing on a few radio shows and the odd TV interview. Relax! He doesn't know about us. He suspects I am alive, that's all.'

'That's a risk by itself.'

'It's no risk to the campaign.'

The accountant thought it through quickly and nodded reluctantly. Gunner had a point. What could Grogan do? Nothing. He and the ex-convict were like two prize fighters circling one another in a ring. *Let them go at each other. We're safe.*

'You plan to take him down?'

'No. I'm going to crush him,' Gunner said menacingly.

Mease couldn't suppress the shiver that ran through him. 'Do what you think is best,' he said calmly. 'Remember the big prize, though.'

'I have two prizes,' the Lions' founder rumbled. 'One of them is Grogan. He's like the icing on the cake.'

80

'You're good at surveillance.' Nails crouched in front of Darrell and looked him in the eye.

'I think so, sir,' the teenager stammered as he fought to keep his voice steady.

'Sir. You heard that? None of you ever call me that,' the Brownsville leader chuckled as he straightened and faced his men. He clapped his hands to draw attention. 'Listen up ... no, not you,' he told the sentries at the edge of the lot. 'You keep watch. We don't want the pigs to roll up on us.'

'We've got an assignment,' he told the rest of the gang. 'A hit.'

Darrell's chest pounded when a murmur swept through the thugs. A hit. That meant—

'I'll be the shooter. I'll pick four other men. I'll decide who they'll be later. But first, we need to do some recon. Darrell here will check out the place.'

'Where's that?' Marv called out.

'All in good time. For now, only he'll know. You're good at keeping secrets, aren't you, Darrell?'

The boy nodded dumbly, aware of everyone's eyes on him.

'Great—'

'I'll tag with him,' Manuel intervened. 'He and I are best buds.'

'You didn't hear what I said.' Nails' voice hardened. 'He goes alone. No one else. It's surveillance, not a street deal. Got it?'

Nails clapped his hands again when Manuel flushed and looked away. 'Get back to work. We have powder to sell.'

Darrell couldn't help shuddering when the leader placed a hand on his shoulder.

'You excited, boy?'

'Yes.' He nodded furiously and looked Nails in the eyes before crouching again.

'You know that bodega I held up? On Lafayette?

The student's eyes widened.

'Yeah, that one.' The gang leader smiled at his reaction. 'You need to watch it. Find out what time the owners come in and go. Their routine. When they're alone. Do the cops roll by? If they do, is there a schedule? Any regular customers. What time they drop in. The works.'

Darrell's heart was pounding so hard in his chest that he feared Nails would hear it, but it looked like the gangster took his expression for excitement. He clapped the boy on his shoulder and made to leave.

'Why them?' the student asked.

'You mean, why have we decided to kill them? Boss's orders.'

'I thought you ran this gang yourself,' the teenager dared to ask.

'Nah.' Nails laughed, clearly flattered that Darrell thought so highly of him. 'I report to someone. There are many others like me; we all report to the same person.'

'He never comes here? Your boss?'

'Nope. Too risky. I meet him regularly.'

'Here?' Darrell looked around in surprise.

'No. Another place. Not far from here. Get to work tomorrow.' Nails fist-bumped the teenager and left.

Calm down, the teenager told himself when he was alone and returning home. He took deep breaths and walked steadily, letting the breeze cool the sweat on his face. The thumping in his chest slowed, but the sickly feeling inside him didn't go away.

He knew Cutter was friendly with the store's owners. He had worked that out from the Fixer's actions during the holdup and the TV coverage that followed.

I should warn him.

What can he do? He'll be there with the cops and they'll arrest Nails.

Would that be sufficient to get him and Mama witness protection?

He didn't think so.

Besides, he didn't know when the hit would go down.

No, it was better to carry out the recon and warn Cutter when he had all the details.

He nearly tripped when another thought struck him.

What if I record Nails meeting his boss?

81

'You've got nothing else from his phone?' Cutter referred to Knowles' cell.

'Nope.' Beth pursed her lips. 'Thrice. That's how many times we told you. That's not counting how many times we told you yesterday.'

He grabbed his coffee mug and drank distractedly as he checked out their office. Empty, except for the three of them.

'You can run voice analysis?'

'Against what?' she asked him patiently. 'One voice is Patchey. We know how he sounds from NYPD's files. Sheller ... we don't have anything for him.'

'ADX?'

'Yeah, there's a lot of video and audio of him from there, but that's not the problem. What you've got on that call ... that's not big enough to run a sample.'

'Why do you need confirmation it's him? You know it's him, don't you?' Meghan peered at him.

'I need to know where he is!' Cutter ground out in frustration. 'And if that was him—'

'We've already run his voice prints and done a social media check,' the older twin interrupted calmly. 'We got no hits. We could have checked out the cameras at the club to see where he disappeared. But when we EMP-ed them in the evening, all of them went out. That was the only way we could protect you. Even the ones outside the club.'

'We got nothing, then?'

'I wouldn't say that,' Beth smirked. Her fingers flew and a brief video appeared on the screen. A boxy-looking SUV speeding along an avenue. 'That's his getaway vehicle.' She held a finger up to silence him. 'Watch.'

He obeyed. The ride raced down the street and slowed at a traffic light. Its rear was illuminated by the lights of another vehicle and, even through the darkened windows, the shape of a man was visible.

'Bald head. Rear seat. We ran comparisons against all the footage we have from ADX. Werner says there's a high probability that's Sheller in that vehicle. Going north on Fifth Avenue.'

Cutter leaned forward in excitement. 'If we can track where that vehicle went,' he half-spoke to himself.

'We hit a block there,' Beth said regretfully. 'We got lucky with that one street camera, but—' She brought up another image, a parked SUV. 'That's the vehicle we were tracking. It was left on West 53rd.'

'They switched rides,' he guessed.

'Yeah, and we lost them there.'

Harlem, Bronx, Yonkers, they could be anywhere.

He glanced at his watch and got to his feet.

He had one more card to play.

NYPD POLICE COMMISSIONER BRUCE ROLANDO TOOK OUT his wallet and passed two ten-dollar notes to Quindica and Difiore.

'It's your fault,' he told Cutter as he burst into the conference room in the afternoon. 'Gina and Peyton were adamant you would insert yourself in this meeting.'

'Cutter,' Jamison greeted him from DC.

'Sir,' he nodded at the video conference screen and turned to his friend. 'I had to represent myself.'

Difiore snorted, turned it into a coughing fit and was studiously impassive when he looked at her suspiciously.

'This idea of yours—' the FBI Director began.

'Is the only way we can draw out Sheller, sir.'

'It's risky.'

'Yes, sir. Is there any other option? Detective Difiore and Special Agent in Charge Quindica haven't made much progress.'

He held up his hand quickly before the cop exploded. 'I mean your task force is held back by procedures, and then there are the dirty cops—'

'We got your point, Cutter,' said Rolando, granite-faced. No one liked to hear they had corrupt employees.

'How will it go down?' Jamison filled the awkward silence.

'Quindica and Difiore will hold a press conference. Announce they have a significant lead.'

'In what? The Task Force is not public knowledge.'

'On The Elitist, the race crimes, Crump, Martinelli ... they'll say they've found a link. A common thread.'

'That alone will not be enough.'

'I'll go on TV. Say my statement will blow apart the establishment. I will reveal some details of my past—not the classified parts, but I'll drop enough hints that Sheller will know I'm talking about him.'

'We'll have to put you up in a safe house,' Quindica said. 'We have several in the city.'

'We have them, too,' the detective chimed in, 'but—'

'Yours might be compromised.' Cutter shook his head. 'The Feds' too. I'll find one.'

'You think he'll take the bait?' Rolando polished his reading glasses.

'Yeah. I'm the one who knows the most about him. On the law enforcement side. He won't want his cover blown.'

'Only if Knowles had talked.'

Cutter started to nod, but caught himself quickly when he found Quindica and Difiore staring at him. 'There was no opportunity to question him?' he asked smoothly.

'Nope. He was dead before we arrived.'

'You found out who that club member was?'

'Vance Trent. But the real member is in Cancun, where he's got a second home. He hasn't been to the club in months. This intruder faked his appearance and membership card.'

'He also hacked into Trent's email,' Quindica added, 'and sent a confirmation to Tizzard's team that he was attending. That's serious chops.'

'He's got a team behind him,' Cutter asserted. 'There's no way he could do all that himself.'

'How do you figure that?' Difiore asked him when everyone's eyes swung his way.

'I haven't come across many lone operators who can do everything. Good at disguises, hacking ... nope. Fake Trent wasn't acting alone.'

'We've found no signs that there was anyone else with him, sir,' the detective told her boss. 'We're still investigating, however.'

'What about these rumors on social media? That Sheller would turn up at the rally?' Jamison's chair squeaked in protest when he leaned back and stretched.

'No one who looks like him at the event, sir,' Quindica replied. 'We ran facial recognition on all the attendees. However, all cameras burned out earlier in the morning—'

'All?' Jamison frowned.

'Yes, sir. We're looking into that, too. The club installed new ones, but not all were replaced. We don't have full coverage of the inside.'

'They burned out in the evening, too, didn't they?' Rolando growled.

'Yes, sir. Grogan's right. The impersonator had help.'

'Find out who he is. And set this up. Cutter's idea—crazy as it sounds, it just might work.'

'Yes, sir.'

82

Darrell was nervous, sweating, when he took up his position opposite the bodega.

He had gone to school in the morning and then slipped out during a change of class. He had raced back home and changed into a Tee and jeans.

Not feeling well, he texted Manuel.

Liar. You're going for recon.

Darrell didn't respond. He deleted the texts and went to the subway. Hoped and prayed his mom wouldn't find out that he had skipped school.

The store was easy to find. It was the only one of its kind for several blocks, and Nails' description had been accurate.

He drew out a bar of chocolate from his pocket, unwrapped it and bit into it as he watched.

AT TWELVE PM, DIFIORE WENT IN FRONT OF THE PRESS. SHE and Quindica decided the SAC wouldn't be with her.

'Let's not mention the Task Force. That will raise more questions.'

The detective had agreed.

She straightened her suit, drank from a glass of water and took the first question.

'The NYPD's giving us the runaround,' the reporter growled. 'The last few weeks have seen a rise in crime and shootings. The commissioner has nothing to say about those. He repeats his stock phrases—'

'Is there a question in that?' Difiore interrupted the journalist, who was from a tabloid that attacked the cops at every opportunity. There was no love lost between the publication and the police.

'What's happening with the crimes?' he yelled, red-faced, as a snicker went around the room.

'You should have led with that,' she replied and launched into details of the monthly stats on crimes and how they compared to previous periods.

'That's not what I asked,' the reporter raised his hand again, but she ignored him and pointed at another journalist.

She took question after question, surprised to find that she was enjoying the thrust and parry with the reporters. *Peyton must be smirking. She was sure I would do well. I was the one who was hesitant.*

It was toward the end of the press conference that she released her bombshell.

'We've got a confidential informant,' she said, 'who has proof that Assistant Chief Crump's killing is related to that of Officer Martinelli's. The two murders are connected to several other crimes in the city. Hold on!' she raised her hand when the reporters broke into a clamor, shouting questions, demanding answers.

'That's all I have for you for now,' she told them when they had quieted. 'Those are active investigations; we'll have to verify his account—you know how police work goes.'

She couldn't hold back a smile when the first journalist fired back. 'Not very well.'

'Your snitch is a man?' another reporter asked.

'I can't comment on their identity,' she deflected.

'You'll put him up in a safe house?'

'No other questions.'

GUNNER KEPT WATCHING WHEN THE DETECTIVE DISAPPEARED. A TV host came on screen and recapped the conference.

He looked away blindly when she summarized the key statements. He knew what they were.

He was cool. Calm. His breathing was steady.

He knew he was at his most dangerous then.

'Cray,' he called the hacker.

'Yes, boss. I saw it. You think they've got Grogan?'

'I don't know. I'll make some calls. Where is he?'

'He's not answering his office phone. I can send someone to check it out in person.'

'Do that. At his apartment, too.'

'He's got cameras there.'

'Get someone to walk up and down the stairs. Casually. Like a visitor to another floor.'

'Gotcha.'

He called the deputy chief he had spoken to earlier.

'Trejo, what was that about? That press conference?' he growled softly.

'Beats me,' the high-ranking officer confessed. 'It took us all by surprise. Difiore keeps to herself, like I said before—'

'Who's her informant?'

'I don't know. No one does. I tried to find out. I just finished a meeting with the commish. Asked him too. He brushed me away.'

'Find out. And where they've stowed him.'

He made more calls and got the same responses. It looked like the press conference had been authorized by Rolando himself, and other than he and Difiore, no one at the NYPD knew what was up.

None of my contacts, Gunner corrected himself.

He called Mease.

'Ring your NYPD friends,' he told the strategist. 'Find out what that press conference was about. ... You don't know? It would help if you watched other news rather than just the campaign coverage.' He broke it down for the accountant, who sucked in his breath sharply.

'Have they connected you?'

'That's what I want you to find out,' Gunner raged and ended the call.

THREE PM. DARRELL WAS EXHAUSTED, BUT HE STILL WATCHED. He didn't stick to one spot. He kept moving, finding different observation posts on opposite sides of the street as he made notes discreetly.

He could see the Chinese couple and the third owner, Moshe, occasionally through the windows. They had a smile for customers and frequently came out of the bodega and greeted passersby.

He could guess who the regulars were by the way they were greeted and made a note of their arrival times.

He would hang around till seven pm, and then he would head home.

CUTTER RANG SOME OF HIS FAVORITE TV REPORTERS AND invited them to a hotel room for an interview.

'It will be explosive,' he promised them. 'However, you cannot tell anyone beforehand that you're meeting me. Or where it will be held.'

'That's—'

'That's the only way it will go down. And it has to be live.'

A few reporters protested, but most went along. He provided

good sound bites, and his teasers, on the back of Difiore's conference, were enough to hook them.

Cutter booked a suite in a downtown luxury hotel and made arrangements with the manager, whom he knew.

'No shooting,' Dom Perez warned him.

'There won't be. It's a press conference.'

The manager, who had served with him, looked at him cynically. 'I know you, Cutter. The last time you booked a room with us, cartel shooters invaded my hotel.'

'Hey, that was over a year ago. Besides, you got good publicity out of it. These are well-known TV hosts,' he dropped a few names. 'No hitters this time. I promise.'

'I gave you the best suite,' his friend said grudgingly.

'Appreciate it. However, your front desk should take their phones and only then give them the room details. Security,' he said hurriedly, when Perez raised an eyebrow. 'I don't want anyone to know which room I'll be in. Not until the last minute.'

'I'll deploy some security personnel.'

'You're a rock star.'

'Flattery won't get you anywhere ... but an introduction to Ellen Ronning might.'

'Done.'

The TV journalist, a friend, was a highly respected reporter who was also single.

'She's a good person,' he cautioned his friend.

'And I'm not?'

At seven pm, Ronning and several other TV news anchors crowded the hotel's lobby, along with their crews.

Darrell was in the subway, clutching his notebook.

Cutter was in the suite, readying himself. The Fixer had an image. He had to maintain it. Checked red shirt tucked into blue jeans, a dull leather belt at his waist. Sneakers on his feet, customized with Vibram soles.

He surveyed the room critically and hid his Glock and spare guns in several strategic locations. He wasn't expecting intruders, but being prepared had been drilled into him enough to become habit.

Finally, he checked his escape routes.

One would be through the service door. Another through the elevator shaft and a third from the roof, where he had stowed another base-jumping kit.

He waited for the reporters.

'THAT'S GOOD WORK.' NAILS STUDIED DARRELL'S NOTES. HE took a photograph with his cell phone and handed the journal back to the teenager. 'Go back tomorrow and keep watch.'

'But—'

'Will that be a problem?'

The student moistened his lips and shook his head. *I'll have to skip school a second day. If Mama finds out, there'll be hell to pay.*

'YOU MIGHT HAVE HEARD DETECTIVE DIFIORE'S PRESS conference today,' Cutter began when Ronning signaled they were ready.

Six TV reporters seated on chairs, facing him. Their camera crews behind, filming the scene. He was on a couch, relaxed, left arm stretched out, right hand close to a cushion beneath which was his Glock.

'I'm the NYPD's informant,' he smiled.

83

Gunner's spoon stopped in midair. His eyes bulged when he took in Grogan's face on TV. He thumbed up the volume on the remote and pushed away his half-eaten dinner. What the Fixer had to say was more important.

'Why have you come forward?' Ellen Ronning answered. 'Aren't you risking the investigation?'

'What's there to risk?' He smiled broadly. 'I'm not going to reveal any inside information to you. Back to your first question ... I am hoping this gig'—he gestured at the cameras—'will encourage others. There will be many who know exactly what's gone down and who's behind it. Some of them will be troubled; their consciences will be pricking them. My message to them is: Step out. Tell the NYPD what you know, help them take the masterminds down. The cops will protect you.'

'We don't see any police here,' another reporter called out.

'You won't see them.' Grogan smiled confidently. 'They're there, however. I'll be going into a safe house after this interview.'

He waggled his fingers to invite questions, and they came thick and fast. Many of them were about what he knew, who Crump's killer was, who the shadowy perps were. He smiled, deflected some but answered other ones. With his dark hair slicked back, his green eyes standing out in the hotel room, Grogan had even the experienced TV hosts eating out of his hand.

Gunner became aware of a sound, like the hard scrape of rocks, and realized with a start that it came from him. He was gritting his teeth. He stopped himself and forced himself to stay calm until the interview was over. He turned off the TV and flung his dinner plate against the wall. His rage partly vented, he picked up his phone. There were already several missed calls. He took the most important ones.

'Trejo, stop talking and listen,' he rapped out when the cop's voice rose. 'He knows nothing. He and the NYPD are playing a game. Do you think you'd still be in your office if he had real information? You'd be arrested by now. I'll take care of it. Where's Difiore?'

'She's with her task force. I checked. She and that FBI woman were watching the interview.'

'Find out where this safe house is.'

'I'll try, but you'll—'

'I'll take care of it.'

He called another assistant chief, a deputy, several lower ranked cops and several politicians. He repeated the same message, that he would take care of it.

Mease was last.

'You saw it?'

'Yeah,' the accountant replied. 'How worried should we be?'

'Not at all. Grogan's playing a game—'

'Are you sure?'

'Did cops burst inside your house? Has Rubin been arrested? I'm still here. He's got nothing. I'll take care of him.'

'There should be no blowback.'

'There won't be.'

He called his cell leaders and checked that business was uninterrupted. It was.

'Nails, did you see the interview?'

'What interview?' his Brownsville leader asked. 'I've been on the street.'

'All good?'

'Yeah, why do you ask?'

'We need to meet. Same place.'

'Cray,' he yelled on his next call, 'why haven't you found where Grogan is?'

'Boss, he's gone off the radar.'

'GONE OFF THE RADAR?' Gunner roared. 'He was on TV, live, just a few minutes ago. Didn't you see that?'

'I did, boss. I'm checking with hotels to see where it took place.'

'He would have already left by now. Reach out to our contacts in TV. They'll know. What about that snitch? Why're you taking so long?'

'None of Nails' men called Grogan. I checked their call records. Our rat must be using some other phone or meeting Grogan somewhere. I'm checking out his office—'

'Why would they meet there?'

'Hiding in plain sight, boss. Like you've done all these years. It's so effective.'

'Find him. I don't care how. AND FIND GROGAN.'

DARRELL TEXTED HIS MOM TO SAY HE WOULD BE LATE AND shook his head when her usual reply came back. Anxious. Concerned. Angry.

It won't be for long, Mama, he told himself. He wasn't so sure about that, however. Cold dread filled him whenever he thought of Nails' hit. The store's owners seemed like nice people. *I should warn Cutter. But not yet. I need to know when it will happen.*

He ducked behind a car when Nails, whom he had been tailing, stopped to take a call on his cell. He had hung around discreetly after the gang split up in the evening. Finding out who the boss was would be his ticket to witness protection. For which he had to follow the gang leader and see if he met the mysterious person.

The gangster hadn't been in any hurry. He had walked the length of Rockaway and spoken to several dealers. Had checked out street corners and parking lots where deals went down and had then disappeared into a restaurant.

Darrell was worried that was where the boss would be, but when he saw Nails alone at a table, he was reassured. He brought out his last snack bar and had a cold, unsatisfactory dinner while the gang leader feasted on chicken thighs and lamb chops.

It was two am when Nails finally made a move. He walked back on Rockaway and took a circular route to Mother Gaston.

Darrell followed him from a distance, which wasn't difficult since he was small and could blend into the shadows. They passed their usual hangout and arrived at a fenced-in yard littered with trash.

A shadow moved and approached Nails.

Was that the boss?

No. The gang leader said something, climbed over the barrier and disappeared from sight.

There were a few abandoned vehicles right in front of the yard, but there were also some men who seemed to be a protection unit.

Darrell breathed shallowly as he crouched low and stepped off the sidewalk. No vehicles in sight. Store signs and dim street lighting cast a glow, but the sentries, four of them, were alert for vehicles and cops, not a small-sized teenager.

His heart in his mouth, he got as close as he could and rolled swiftly underneath a truck when a guard looked his way.

Had he been spotted?

He heard a chuckle and a soft murmur. A lighter flicked. A passing car illuminated him, but no one was paying attention.

Darrell crawled on his hands and knees and came to the hood of the vehicle. Checked the coast and found the next vehicle was an SUV. He held his breath and crept forward quickly and squeezed beneath it.

The yard was to his left.

He inched forward until he had the best view and let his eyes adjust to the darkness.

He could see Nails' faint outline as he shifted weight from one foot to the other.

He's alone. Did the boss leave? Why would the sentries still be there if he had?

The darkness in the yard seemed to part half an hour later. Something large and big moved.

That's the boss!

He was huge. He clapped Nails on the shoulder.

He seemed to be bald; his head gleamed faintly.

Darrell clawed at his chest and extracted his phone from the tape. He froze when his head bumped against the chassis. The guards' murmur stopped. It felt like the earth stopped for long moments, and then a laugh reached him.

He relaxed, held up the phone with trembling fingers, and aimed its camera at the two men in the yard. He zoomed in as much as he could and turned on video recording.

'Have you got everything for the hit?' Gunner rasped at his cell leader.

'Yesterday was our first recon, boss. There'll be another run later today, and we hit tomorrow.'

'No time for that. Take them out today.'

'Boss—'

'You heard me. IT HAS TO HAPPEN TODAY,' Gunner

repeated loudly. His guards glanced his way, prepared to come with guns blazing, but he stood them down with an angry wave.

'It's risky, boss,' Nails protested. 'Grogan nearly got me the last time.'

'I want him to come, don't you get it? It's a trap to sucker him. I thought I explained it to you. Are you stupid—' He broke off and breathed out harshly and then said calmly, 'Do it today. Around lunchtime.'

'There could be customers.'

'Don't care. I'll send more hitters. They'll grab Grogan when he shows up. They'll have getaway vehicles and fire on cops, too. We've done this before.'

'Yes, boss.'

'Who will you take?'

'Marv and Chino. The three of us are the best shooters in my cell.'

'Don't fail. That Jew and the Chinese should die tomorrow.'

And if everything went to plan, Grogan would be captured. Once that happened, it wouldn't matter if Nails or Cray couldn't find out who the snitch was.

Gunner would extract the information from the Fixer.

Slowly and painfully.

84

Cutter stopped taking calls at ten am. They had started after his interview. Journalists, bloggers—everyone in the media who knew him rang to get more details on the story.

He got tired of saying, *I said everything I had to say*, or, *you saw the interview. I've nothing more to add.*

Rolando and Jamison messaged to check how he was doing. *Still alive*, he replied.

Difiore displayed her tender, loving side with: *We'll assume you're dead if you don't reply*.

Sorry to disappoint you, he messaged her.

He yawned and stretched and climbed out of his SUV, in which he had spent the night parked near Javits Center in Hell's Kitchen. He checked into a tourist hotel and showered, then drove to Times Square, where he parked illegally. He went to a fast-food joint where he had breakfast and, for a moment, forgot about his assignment and Sheller and the world and watched tourists snap photographs. That reminded him of Riley, and he shut down those thoughts and glanced at his watch.

'Key and access code are in a downtown lockbox,' Meghan replied crisply when he called.

'This is a mansion,' he protested when he checked out the place on his maps application. He had gone to them for help and the Petersens had come through.

'You want it or not?' Beth's impatience coming through plain and clear.

Cutter studied the images they had sent. A townhouse on Henderson Place on the East River. Red brick front. Sturdy door with knocker. Four bedrooms and equal number of bathrooms, but those didn't interest him. Five floors. Terrace on the floor that overlooked the street. A fire exit at the back of the house opened into a central yard, from which there was egress.

'We've used it several times,' Meghan said, seemingly reading his thoughts. 'That's almost like a private street. It's easy to seal off and protect.'

'Whose is it?'

'Why do you need to know?'

'He's worried we'll send a bill,' her sister snickered.

'Cutter,' Meghan replied impatiently. 'That's a good place. Secure. It can house an entire NYPD precinct—'

'I'll take it,' he said hurriedly, before she changed her mind.

'That lockbox has everything. Keys. Security codes, camera locations.'

CRAY HAD IMAGES TO SIFT THROUGH. HE HAD HACKED INTO the security cameras around Grogan's office and copied two months of their feed. He ran a social media face-recognition algorithm that matched everyone who entered the building to those who had online accounts.

He eliminated the building's occupants and other office residents by looking up the tenants and working out the employees. He checked off delivery drivers, too. He could circle back to those later if he found no one suspicious.

It wasn't easy. He had to write programs, some of which were to hack into the DMV database, the Social Security one. He got out of his chair, massaged a crick in his neck, and went to make coffee. The search would work in the background and create a list of possible suspects whom he could investigate.

Darrell took up his position a bit later than the previous day. He had to escape from school, and then he had to shake off Manuel, who kept asking annoying questions.

The bodega owners were there, visible through the windows. A customer walked in as he watched, and placed an order. The teenager's mouth watered and his stomach rumbled as he imagined the smells of fresh baking. He searched his pocket for his usual—*What the?*

Nails! What's he doing here? Marv and Chino, they're there too.

Fear gripped him as the three gangbangers walked up the street, apart from one another, as if they were strangers. The Brownsville leader slowed when he took a call, finished it quickly, searched the sidewalk and found him. Gave him a hard stare and made a discreet gesture.

I have to keep watch and alert them.

His mouth went dry when the implications hit him.

They're going to kill the owners.

85

Luck played a role.

Cutter was back on Lafayette, drinking coffee on the sidewalk, leaning against the storefront, checking out the outside of his building and the street for surveillance when he got the call.

'IT'S ME. DARRELL. NAILS IS GOING TO KILL YOUR FRIENDS. HE'S MINUTES FROM THE STORE. MARV AND CHINO—'

'HEY!' another voice broke in. 'Give my phone back. How dare you—'

The call cut off, but it didn't matter anymore. Cutter had moved before it ended.

His coffee cup fell to the street. He was several feet away when the liquid sloshed out and spread across the concrete. He was racing at full sprint, shouting, urging, cursing and pleading for people to make way for him.

He tried the bodega. Got a busy line. Called Difiore and Quindica. Got their voicemails. It was a repeat of the holdup.

SHOOTING'S GOING DOWN AT THE STORE, he said in a terse message. He stuffed his phone into his pocket and ran. His eyes scanned the sidewalk crowd, found gaps through which he could slide, a brush against a body here, a leap over a trash can there, a startled squawk from someone. He ran heedlessly, working out how it would go down.

He'll make them suffer. Beat them up. Sheller will want that.

It was also a trap to draw him out. Which meant the Lions' founder would send more hitters.

Cutter cut across Lafayette recklessly as brakes jammed, horns blared and windows rolled down to let out angry swears. He continued down Howard Street, turned left on Center Street and sped up.

Towards the back of the store.

Rear entrance. Window on the low, sloping roof.

That would be his way in.

He hoped he wasn't too late.

86

Nails took the call just as they neared the street.

'Yeah?'

'It's me.'

He straightened when he recognized Gunner.

'Are you—'

'Boss, we're outside the bodega. The hit's going down.'

'Call me when it's done. Support's on its way.'

The Brownsville leader pocketed his phone and nodded imperceptibly at his men. No change to the plan. They had worked together for so long that words were unnecessary.

He searched for Darrell and found him. The teenager shook his head, which meant the coast was clear. No cops in sight.

His two shooters went inside the store.

Chino went to the counter with a smile on his face. The grin remained in place as he leaned over and yanked the phone so hard its cable slipped out. He flung it to the floor and caught the Chinese man by his collar and spat on him.

'WHAT—' the Chinese woman shrieked. She ran from behind the dessert counter and slid to an abrupt stop when Chino and Marv produced their guns.

The Jew came from behind an aisle, his eyes sharp. He

slowed down and raised his hands when Nails shut the door, locked it from the inside, turned the *OPEN* sign to *CLOSED* and lowered the blinds.

'Last time was a holdup,' he said with a chuckle when the owners seemed to recognize him. 'This one's a killing.'

He shoved a stand and sent it crashing against the wall display. That made more space in front of the long counter.

'Get over here,' he ordered.

'PLEASE DON'T DO THIS. TAKE OUR MONEY—' He slapped the woman so hard she reeled against the counter. Blood flowed from her split lip.

He caught her, heaved her across the counter, then shoved her against it.

'You two,'—he waved his gun at the husband and the Jew—'join her.'

'PLEASE—' the Chinese man began but cut himself off when Nails raised his gun.

They shuffled over to flank the woman, all three of them standing with their hands raised.

'She's quite a babe,' Marv leered.

'She's old, isn't she?'

'They're the best.'

'You want to have some fun?'

'We have time?'

'Go ahead. Darrell will warn us. Boss is sending support. Chino, check the rear.'

'All good here,' the hitter called out from the back. 'Door's closed.'

'Stay there. Watch out for Grogan.'

Nails stood back and grinned as the woman moaned and made to escape, but Marv slapped her again and ripped the front of her shirt.

Front and rear were secure. Grogan would most likely come down Lafayette, where he would receive a warm welcome. They needed to stall until he showed up, however, which was why he had encouraged Marv to assault the woman.

His loins stirred at the sight of her full undershirt. *Never had a Chinese before*. *Nope*. He couldn't get involved. *Make it spectacular*, Gunner had told him. *And then kill them*.

Raping the woman in front of her husband was spectacular enough.

'You,' he prodded the Jew, who was impassive, his dark eyes still, watchful. 'You don't look scared. You haven't said anything. You haven't begged. BEG!' he roared and slammed the barrel on his forehead.

The Jew fell back with a small groan, but he didn't speak. The Chinese man swore and lunged at the leader. He skidded to a halt when Nails jammed his gun against his mouth.

'You can die right now. You want that?'

The man raised his hands and backed off, venomously. Nails' smirk turned to a laugh at the sounds of a scuffle. The woman struggling furiously, silently, with Marv.

'You can't control her, bro?' He sneered and looked at the window when tires squealed outside. He covered his captives with his gun and shuffled to the window to peer through the blinds.

Two SUVs at the curb in front of the store. Both of them filled with hard-faced white men.

'Help's here. Take her, Marv.'

87

Cutter was still several doors away when he took to the roof.

He planted a foot against a white-painted wall and leapt into the air. Grabbed a drainpipe and clambered up the side of the two-story building and ran down the length of its roof.

A rooftop sunbather leapt and grabbed a towel to cover herself. She yelled at him, but he was past listening.

He reached the edge of the roof and looked down. The line of buildings broke down to a row of stores, with lower roofs. The bodega was the fourth from where he was. Center Street visible from his vantage point. Busy as usual. No gun-toting thugs outside. No cops, either.

He got to his knees, hung off the roof by his fingertips, and let go. Slid down the vertical wall with his feet jammed tight to slow down his fall, then pushed away. He landed on the lower roof and rolled smoothly. Increased surface area to absorb the impact. Muscle memory triggering automatically from his parkour training.

He got to his feet and sprinted, conscious of the clock ticking. Straining his ears for the sounds of gunshots. First store roof navigated. An assistant at the back entrance looked at him and gawped.

Second roof had air-con equipment that he lost precious seconds circling around. The third roof was smooth and obstacle-free, and he slowed there and crouch-walked.

Rear of the store was empty. Next roof was the bodega. He crossed over to it, his moves liquid-easy.

The window was wide open to let in air. No signs of anyone at the back, on the outside.

He got to his belly and crawled forward.

Peered forward carefully. Back door closed. A shape ... yeah, that was a shooter. Gun down his side. Relaxed. Face turned to the inside of the store.

From where Cutter heard Lin Shun scream.

88

Nails, Chino and Marv. Three men, one of them at the back. Another seemed to be assaulting Lin Shun. No shots that Cutter had heard.

The animal inside him yapped when another muffled shout came to him.

She's alive. Chang and Moshe, too. Nails will make them watch, he concluded, and with that, he acted.

Speed and shock.

Cutter used them to his advantage as he threw himself through the window, his elbows raised to cover his face.

He landed easily, the familiar cold filling him as the hitter started to turn with a grunt of surprise.

'Don't,' he snarled.

He jammed his Glock tight against the back of his neck, caught him by the left shoulder and pushed him ahead.

Small passage. Storage racks on each side. A bathroom. The rear of the inside of the store. The dessert counter to his left. The central stand to his right, fallen to its side, display items strewn on the floor.

Lin Shun half-sitting, her shirt torn, her lips bleeding, her eyes wild, scrabbling with a hood. Who stopped and cursed when Cutter entered—and there was Nails, who was equally startled at his sudden arrival.

Lin Shun gasped and cried, 'CUTTER!'

He shot her attacker in the face.

His captive snatched the opportunity to dive out of the way and turned around to bring up his gun.

Cutter anticipated the move and fired into his body without shifting from his position because Nails was there, ahead of him and the gangbanger's gun was rising as well and he had to paint himself as a target.

That was the only way he could save his friends—and he jerked when the first bullet caught his armor and another grazed his neck.

His Glock returned fire, spent shells rising out of it and spilling onto the floor as each pull got the firing pin to strike the primer, which got the gases to propel bullets out at one thousand two hundred and thirty feet a second. Two struck Nails and brought him down, but Cutter wasn't done.

A fast-change and a new magazine. He stood his ground and shot Nails in the face to make sure, and that was when he saw the shadows move outside the store.

'GET BEHIND THE COUNTER,' he yelled, just as the door crashed and two hitters fired as they rushed in. Their rounds went wide. Cutter's didn't.

He shot them down as another banger showed up who fired from behind the falling bodies and he jerked as another slug got him in the chest.

He fell to his knees, slapped in another magazine as the sirens seemed to flood the store and the sounds of pounding footsteps and shots reached him. No other gangsters showed in the door.

'POLICE! STAND DOWN,' a voice yelled.

Cutter dragged himself back and rested against the cake counter. He blinked and wiped the sweat tiredly from his face.

'I'm good,' he whispered when Lin Shun tore around from where she was hiding and came over to him.

'Armor. It saved me again.' He smiled weakly and raised his eyes when two shadows fell over him.

Difiore and Quindica.

The warm reception had arrived.

89

'We were in a meeting.' The detective held her phone up.

It was the nearest she had ever come to an apology.

Cutter nodded. He drank greedily from the water bottle that she thrust at him and wiped his mouth with his sleeve. Cops from the Emergency Service Unit were everywhere. Armed, alert, they checked out the inside of the store, conferred briefly with their officers and the detectives, and declared the store free of threat.

'We got a bunch of hitters.' Quindica nodded her head at the street. 'Looks like the plan was to shoot you when you showed up.'

'Lift me.'

'What?'

'Sheller would have asked them to grab and get me to wherever he is. Killing me on the street isn't what he would have wanted. You got anyone else?'

'Just them.'

'Civilians?'

'None injured. No cops, either. A few broken windows; that's the only damage. There were two SUVs filled with men. Some of them opened fire on us, but many of them escaped.'

Darrell got away!

Nails must have posted him as the sentry.

Why did he warn me that late? He must have known of the plan. He could have called earlier. I would have called the cops. We could have captured Nails alive and got where Sheller is from him.

NYPD technicians filled the store and started recording the crime scene. A paramedic came over to him, bathed and dressed his wound. 'It'll heal,' she informed him. He thanked her and leaned back as his body dealt with the remnants of adrenaline.

'Cutter?'

He opened his eyes as Difiore loomed before him.

'You okay?'

'Yeah.'

'Walk us through it.'

He started with his arrival through the roof.

'No,' she frowned. 'Track back. Why didn't you come down Lafayette? Someone warn you?'

'That's what I was doing. I spotted the blinds and *Closed* sign. Took me back to the holdup. That's when I took to the roof.'

'Your phone,' she demanded.

He watched as she scrolled through it and handed it to Quindica for a double check. He had deleted Darrell's call from the logs when they had been with the ESU commander.

'You've got to believe me, Difiore.'

She snorted in disbelief and motioned for him to continue narrating. Listened silently with no expression on her face and sized him up when he had finished.

'Those plates?'

'Don't go without them.' He tapped his armor. 'Ever since those thugs hit my apartment.'

She turned away when a cop came to her and spoke softly.

'She always like that?' he asked Quindica, who was wearing an amused smile.

'Nope. She doesn't like you.'

'I wouldn't have guessed!'

'None of them are talking,' the detective reported. 'Those hitters have clammed up.'

'They must be Sheller's best men. They know he'll take care of them.'

Difiore and Quindica nodded in agreement and stepped away when his friends came to him.

'You took your time,' Moshe said accusatorially. But his eyes belied his words, and his hand reached out to squeeze Cutter's shoulder in silent thanks.

'How're you?' Cutter asked Lin Shun, who responded by hugging him hard and burying her face in his chest.

'I thought ...' she trembled and trailed off.

He held her until her shaking eased and she drew off and went to her husband, who raised his shoulders, lost for words.

'Hey.' Cutter tried to lighten the mood. 'You would have come to my aid, too.'

'Maybe,' Moshe said, pausing to think about it, 'or maybe not.'

Cutter grinned as he sized his friends up. *They'll come through. They'll chalk it up to another life experience. Lin Shun is tough. She won't let this attempt affect her. Moshe ... this is nothing for him.*

He looked up when Difiore beckoned at him.

'It's time?'

'Yeah,' she said.

He and the cops had one more move to make.

90

'None of them are talking,' Cray said nervously as Gunner watched the TV in the Harlem bar.

Fixer Fixes Thugs!

Brownsville Gang Revenge Attack Fixed!

One sensationalized banner followed another as Grogan's dramatic intervention was covered by every TV channel. Journalists interviewed witnesses, onlookers, police officers, hostage negotiators, anyone they could get hold of, to embellish the story, which was that Cutter Grogan had interrupted the Brownsville Gang yet again and had taken out its leader, Steve Patchey, and two of his senior men. Several other gang members had turned up and there had been a brief firefight with the cops, who had arrested many of them, while the rest had escaped.

'We don't know why they returned to this store,' an NYPD spokesperson replied to reporters. 'Mr. Grogan was in the vicinity and acted.'

Detective Difiore came on, but she offered very little detail. 'We're investigating,' was her stock answer. 'Yeah, we've arrested some of them.'

'They won't talk, boss.' Cray moistened his lips when Gunner looked at him coldly.

The Lions' founder didn't say a word. He turned off the TV and went behind the bar. Poured himself a drink and gulped it down in one swallow. He slammed the glass on the counter and wiped his lips.

'Nails and Knowles,' he growled. 'Two of my best men. I was going to promote them. Split our New York operations between them.'

'HOW WAS GROGAN THERE?' he roared and grabbed Cray by his shirt. 'HOW DID HE KNOW?'

'It ... must ... have ... been ... that ... snitch,' the hacker stammered as he tried to breathe.

'WHY HAVEN'T YOU FOUND HIM BY NOW?'

'It takes time, boss.' Cray staggered when Gunner flung him away. 'I'm running algorithms—'

'I DON'T WANT TO KNOW. COME TO ME WHEN YOU'VE FOUND HIM.'

He had collected himself when he met Mease in the Melrose parking lot.

'How bad is it?'

'Nothing I can't handle,' he scoffed. 'I know every one of those men who've been arrested. I sent them myself. They won't talk.'

'If they did?'

'What do they know? That I'm alive? So what? There's nothing to connect me and the Lions to Rubin.'

The strategist stroked his chin and nodded finally. 'What will you do about them?'

'They're lawyered up already. Their story is they were hanging outside the store. They didn't know what was happening inside. They've got no connection to Nails. They panicked when the cops arrived and fired on them. They'll do some time for that. Nothing more.'

'What about Grogan?'

'I've got plans for him.'

'You saw his interview on TV? He's turned informant.'

'I saw. He knows nothing. He'll say I'm alive. That this Brownsville Gang is the Rising Lions. It's his word. We've removed all traces of my gang.'

'HE SAID HE KNOWS ABOUT CRUMP'S KILLING.'

'He's just talking,' Gunner replied flatly, unmoved by Mease's shrill yell. 'He wants publicity. That's how he gets business. I told you I would take care of him. Besides,' he said savagely, 'it's not as if you and Rubin aren't using this. He went running to the TV cameras when this shootout happened. He condemned gang culture. I saw the polls, too. He got an uptick, didn't he? You're benefiting from what's going down.'

'*We* are benefiting,' Mease corrected him. 'We're in this together.'

'You seem to be forgetting that yourself.'

Gunner spun on his heel and walked off without a further word.

When he was alone, he called the deputy chief. 'Trejo, find out where Grogan is hiding. Where's that safe house?'

'That'll be difficult,' the cop replied nervously. 'I told you. Difiore does not share—'

'Trejo,' Gunner snarled. 'I don't care what you have to do to get that address. Even if they find out you're my informant. I want that address. Do whatever it takes.'

91

'What is this place?' Difiore exclaimed as Cutter escorted the detective and Quindica inside the townhouse.

'The safe house I was telling you about.'

'This?' the SAC's jaw dropped as she took in the high ceiling, the chandelier and upscale fittings. 'How did you find this?'

'Grogan, did you break into it?'

He chuckled when the detective looked at him suspiciously. 'Nope. Everything's legit. Some friends got it for me. We can use it for as long as needed. Go, check it out.'

'Five floors!' Quindica shook her head when she and the detective joined him later at the kitchen island. 'The FBI's got some neat places, but this beats any of them by a mile.'

'Let's not even talk about the NYPD safe houses,' Difiore muttered. 'Alright,' she addressed Cutter, 'what else have you got for us?'

He had driven the two of them in his SUV after they finished the procedural stuff at OnePP. She had taken in the false number plates but made no comment. None of them had commented on his counter-surveillance maneuvers on the way up.

'Henderson Place.' He brought up the street on his maps

application. 'This is where we are,' he said, pointing to the house. 'Carl Schurz Park at the back and the East River beyond.'

'I saw the views,' Quindica sighed. 'I'll have to sell my kidneys, both of them, my legs, and even then, I won't be close to the down payment.'

'A back entrance opens to the private yard,' Cutter grinned. 'It isn't overlooked. High metal fence at the back, which leads to the park. Two entrances at the front. One through the main door, which is teak but has reinforced steel inside, and a side entrance—'

'I didn't see that.' Difiore craned her head. 'Oh, there, between this and the neighboring house?'

'Yeah. The two homeowners worked together to build it. Shared access that opens into both gardens through two doors. You wouldn't see it from the street, camouflaged to look like the front wall. Security system, which has alerts into the 12th Precinct.'

'We won't want that.' Difiore took charge and nudged him out of the way.

Cutter left them to work out the security details. He pulled out his phone and punched Darrell's number. Was about to make a call when he stopped himself. *Can't call his phone. Sheller will suspect they have a snitch.* He tried his mom, got her voicemail and left a message for her, asking her to call him when she was home.

'We have a problem,' Quindica announced when he joined them. 'All these houses will have security cameras. They would have recorded our arrival. If Sheller is as smart and well-connected as we think he is—'

'None of those are working. Yep,' he shrugged at their expressions of disbelief. 'You can check for yourselves.'

Both reached for their phones and made calls. Hung up and looked at each other and then at him.

'How did you organize that? This is an upscale neighborhood. Such residents like their security.'

'All the townhouses in Henderson Place are empty. Vacation season.'

'All of them?

'There aren't that many. This is a cul-de-sac. Six houses on this side of the street, another six on the other. Bankers, CEOs, a few foreign investors own or rent the rest of those properties. They'll be in their villas in the Hamptons or Europe or wherever the super-rich go for their vacations.'

'You sure of this?'

'I'll stake my life on it.'

'You'll be doing just that.'

Beth and Meg said they'll be empty. I'll take their word any day.

'That's even better.' Difiore looked at the SAC. 'We can position our team across the street. Snipers on the roof. Plainclothes members in the park.'

'We need to familiarize ourselves—'

'Stay the night,' Cutter offered. 'I'll cook … and brew some of that coffee.'

'That still won't make us friends,' the detective warned him, clearly tempted.

'Such is my life.'

92

It was late at night when Cutter got time for himself.

Quindica had opened up about herself and had also gotten him to talk. Difiore had been her usual self; a little more relaxed, but not by much.

No one else knew of the safe house. The detective and the SAC would check out the neighborhood and only then would they call in the rest of their team. His stay as an informant had begun, however.

'We'll protect you tonight,' Quindica assured him.

He didn't doubt her. From their files he knew the two of them were as badass as any operators he had worked with.

They had taken two of the bedrooms on two floors, while Cutter took the couch in the living room. This was no hardship; it was ten feet long, three feet deep and as comfortable as a bed.

He turned on his laptop and checked his phone for any activity from the cloning software. There didn't seem to be ...

He stopped when he spotted the recording.

'Yeah?'

'It's me.'

'Are you—'

'Boss, we're outside the bodega. The hit's going down.'

'Call me when it's done. Support's on its way.'

Nails, and that second voice was surely Sheller's. He searched feverishly for previous recordings and compared them to the segment he had gotten from The Elitist.

No doubt about it. The club recording was very brief, but there was no question that hard, authoritative voice was the Lions' founder's.

Where is he?

Bronx, the software told him. He cursed loudly when the program didn't give him any more detail on the address.

He checked the time. Eleven pm. *Will they be awake? Should I call?*

He called.

'Cutter,' Meghan answered at first ring. No traces of sleep in her voice.

'Did I wake you?'

'I'm talking to you, aren't I?'

'I'll call later—'

'What is it? We were leaving the office.'

'That software got a hit on Sheller's phone. However, I don't have an address.'

'Hold up.'

The sound of background voices. Beth's coming across loudly. 'We should send him a bill. You heard that, Cutter?'

'Yes, ma'am,' he replied.

'Okay,' the elder twin came on presently. 'I see that recording. Earlier today, right?'

'Yeah.'

'Bronx.'

'That's all I've got. Can you find an address?'

'Nope, that call was so short it bounced off only one tower. That alone isn't enough to narrow down the location. That SIM's out of commission now. Sheller probably destroyed it, and the phone as well. Nails' phone—'

'Is with the Task Force.'

'He won't call it again. Darrell is your best bet.'

'He won't get close to Sheller. That's not how he works.'

'You'll need some luck, in that case.'

Luck was on Cray's side.

His algorithm had flagged several possible suspects, people who had entered Grogan's office building. Facial rec and social security programs had worked together to give him identities. He sat at his screen and checked each one of the twenty-eight names.

Jared Twinnings, Building Inspector. Nope.

Kayla Hart, Insurance Clerk. She wasn't part of the gang.

Pieter Ditchman, Sales Rep. Cray had never seen the man in his life, and he knew every member of Nails' gang.

He ran down the entire list and sat back, defeated, when every one of them had been crossed out.

What else could he do?

He swept his arm across his desk in frustration, scattering the printouts to the floor. Swept his hand through his hair and composed himself. Rage and anger clouded thinking. He had to be more like Gunner, who rarely lost his cool.

He bent and picked up the photographs and returned to the table. Sat down abruptly when the uppermost one seemed to ring a bell.

Carmel Ward. Clerk in a law firm on Grand Street. Not far from Grogan's office. Facial rec had identified her from an internet moms' group.

What was it about her that pinged his radar? There were no women in Nails' gang. Heck, none in all the Lions' cells.

Ward.

Wasn't there someone—

Darrell Ward!

That disposable kid in the gang.

Carmel Ward was his mother.

93

Gunner's massive fists opened and closed as he took in Cray's account. He kept looking at the photographs of the mom and the kid.

'I called you last night, boss,' the hacker said apologetically.

'I was asleep.'

'I called Peels. He agreed to open the club this early for us—'

'Stop talking.'

It was only the two of them in the Bronx club. The Lions' founder sipped the coffee Peels had brewed for him before he left the two alone.

'He's a disposable.'

'Yes, boss.'

'Why did his mother go to Grogan?'

'No idea, boss. But it's not a coincidence. Darrell knew about the holdup. He was the lookout for the hit. He must have used some other phone to—'

'Cray,' Gunner said softly, 'I can think for myself.'

Silence fell in the bar.

The Lions' founder closed his eyes momentarily as the fury rose in him. A vein in his neck ticked angrily. 'Where is he?' he asked roughly.

'At home. I placed his phone there.'

'His mom?'

'She's at home, too. It's seven am.'

'Lift them.'

Darrell hadn't slept well. He had been jumpy and nervous the previous day as he had watched the cops take down the extra hitters Gunner had sent. He hadn't seen what went down in the store until he caught the NYPD press conference on TV in a storefront.

Cutter's alive!

Relief had swept over him as he headed home. Fear had replaced it soon after. What would happen to the gang? How would he get intel?

The recording he had made the previous night was unclear. All he could make out was a bald head, a large shape and a few indistinct voices.

There was no doubt the mystery man was key. The way Nails had deferred to him made it clear he was the boss.

Maybe the gang will dissolve, he thought as he buttoned his shirt. That would be ideal. It would free him immediately, and his life could return to normal.

Cheered up, he went to the living room and surprised his mom by hugging her tightly.

'What brought that on?' she said, laughing and ruffling his hair.

The buzzer sounded before he could reply.

'Yeah?'

'Delivery for Ms. Ward,' a tinny voice sounded.

'You expecting something, Mama?'

'It's from the law office.' The man seemed to have heard them.

'Must be some case papers,' his mother frowned. 'Why would they—'

Darrell opened the door before his mom finished and fell back with a yell when the hitters barged in and whipped him with a gun, and the last memory he had was of his mama screaming.

94

Gunner paced the eleventh floor in the Melrose building. Scaffolding around it. Bags of concrete, cables, tools, wooden planks strewn untidily. The builders had left in a hurry when the city had served them with a Stop Order for violating several codes. It had remained incomplete, abandoned, until Rubin's company had acquired it. The Lions' boss had urged him to leave it unfinished, to be used as a meeting place and interrogation center.

He went to the edge of the floor and peered down. Melrose Avenue to his right. East 154th ahead of him; another high-rise, completed and occupied, beyond. He wasn't worried about being spotted. He had guards on the ground and several escape routes. Besides, he and his men would be hardly visible from anyone watching from the other building.

He turned at a sound.

The mother had come to. She looked at him, dazed, and then at his men. Cray among the ten of them.

'What—? Who are you?' Her scratchy voice gathered strength. 'Why are we here? WHO ARE YOU? LET US GO!' She ended with a shout as she found she and her son were tied up.

Darrell's eyes flickered at her voice. He shook his head groggily and licked his lips when awareness returned.

'Mrs. Ward,' Gunner rasped. 'Don't waste your breath. No one can hear you.'

'WHO ARE YOU?'

'Why don't you ask your son.'

'DARRELL! WHAT DOES HE MEAN BY THAT? WHO ARE THESE MEN? WHY HAVE THEY BROUGHT US HERE?'

'Mama,' the boy began. He trembled and broke away from her eyes. His shoulders shook as he sobbed. 'I'm sorry, Mama—'

'Mrs. Ward,' Gunner said emotionlessly, 'It looks like your son has kept you in the dark. He's part of my gang. We are the Rising Lions. No,' he spotted the surprised expression on the teenager. 'You haven't heard that name. Very few have. All you know is Nails—'

'DARRELL, IS THAT TRUE?' the mother cut in. 'HAVE YOU BEEN IN THIS GANG?' Her lips curled spitefully. 'WITH THESE MEN?'

Gunner chuckled mirthlessly and backhanded her casually. She fell to the floor with a scream. The boy shouted in anger and struggled, but he was bound tightly to his chair and all he could do was swear and curse balefully.

'Some respect, Mrs. Ward.' The gang founder went to the fallen woman and righted her chair. 'Your life and your son's are in my hands. Yeah. That's the answer to your questions. Your precious boy has been working with us. Running errands, hustling drugs, keeping watch, like the good disposable that he is. But he wasn't that good. Were you, Darrell?'

Gunner punched the teenager in the belly and followed it up with a slap that broke his lips.

'This was on your phone.' He held up the cell and played the recording on it. His meeting with Nails. 'You were the snitch. You informed on us to Grogan. There's only one reason you're alive. Who else has gotten this? Who knows what about us?'

He grabbed the boy's hair and forced him to look at him.

'TALK!'

The teenager was struck dumb with fear. His eyes darted here and there, landed on his mother and flitted away in shame.

'Jude?'

'Yes, boss?' One of his hitters stepped forward.

'You told me once you always wanted a black woman. There she is. Take her.'

Carmel Ward screamed. Darrell lunged forward in fury and fell back when Gunner hit him in the chest. Jude, a swarthy man, stepped in front of the mother and unzipped his jeans.

'Don't be afraid, babe,' he crooned.

'DARRELL!'

'CUTTER'S GOT IT. HE'S GOT EVERYTHING. YOUR MEETING WITH NAILS. WHERE YOU LIVE. EVERYTHING.'

'I don't believe you.' Gunner watched as the mother flinched and shuddered when Jude cupped her face. 'Why don't we watch your mama? That's what you call her? It'll be a good show.'

'NO. PLEASE. I'M TELLING THE TRUTH. CALL HIM. DON'T TOUCH HER.'

'Go ahead, Jude. You shy?'

'No, boss. I been wanting something like this a long time.' The thug kicked off his jeans and paraded in his underwear.

'Please don't do this,' Carmel Ward sobbed as she tried to shrink from the advancing man. 'He told you. Let us go—'

'He lied to you. How do I know he's telling the truth?'

'I am,' Darrell pleaded. 'You've got to believe me. I swear—'

Gunner punched him so hard that he toppled sideways. His mother shrieked and tried to rise but fell back when Jude shoved her down.

The Lions' boss grabbed the teenager and righted him. Clicked his tongue impatiently when he found the boy was out.

'Cray, you believe him?'

'It's possible, boss.'

'Jude, stop. Dress up.'

'But—'

'You'll get your chance. I promise you.'

'Cray?'

'Yes, boss.'

'Call Grogan.'

95

'We're good to go.' Quindica swallowed a mouthful of French omelet and leaned back with a sigh. 'As soon as you brew some more of that coffee.'

Cutter grinned as he filled their mugs and presented them with a flourish. He had whipped up breakfast while they went out for their surveillance run. The place was ideal; that was their summary when they returned.

'Yeah,' he agreed as Difiore toyed with her phone.

'Let's do it,' she said as she finished her coffee. She was thumbing a number just as Cutter's phone rang.

'One moment.' He held up a finger and checked the number. *Darrell. Should I take the call in front of them? It won't matter if I don't mention his name.*

'What's up, buddy?' he answered cheerfully.

'Grogan. It's been a long time.'

He froze for a moment. Checked the caller ID and returned it to his ear.

'I hear you're looking for me,' the voice rasped.

Who is it? Difiore lipped, reading his body language. Quindica stood up and checked the street through the windows, alert for any threat.

'You're thinking how I got this phone. Where Darrell is—'

Difiore snatched the phone from his hand, put it on speaker and placed it on the island.

'Stop wondering.' There was a sound of flesh striking flesh and a voice screamed.

'CUTTER, HE'S GOT US. MAMA AND ME!'

'You heard the boy, Grogan—'

'What do you want?'

'You. I have been looking for you, too. But not just you. Bring the recordings from Darrell's phone. Everything.'

What recording?

'You may choose not to come. Or you may bring cops along.' A slap followed by a woman's shriek. 'You can guess what will happen. We'll disappear. My boys will play with Mrs. Ward before I cut her and her boy to pieces. And then we'll hunt you.'

'Where do I meet you?'

'I'll tell you where.'

Cutter gripped the edges of the marble top so tight that his fingers turned white. There was a roaring in his ears ... it was Difiore, who was yelling at him furiously.

'THAT WAS SHELLER! WHO DOES HE HAVE? WHAT RECORDING DO YOU HAVE? WHAT THE HELL'S GOING ON?'

'His name is Darrell,' Cutter responded dully. He slumped in his chair and told them about Darrell and how it had started. There was nothing to play for by holding back information from them.

Difiore and Quindica stared at him for long seconds when he had finished.

'You could have come to us. We would have found a way to—'

'He doesn't trust cops, Difiore,' he said wearily. 'Don't you get it? Going to you was the first advice I gave him. He asked—'

'Enough,' Quindica slammed her palm on the island. 'We can get him. Where's this recording?'

'I don't have it. I don't know what he's talking about.'

He raised his hands helplessly at their expressions. 'It's true. Darrell must have caught Sheller on his phone.'

'He bought time.' Quindica caught on fast. 'By saying he's given it to you.'

'When this is over,' Difiore said venomously, 'I'm going to—' She caught herself and put on her game face. 'We'll wire you. Fake some recording—'

'I have something,' he told them about the cloning software and The Elitist and waited for the storm to break, Difiore's fury to rage.

She surprised him. She didn't shout, yell or come at him physically. She and the SAC traded glances.

They're amused?

'We suspected you knew more than you were letting on,' Quindica waved vaguely. 'All that for later. Our tech people might be able to track his phone.'

They won't. If Beth and Meg can't, no one can.

He kept his silence, however; he logged into his laptop and phone and turned over everything he had to them.

Difiore made calls and joined Quindica at the island. They listened to the recordings from the software and made notes.

'Sheller can find this place.' The detective raised her head. 'He's got your number.'

'He can't. My calls get forwarded, bounced ...' he trailed off.

'You duped us. When you were at the club.'

He shrugged. Those events felt like a million years ago. They didn't feel relevant, not with the taste of defeat in his mouth.

He paced and brooded while they spoke softly, made notes, and established timelines. *Difiore's right. I should have ignored Darrell. I should have gone to her.* He was cursing himself for his negligence when the buzzer sounded.

'That'll be our team.' Quindica started to rise.

He waved her down and went to the door. He needed an

outlet for his self-directed anger, and any physical movement helped.

It was how he was feeling, he would say later, the bitterness inside him that made him ignore the video monitor at the door.

He opened it. Felt his radar ping, but it was too late.

A blow knocked him out.

96

The sound of soft voices. Footsteps shuffling. Bright lighting. Something squeaking ... a chair. The feeling of being restrained.

Sounds, impressions and smells came to Cutter as he regained consciousness. He kept his head bowed, his eyes open a fraction as he checked out his surroundings.

He was tied to a chair. Dirty concrete floor. Several people present. He could see feet at the edge of his vision. Difiore's shoes.

They're here, too.

He didn't curse himself. There would be time for self-recrimination later.

If we live.

Someone sobbed in the distance.

That's Carmel. Darrell should be here, too.

It felt like they were somewhere high up, with a breeze playing. The distant sounds of traffic. *We're in the city, but somewhere remote.*

He gasped and shuddered when cold water fell on him.

'Wake up, Grogan, and join the party.'

Jeff Sheller stood in front of him, his thumbs hooked in his waistband as a flunky came from behind Cutter and placed an empty bucket on the floor.

He's huge.

That was his first impression. The Lions' founder dominated with his presence. Taller and broader than everyone else around him. His command over his men apparent from the way they deferred to him. His eyes were small, slitted. Light shone off his shaven head. The loose shirt he wore didn't conceal the flex of powerful muscles.

'It's been a long time, Grogan. I wish it was longer. I wish I'd killed you in ADX. Never mind. You aren't going anywhere tonight.'

Cutter rocked back in his chair and fell when the slap struck him. It wasn't a hard blow, but he wanted to make it look like it was.

He lay gasping on the floor and groaned when the ex-con grasped his Tee and righted his chair roughly.

He coughed and wheezed and shook his head.

'Come now, Grogan.' Sheller chuckled. 'I didn't hit you that hard. I was worried my men put you into a coma at that fancy place, you were out for so long.'

Ten men. One of them working on a laptop. Everyone else armed. We're on the floor of some under-construction building. Wired up for ceiling lights.

He could see the night through the open structure, which had no walls. He was to the left of the remaining prisoners: Difiore, Quindica, Darrell and then Carmel Ward. The boy and his mother were looking on with shock and fear; the detective and the SAC were impassive.

His gut tightened when he noticed the mother's ripped shirt.

'There's no escape, Grogan,' Sheller continued. 'Heck, I'll even tell you where we are. Melrose. In a deserted building. Eleventh floor. No getting away from here. That high-rise over there.' He jerked his head toward a property that seemed to be across the street. 'None of their residents will be able to see clearly. They might with binos, but I've got people on the ground. They'll warn me. Besides'—he leered at Difiore and Quindica—'we have other informants.'

'Let them go,' Cutter told him. 'You've got me. Your beef's with me.'

He didn't have to pretend anymore when Sheller's fist crashed into his belly. He groaned and fell over and lay dazed on the floor until the Lions' man picked him up and straightened his chair.

'None of you are going anywhere.'

'I'm a cop,' Difiore said sharply. 'She's an FBI agent. You touch us, every LEO will be looking for you.'

Sheller looked at her the way a hawk watched a mouse. His left hand struck her on the face and sent her sprawling to the floor.

'That's how much I think of cops.' He spat at her as a thug went to her chair and set it upright. 'Cray?'

'Yes, boss?' the man with the laptop replied.

'What have you got?'

'Nothing much on Grogan's phone, boss. Just those recordings. Your call with Nails. That snippet at the club.'

'His laptop?'

'He rigged it some way, boss. It wiped itself when I tried to unlock it. I'm working on recovering it. It'll take time,' he said apologetically.

Sheller went to a hitter, who handed him a pair of gloves. He slipped his hands into them and flexed his fingers.

'Tell me where the recording is. You were going to tell the NYPD everything. Those weren't just words, were they?'

'Let them go.'

'There's no deal to be done here, Grogan.' Sheller shook his head pityingly. 'Here's what's going to happen. I am going to beat you to death. Sure, I can shoot you, knife you, but what would be the fun in that? Then, my men are going to have some fun with these women. Cray, this FBI woman, she's Chinese?'

'Chinese-Hawaiian, boss.'

'Any of you had such a woman?'

His men shook their heads.

'I might stop beating you and let you watch. But they'll die, too. Stop—' he thundered when Quindica made to speak. 'Don't say a word. I've been dead all these years. You think I can't get away with this?'

Cutter saw the punch coming, tried to evade it, but couldn't escape it. He took it high on the chest and toppled when a second blow followed, in the neck.

'You ... never ... beat ... me ... even ... with ... your ... men ... with ... you,' he panted.

Each breath was labored, but he wasn't hurt badly.

'Free ... me ... then ... we'll ... see ... how ... tough ... you ... are.'

'This isn't a Hollywood movie, Grogan,' Sheller sneered as he picked him up. 'The sooner you give me what I want, the quicker this will end for you.'

I've got to make it last. I've got to buy time.

The Task Force was probably aware Difiore and Quindica were missing. They would be searching. *They'll go to Rolando and Jamieson. NYPD and FBI will throw everything they have at finding them.*

All he had to do was survive as long as he could, and with that thought he let out a loud yell and heaved himself at Sheller.

It was clumsy, graceless; he was hampered by the chair, but his body-charge took Sheller by surprise; he fell back under Cutter's weight and his lips burst when Cutter head-butted him.

The gangbanger roared furiously. He grabbed his attacker and tossed him away as if he weighed nothing.

Cutter didn't roll. That was impossible with the furniture attached to him. He slid and scraped on concrete, his skin burning.

He felt himself being hauled back and turned his head just in time as a massive fist sailed past his neck. He reared forward and caught Sheller's ear between his teeth and bit hard.

The felon howled in pain and pounded Cutter with meaty, heavy blows, but there was no give in him, and the shout turned to a shriek when the thug's flesh tore. He staggered back, his eyes widening in shock when he saw the ear in his attacker's mouth. Cutter spat it away.

The ex-convict charged with a curse, blood streaming down his face, killing rage in his eyes. He picked Cutter up bodily and threw him to the floor. The Fixer took the impact on his shoulder and slid several inches, a groan escaping from him as lights burst behind his tightly closed eyelids.

The chair broke. Its back snapped free from the seat, freeing the chair's arms and front legs from the frame.

Cutter lay on the floor, his chest heaving, his eyes slitted. It felt like his whole body was on fire. That lancing pain in his side —that was probably a broken rib.

But to an extent he was free. He could move his hands, which still had the chair-arms tied to them. The furniture legs were tied to his calves, but they felt loose; there was give in them.

The animal in him gathered itself. He didn't let on that he could move with relative ease. He had to use every little advantage he had.

He lay to the front and left of Difiore and Quindica, whose harsh breathing he could hear. Beyond them, Darrell and his mom were sobbing and praying.

Sheller's men had gathered in a loose circle, fascinated by the fight. Even Cray had left his screen to join them.

And that's when Cutter spotted it.

A red dot on the floor in front of him.

Difiore breathed sharply as it moved almost lazily and climbed up one of the thugs. Just as Sheller shouted a warning, it centered on Cray.

The bullet split his head like a melon.

97

The hitters watched in disbelief as Cray's body fell. It took time for what had happened to register on them.

Cutter acted in that moment.

He heaved off the floor, the chair's frame clacking against his back. He lunged forward, a large step. Another to gain speed. It was ungainly, but grace wasn't what he was going for. On the third step he leapt high and stretched his left leg forward in a balletic move, hooked his right behind it and toed the chair's leg as hard as he could, getting its shattered edge to project beyond his heel.

Sheller sensed his approach and spun around, his yell becoming a scream when the makeshift spear pierced high on his right side, just beneath the shoulder. He staggered back from the momentum and swung a beefy arm as he was falling, to send Cutter crashing to the floor with a clacking of wood.

'KILL THE WOMEN!' The Lions' founder roared as he rolled on the floor, clutching his shoulder.

His shout, Cutter's attack, snapped the thugs out of their shock. Several grabbed their AR-15s and brought them up, but before anyone could trigger, the mystery sniper shot off another head. A third hitter's chest turned into blotches of red as two shots sent him reeling to the floor.

'WE'RE EXPOSED!' someone cried.

Cutter crawled, got to his feet, blinked furiously to shake off sweat, was aware of his loud, harsh breathing, felt a large mass approaching but didn't turn from his mission, which was to break Difiore's chair leg with a savage blow using the wood still tied to his right hand.

She shouted a warning as she fell, but it was unneeded as he felt a vise-like grip clamp on his shoulder, turning him around. The approaching fist crashed into his chest with the force of a sledge-hammer.

Sheller—bloodied, swaying but still appearing indomitable, rage and fury working his face—was snarling.

He smashed Cutter repeatedly in the chest, belly and neck, hitting so fast that the Fixer couldn't counter-attack, holding him so tight that he couldn't escape, even as the mystery shooter kept up the deadly fire, seeking out and cutting down the thugs, who had given up on shooting the prisoners.

Cutter brought his right hand up defensively, and it was more by luck than design that the chair's arm still tied to it blocked a blow from Sheller, who yowled as his knuckles met hard wood.

Another slash of his hand and the shaft crashed into the felon's head; he roared and flung his captive away.

Cutter stumbled back. Every breath was like taking in fire. He knew he couldn't last long. He was dimly aware of shouting and yelling as Difiore had managed to free herself and Quindica and the two had overpowered one hitter. The sniper seemed to be helping them by taking out gangbangers.

He wheezed and looked down when the chair arms slipped out of their binding and fell to the floor. He grabbed them and brought them up just as Sheller charged with a ferocious yell. His kata moves came to him instinctively, improvised from years of training and practice.

The left shaft deflected Sheller's haymaker as he ducked

beneath it and jammed the right staff right against his mouth. Two of the felon's teeth cut through his flesh and fell to the floor. He howled and retreated, brought his hands to his mouth and stared at the blood on them. Uttered a blood-curdling yell and charged again.

Cutter, running on adrenaline fumes, separated his mind from his body, which was one big hurt. He jabbed, parried and thrust, each blow striking the ex-convict wickedly, drawing grunts and groans, raising welts and drawing blood. But still Sheller came charging.

Can't retreat. Darrell's behind me.

There was no room to evade, and then the felon's massive arms were around him, lifting him effortlessly, his breath on his face, his eyes glittering in triumph as he squeezed.

The chair's back, still attached, was an impediment. It cracked, which momentarily loosened the hold, which gave room for Cutter to smash the shafts on Sheller's temples, who groaned but kept on tightening his hold.

Can't breathe!

Cutter sucked air painfully as he kept hitting the ex-con. Sweat poured down his face. Someone yelled, faintly in his ears. His vision swam as he took in the detective, who was at a distance, shouting at him, waving an AR-15 and then the fury was rising in him, too. If Sheller could withstand his blows, he could take punishment too and that spike of adrenaline drove him to bite the felon's shoulder so hard that his jaws felt like they might dislocate, even as he kept up a metronomic beating with his improvised clubs.

His sight was fading. No, it wasn't. The lights were going out, being shot out by the sniper until the last one remained. Just as Cutter thought he couldn't bite any harder or longer and couldn't club Sheller any more, the man groaned, stepped back and his arms fell away.

Cutter sobbed when his feet hit the floor. The clubs fell from his limp fingers. He was ready to give up, but then his eyes took in the felon, who was breathing stertorously, his hands clasping and unclasping unconsciously, his head bowed.

That brought back the memory of Gruber dying in his arms. Dark fury flooded him just as the last light went out, and under the cover of the cold night, Cutter leapt forward, got his arm around Sheller's neck, and dragged him to the edge of the floor where the building ended and the rest of the city began.

'GROGAN, STOP!' Difiore yelled.

He was beyond listening. The ex-con had blood on his hands. Gruber and Horstman were just two of his victims. He remembered the man's taunting voice, urging his men to rape the women. Lin Shun's torn shirt.

With that sneering laugh echoing in his mind, Cutter Grogan, the Fixer, pushed Jeff Sheller with all his strength and sent him windmilling into the night.

98

It seemed like an eternity but must have just been a few minutes before Difiore trained a flashlight on him.

Where did she get that? he thought drunkenly.

'Are you alright?' She leaned over him and touched his shoulder gently.

He nodded and winced. Every move hurt. Even drawing breath felt like walking on hot coals. He was on his knees, his hands braced on the floor.

'I told you to stop.'

'I did. I slipped and fell. Why? Where's Sheller?' The way he was feeling, he didn't need to make an exaggerated show of looking behind him. The grimace, the sharp breath, the clutching of his ribs, came naturally.

'You threw him out of the building,' she accused him.

'I did not,' he defended himself stoutly. 'I fell. I must have blacked out for a moment. Next thing I know you're prodding at me. He must have fallen off the edge. He was in bad shape. Judgment's gone at that stage.'

'You expect me to believe that?'

'You saw it yourself?'

'Saw?' she sneered. 'It was dark. No lights. We saw nothing.'

'I'm on the verge of dying here,' he said, forcing some spirit into his voice. 'Anyone else would have tried to help me and shown some sympathy.'

'Dying!' she snorted but knelt over him and helped him up gently and brought him to the center of the floor, where it was warmer. She uncapped a bottle of water. 'Gang's,' she explained, and held it to his mouth. He drank deeply and sighed gratefully when he had finished.

He settled to the floor wearily and squinted beyond the glare of the light. Saw Carmel Ward to the side, hugging Darrell tightly. Quindica on a phone. Three thugs on the floor, their hands behind them, their feet bound. A pile of weapons on the floor. Bodies of the dead hitters where they had fallen.

'How did all that happen?' he whispered.

'You don't remember?'

'I was occupied.' His chuckle turned into a groan.

'You broke my chair. That helped me get free. That shooter helped. We got—who was that?'

'I don't know,' he wheezed.

'Grogan. You can't hold back anymore. Not after what's happened.'

'I swear,' he insisted. 'I don't know who that was.'

It was true. He could make a good guess, but he wasn't certain.

'You should search that other building,' he bobbed his head at the night. 'You might get him. Or her.'

'You're telling me how to do my job?'

The first wail of a siren sounded as Quindica came over to them.

'He looks bad. How's he?'

'Grogan will live,' Difiore said unsympathetically.

'I'm right here,' Cutter sighed, but they didn't pay him any attention.

. . .

DIFIORE'S TASK FORCE BURST ONTO THE FLOOR. SEVERAL ESU members and armed cops followed. Paramedics rushed in and hovered over Cutter at the detective's command.

He didn't resist their help. His consciousness was slipping. Events were blurring, and when he heard Difiore instruct the medics to *take care of him* and felt her squeeze his forearm, he knew he was dying.

99

Cutter woke to a soft, fluffy pillow, a firm bed and the whir of machines.

He was alone in a hospital room. Plain walls framed with art, a cartoon drawing, a flower vase on a table, beside which was a jug of water and a glass.

It looked like he was still alive.

He grunted when he leaned over and poured himself a glass. Drank deeply and replaced it. Checked himself out. He was bare-chested. Shorts. Tape around his ribs. Angry red bruises on his shoulders. Knuckles red and scratched. His legs felt like he had run a marathon. He found more bandages when he fingered his neck and temple.

He was alive, however, and if he ignored the way his body felt, he seemed functional.

He lay back and closed his eyes. Promised himself it would be just for a few seconds.

He felt much better the second time he woke. His body still hurt, but instead of the lancing pain, it was a dull ache.

He climbed out of bed and stood up gingerly. He didn't sway

or feel like blacking out. His clothes were neatly folded on a chair. He grimaced at the tears and blood and dirt on them but slipped them on quickly. Went to the bathroom and looked away quickly at the sight of the blue-ish bruises on his face. Washed and slipped into his shoes. He didn't find anything else. His phone was missing, as were his wallet and watch.

It didn't matter. He peered out cautiously into a busy hallway. Nurses and doctors going about their business. A uniformed cop helping himself at a coffee machine.

He snuck out before the officer returned and went down the stairs. No one stopped him when he walked out, though he got a few stares.

Montefiore Medical Center in the Bronx, a signboard said. He flagged a cab and gave his Lafayette address.

'I don't have money on me,' he told the Middle Eastern–looking driver, who looked at him suspiciously. 'But I'll pay you when we get there.'

'You sure, buddy? I just had my lunch. I'm feeling good. I don't want you to ruin my day.'

'Yeah.'

'You don't look so good.'

'I don't feel so good. Can you drive?'

'Maybe you should see a doc?'

'I've been to one,' Cutter sighed. Why did every New Yorker have to have an attitude? 'He said I should rest at home.'

That seemed to remind the cab driver that he had a job to do.

Cutter fiddled with the entertainment screen at the back and brought up a news channel.

Shootout in Melrose. FBI and NYPD Task Force take out a gang.

The details were sketchy. All the journalist could report was that a few gang members had been killed and that the commish would make a formal statement in due course. *It's still an active investigation,* the reporter said in signing off.

They didn't mention anything about the Lions or white supremacy.

He wondered why. The answer came to him when the cab drove up to his building.

Difiore and Quindica don't want to tip off Sheller's network.

He went to his apartment and returned with cash, tipped the driver generously and returned. Climbed into bed with a sigh and was asleep in an instant.

CUTTER WOKE TO STILLNESS. THE SORENESS AND PAIN IN HIS body were a reminder of the punishment he had taken. He lay motionless, wondering what it was that had woken him up. *Nothing, don't get paranoid.*

The sounds of the kitchen tap dripping in the sink, a faint honk coming from the street. Nothing else.

The tap! His eyes flared open. He was particular about turning those off, since he hated the metronomic sound of water leaking.

There was someone else in the apartment.

100

He pressed his palm against the wall at the foot of his bed. A concealed safe door sprang open and a tray slid out noiselessly. Cutter grabbed the Glock and spare magazine and rolled out of bed silently.

He padded barefoot out of the bedroom. No one in the kitchen or in the spare bedrooms.

Down the hallway, his gun held high, alert. Shoot first, ask questions later, since he wasn't wearing armor.

Living room. Couches empty—

'Don't shoot,' Quindica called out from the dining table.

She and Difiore at their screens, both of them turning at his stealthy approach.

'That can get you killed,' he growled as he lowered his gun. 'How did you get in?'

'You're not the only one with fancy tricks,' the detective smirked but offered no explanation. 'Why don't you get changed?'

He took the hint and hit the shower. Took his time underneath the spray, letting it wash him down. A wry grin twisted his lips at the way the two women had intruded into his apartment. *They helped themselves to my coffee, too.*

'Walking out of the hospital like that wasn't nice,' Quindica reprimanded when he joined them.

'Nothing wrong with me. The ribs will heal themselves.'

They surveyed him critically and shook their heads simultaneously.

'Your face ...' Difiore snickered. 'You've lost your looks.'

'Just bruises. They'll go away.'

He wasn't vain. His appearance was down to genes, nothing more. He checked them out in return. Fine lines around their eyes and lips. Faint shadows of exhaustion.

'Did you two take a break?'

'We slept some,' the SAC admitted, 'but there's a lot to do. Connecting the dots. We needed to get away from OnePP. Your place is quiet ...'

'You were concerned for me!' he chortled.

Difiore snorted at that. 'We found the shooter—traces of him ... or her,' she corrected herself when he looked up in surprise.

'Rooftop of that building across the street. Smudge marks in the dust, but no clear footprints or fabric traces. Nothing there except those and the signs of a tripod. Close to eight hundred yards, downward range, no wind. That was good shooting.'

'McMillan Tac-50,' Quindica held up a baggie containing a deformed bullet. 'Not common, not rare either. Task Force is locating all such weapons in the country ... it's an impossible task. There will be enough of those with gangs and criminals, but we've got to do it.'

'Who was it?' the detective demanded.

'I don't know. We've been through this before.'

He braced himself for a hard interrogation, but she surprised him by not pursuing it.

'You meet them,' she said gruffly, 'thank them for us. They know you.' She stopped his protest with an imperiously raised finger. 'That's the only reason they didn't shoot Sheller. They know your history with him.'

'Huh? You figure a friend would let me get beat up like that?'

'Yeah.' She bobbed her head. 'That was a good way to wipe your smug grin.'

'I don't grin—'

Quindica squeezed his forearm. 'Thank them.'

He didn't reply. *If I acknowledge her, I'll be admitting the sniper is someone I know.*

'How have you explained it?' he asked after a while.

'Task Force shooter,' the SAC said simply. She met his eyes squarely. 'Gina and I talked about it. Surviving gangbangers think it was a police shooter. So do the Wards. No reason to present a different story.'

'Bigger picture is more important,' Difiore said. 'Whoever they are, NYPD or FBI aren't interested in them.'

'Darrell and his mom?'

'He taped his phone to his chest and recorded gang meetings. He wanted enough information to strike a Witsec deal.'

'I know about that, not about the phone,' Cutter admitted. 'I tried to talk him out of it—he was stubborn.'

'He followed Patchey one night and caught him talking to Sheller. Images aren't very clear, and there's nothing audible. Not of use. He let on that he had much more; that he had passed it over to you.'

He nodded as the dots joined. *Darrell bought time for himself and his mom.*

'His mother hit the roof when she heard all this,' Quindica smiled in recollection. 'There was quite some yelling and shouting there. They're good, though. You should pay them a visit.'

He looked up at that. 'They're—'

'Back home, Grogan,' Difiore said impatiently. 'What do you think we are? He was our CI. Our snitch. That's how we've logged him. They'll be protected. Witsec too, if they want, but with Sheller gone, that may not be needed.'

'Thank you,' he said gratefully.

. . .

SHE BRUSHED IT AWAY AND BROUGHT UP AN ARRAY OF IMAGES on her screen. 'These are from Sheller's phone and from that dude's laptop. Cray. He was a hacker, did time at Lompoc for hacking into the NSA. Looks like he was Sheller's tech expert.'

'That's a judge,' she said when Cutter clicked on the man's photograph. 'Southern District of New York. Lawyer.' When he moved on to the next image, 'white-shoe firm in the city.'

City council members, doctors, bankers, doormen, delivery drivers, mechanics, senators, congressmen; Sheller's network was widespread and across the country.

Her face tightened at one of the photographs. She didn't speak when he looked at her.

'Deputy Chief Trejo.' Quindica gripped the detective's hand hard, empathetically. 'NYPD. He ratted on us at Henderson Place. He's been leaking inside information.'

'You hadn't logged the address.'

'No, but Gina and I had called the commish and the FBI director. They knew where we were. Rolando made a note on his scratchpad. Trejo sneaked into his office when he was away ...'

'He's had to take a sudden vacation,' Difiore almost snarled. 'That's the official statement. He's at a safe house. Our team's interrogating him.'

'The Feds?'

Quindica's turn to clamp her lips tightly. 'There are a few,' she admitted. 'As high as SACs. In Wyoming, Texas, Montana, California, a few in DC too. All of them being questioned.'

'What about the politicians?'

'We haven't acted on anyone else. We don't want to tip them off just yet. That's why we've kept a tight lid on the shootout. All we've told them is a violent gang was busted. We need time to go through everything we found, put the jigsaw together. Just what Sheller was involved in.'

'Drugs, kidnapping, extortion, usual gang business,' Difiore chipped in. 'What we've gotten so far.'

Cutter nodded absently as he flicked through photographs, many of which had names and titles at the bottom. 'Good work,' he commended them. 'Identifying all these must not have been easy.'

'It wasn't. There are still a few more we need to tag.' She reached over and had begun scrolling quickly when he grabbed her arm.

'Go back.'

'Huh?'

He nudged her hand away and took over. Flipped back several images and stopped at one.

'We haven't identified that one. No facial rec, no social media, nothing about him ...' She read his expression. 'You know him?'

Cutter stared at the person on screen. Middle-aged, clean-shaven. Narrow face. No special features, scars, nothing remarkable about him.

'Are there any call recordings?'

'There's a lot in that laptop, but all of it is encrypted. Our team is working on it, but we've got nothing at the moment. These photographs are from the phone directory, which was duplicated on the machine. Why? Do you know him?'

'Can you do some 3D fancy stuff?'

'I'm sure our team can do that ... Grogan, do you know him?' she repeated sharply.

He didn't reply even then. That faint memory returned, when he had seen the second person in that Livonia bar's parking lot.

Quindica took over the screen, played with the keys until she got the photograph inserted in a rendering program.

'We've got some fancy tools,' she said and played with the image until it had fleshed out and presented it in different angles. Front-facing. Profile, looking right, profile, looking left.

'STOP!'

She froze at Cutter's yell.

'I've seen him.'

101

'That time in Livonia. I told you I stopped at a bar for a call. That's when I saw Davis meet—'

'Yeah,' Difiore waved him to move on. 'We remember.'

'Mystery Man was in that vehicle. With Sheller.'

'You're sure?'

'That face in profile, it's him. But it's not just there. I know him from someplace else.'

'Where—'

He reached for his phone and dialed a number, which rang several times before a gruff voice answered, audible even though the call wasn't on speaker.

'ADX Florence, Warden's Office. Brodsky here.'

Cutter ignored Difiore's sharp breath and Quindica's stiffening. 'Joe, Cutter here. I need your help.'

'Nothing good ever comes of that,' the officer grumbled. 'I was about to leave for home. A warm dinner and my kids. They're a damned sight more tempting than talking to you.'

'Please. This won't take more than a minute. I wouldn't call if it wasn't important.'

'The last time you called, I had a brutal killing in my prison.'

'Mr. Brodsky.' The SAC snatched the phone and turned it on speaker. 'This is Peyton Quindica, FBI Special Agent in Charge, New York Office, sir. Detective Gina Difiore of the NYPD is with us as well. She and I are leading a joint NYPD-FBI Task Force looking into several high-profile crimes. Mr. Grogan's previous calls to you, sir, those were personal. This is official. I'll be happy to get FBI Director Bart Jamison to give you a call to verify my credentials, sir.'

A long silence. A chair creaked. A bottle opened and a sigh.

'Cutter?'

'Yeah, I'm right here.'

'This lady is who she says she is?'

'Yeah.'

'I'm going to shoot you next time I see you.'

'I'll give you the opportunity.'

'What do you want to know?'

'I used to meet you when I was in prison.'

'I remember, Cutter. Let's not rehash history.'

'One time I came to your office, you were watching a meeting on your screen. Jeff Sheller had a visitor.'

'Gunner? Heck, Cutter, you expect me to remember all his visitors from all those years ago?'

'He wouldn't have had many. You'll have recordings. You don't destroy them.'

'We don't record their conversation.'

'It's the video I'm interested in.'

Brodsky grumbled and cursed, but Cutter knew it was an act.

The warden had to be taken into confidence for Farhaan Zaidi's insertion in the prison, and over time he and the special forces operative had become friends. That the official had been a Ranger helped create a bond.

'I have close to fifty videos with me. Where do I start?'

'Do you have a record of when you and I met?'

'My life was good before you entered it, Cutter,' Brodsky grouched. A drawer opened. Stationery rattled. 'Let's see ...' he said to himself. 'Yeah, here we go. Good thing I keep a journal.'

The sounds of pages flipping, a toneless whistle, a grunt. 'Here we go. There's just one day that our meeting coincided with a visitor. I've got the clip with me. Where can I send it?'

Quindica gave him a cloud address and swiveled the screen toward herself to log in.

'Got it, sir,' she nodded.

'Can I go now?'

'Stay a moment,' Cutter requested. 'Let us go through it.'

The SAC opened the file, turned the screen towards them and pressed play.

It was years old, but the camera angle was good. Sheller, bull-like, his back to them. His visitor seated across from him at a table in a large empty room. An armed guard in the distance.

'That's him,' Difiore said, comparing the video to the photograph she had on her phone. 'No doubt about it.'

'You got a name for him, Joe?' Cutter asked his friend.

'I figured you'd ask me that. Doug Mease. Sheller's cousin from Texas. Take down his address. That's the only time he visited.'

'Did Sheller have any other family visit?'

'Nope. Only his lawyer.'

'Thanks, Joe. I owe you one.'

By the time Brodsky had hung up after more grumbling, Quindica and Difiore had gotten on their phones.

'That address is fake,' the SAC said presently.

'I doubt that's his cousin. As far as I know, Sheller had no family.' Cutter wrinkled his brow.

'I got a hit.' The detective snapped her fingers, drawing their attention. 'There's a Doug Mease who did time ... here's his record. Partner in an accounting firm. Convicted for tax fraud. Served in Otisville. Here's his prison photo.'

It was a match.

'Where's he now?'

'No record. Dropped off the face of the earth.'

Cutter looked down the hallway blankly as he tried to make sense of it. Why would a convicted accountant be so important to Sheller? Did he keep the Lions' books?

'Anything from your task force?' he asked his visitors. 'Cray's laptop might have something on Mease.'

'Not yet. He's likely to be just another white nationalist, a fan of Sheller's. The gang made use of his accounting experience.'

He nodded. His guests were thinking along the same lines as he was. But something nagged at him.

Otisville ...

He did an internet search for the prison on Difiore's laptop. The first few hits were of notable prisoners. He browsed past them, conscious of the women looking over his shoulder. Ponzi scheme convicts, former politicians, conman hustlers ...

His fingers stopped scrolling at a name just as Quindica gasped.

Kevin Rubin.

102

'They were in prison at the same time,' Difiore exclaimed as she brought up the presidential candidate's rap sheet. She read it aloud, searched for his records and found no link to Mease.

'Nothing beyond their time in Otisville. Cutter? CUTTER?' She shook his shoulder.

He focused on her.

'You drifted off. Are you okay?'

'Yeah,' he replied distractedly.

'What's on your mind?'

'Something Jake Horstman said. That Sheller was working on something big. Mease, Rubin, the Rising Lions.'

Difiore turned pale. She pushed her laptop away and turned to him.

'Do you realize what you're implying?'

He nodded slowly. 'Kevin Rubin, who has a good shot at being president, is a white supremacist. Everything about him since he left prison is a sham.'

The only sound that followed was their breathing.

'No,' Quindica said hollowly. 'It's just a coincidence. Mease met Sheller in ADX for his own reasons—'

'Look at the timeline,' Cutter urged. 'Search for Rubin's TV appearances.'

Difiore brought up a schedule of the candidate's interviews.

'The holdup at the bodega. Several other stores were hit that day. Rubin went on TV afterwards and criticized them. Tizzard's rally—'

'That was in Arizona. And—'

'Wanna bet Tizzard and Sheller didn't know each other? The shootout at the bodega again, The Elitist ... every white nationalist violent incident, Rubin goes to the media. You still think it's a coincidence?'

Quindica bit her lips, played with a loose curl of hair and moved uneasily on her chair. 'Grogan, if this is true ... this is big.'

'Understatement,' Difiore said drolly.

'I can't go to the director with just this,' the SAC said helplessly. 'He'll want more. You can't move against a presidential candidate, one as high-profile as him, with something so circumstantial.'

'It's brilliant,' Cutter replied unheedingly. 'Mease and Rubin come together in Otisville. We'll never know whose idea it was unless they confess. He comes out of prison and makes a show of reforming. Sheller throws in with them. He orchestrates supremacist violence. That's the plank for the candidate. He denounces it. Calls for tougher policing, better law enforcement ... it goes down well. Who doesn't want that?'

'Their end goal?'

'Power. Imagine what they can do when they have the country in their hands.'

His lips thinned grimly when Difiore couldn't hide her shudder.

'Grogan, did you hear me? Jamison will throw me out of his office if I go with this.'

'Your task force might find something on Cray's computer.'

'If they don't?'

'I have an idea.'

103

'Have you heard from Gunner?' Mease asked Rubin the next morning as he accepted the cup of coffee the candidate handed over.

'Me? No. You have the communication line with him. We agreed about that.'

'He's not answering his phone,' the strategist frowned as he looked out at Central Park. 'We talk every day.'

'He must be busy. He's got a gang to run.' The candidate looked up sharply. 'That report on the news. Melrose building. That's where you meet, right?'

'Yeah. It's cordoned off by the cops. What have they told your company, the one that owns it?'

'What's on TV. They busted a drug gang. You think it was the Lions?'

'Nope.' Mease shook his head decisively. 'Gunner would have told us. Besides there's no way the NYPD could have contained that. Our sources would have told us, as well. I tried Trejo; he's gone on vacation and not answering either. But no. Whatever went down there doesn't affect us.'

'Good,' Rubin smiled broadly, 'because I've got news. Guess who's coming to interview me tonight?'

'Kevin,' Mease said irritatedly, 'you know I don't do guessing games.'

'Ellen Ronning!'

The strategist gaped at him. 'Ronning?'

'Yeah. Her team reached out yesterday. They want to do a live profile on me. Farley accepted instantly. He and Parsons are on the moon.'

The former accountant was stunned. Ronning, who had one of the highest viewerships in the country, was known for making or breaking politicians with her incisive questioning and exposés. She was at the forefront of every presidential election, interviewing the front-runner candidates, picking apart their policies and pledges. She didn't endorse anyone, but there was correlation between a favorable interview by her and the election winner.

She had stayed away from Rubin, however. She had declared publicly several times that any interview with him would be biased because of his distasteful past.

'She's tough,' Mease warned, though he couldn't keep the excitement out of his voice.

'She sure is. Farley and Parsons have been prepping me all day. We've been doing mocks. You caught me in between.'

'I'll listen in,' the strategist nodded to a neighboring room. 'Usual protocol.'

He had access to Rubin's private elevator, and no one questioned his presence. In any case, Schillum ran a tight ship and only the most trusted and thoroughly vetted had access to the floor.

'Wish me luck.'

'You don't need it ... President Rubin.'

He thumped the candidate on his back and left.

. . .

'IF THIS GOES SOUTH,' RONNING SAID BENEATH HER BREATH TO the burly man beside her as she and her crew rolled up to Rubin's building, 'I'll have your ass.'

'You'll have to join the line,' Cutter mumbled as he lugged a large case that contained lighting equipment.

'I said I would never interview him.'

'You changed your mind. It happens often in journalism.'

Ronning glared at him and swept into the building's lobby. She smiled at the head of security, who introduced himself as Ricky Schillum.

'Gene Salter,' she introduced the cameraman and then the rest of her five-person crew. 'And this is Tony Vecchio, my man Friday.' She pointed at Cutter.

The security head checked their faces against images that the TV host had sent ahead. He beckoned at his team, who inspected every piece of equipment.

'No phones, wallets, no personal stuff, no recording equipment other than the cameras.'

'That's what we agreed,' she said, smiling.

Cutter got wanded and patted down expertly. His shoes were inspected before he got waved toward an airport-style security gate.

Up an elevator and onto a thickly carpeted floor.

'No recording until the interview starts,' Schillum warned the arrivals and handed them over to the campaign manager, who introduced himself as Scott Farley.

'We spoke before,' Ronning beamed, giving him the full treatment, turning him to putty.

'You've got an hour to set up,' he stuttered and ushered them into an enormous living room with views of Central Park. 'Will this do?'

'This will do.' The TV anchor checked out the room critically, conferred with Salter, and pointed to a corner. 'Mr. Rubin will be there. That will give us the best view and backdrop.'

'Remind me again,' she whispered to Cutter, who was making

himself busy helping the crew set up the cameras, lights and broadcast equipment. 'What's this for?'

'The biggest scoop of your career.'

'The number of times I've heard that.' She rolled her eyes. 'Is it dangerous?'

'Not for you.'

She looked at him shrewdly. 'Cutter, just what's going on? In all these years, you've never asked for such a favor. To be tagged as my crew. Who were those women with you?'

'They are helping out on this assignment. I can't tell you more. You'll see it go down yourself.'

'You didn't introduce them. You know I can check out who they are.'

'Ellen, after this evening, you'll be flooded with offers from rival networks. The world will be at your feet. Forget those women. Think big.'

'Is Rubin involved in something?'

'Patience is a virtue,' Cutter said nobly and skipped out of the way of her discreet kick.

'Mr. Rubin,' Ellen Ronning began the interview, 'why should the citizens of our great country trust you?'

104

Cutter watched from the back of the room as Ronning started her background questions. His early years. Family life. She was known for painting the big picture before going for the detail.

Farley was in front of him, standing next to Rubin's chief of staff. Schillum had upheld his side of the agreement. Just one security guard in the room, a suit near the door, who was engrossed with the interview.

Cutter drifted to the exit and bent his head to the sentry. 'Bathroom?' he whispered.

'Outside. Turn right, follow the hallway and right again.'

He nodded his head in thanks, held his breath and pressed hard on a section of his jacket's lining near the bottom. The guard's pupils dilated briefly, then returned to normal. He stood aside without resisting when Cutter nudged him and stepped into the hallway.

It worked, he marveled.

Beth Petersen had called it Zombie Gas, a nerve agent that temporarily took away a victim's will. They remained conscious, aware of what was happening, but couldn't act on their own. They would obey orders blindly, which was why she'd given it the imaginative name. She had injected him with an antidote so that he could use it without being affected.

Two guards outside. One at the elevator and the other near the entrance to the interview room. One camera in the ceiling, but there would be others. No sign of Schillum. *There's got to be a control room from where he's watching. On this floor, since he'll want to be close to Rubin.* Other staff were likely to be there, huddled around a screen.

'I'LL SEARCH THE FLOOR,' HE HAD TOLD DIFIORE AND Quindica. 'A conspiracy of this scale and for so long ... Rubin's likely to have something incriminating, maybe in his study, his bedroom or somewhere else. Mease might be there, too.'

'You're hoping!' the detective had said scornfully.

'If I find nothing, I'll confront Rubin. On camera. With the world watching.'

That had got their attention.

I'LL HAVE TO GET PAST THE GUARDS FIRST. INTERVIEW ROOM Man was hard-faced and barely acknowledged Cutter. He stared at the wall impassively, his hands crossed behind his back. Former cop or military, Cutter guessed from the man's posture and buzzcut. Elevator Man was younger and had nodded to him. *I'll go at him.*

He walked past the older sentry and pressed another lining pocket. Went down the hallway in the opposite direction, as if deep in thought. Slapped his forehead with an exclamation and returned. Brushed Interview Room Man with his shoulder; he took a step back without protest.

He's down.

'Hey,' he smiled conspirationally at the second guard. 'I'm looking for the bathroom.'

'Down there, sir.' The sentry bobbed his head at the far end.

'This is some place.' Cutter shook his head admiringly. 'This carpet, heck, it's softer than my bed at home.'

'Yeah,' the man chuckled. 'Mr. Rubin spent a lot on it.'

'You've been with him a long time?'

'Ricky hired me. I've worked protection details with him.'

'Where is he? I thought he would be watching the interview.'

'He is.' The man glanced involuntarily to his right.

'Security room's over there?'

'I can't tell you, sir.'

'You know,' Cutter lowered his voice, 'I'm Ellen's assistant. I've been with her for a long time. You heard about that movie deal she signed?'

The guard nodded.

'They've started casting.' He took a step back and sized up Elevator Man thoughtfully. 'You're just right for some of the scenes. You'll get credits too. I can pass your deets on—'

'Chaz Huntington, but everyone calls me Hunter,' the suit tried to control his excitement. Hollywood. Fame. Babes on his arms.

'Even that name.' Cutter shook his head admiringly. 'I'll tell Ellen the moment this interview is over. She'll want to talk to you.'

'I can't socialize, sir—'

'Oh, come on. I can see several doors here. We can slip into one of the rooms. Ten minutes, that's all. Ellen meets every hire. She's a quick mover. She'll say yes, come on board. I'll guarantee it.'

'Well ...' Hunter was torn. 'There's an empty room. Down there.'

'That one, where the hallway turns off?'

'No, sir, that's Mr. Rubin's study. No one goes there.'

'It's locked?'

'No sir. We cover the entire place. There's no need for locks. You see the door before that? We can meet there—'

'Great. I'll take Ellen there, *accidentally*,' he said, making air quotes, 'once we finish the interview. That's your cue. You come after us and that'll give us time. Best ten minutes of your life. Hollywood. That's where you belong, Hunter, not here, standing in hallways.'

'You've got to go, sir.' The guard licked his lips nervously. 'Dieter'—he cocked his head at the older sentry—'will notice. Ricky might spot us on the security cameras.'

'I'm off,' Cutter assured him and pressed his lining.

Hunter was out by the time Cutter reached the end of the hallway. He went to the bathroom, checked that it was empty and washed his hands. He wiped them on his jeans as he emerged. Walked the entire length of the hallway, gesticulating as if thinking aloud. He would say he was going over a speech he had written for Ellen if anyone accosted him.

Two rooms on his side of the elevator, the study and the spare room. Three more flanking the living room. He tried a door and found a large dining room. The other one was a bedroom the size of a tennis court. *Last one's the security room.*

He returned to the study and slipped inside silently. He held his breath and waited. No pounding footsteps, no shouts of alarm. *Schillum's watching the interview. He's ignoring the camera feed.*

Cutter went deeper inside. More soft carpeting. A coffee table next to a window with Central Park views. Chairs. Newspapers and magazines. To his left was a floor-to-ceiling bookcase filled with hard-bound copies, paperbacks and journals on a variety of subjects. A gleaming walnut desk on which was a computer, a notebook next to it. He flicked through it quickly. Media appointments, interview notes. Nothing incriminating. He opened drawers and searched through legal pads and diaries.

'Who the hell are you?'

He turned slowly at the voice.

Doug Mease.

105

'Doug.' Cutter grinned disarmingly, realizing as he approached why he had missed seeing the man.

A deceptive-looking wall, on which hung a large painting, had given the impression the room ended there. It didn't. Around it was an entertainment area in which a TV played silently. A couple of couches, one misshapen, indicating that Mease had occupied it.

'Who are you?' the former accountant repeated in growing anger.

'You don't know me?' Cutter asked in surprise, then removed his fake nose, cheek pads and the chest padding beneath his shirt. 'I'm sure Sheller must have mentioned me to you and Rubin.'

Mease's jaw dropped. Alarm spread over his face. He lunged at his couch, for his phone.

Cutter caught him before he could yell. Clamped his palm over the man's mouth and punched him in the belly.

We don't need any other proof, he thought triumphantly as the ex-convict sagged into his arms.

He released more nerve agent and temporarily turned Mease into a robot. Searched the study for anything that would act like a wedge and found a cue stick. Wondered momentarily why it was in the room and then spotted the folded pool table against the wall.

He pushed Mease out and directed him toward the living room, head bent, as if the two were in deep conversation.

He held his breath when he opened the interview room and got the felon inside quietly. Parsons and Farley didn't look his way, their attentions on the interview.

He jammed the cue stick beneath the door handle and only then noticed the door could be locked from the inside. Turned the knob to secure it and looked up to see Salter and two more of the TV host's crew looking his way. He frowned at them furiously. Message received, they turned back to their work.

He directed Mease to the back of the room and stood him against the wall. Straightened his clothes and patted his hair into place, nerve-agented Parsons and Farley, grabbed a chair, ignored Salter's whispered hiss of protest—and stepped in front of the lights.

'Ellen,' he smiled at the journalist. 'I have a few questions for Mr. Rubin.'

106

Ellen Ronning showed why she was one of the best journalists in the country.

She didn't miss a beat, didn't pause, didn't appear flummoxed.

'Mr. Rubin,' she turned smoothly to the presidential candidate, 'you know I usually conduct these in front of live audiences. We don't have that in your home and decided to improvise. Meet Cutter Grogan. You might have heard of him. He calls himself The Fixer. He's made the news most recently for being an NYPD informer.'

The billionaire recovered swiftly. 'This is a surprise, Ellen. No, I haven't heard of Mr. Grogan. I don't watch TV, and the only news I follow is that of my campaign,' he said with a laugh.

'Mr. Rubin, you did time at Otisville,' Cutter asked him.

'Yes, I covered that with Ellen. I'm not proud of who I was and what I did,' he explained, 'but I'm a different person now. I believe every one of us can choose a new tomorrow.'

'Did you really?'

'Yes,' Rubin exclaimed. 'I've lived my life in the open. No secrets, nothing to hide. That wouldn't have been possible'—

another chuckle—'with the amount of coverage I get, the reporters and paparazzi chasing me.'

'Do you know Doug Mease?'

'Mease?' Rubin frowned. 'That name ... nope, it doesn't ring any bells. But I meet a lot of people—'

'He was a convict at Otisville, too. You and he were close.'

'Mease? Doug Mease? Oh yeah, now I remember.' Rubin laughed uneasily. He glanced at Farley and Parsons as if for support. None came. 'It's been a long time since I heard of him.'

'You haven't met him since then?'

'No.' Rubin gave Ronning an irritated look. 'Ellen, is this going somewhere?'

'It is,' Cutter interjected before the reporter could reply. 'Do you know Jeff Sheller?'

'Ellen—'

'Answer him, Mr. Rubin. My interviews are no-holds-barred. You knew that when you signed on.'

'I don't know this person, Sheller, whoever he is.' A thin line of sweat on the candidate's face. 'I don't see what all this—'

'Sheller was a leader of a gang of white supremacists, the Rising Lions. He—'

'I don't know him. I quit all that after I left Otisville. Ellen, we talked of this—'

'Did you really?' Cutter asked softly. 'Sheller was a dangerous criminal. He served his sentence in ADX Florence. Your friend Mease met him there—'

'I don't know anything of that.'

'Mr. Rubin,' Ronning caught on. She gave Cutter a speculative look and leaned forward. 'Are you still a white nationalist? Do you believe people of other races, ethnicities, origins, are inferior?'

'What?' Rubin thundered, then quickly controlled himself. 'Of course not. I find these questions offensive. I'm surprised Scott allowed you to ask them.'

'No one tells me how to run my interviews, Mr. Rubin.'

'You have lost contact with Doug Mease.' Cutter raised a finger. 'You don't know Jeff Sheller.' He extended another digit. 'Do you know he died? He was killed in a shootout a couple of days ago. In Melrose. In a property one of your companies owns.'

Rubin turned white. He grabbed a glass of water and drank it. His eyes searched beyond the bright lights of the camera, trying to find his campaign manager or chief of staff.

'It's news to me—'

'Sheller organized attacks on businesses owned by people of color. You went on TV and condemned them. That timing ... you seemed to know when those events would happen; you were ready, prepped—'

'This is preposterous,' Rubin composed himself. 'This interview is over, Ellen. Your CEO will—'

'Are you a white nationalist?' her eyes glittered. 'Is your campaign fake?'

'NO!'

'Really,' Cutter scoffed. 'Sheller confessed to the cops that he—'

'I DON'T KNOW HIM. I'VE NEVER MET MEASE AFTER OTISVILLE.'

'Funny you should say that. He was in your study a few moments ago, watching the interview. There he is, at the back.'

Rubin rose out of his chair, as if stung, when a camera light illuminated Mease.

His mouth opened. No sounds came. He swallowed. 'That's ... He's ... Doug and Jeff,' he burst out, 'it was their idea.' His face whitened as he realized the importance of his words.

'INTERVIEW'S OVER,' Schillum roared as he crashed through the door and burst into the room with several guards. 'TURN THE CAMERAS OFF. GET OUT. NOW!'

Cutter caught Ronning by the elbow and hustled her out as the room exploded with yelling.

'Leave it,' he barked at Salter when the camera-man tried to gather his equipment. 'Move, quickly.'

His message got across. Ronning's crew gathered behind him and got into the elevator. Rubin came into view just as the doors shut. Haunted. Yelling. Gesticulating furiously, surrounded by his protection detail, and then they were going down, being hustled out of the building and into their van.

'Drive!' Cutter ordered. 'OnePP. Don't stop for anything. Cut through lights.'

He allowed himself to relax when they were several blocks away. Found Ronning's eyes on him.

'You knew,' she accused him.

'We suspected,' he countered.

'We?' Her forehead cleared. 'Those women—'

'You never met them. You can't mention them. Are we clear?'

She nodded slowly and looked behind.

'You thought they would shoot us?'

'It was a possibility. Schillum ... I didn't know how he and his men would react. That was good thinking,' he congratulated Salter. 'You turned the cameras on them. That stopped them from being more aggressive.'

'Man,' the technician mopped his sweat. 'That was close.'

Ronning punched him furiously in the shoulder. 'Give us some warning next time,' she raged, but that turned to laughter when reaction set in, and by the time they reached the NYPD headquarters she was beaming, her phone buzzing repeatedly with messages and calls.

'You know what we did there?' she addressed her team. 'We brought down a leading presidential candidate. On live TV. No one's ever done that. No one ever will. Why are we here?'

'You'll need protection. Until this blows over.'

107

The interview had out-trended every other by the time Cutter made his breakfast the next day. He caught up with the headlines as he ate.

It had come crashing down on Rubin while he was asleep. The Task Force had cracked Cray's computer. They had found recordings of Sheller's meetings with Mease and Rubin. They had secured arrest warrants, which had been executed at JFK as the candidate tried to flee on his private jet.

Jamison and Rolando addressed the media jointly, spoke of the conspiracy to subvert American politics, and promised more arrests across the length and breadth of the country.

'No one is too powerful, no one is out of the reach of the law, no one is more equal than others,' they said grimly as they signed off.

It's over, he thought as he turned off the TV and scrolled through numerous missed calls and messages. Only two were important. One was from Arnedra, checking if he was okay.

All good here, he messaged.

Good? She replied with astonished emojis. *Is that all you can say?*

He grinned and made a mental note to call her later. The other message required a visit, not a reply.

'I DIDN'T KNOW IF YOU WOULD COME,' CARMEL WARD SAID and hugged him tightly when she opened the door.

She led him inside and there Darrell was, lounging on a couch.

'She made me take a day off,' the boy said defensively at Cutter's quirked eyebrow.

'Quiet,' his mom ordered her son, directing their visitor to another couch. 'Tell me everything.'

'Darrell hasn't?'

'What he knows. It's bigger than the Brownsville gang, isn't it?' She waved at the TV.

'Yeah.' He launched into it.

'Wow,' she replied when he had finished, lost for words.

'I changed the presidential election?' Darrell's eyes were like saucers.

'You sure did, buddy.'

'What about us?' his mom asked. 'What happens now?'

'Difiore—'

'I want to hear it from you.'

'She's good. I trust her.'

'You do?'

'Yes, ma'am. What she said will happen. Your name will not be in the media. No one will ever know about Darrell's role in the gang. You can continue living your life like this. Or you can go into Witsec. The choice is yours.'

'I am tired of change,' she said, rubbing her eyes. 'I don't want any more surprises. No witness protection. I've discussed it with Darrell. He agrees with me.'

'What if Manuel asks you to go with him?'

'I'll drop him,' the boy said resolutely. 'I'm done with gangs.'

'You'd better be,' his mother said in a hard tone. 'If you don't, I'll tell the cops to arrest you, myself. Are we clear?'

'Yes, Mama.'

'We didn't discuss your fees,' she told Cutter when he was leaving.

He took in the lines and wrinkles on her face, at the eyes, weary but hopeful. A mother who worked two jobs just so she could give her son the best break in life. He looked beyond her at Darrell, who was playing on his phone.

'My phone's ringing off the hook, inquiries from new clients,' he said, grinning. 'Fees? We'll never discuss that.'

He held her close as she sobbed into his shoulder.

'How can I thank you?' she whispered.

'You did.'

He didn't explain that helping folks like her was why he did what he did. Why he called himself the Fixer. It didn't matter.

Carmel Ward had closure.

That was more important.

THE MESSAGE CAME TO HIM WHEN HE WAS RETURNING HOME.

Meet us. OnePP. Right now.

No signature. An unknown number, but judging by the tone, there was only one person who could have sent it.

108

Difiore led him up the floors to Rolando's office. Cutter stopped short when he saw who else was in the commish's office. Peyton Quindica, as he had expected, but sitting across from the commissioner was Bart Jamison.

'Everything is off the record,' the FBI director waved him to a chair.

'We're taking heat,' the commish explained. 'Politically. That Ronning's interview and your intervention were staged, at our request.'

'We would have gotten Rubin,' Jamison spread his hands. 'Once we cracked Cray's computer.'

'How long would it have taken for him to be tipped off?' Cutter said heatedly. 'What I did gave you freedom to open an investigation on him. Even if you had found nothing on that laptop.'

'We get that,' the commish admitted. His hawk-like eyes gave Cutter a piercing look. 'Some folks are saying Gina and Peyton allowed their personal prejudices to get in the way. That their investigation was biased.'

Cutter blinked. 'Detective Difiore and Special Agent in

Charge Quindica didn't know what I was planning. Nothing. I got Ronning to reach out to Rubin's people and set up the interview. It was all me. I can arrange a press conference and say that. That should take some heat off you.'

'No thanks. We can fight our own battles. How did you know Mease would be there?'

'I didn't. But where else would he be? No politician turns down a Ronning interview. That was the biggest moment of their campaign. I suspected he would want to be close.'

'You're damned lucky to get away alive.'

'Yes, sir.'

'Cutter, who was doing the shooting at Melrose?'

He hid his grin. *That's what this is about. Bruce and Bart aren't happy about that loose end.*

'Some NYPD sniper, sir,' he replied innocently. No first names. That was only when he was alone with them.

'Save it,' Jamison growled. 'I told you this is off the record. You're among friends. That was no FBI or police shooter.'

'I don't know who it was, sir. I was trying to stay alive.'

He stuck to that, even though they badgered him.

'We don't want vigilantes in the city,' Rolando said at one point.

'This vigilante saved the lives of Difiore and Quindica, the finest law enforcement officers I've worked with,' he shot back.

The commish narrowed his eyes. He seemed to suppress a smile as he glanced at Jamison. 'Better than the two of us?'

Cutter got to his feet. 'Are we done here?'

'You're not going to tell us anything, are you?'

'Sir,' he replied, straight-faced, 'I thought I was coming for an award presentation. Not for the third degree I've just experienced.'

'Get out,' the police commissioner grunted, 'before I throw you out.'

. . .

'You meant that?' Difiore asked him on the way down.

'Yeah,' he said, knowing what she was referring to.

She didn't say another word but surprised him by shaking his hand.

'Are there cameras here?' he said, looking about the lobby. 'Can I get a clip of that?'

'Go away,' she sighed.

✠ 109 ✠

Terry Kobach was escorted into the yard at dusk.

'Forty-five minutes,' the guard told him and went to stand by the door.

This had been the routine ever since he was sent to solitary for killing Horstman. The guards came to his cell in the evening, brought him out for his exercise and took him back after his allotted time. It was the only time he got to see the sky and breathe some fresh air.

He lay down on the weight bench and put his hands to the bar.

'Shall I spot you?'

He jerked upright and stared at the stranger. Green eyes, dark hair.

'Who are you?'

'Got transferred from Lewisburg.'

'How come you're here?' Kobach asked suspiciously. 'There's no one else around when I train.'

'Dunno, dude. Guards brought me.'

'Where are they?'

'How the heck do I know? It's my first day out.' The stranger moved away irritatedly. He picked up a barbell and started exercising.

Kobach stared at him for a moment and looked around the yard. The lack of guards ... that had never happened. He shrugged. Who knew what the prison officers were up to?

He got back to his position and lifted the bar.

'Come, spot,' he ordered. He was an alpha, even if he was in solitary. A new convict had to know who was boss.

'What're you in for?'

'Rape.'

'You have a name?

'Bo Trice. You're Kobach?'

'How do you know my name?'

'Everyone does.'

The killer grunted when the newcomer added more weights and helped him lift.

'Slow,' he gasped when Trice pushed down with his hands.

''WHAT THE HELL ARE YOU DOING?' he panted when the felon didn't stop.

'Did you stop when Jake Horstman pleaded?'

Kobach's eyes widened. He took in the convict as if seeing him for the first time. He let the bar fall on its holders and sat upright.

'Who are you?'

He felt no fear. He could take on any prisoner at ADX; pretty boy was no threat.

CUTTER SLAMMED THE TWENTY-POUND DUMBBELLS INTO Kobach's chest who fell onto the bench with a groan. He cursed when the convict sprang back to attack with a guttural roar. He had underestimated the man's capacity to absorb punishment and overestimated his own recovery.

He retreated rapidly as he swung with the weight, stumbled

when he stepped on a loose disc, and went crashing down when the felon slammed into him.

'WHO ARE YOU?' Kobach raged as he smothered his attacker with his body and clamped massive hands around his neck.

Got ... to ... finish ... him, Cutter panted as he brought the bells down on the convict's head. His breath was stuttering and his vision was already dimming as the prisoner's vise-like grip tightened and cut off his air.

He kept going however, hammering away with the weight, which was feeling heavy to lift. Breathing was becoming impossible, but he kept swinging, pounding at Kobach's head until it turned bloody.

The convict's eyes faded and his grip faltered but Cutter kept hitting even when the body turned still and heavy, and only then did his hand fall away.

He gasped and panted and sobbed as clean air filled his tortured lungs and his ribs felt as if a tank had driven over them.

Cutter heaved the dead man away and got to his knees. Forced himself to crawl to the bench and sat heavily on it. He sat there until the earth stopped spinning crazily and the lights and colors behind his eyes faded.

He limped out of the yard without a second glance and entered the hallway. Walked through the prison, which had filled with cacophony. Alarms sounded and prisoners yelled as they pounded their cell doors. No guard accosted him. Those at their stations were at their screens, which seemed to be down. He heard snatches of frantic conversation and then he was out, under the enormous canopy of the night sky, where his cab was waiting for him.

They sped off just as the first fire truck nosed inside the prison's compound.

'Some kind of fire,' the cab driver said, relaying the news. 'In the dining area. It seems to be serious.'

Cutter didn't reply.

He had called the same three-star general who had arranged for Jake to meet him. The officer had listened silently as he had made his case.

'It'll be difficult,' he had hedged.

'You can make it happen. If Zaidi could take out Mansoor, this is nothing.'

'Do you know what you're asking?'

'Yeah,' he had replied.

'It will cost you,' the general finally agreed.

Cutter knew what that meant.

The covert world would come calling one day, asking for the favor to be repaid. He wouldn't be able to refuse.

It was a trade he was willing to make for Jake Horstman.

110

'Did you have anything to do with it?' Joe Brodsky asked him angrily.

'Did I have anything to do with what?'

'Kobach!' the warden yelled. 'He was killed yesterday, just as a fire broke out in my prison.'

'Huh? You think—'

'Save the innocent act,' his friend snapped. 'My security cameras went down mysteriously. Guards were drawn away from their stations by panic alarms. All of them were false. No witnesses. No one saw anything.'

'I am a lot of things,' Cutter said spiritedly, 'but I am not a magician—'

He grinned when the warden hung up abruptly. He stretched and winced when the aches and pains started all over again.

Good thing, Joe wasn't on a video call. The way I'm looking and feeling, he would know it was me.

'Look who's here.' Beth grinned when Cutter limped to their table.

It had been easy to locate Zeb and his team. The crew

frequented Kolumbus Koffee, the café near their office, when they were in town.

'You sure you should be up and about?' Bwana hugged him carefully.

'Wheelchair,' Chloe declared, 'that's what he needs.'

'Nah, he's too vain for that,' Meghan smirked. 'The Fixer's image will take a beating.'

Cutter gripped the back of Broker's chair as he took their joshing. He shook his head when Zeb pointed at an empty seat.

'Got to be somewhere else,' he said. 'Thank you,' he said softly. 'If you hadn't taken those shots ...'

'I was the sniper? What makes you think that?'

'I thought—'

'You thought what?' Beth jibed, 'That only Zeb can shoot?'

'No, that's not what I meant—' Cutter floundered. Every one of the Agency operatives was a crack shot.

'After all we did for him,' Meghan scowled, 'he thanks Zeb. As if we were twiddling our thumbs.'

'Men are like that,' Chloe agreed. 'They think we women can't—'

'Sorry,' Cutter said hurriedly, addressing them all. 'I *am* grateful,' he insisted, 'truly,' and retreated as gracefully as he could.

MEGHAN SNORTED AND BURST OUT LAUGHING WHEN SHE caught sight of him hurrying away, red-faced in embarrassment.

'That *was* good shooting,' Zeb told her.

'Teamwork,' she said, bumping his shoulder.

Bear and Chloe had been the drivers in two getaway vehicles. Beth had been her spotter. Broker, Bwana, Roger and Zeb had been in the shadows on the ground, to provide forceful support in case the fight went south.

The elder twin could have taken out Sheller if she wanted. They had agreed, however, that Cutter needed to end the gang-banger's reign.

'Should I delete the software on his phone?' Beth asked. 'We can track him even now and see if he's in trouble.'

'Leave it,' Zeb said. 'He's one of ours.'

They would always have Cutter's back, even if he wasn't Agency. That was how they worked.

CUTTER GRINNED WRYLY AT THE WAY HIS FRIENDS HAD suckered him as he made his way across the city to Lafayette. *Serves me right for assuming it was Zeb who was the mystery shooter.*

He had known the moment the first shot had taken out Cray, that his friends had come to the rescue.

He pulled out his phone and inspected it. *Beth and Meg must have been tracking it, that's how they knew where I was*. He thought about getting a new phone and number. Considered it for several moments and then shrugged.

Let them track me. He worked alone, but it was good to have friends watch out for him. *Friends*? he snorted. *They're family*.

IT WAS EVENING BY THE TIME HE REACHED THE BODEGA, where Lin Shun was stocking up the counter with a fresh batch of baking.

'Just in time,' she greeted him. She placed two slices on a paper tray and handed them over. 'Pineapple and lemon tarts.' She cocked her head when he took the first bite.

He rolled his eyes in delight when the sweet-sour flavor hit his taste buds and gave her a thumbs-up. Moshe appeared silently and shook his head at Cutter's condition. He went to the door and turned the sign to *Closed.* Chang lowered the blinds and pulled out a table and four chairs. Lin Shun brought steaming trays of food, and they were digging in when there was a pounding at the door.

Moshe went to get it and returned with Difiore and Quindica, both impassive and hard-faced.

'Room for two?' the detective asked. They dropped into the two chairs that Chang and Moshe returned with.

'Difiore,' Cutter greeted her.

She nodded regally and reached down to bring out a bottle of wine.

'I don't drink.'

At that, Quindica held up a bottle of juice and poured into a glass for him.

'Peyton,' she said, pointing at herself. 'And she's Gina, from now on.'

'Don't read too much into it,' the detective warned him, impassive as ever. 'We'll still nail your ass to the wall if you give us reason.'

'But,' the SAC added as she slurped her noodles, 'since we're on first-name terms, we'll cut you some slack.'

'We'll let you choose the wall,' Difiore cracked.

Cops. They always had to get the last word.

MORE BOOKS

Check out Powder Burn the next thriller in the series.

Check out Incoming the most recent in the Zeb Carter Series.

Join Ty Patterson's Facebook group of readers.

BONUS CHAPTER FROM POWDER BURN

'That's close enough,' the bearded man snapped.

Cutter stopped in the clearing and raised his hands as wide as he could.

'I'm alone.'

'Do you have the money?'

'What do you think I'm carrying in this?' he retorted. He dropped the heavy gym bag to his feet and massaged his fingers.

'Piotr, count it.'

'Not so fast,' Cutter warned the gangbanger. 'Where's the girl?'

The thug nodded at another heavy, who disappeared into the darkness and returned with a teenage girl. Her eyes were wide with fright, her mouth was taped and her hands were bound behind her.

'Amy?' Cutter recognized her from her photographs. 'This will be over soon. I'll take you to your mom and dad.'

She nodded rapidly and sobbed in relief.

'Count it,' he told the leader of the kidnapping gang, at whose shoulder jerk two gunmen came forward with counting machines. They opened the bag and placed the bundles of used notes on their trays. For long moments, there was nothing but the sounds of the whirring devices and the girl's dry heaves.

'Three million,' one shooter announced.

'Just as we agreed. Let the girl go.'

'I think not,' the leader said with a smirk. 'We have the money, the girl. You are alone. We'll kill you here.' He hefted his AR-15. 'It's a remote part of the Catskills. No one will hear a few shots. It'll take days or weeks for your body to be discovered.'

'You think you'll get away?'

'We know we'll escape. It's not the first time we've taken the money and run off with the girls. Who'll stop us?'

Cutter clamped his lips tight as rage flared.

Abraham Zinov, a Russian gangster, had made a successful business of kidnapping the children of millionaires and escaping with the ransom money. In most instances, the victims weren't seen again.

He was wanted by the FBI and by every law enforcement agency in the country, yet he had evaded capture.

Amy Sorkin was his latest victim. He had grabbed the eighteen-year-old as she was emerging from her upscale private school in Brooklyn Heights. He had sent the ransom demand to her father, Travis Sorkin, a multimillionaire hedge-fund owner, who had contacted Cutter.

'No cops,' the distraught father had insisted. 'I know how it's gone down before. More than half of the kids are still missing.'

'You need to trust the FBI and the NYPD. I'm by myself. I'll—'

'No!' the dad had yelled. 'I'll pay. Three million is nothing. I would give away thirty, everything I have, to get back Amy. Take it to them and get my daughter back.'

Cutter tried his best to convince the parent, but his arguments fell on deaf years.

'You cannot go to the cops either,' Sorkin told him. 'You've got to promise.'

Cutter had given him his word and agreed to go to the drop-off in the Catskills.

'You think I'm alone?'

'That trick won't work,' Zinov boasted. 'We followed you when you entered the forest. We've searched you. No phone, no tracker. You're surrounded by thirteen men. Yeah, I think you're alone. You're bluffing, and you'll die.'

Amy screamed when he raised his gun.

Her shriek turned to a startled gasp when the gangbanger holding her fell to the ground as his head exploded.

Cutter dived to his left and caught his left shoe as the rattle of guns burst the silence.

'POLICE. GIVE YOURSELF UP,' came the order from a loud-hailer.

Zinov grabbed the girl and fired wildly into the dark.

Cutter scrabbled away as the kidnapper turned on him. He tore the bottom of his shoe away and removed the composite 3D-printed gun and took aim.

He didn't flinch when a bullet smacked into the ground next to his face, spraying him with dirt and leaves.

'I'll SHOOT HER,' Zinov yelled as his men disappeared into the woods. He crouched behind Amy, holding her hostage.

Cutter could see the side of his face and was aware of voices and shouts as cops captured the escaping gang, and then he saw nothing but the gangbanger's forehead beyond the sight of his gun.

'No, you won't,' he whispered and triggered.

'I told you, no cops,' Travis Sorkin said as he hugged his daughter tight.

They were at the FBI's perimeter, half a mile from the scene of the drop-off. The father's face was streaked with tears and lines of worry.

'I gave you an order,' he bellowed.

'I didn't go to the cops, sir,' Cutter replied.

He hadn't. He had confided in Zeb, who had alerted the Feds who had worked with him to set up the trap. An ingestible GPS tracker that he swallowed had enabled the federal agents to track him down. The ceramic gun had been his improvisation.

'How did they know?'

'Dad!' His daughter caught his lapels and shook him. 'I'm safe. Alive. Mr. Grogan got me out. Isn't that important?'

Her father burst into sobs at that and blindly reached out and squeezed Cutter's shoulder.

'You didn't have to shoot him,' Peyton Quindica, FBI Special Agent in Charge, told him with a frown.

'I didn't have to,' he agreed. 'I could have let him shoot Amy and me.'

'We would have taken him down.'

'I couldn't risk it.'

'I told you not to be a hero.'

'I was trying to stay alive and keep Amy safe.'

She grinned wryly as she shook her head. 'We'll need that,' she said, gesturing at his gun. 'That escapes the detectors?'

'Yeah, it's made of a composite material that the NSA is testing. I wouldn't be alive otherwise.'

'You'll keep that to yourself?'

He searched her eyes under the glare of flashlamps and nodded. *If that gets out, every terrorist and criminal in the country will be printing guns.*

He grinned as he searched over her shoulder. 'I'm half-expecting to see Difiore.'

Gina Difiore, Detective First Grade with the NYPD, the FBI agent's partner. He had come across them in a previous assignment, and the initial antagonistic relationship had turned into a kind of friendship.

Sort of, he told himself.

Cutter called himself a Fixer, someone who helped those

whom the system couldn't. The detective considered him to be a vigilante and treated him with disdain.

'This is an FBI operation,' Quindica said, smiling. 'We aren't joined at the hip.'

'She knows I was involved in this?'

'Yeah. She said the world would be a better place if I let you get shot.'

'Sounds like her.' He high-fived her and went to his SUV.

Leaned back wearily when his phone rang.

'Yeah?' he asked. *That's a West Coast number*.

'Is that Cutter Grogan?'

'That's me.'

'Mr. Grogan, I'm Diego Cruz, detective with the LAPD.'

'What's this about?'

'I have bad news. Arnedra Jones and her sister were killed in a gang shooting.'

AUTHOR'S MESSAGE

Thank you for taking the time to read *Break*. If you enjoyed it, please consider telling your friends and posting a short review.

Sign up to Ty Patterson's mailing list and get The Watcher, a Zeb Carter novella, exclusive to newsletter subscribers. Join Ty Patterson's Facebook Readers Group.

BOOKS BY TY PATTERSON:

Most recent first

Cutter Grogan Series (Zeb Carter Universe)

Two books in the series and counting

Zeb Carter Series

Seven books in the series and counting

Zeb Carter Short Stories

One book in the series and counting

Warriors Series (Zeb Carter Universe)

Twelve books in the series

Gemini Series (Zeb Carter Universe)

Four thrillers in the series

Warriors Series Shorts (Zeb Carter Universe)

Six novellas in the series

Cade Stryker Series

Two military sci-fi thrillers

ABOUT THE AUTHOR

Ty has been a trench digger, loose tea vendor, leather goods salesman, marine lubricants salesman, diesel engine mechanic, and is now an action thriller author.

Ty is privileged that thriller readers love his books. 'Unputdownable,' 'Turbocharged,' 'Ty sets the standard in thriller writing,' are some of the reviews for his books.

Ty lives with his wife and son, who humor his ridiculous belief that he's in charge.

Lightning Source UK Ltd.
Milton Keynes UK
UKHW010819200222
398952UK00002B/414

9 781916 236981